Dedicated to all readers of fantasy romance who, like me, believe in happily ever after

The Golden Key Legacy

AJ NUEST

Harper*Impulse* an imprint of
HarperCollins*Publishers* Ltd
1 London Bridge Street
London SE1 9GF

www.harpercollins.co.uk

A Paperback Original 2016

First published in Great Britain in ebook format by Harper*Impulse* 2015

A catalogue record for this book is
available from the British Library

ISBN: 9780008170851

Automatically produced by Atomik ePublisher from Easypress

Printed and bound in Great Britain

A Furious Muse

Chapter 1

The low caress of a maniacal laugh raised the hair on her arms, and Faedrah paused in her flight up the stairs. Slamming her back to the wall, she searched in the dim light of the first landing above, swiveled her head and squinted into the murky shadows swallowing the steps below.

On which level did he linger? The evil laugh had echoed in from every direction.

"You cannot hide from me, Faedrah." The rustle of black robes, the morbid stench of decay wafted in from the haunting depths and she sprinted up the staircase. "The flutter of your pulse gives you away."

The sharp corners of the banister's wooden dowel bit into her palm as she rounded the landing and dashed up the remaining five risers to the second floor. Where was the door? She glanced left then right, but the long corridor to either side stretched into obscurity. Only one choice out of many led to safety. Behind only one would she find her escape.

"Come, my sweet." A fetid breath skimmed the nape of her neck and she skittered forward, whirling around. Reaching over both shoulders for her short swords, she bit back a roar of outrage as her hands clawed empty air. Goddesses' tits, how many times had she forgotten? Her weapons did not accompany her into this realm.

Yet the stairwell remained vacant.

Her jaw firmed as she lowered her hands to her sides. And on how many occasions had she fallen prey to this wizard's seductive ploy? He purposely kept her off balance, setting his evil whisperings upon her ear. If just once he would cease in his trickery, she would happily banish him back to the netherworld from whence he came.

"All I ask of you is the key."

Rage trembled through her taut muscles and her nostrils flared. He lied. The key would merely be the first of his demands. "Never."

His wistful sigh dallied about the high ceiling. "You are so like your mother."

Her fingers curled in on themselves against a hot shard of despair. She was not like the White Queen of prophecy. No matter how hard she toiled, she would never be as strong or as beautiful.

A spin on her toe and she raced down the corridor on her left. Wicked shadows leapt from the baseboards, but she hurtled past the sinister phantoms and kept moving. She could not surrender. With Helios as her witness, she would never consent.

The golden key bounced against her chest. Her braid echoed the heavy rhythm down her back. Doors flew by, yet she sprinted on. Perchance this was the opportunity she could finally take to prove herself. She would reign victorious and attest to all in the realm she was worthy.

The myriad switchbacks muddled her sense of direction. Skidding to a stop, she retreated from a dead end. How long must she withstand the torture of this labyrinth? How many countless nights must her soul be splintered before she gained release from this hell?

Stopping before a door she'd not yet encountered, she twisted the knob and shouldered into the room. May the goddesses grant that, at long last, she'd found the right one.

Her eyes darted along the wooden walls and disappointment crashed down upon her shoulders. Hot tears of defeat stung her eyes.

No armoire. No mirror.

"You lose."

A pair of obsidian eyes swarmed her vision. A jagged dagger plunged toward her chest, and Faedrah screamed...

Drawing a deep breath, Princess Faedrah Austiere fought to clear the disturbing nightmare from behind the pulsing canvas of her closed eyelids. The comforting pattern of the training mat's woven reeds cushioned her bottom. Spine straight. Hands relaxed on her thighs. Knees bent and ankles crossed. She envisioned the terrifying images escaping the top of her head for the ceiling and slowly exhaled, easing the tension from her body. She had returned to the realm of the living, was in the sparring room awaiting Vaighn, and must focus if she intended to win out the day.

The door creaked open and she peeked through the dark fringe of her lashes as her elder cousin entered.

"Good morning, Poppet."

His use of her childhood nickname made her jaw clench. His tousled locks and the disheveled slouch of his untucked shirt forced her lips into a sneer. "Been tossing the sheets with another courtier, have we? Who was the recipient of your bumbling affections this time?"

A lop-sided grin deepened the dimple in one of his scruffy cheeks. The merry twinkle in his amber gaze relayed she'd targeted the cause behind his late arrival. "No one you need concern yourself with."

"Good." She closed her eyes and feigned the continuance of her meditations whilst, in reality, she kept both ears sharply tuned to his motions about the room. Ruse or not, she would not fall victim to Vaighn's casual demeanor. She'd done so before only to have her ass presented back to her on a platter.

A labored sigh lifted her chest, and her fingers involuntarily tightened on her knees. Vaighn's reputation as a rogue plagued her more often than not, all thanks to her position in the realm and her father's coddling eye. Though cousins by blood, most in the kingdom had branded them siblings, and the vast contrast of her untouchable purity to his scandalous escapades oft lay the

5

sour taint of jealousy upon her heart.

Another peek as he bracketed his hands on the base of his spine, and a smile twitched her lips whilst he worked out the kinks in his back. Mayhap, this day, she could exploit his lack of restful slumber to her benefit. For once, his fatigue matched hers and she'd been presented the opportunity to trounce him sound and true…and, in the process, leave him no alternative but to advance her training to the Gantlet. A reward that, once accomplished, would serve both their goals.

Yet he would never concede unless she proved herself the more adept adversary. She tipped her head side to side, rolling the rigid set of her shoulders. To cheat and grant her sanction merely because they shared a familial bond went against everything he believed in. For all her impatience, it went against everything they *both* believed in…and would incite the wrath of her father in ways neither one of them were prepared to pay.

As a seasoned warrior ten years her elder, Vaighn was poised to succeed Denmar Emsworth as Captain of the Royal Guard. A position Vaighn had fought hard to attain since his father's desertion and fateful disappearance, and one Denmar would not relinquish until Vaighn's abilities as a mentor were proven through her skill.

Yet, if any heart in the realm understood the overwhelming pressure Vaighn bore to validate his worth, 'twas the one which beat in her chest.

A princess by birthright, her place within the kingdom had been plotted. The events of her life charted and coursed. As the single heir to the half-blood gypsy king and his prophesied white sorceress, Faedrah's path to the throne was assured, though her doubts were many she'd ever be granted the undying adoration lauded upon her parents. Their achievements had simply set the bar too high, and her tedious ascension through the guard fell far short of their glorious salvation of every soul in the kingdom.

Even though her mother and father steadfastly professed she'd one day rule with benevolence and grace, she'd yet to gain the respect of the Council…not to mention the admiration of the realm.

The only opportunity for her to do as much was to earn her crest. If only she could prove to Vaighn she was ready…if she could follow her mother's shining example and be only the second woman in Austiere history to gain entrance to the Gantlet then, at long last, she would have finally made a step in the right direction.

"Do you plan to deliberate your defense all morning or shall we get started?"

Hah! As if she were a first year recruit. "I was prepared for your assault the moment you entered the room."

Faedrah blinked and stretched her arms forward, fingers linked and palms aimed toward the wall. Vaighn fisted the back of his shirt and whisked the collar over his head.

Releasing her hands, she scanned his bare torso as he tossed the clothing aside. Muscled and lean, his shoulders and chest bore the scars of his battle-worn talents. The chiseled planes of his stomach bespoke a life spent dedicated to training hard and playing harder.

Not that she found his physique the least bit appealing, especially in lieu of their familial ties and his unwavering aversion to any moral compass.

Several dark bruises marred the tanned skin of his throat, and she lifted a shrewd brow at the stark evidence of the latter. "Your latest conquest was a biter, I see."

He chuckled and retrieved his sword, swiping the blade in a wide arc on either side of his hips. "Oh fair Lindeen. What she lacks in beauty, she offsets in enthusiasm."

Faedrah huffed. And no doubt the poor girl would appear at her chamber door two days hence, begging Faedrah to deliver Vaighn a scented missive wrapped in a hankie…which he would decidedly ignore.

Pressing her palms to the floor, she uncurled the length of her body and pushed into a handstand. Her braid tumbled past her shoulders and hit the mat with a heavy *plop*. She closed her eyes and focused on centering her balance, all while presenting Vaighn the two short swords crossed at her back. "For far too many reasons than I care to count, I cannot wait to cram my boot up your—"

"Now, now, Poppet." Reeds crinkled as he stepped onto the sparring mat. "Is that truly the proper way to address your superior?"

Sweet tits of the nine. If only today were the day *she* could teach *him* a lesson.

Wait for it...

The whisper of honed silver sliced the air a moment before she flipped to her feet. Utilizing her momentum, she sprang hands to heels away from him as he advanced, the tip of his sword slashing a scant mote from her body. A spin on her toe and she unsheathed her weapons.

Lunging forward, she crossed her blades overhead to arrest his attack. A twist of her wrists and his weapon was trapped, lodged between the edge of her sword and its long u-shaped quillon. A thrust of her boot against the wall of his chest and he stumbled back, hilt torn from his hand and blade careening to the mat with a dull chime.

"Very good." He nodded, raking his ebony hair back from his brow.

"Not good enough, you mean."

His eyes widened as she sprinted at him full force. A moment before they collided, she dropped to one knee and swept her leg in a wide semi-circle. His feet were wrenched from beneath him. A grunt burst from his chest as his back slammed the floor.

She grinned and rolled onto her shoulders, hands braced on either side of her head. As he struggled to his feet, she pinioned her heels against his ribcage, using the strength of her thighs to knock him askew. He stumbled sideways, but the distance allowed him to reclaim his sword.

Son of a whore!

Whirling around, she charged for the far wall. Three steps up and she flew back, body extended. Her braid whipped the air as she jabbed his defenses from above. Silver clashed and a dense vibration pulsed up the bones of her arm.

The impact threw her landing off balance. His fist shot out and pain exploded through her shoulder. Numbness tingled into her fingertips. The breath was thrust from her lungs as he drove the top of his head into the pit of her stomach.

Pounding his back and kicking her feet, she gritted her teeth as he hefted her onto his shoulder and carried her to the center of the mat. An *oopf* blurted from her lips as he deposited her on her ass with an unceremonious thump.

"Goddesses' tits, Poppet. What deviltry has gotten into you today?" Hands braced on his knees, he panted and shook his head. "I think you may have cracked one of my ribs." A wince squeezed his eyes tight as he straightened and pressed a palm to his side. He groaned.

Propping her elbows on her knees, Faedrah swallowed past the hard knot of defeat crowding the base of her throat. Whatever wounds she may have inflicted didn't matter. She'd still lost. The error in her strategy had ensured as much the moment she raced for the wall. "I was not high enough, was I?" How many times had he warned her to estimate her ascent to the height of her opponent? And if not enough space to strike without risking injury, to alter the angle of her attack. "I should have never engaged you from overhead."

Someone cleared their throat and she and Vaighn looked toward the doorway.

The queen stood resplendent in her gray leather warrior's ensemble, cheeks rosy and a glint of humor sparkling in her emerald eyes, unbound hair sheeting past her shoulders like bolts of silver-spun silk. She crossed her arms and shifted her weight onto one hip. "If you two can spare a moment between maiming each other, your father and I are ready to break our fast."

Faedrah frowned. Normally, the king and queen dallied about a morning ride before breakfast. Or rather, they dallied about whatever shameless activities they shared whilst hidden amongst the trees. This delay was rare occurrence, indeed. "Has something happened, M'ma?"

"Denmar and Fandorn have asked to join us this morning." She smirked. "But don't worry. I'm sure your father will insist we have our ride before the day is through."

Vaighn chuckled at her veiled meaning, scratching at the unkempt bristle under his chin.

Faedrah grimaced and kicked the side of his ankle. "Please."

Though it was well bandied about the castle the king and queen still enjoyed a torrid love affair an abundance of years into their marriage, she didn't need the reminder. Certainly, amongst the entire kingdom, she was the only girl of twenty to have never been kissed. While most courtiers her age enjoyed a variety of dalliances, and the proposals for her hand in marriage still filtered in with the same profusion they had since her sixteenth season, her father had yet to entertain even one of the suitable candidates. Not even her mother's insistence Faedrah was well into the age of eligibility swayed his decision.

No, he preferred her days be filled with swordplay, presiding over provincial disputes and the droning of the council in matters of state.

"Come." The queen tipped her head and disappeared from the doorway, and Faedrah sheathed her swords before awaiting Vaighn to trail after her.

A grim apprehension sparked along her nerve endings as she climbed the stairs at her adoptive brother's side, yet it wasn't the impromptu summons to the king's chambers which tautened her nerves. For as long as she could remember, her family had taken their meals together. A rule her mother insisted upon whenever she and the king were in residence.

The uneasy comings and goings of the guard is what made her peek askance at Vaighn, and when the glint of anxiety in his gaze mirrored her own suspicions, she quickened her pace as he lengthened his stride.

Something was amiss in the kingdom.

A pair of obsidian eyes streaked across her vision. She shuddered and fisted her hands at her sides. May the goddesses grant whatever had occurred was not the least bit connected to her nightmares, and the horrifying dreams were merely an offshoot of her wearisome shortcomings…or her unsatisfied libido.

Her mother led them to the king's receiving room and, upon entering, Vaighn strode directly toward the long wooden table centered before the hearth. Nodding a greeting to Denmar and Wizard Fandorn, he bowed to her father and assumed his appointed seat on the king's right.

His position of honor was not questioned by those in the room, nor was the ease with which her father clasped a welcoming hand on Vaighn's shoulder, and Faedrah clamped down hard on the twinge of envy deepening her pulse.

Such courtesies had not always been granted the direct descendant of Braedric Austiere, her father's half-brother and their kingdom's most treasonous enemy. Following the charges levied against his father for crimes against the crown, Vaighn's mother had fled in shame back to her homeland. At the tender age of ten, Vaighn had been set adrift, homeless and alone, without guardianship in the kingdom.

Bearing witness to his nephew's suffering had reminded King Caedmon of his own torturous childhood. He'd survived firsthand the terrible stigma inherent in the iniquitous opinions of the court, branded impure simply because of the gypsy blood which flowed through his veins. Despite the agitation his decree sent rippling through the kingdom, he had welcomed Vaighn as an adoptive son and future leader in their kingdom…for, in this, he'd made his ruling clear.

Under the reign of King Caedmon Austiere, the sins of the father would not be visited upon the son.

In the seasons since, Vaighn had not once shown anything but the utmost respect and allegiance to the Austiere throne, though few but Faedrah fully gleaned the reason why. Due his desperate need to demonstrate he was unlike his father, Vaighn could offer no less. To do as much would betray the oath he'd sworn to the one man who'd offered him sanctuary, and the uncle he grew to love as father and king.

The four men lowered their heads as their conversation resumed, and Faedrah hastened across the room to join them. Yet she was waylaid when the queen skimmed a hand down her forearm and pulled her near the high stained-glass window...and, more specifically, the roosting stand of her beloved falcon, Dart.

"Give them a moment, Faedrah. Your father agrees the day's affairs would best be addressed after a hearty meal. Let the men banter about the latest grievances of the council while you and I catch a breath of fresh air."

Uh oh...

Never, in all the days since Faedrah's birth, had her mother drawn her aside for a clandestine conversation. If one thing above all was abundantly clear, the king and queen did not keep secrets from one another.

A cool spring breeze filtered in from the surrounding mountains, ruffling her mother's white tresses and soothing the weariness from Faedrah's brow. She kept her attention firmly fixed on the falcon, running the back of her index finger down his silky spotted breast. Yet she did not speak. Her time navigating the intricacies of the court had taught her well. Holding one's tongue in times of doubt was always the more prudent course.

She instinctively leaned into her mother's hand when the queen lightly combed her fingers through the ebony stripe marring Faedrah's otherwise light-blonde hair. Her father had often teased that, other than her dark eyes, the strange anomaly was the only trait she carried of her gypsy heritage.

"Are you quite right, dove?"

Ah. Of course. The strain in Faedrah's shoulders eased a degree and she softly smiled. After a lifetime together, her mother understood better than most the king's propensity to worry, especially when those he loved were in question. The queen would certainly validate any misgivings which had snared her attention before voicing her concerns to the king. "I'm fine, M'ma. Truly. A few restless nights, is all."

The queen cupped Faedrah's face in both palms and placed a gentle kiss on her forehead. "You must remember, my heart. I was nearly ten years your elder before I'd earned my chance to contest in the Gantlet. Comparing your path to mine does not serve you well. And neither is it wise you should compare yourself to Vaighn."

Faedrah slumped. How easily her mother had honed in on her frustrations. She must be as transparent as glass. "But you achieved as much in two passings of the seasons, M'ma. Four passings now, and I've still not earned my chance."

"You fret too much." Pressing their brows together, the queen smiled into Faedrah's eyes. "Just like your father. I promise one day soon your time will come, and when it does you shall shine brighter than all of Helios' diamond offerings in the sky."

She withdrew and tipped her head, a musing frown pleating the skin between her brows. "In the meantime, I really must insist you get some sleep. Promise me you will tread lightly on yourself or I fear your father may order you abandon your training altogether."

Alarm jabbed the pit of Faedrah's stomach and tears of exhaustion flooded her eyes. "No, M'ma." She clasped her mother's wrists to emphasize her distress. "He mustn't. Not when I'm so close to advancing."

"Your father and I just want what's best for you, Faedrah." The queen sighed and shook her head. "Not one amongst the court measures themselves against the lofty ideals you've established for yourself. Helios forbid they ever would." She pulled Faedrah into her arms and held tight. "I will buy you some time, but that is the best I can offer. Now please promise me you will try to get some sleep."

The king cleared his throat. "Is everything quite right over there?"

"Right as rain." Her mother leaned back with a smile, applying a squeeze to Faedrah's shoulders. "Come now and let's eat."

Faedrah trailed her mother to the table and sat in her appointed position on the queen's right, yet before she'd wet her lips with her first sip of wine, her father sat back from his plate and pinned her with an arched brow.

He tapped his cheek.

Faedrah rolled her eyes and stood, rounded the table and pecked the spot above the trim salt and pepper beard accenting his square jaw. "Good morning, P'pa."

"That's better." He nodded once curtly, pursing his lips against smile, though the weight of his gaze lingered on her back as she circled the table and reclaimed her seat.

Her heart sank the same distance she lowered onto her chair, and she avoided his inspection by tipping her wine goblet to her lips. Whilst her mother spoke true and her father did worry, the circumstances surrounding his impending decision left her few choices. Either she confessed the true reason behind her fitful slumber or she remained silent. Regardless, the outcome would furrow her around to this exact same position. Her parents would become agitated…perchance even angry she'd kept them unaware, and they would insist she break from her training until the source of her nightmares had been found.

The conversation resumed where it had apparently left off—Councilman Vlandross' yearly petition to increase taxes, and his heated response to her father's adamant refusal. Faedrah concentrated on rearranging the smoked fish and fruit on her plate. She had heard both sides of the argument several times. 'Twas the same every spring. Much to Artemis Vlandross' annoyance, her father rejected the notion of lining his coffers with the hard-earned profits borne off the sweat of his subjects' brows. And, history had shown, he'd made the proper choice. Under his reign, their kingdom had prospered, trade had increased. The Austiere Realm had enjoyed a season of peace they'd not encountered in centuries.

Faedrah selected a hard roll from the silver bowl on the table and tore the loaf in half, balancing each end on either side of her plate. If only she could unearth the reason behind her nightmares, then perchance she could vanquish them once and for all. She chewed the inside of her lip. Her mother had promised her a bit more time and, to succeed, she must use it wisely. But, sweet tits of the nine, where did she even begin? She held no more sway over her dreams than, evidently, she did her future.

The king slammed his fist to the table and Faedrah snapped out of reverie. "What quality of monarch willingly filches the coins from his subjects' pockets only to then turn around and demand allegiance from those same men?"

"Or women," the queen interjected.

"Yes, quite right." Sunlight winked off the thin gold band bisecting the king's brow as he nodded down the table toward his queen. "To do as much undermines the very principles upon which Rowena and I have based our sovereignty. I shall not ask our kinsfolk to forfeit their comforts in exchange for that which we do not need. For then, as much as they prosper, it is my utmost belief they shall heed my call to arms should the occasion arise."

Denmar propped his elbow on the table and stroked the point of his wiry gray beard, one steely blue eye squinting at the king, the empty socket of the other hidden behind his black leather eye patch. "That same occasion may very well be upon us, Sire."

Faedrah's pulse leapt and she jerked her focus back to her father. He held up his hand, darting a sharp glance about the room. "Leave us."

The servants quickly deposited their serving platters and wine vessels on the table, bowed and backed toward the exit. Two of the queen's personal guard secured the chamber and stood stiff as boards inside the door, an armored wall of flesh sworn to protect her by an oath as strong and true as the deadly swords at their sides.

15

The king leaned his forearm on the table. A subtle peek at the queen, and he refocused on the captain of the royal guard. "What news of the black infestation?"

Faedrah collapsed against the back of her padded seat. *What black infestation?* Her stomach lurched and she swallowed the acidic bile crawling up the back of her throat. She locked onto Vaighn, but the surprise lifting his brows displayed no deception. Whatever secrets were about to be revealed, he'd not been given the slightest forewarning.

At least, in this, they remained equal.

"Reddeck and his Dregg legions have been unable to locate the source." Wine glugged from the ewer as Fandorn refilled his goblet. A droplet of claret left the lip to stain the linen tablecloth like a bead of red blood. He lifted the golden rim to his lips and his Adam's apple bobbed beneath the weathered skin of his neck.

Faedrah clenched her jaw against the urge to gag. Sweat broke the surface of her skin and trickled down the nape of her neck. Since the time of her birth, a clan of large bat-like Dreggs had served the king and queen with a loyalty nigh to obsession. She must concentrate if she hoped to glean the reason behind their concerns.

"Yet the trees continue to wither and die at an alarming rate." The aged wizard twirled the stem of his glass between his bony fingers. "The epidemic is spreading."

A wave of vertigo pitched her off-center, and Faedrah seized the arms of her chair. What was happening? Not a morsel of food had passed her lips, so why was she suddenly ill?

"They have but one conclusion, of course." Denmar crossed his beefy arms and the stench of rotting flesh permeated her senses. "They fear for Gaelleod's return."

"Helios save us," Vaighn whispered. "The black wizard rises."

The floor heaved, and Faedrah stiffened in her seat. Her lungs constricted despite her desperate need for air. What were they talking about? No, no, the black wizard couldn't be real. He was merely a figment of her imagination.

A pair of dead, stygian eyes coalesced in the space before her. A malevolent chuckle floated past her ear. *"I warned you, Faedrah. You cannot hide from me…"*

Yet he was here. In her realm.

"Faedrah?"

She spun toward her mother and opened her mouth, but words refused to form on her lifeless tongue. Why had they not told her? She pounded her fist on the table. Shook her head and grappled with her frozen throat. By striving to protect her they had condemned her to hell!

"Caedmon!" Her mother leapt to her feet. "She's not breathing! Caedmon, *she's not breathing*!"

The din of clanging silver erupted amid the shattering of china plates. Shadows flickered at the edges of her vision. Faedrah seized her mother's outstretched arms, dug her nails into the leather sleeves. "The…key…"

She choked; toppled forward.

Her mother's scream rebounded inside her skull as darkness swooped in to swallow her whole.

Chapter 2

"We should have confessed the truth to her long ago."

The profound sadness in her mother's voice tugged Faedrah from the quiet gloaming of slumber and, with her ascent into waking, she inhaled a full, sweet breath. Based on the hint of night-blooming jasmine her mother enjoyed sewn into sachets and hidden beneath her pillows, she lay in her parents' private chamber, tucked safely beneath the coverlet on their bed.

She drew another blessed breath, and a prayer of gratitude floated heavenward with the ease of her exhalation. Thank the nine, whatever specter had cast its loathsome pall over her body, it had released its deathly grip. Henceforth, she would never again discount the simple task of drawing air.

"We discussed the topic at length, my love. On several occasions." Her father sighed, the heels of his boots tapping the continuous pace of his long-legged stride across the stone floor. "She displayed no outward signs of her laments, and must understand we merely kept silent to protect her."

Skepticism laced her mother's soft chuckle. "She's displayed the signs since childhood. Or do you not recall how often we discovered her in this very room, standing before the armoire, staring at the doors as if her spirit had been transported to the other side? Not to mention her persistent questions regarding the key. I lost track of the evenings she begged you to recount the details of our meeting."

Images from Faedrah's youth floated in on the wistful strands of her memories and coalesced to a vivid picture in her mind. Whilst 'twas true, the mesmerizing lure of the armoire had been a perplexing distraction ever since childhood, she'd never believed her spirit transported to another realm. 'Twas more as if she found untold comfort in the armoire's presence. As if, in her father's retelling of the golden key and magic mirror hidden inside, a strange vacancy had been banished from her soul.

Only after acquiring her parent's solemn promise that, one day, the armoire would pass to her, had she surrendered her insistence to remain within its reach. Though not for one moment had her fascination with its mysterious contents faded. Even now, as she nestled within the haven of her parents' sleeping pallet, the appeal of the armoire called to her from across the room.

"Those were nothing more than the fleeting fancies of a little girl." Her father's footsteps paused and, behind her closed eyelids, she envisioned the way he habitually raked his hair back from his brow. "She's not shown interest in such tales since she was small enough to bounce upon my knee."

Tension filled the silence which followed, at odds with the gentle snap and crackle of the fire in the hearth. A log shifted.

"She was too young then to fully comprehend the dangers we faced at the hands of that vile bastard." Her father's words were clipped. "Helios save me, I prayed such horrors would never be imposed upon her heart."

"As did I." The tender caress of her mother's palm warmed the back of Faedrah's hand. The queen twined their fingers together and lifted. Her soft lips bestowed a tender kiss.

"She has not been sleeping of late." The bed dipped near Faedrah's right foot, a fitful anguish sharpening Vaighn's tone. "I should have reported my suspicions the moment they occurred."

"Do not take the blame upon yourself." The supple curve of

her mother's cheek brushed the inside of Faedrah's wrist. "Despite my best efforts to share in her worries, she's always preferred to suffer in silence. I've oft wondered if our vigilance to keep her safe has done more harm than good. Instead of speaking her fears, she secrets them away in hopes of lessening our concerns."

"Mayhap we should invite the princess' council in the matter." Fandorn spoke on her left and every muscle in Faedrah's body tensed. He'd been so quiet, she'd not detected his presence in the room…and nothing ever went unnoticed by the ancient wizard's eye. "She is awake and has been eavesdropping on our conversation for quite some time."

She blinked and glanced around the faces in the room, all displaying varying degrees of surprise. Except for Fandorn, occupying a chair beside the bed, his gray eyes glittering with curiosity from behind his steepled fingers.

Vaighn's features were the first to break into a smile. "You gave us a proper fright, Poppet." He grabbed her ankle through the blankets and applied a gentle shake. "Do you yet feel strong enough to relay what happened?"

To be certain. In fact, if anything, her muscles were more relaxed, her mind sharper and her body better well-rested than what seemed in a fortnight. Faedrah pushed to sitting and her mother quickly propped the pillows along the ornately carved headboard, arranging them to cushion her shoulders and back. "How long have I been asleep?"

Her family exchanged a round of nervous glances, and her heart stuttered in response. Whatever their impending reply, they feared for her reaction.

"'Tis nearly Apex." The queen resumed her grip on Faedrah's hand. "Two days hence."

What? She bolted upright the same distance three sets of arms reached out and pressed her back into the pillows. *Two days* she'd been lost to her slumber? She batted the hands away and quickly took stock of her surroundings. Impossible!

Several discarded trays of food littered her mother's dressing table, the end tables and floor. Blankets hung crumpled over the arms of two leather chairs and lay spread as a makeshift sleeping pallet before the hearth.

She lowered her head and stared at the white lace cuffs of her sleeping gown, hanging limp and wrinkled off each of her wrists. Her jaw firmed. How dare he? Anger swirled to a hot maelstrom in her chest and, with it, her fingers curled into two rigid fists in the air. What manner of arrogant beast presumed he could reach through the ether of her dreams and steal the very fabric of her life?

"Who is he?" She lifted her gaze and stared hard at her mother and father in turn. If they had been honest with her from the beginning, she would've been prepared for the dangers she faced. All this time, 'twas more than her vivid imagination haunting the wanderings of her dreams. "This Gaelleod you spoke of. Is he not a soulless creature, robed in black, his eyes bottomless pools which spiral into the very pits of hell?"

Her mother gasped at the same moment Fandorn abruptly sat forward. "What do you know of such wickedness, child? Speak clearly now and with an apt tongue. The days of secrecy are behind us."

The wizard brought forth a valid point, and had seen through her frustration to the crux of the matter…something he did with irritating regularity. Her parents' did not bear the fault of these circumstances alone. She had kept silent as well, when candor would have been the more prudent choice. "The black wizard you spoke of haunts me in my dreams."

Her father strode forward and lowered to the bed, grasping her upper arms to commence a detailed study of her face. "Goddesses wept, Faedrah." The profound anguish in his chocolate gaze wrenched her heart, so filled with sorrow…and a direct reflection of the same eyes which stared back at her whenever she chanced by a mirrored glass. "Why did you not bring us this news? For how long have you endured this ordeal?"

How long, indeed? She'd lost count of the endless interludes filled with the dark lord's pitiless cruelty. What had started as the occasional descent into wrestling his invasion of her slumber, had increased to a nightly sojourn of murderous intent. "They've multiplied in frequency since the dawn of the new year."

Her father whisked her close and enveloped her in his arms, cradling the back of her head in his calloused palm. "Nearly three cycles of the moon." His tortured whisper rumbled into the cavern of her chest. She turned her cheek to the soft cotton of his shirt, the musky scent of his skin, the protective nurturing of his strong embrace a comfort to ease the recollection of her suffering.

"And the exact correspondence to when the first whisperings of the black infestation began," Fandorn muttered.

Faedrah withdrew from her father, though the reluctant loosening of his arms bespoke his unwillingness to release her.

He brushed the hair back from her brow and placed a light kiss in her forehead. "Why has this happened, Fandorn?"

"I cannot state with certainty until she recounts the full details of her dreams." The wizard tapped his index finger against his lips. "Tell us, child. What occurs in your chambers between the tolling of the setting bell and daybreak?"

Faedrah glanced toward her mother and received a nod of encouragement before she closed her eyes, delaying a moment to submerse herself in the grim images of her nightmares. "I am in a house filled with many doors, all of them different." A chill tingled through the hair on her arms as the confusing maze of corridors swam into focus. "Only one leads to freedom, behind which awaits the armoire, and yet, despite the urgency of my search, I cannot locate the correct one. Light is strung along the walls, glowing glass orbs which contain no flame. The air carries a metallic taint. I wear the key and the taunting of the black wizard pursues me. No matter my course, I cannot hide from the scope of his all-seeing eye."

She blinked and scanned the horrified alarm etched into the

faces of her family. Yet the worst was still to come, and she gathered her resolve to deliver the last of her warnings. "'Twas the same two days past, at breakfast. Except his promise that I would never evade his clutches came to me whilst Helios hung bright in the sky. And, instead of plunging his jagged knife into my chest, he reached through the ether of my dreams and stole the breath from my lungs."

A long moment of silence wound through the brittle anxiety pervading the room.

"He's broken through to her waking hours." Her mother dropped her focus to the bed. She shook her head and a tear tumbled from her cheek to splatter the dark-blue coverlet. "Dammit, Caedmon. His strength grows even as we sit here unable to provide our daughter shelter from his wrath."

He sprang to his feet and Faedrah carefully studied the rigid set of her father's shoulders, the way his hands had balled into two hard fists at his sides. Once, mayhap twice, in all her days at the castle had she witnessed such profound panic overtake him. Who was this creature which delivered her parents to the brink of dread?

"We must redouble our efforts to uncover the source of the black plague invading the forest." He crossed his arms and aimed a dangerous glare at Fandorn. "Perchance once the disease is eliminated, Faedrah's affliction will cease."

"Indeed." Fandorn sat back in his chair, yet the calculating scrutiny of his gray gaze remained embedded on her. She nervously ran her palm down the back of her hair. He'd studied her with such intensity before, and the perceptive glint in his eyes always left her fully unsettled.

"Yet we must not discount the obvious, Majesty." He shifted his attention to the king. "Shall I tell her or do you prefer the honor?"

Faedrah darted her focus about the chamber. The way her mother and father read the measure of one another's thoughts from across the bed...the flush of embarrassment which reddened Vaighn's neck... Something more untoward than her nightly visitation of a nameless phantom was at play.

"I ask again." She held her tongue until each person in the room returned their attention to her. "Who is he?"

Her father's shoulders fell. He mumbled what seemed a string of obscenities before Vaighn held his palm in the air. "Please, Uncle. Allow me." He swiveled toward Faedrah and raked his fingers through his wavy hair. "Twenty cycles of the seasons ago, before the king and queen were blessed with the joy of your birth, Wizard Gaelleod attended the court of King Seviere. Yet the red king was deceived by his servant, as were many others, most notably my father, Prince Braedric. 'Twas with my father's aid, Gaelleod was given access to capture and torture our dear king for two unrelenting years."

Faedrah glanced at the misery pleating her father's dark brow. Her parents had never recounted the finer points surrounding his captivity. Whenever she'd asked, the details were vague at best. She'd assumed his aversion to discussing the insufferable span he'd languished in Seviere's dungeons had been due his reluctance to relive the past. Not wanting to cause him further anguish, she had kept her queries at bay.

No wonder the slightest mention of Seviere's vile wizard had cast him into a tailspin. Better than any other, he understood the menace which arose from Gaelleod's unholy grave.

Her father's palm landed on Vaighn's shoulder and his fingertips whitened with a firm squeeze. "The agony I endured was not by your hand, Vaighn. To this day, I regret you carry the load of such a terrible burden."

Vaighn nodded, but kept his attention solely affixed on Faedrah. Unspent tears transformed his eyes into glittering amber pools, and her heart rebelled at the evidence he still bore the responsibility of that heavy strain. "The war fought during the Night of Silver Knives did not merely expose Braedric Austiere's deception, Poppet. Nor did it singly denote your father's ascent to the throne. Due the bravery of your mother and with Fandorn's aid, the two of them ensured the battle also initiated an end to Gaelleod's reign."

The outcome of that legendary conflict comprised the totality of Faedrah's world. Moreover, the bravery her mother and father had demonstrated in declaring Prince Braedric a traitor defined the very yoke of inadequacy she wore around her neck. In reigning victorious, no other soul in the kingdom had so fiercely established their allegiance to the throne. Yet neither the king nor the queen had ever mentioned the involvement of Seviere's black wizard… or the courage her mother had displayed in banishing him from their realm.

"Or so we had longed to believe." The queen placed her hand atop the king's, covering Vaighn's shoulder in a show of solidarity. "Gaelleod vanished from sight before we could confirm his undoing. This harbinger of his rising is a danger we prayed none of our heirs would ever face."

Faedrah's eyes fell closed as she collapsed against the pillows. In remaining silent, her parents had hoped to shutter her from danger. They had hidden away the pain and determined she live free of their fate. Over time, with no sign of the dark lord's return, they had assumed their initial assessment the best for her welfare. So much, they had commanded the entire court bide their tongues on her behalf.

How could she blame them their decisions? To do as much would display the very height of rudeness and disrespect. She shuddered as the baleful echo of Gaelleod's evil threats whispered across the province of her mind.

Regardless, this villain from their past had found her. He'd re-emerged from the realm of the undead to threaten the one thing they held dear above all else…and the one who bore the future of their kingdom upon her back.

And yet, one question remained.

How had he done it?

Through what link had the black wizard stretched his sharpened claws to ensure *she* be the recipient of his affections? What connection did they share? Other than in her dreams, she'd not once been granted access to the key. So how had he determined her place in Austiere history?

She opened her eyes and pinned her parents with a determined scowl. "What are you not telling me?"

Alarm nipped at the heels of her query as her father's cheeks flooded a deep red. "Sweet tits of the nine!" He spun on her mother. "She is so like you, betimes I wonder if she inherited a portion of my traits at all."

The queen lowered her chin, but the subtle movement did not disguise her soft chuckle. "Rest assured, our daughter has your penchant for worry, my king."

Fandorn stood and strode toward the armoire, its forbidding presence guarding their conversation like a silent sentry from across the room. "Gaelleod's violation of the princess' thoughts is troubling, to be sure. Perchance her connection to the armoire plays a role. The clues hidden within the framework of her dreams. Did you not recognize them, Majesty?"

"Aye." Her father nodded. "The light with no flame, the metallic taint in the air…" He locked his dark-brown gaze on to hers. "Each night, Faedrah is transported to the future."

Her jaw dropped. Shock blanked her mind as the meaning behind her father's words scuttled home. To the *future*? How was such a thing even a possibility?

"But I hold no connection to my mother's realm." Faedrah opened her hands over the bed as if they could somehow provide the answer. "Not once have I traversed through the veil."

"Oh, but you have, Faedrah." Her mother smiled softly at the king from her spot on Faedrah's left. "You were conceived in the future, my heart."

Every particle in the room froze.

The next instant, a seething inferno rushed Faedrah's veins, raging across her skin, so banked by flames of embarrassment and awareness and the vibrancy of long-lost recognition, she tossed

26

the covers from her legs and leapt from the bed.

No wonder she'd been persistently drawn to the armoire. Closing her eyes, she doubled over at the waist, gathered the folds of her sleeping gown and clasped them near her stomach. A hand grasped her shoulder and she shrugged it from her body.

How often had she questioned her sanity? While standing before the doors, on how many occasions had she denied the painful splintering of her soul? Blessed tears of the nine, the seasons had she wasted, trying to convince herself the emptiness was caused by some deficiency in her personality. She'd been born less than what was expected by all those within the realm.

Fighting back the surge of bile her empty stomach propelled up the lining of her throat, she squeezed her eyes tight and groaned. And how many days had she been ushered from the armoire's presence, confused and afraid, wondering in what parcel of her heart the fault lay, the steps she could take to mend it?

Well, no more.

Setting her jaw, she slowly straightened, releasing the folds of her sleeping gown to the floor. No longer would she languish in self-doubt. The time had come to cast her uncertainties behind her.

She opened her eyes to the guarded expectancy awash on each face in the chamber. From this moment henceforth, she would collect the tattered strings of her destiny and weave her own fate. And if that vile bastard awaited her in the future, she would chase him from her dreams and thrust him back into the dank pit from whence he'd crawled!

"As soon as I am able, I will travel through the veil."

The room erupted into chaos. Her mother and Vaighn sprang to their feet. Shouts of denial echoed off the ceiling and walls, the loudest of which barreled from her father.

"You shall do no such thing!" The thunder of his approach initiated the urge to shrink back, but Faedrah held firm, lifting her chin in defiance. "As your father, I forbid it. As your king, I command you remain in this realm."

27

"The risks are too great, Faedrah." Her mother came forward and clasped Faedrah's hands. "We have no idea what awaits you on the other side."

Oh, they understood exactly what evil loomed opposite the mirror. And so did she. "I am tired of running from him, Mother. Did you not state just two days past my time would soon come? None of us can deny our place in history. Not even me."

"I will *not* allow this to happen." The king aimed a hard finger at the floor. "If needs be, I shall detain her under lock and key."

Faedrah's heart shattered. A sharp pain arrowed into her chest. Did her father not see the outcome of his decision? Condemning her to a ceaseless string of nights filled with fear?

A caustic retort settled upon her tongue, yet she bit down hard against unleashing her anger. Sarcasm would only enrage him further, and prove she was exactly the impetuous child they claimed her to be.

"The princess does present a compelling argument, Sire." Fandorn turned from his musings before the armoire and hope leapt warm and alive through her veins. At last, someone in her family spoke reason. Who, besides her, bore the cost of Gaelleod's evil promises? Who among them but her would recognize the details of his lair? "Yet the perils of traveling through the veil unattended are indeed problematic. Perchance a more detailed examination of the forest is warranted before we outright dismiss the princess' petition."

"I could traverse with her." Vaighn stepped forward and Faedrah nearly collapsed to her knees in thanks. If not in her sleeping attire, she would have leapt into his arms and tossed her arms around his neck. "On my honor, Uncle. I shall die before allowing any harm to come to your daughter."

Not one doubt remained that he would. To atone for the transgressions of his father, Vaighn would be the first to fall upon a sword in her defense.

"Unfortunately, your loyalty to Princess Faedrah is not the issue, my boy." Fandorn plucked his long wooden staff from where it leaned against the side of the mantel and rested the bottom end near his right foot. "Regardless of your honor, the mirror will not allow your safe passage."

Faedrah's hope sputtered and died. *Now* what dismal revelations had the wizard in store?

"Only those hearts bonded in love may be granted entry, as I'm certain the king and queen remember all too well. While I've no qualms you share a strong attachment to your cousin, the two of you have not pledged a vow of love. Unless…" He aimed a bushy eyebrow first at Faedrah, then at Vaighn.

"Oh no! No, no!" She and Vaighn spoke over each other in adamant refusal. Goddesses wept, that was the last complication she needed. Faedrah slapped a palm to her forehead, rolling her eyes.

"Very well, then." Fandorn faced the king and queen. "With your majesties' permission, I shall endeavor to search out Denmar and request he gather a squadron of his best guards to ride for the trees."

"Yes, quite right, and the queen and I shall accompany you." Her father aimed a sharp finger at Vaighn. "You…" He shifted the imposing digit in her direction. "Watch her." With a glance between them, he jerked his head toward the door and followed her mother and Fandorn from the room.

Faedrah slumped as the door slammed behind them. So that was it, then? They were leaving her to rot like some useless moppet unfit to clear the dirt from her face?

"I think I shall see about ordering us up a light meal." Vaighn started after them, his steps unhurried, hands clasped behind his back, and she squinted at the masquerade of his casual demeanor. If anything, he should've been fuming. He'd been assigned nurse-maid duty when a good chance existed he would have preferred to ride out with the guard.

"I was not yet given the opportunity to relay my verdict of our sparring session." He stopped before her and a mischievous smile

29

twitched one corner of his lips. "I am advancing your training to the Gantlet. Given the extent of my injuries, you are ready."

A breath lodged in her throat. That he would admit such confidence in her abilities the same moment her choices had been ripped from her grasp meant...*everything*.

The wave of gratitude which crescendoed through her heart threatened to capsize in a loud *whoop!* She nodded, lowering her chin in a show of respect.

"Now whatever shall you do?" Grit rasped under his boots as he pivoted away from her and sauntered for the door. "A member of the royal guard locked in the king's chamber, only her and the armoire in attendance whilst her parents are absent from the castle walls?"

Sweet tits. She snapped her head up. He couldn't actually be suggesting she purposely disobey their father's—*the king's*—decree?

"And lest you forget, Faedrah." He grabbed the doorknob and winked. "I shall be watching you."

Her brows shot heavenward. He'd just called her Faedrah.

With a quick glance toward the armoire, he swung the door open and left.

Chapter 3

The secret release carved within the top scrollwork of the armoire easily descended under the press of her fingertips. An internal whirring sounded and a small hidden door sprang open, disguised by a square rosette above the top left hinge. Anxiety skittered down Faedrah's spine and she darted a quick glance over her shoulder. On several occasions during childhood, she'd been scolded for surrendering to her curiosity and opening the concealed compartment wherein lay the key. 'Twas no surprise the instinctive bracing of her body bespoke its preparedness to receive a swift, judicious smack on her backside.

She reached inside and her fingers snagged upon the links of a heavy chain. Candlelight winked along the golden cord, snaking from the opening as she withdrew the mysterious treasure. A second glance toward the entrance to her parents' bedchamber, and she carefully lowered the necklace over her head.

Whatever ruse Vaighn had employed to detain the servants, she mustn't dally. Though the onset of spring ensured Helios' delayed descent past the horizon, the king and queen would certainly return soon after Setting…but, by then, their discovery of her disobedience would come too late.

She would not allow their apprehensions to determine her destiny. The Goddesses had placed this task at her feet, and she would follow the path, no matter the risks, until her purpose had been fulfilled.

The soft creak of worn hinges spun her attention back to the armoire, and she withdrew a pace as the door swung wide. A blinding flashpoint zipped around the edge of the mirror's frame. She splayed her fingers in front of her face and squinted past the iridescent shadows impairing her vision. The earth grumbled a warning. The floor pitched and she stumbled to the side as the castle walls heaved a shrug upon their foundation.

Goddess wept. Surely every soul in the realm had experienced the consequence of her forbidden meddling…the results of which guaranteed her parents' homecoming much sooner than she'd originally expected.

Her heart thudded a leaden beat as she reclaimed the distance to the armoire, her knees trembling with excitement and trepidation. There, decorating the back of the door, the veil shimmered and hummed, the flawless glass sparkling like sunlit snowfall upon a winter field.

The view within its frame was dimly illuminated. Beige curtains hung drawn along the far wall of an empty room. A high-backed leather chair sat in the corner, the front legs and padded footstool standing atop the fringed end of a decorative rug. Beside the right arm, a brass fixture sat centered upon a small wooden table, the unwavering light above shaded to a subtle glow.

She lightly skimmed the surface of the glass and her breath caught when her fingers submerged as if she'd dipped them into a silver pool. The reflective liquid stuck to her skin as she withdrew her hand, until the tension broke and sprang back to the mirror, rippling outward as if she'd cast a pebble into a pond.

A door slammed and she flinched. Angry shouts echoed from the king's receiving room. Armor jangled as footsteps neared. The moment for hesitation had expired. Spinning back to the armoire, she closed her eyes, filled her lungs to their capacity and leapt.

Myriad colors pulsed and swirled behind the thin barrier of her eyelids. The corrosive scent of grinding gears, the acrid taint of burnt oil and the coppery tang of spilled blood layered upon her tongue. She tumbled and twirled, arms stretched forward, fingers flexing as she sought purchase on the other side.

The loose strands of her hair whipped a tangled halo around her head. The agitated fanfare of birds taking flight rushed her ears and she was pitched forward, landing on her ass with a solid thump.

The ground teetered unsteadily and she pressed two fingertips to the resonating pulse between her brows. Sweet tits, the disorientation was enough to challenge the most stalwart of men. No wonder her father had balked at the mention of such a journey.

"Well, it's about time you showed up."

She froze; slowly lowered her hand. A lanky gentlemen occupied a tan settee placed along the side wall, his long legs crossed at the knees, fingers curled around the ends of several sheaves of thin, oversized paper he held open before his face.

She frowned. He spoke as if her arrival had been expected.

He turned down one corner of his papers and quickly flipped them back up. "There's a bathrobe behind you. I'm guessing you'll want to put it on."

But…whatever for? A glance down at her naked body and she scrambled to her feet, snagged the garment off a hook beside the armoire and crammed her arms into the sleeves. A jerk to the tie at her waist and she clasped both sides of the collar, twisting them closed beneath her chin.

Movement caught the corner of her eye, and she spun to the side as a dark-haired man entered the room. He glanced at her and his high-pitched scream drilled into her skull. The tray he held clattered to the ground as he slapped both hands to his chest. China shattered against the wooden floor. A small decanter of milk exploded and sugar sprayed as silver spoons bounced and flipped with an ear-splitting clang.

She stared wide-eyed at the mess at his feet before glancing between the two men. Or perchance, she'd not been expected at all.

The man occupying the settee risked a second peek over the edge of his papers, sighed and folded them in half. He tossed his reading aside and stood, tugging on the pointed ends of his buttoned waistcoat before propping his fists on his hips. "Some days, I don't know how I put up with you."

"Well, she scared the bejeezus out of me." The shorter of the two was dressed in much more casual attire than his sharply creased counterpart, yet he affected the same stance, hands punching the hips of his cotton drawstring trousers, the hem of his white shirt bunching above his curled fingers. Though what a "bejeezus" was, she had not a clue. "A little warning might have been nice."

The blond man's brows shot toward his high hairline and he crossed his arms. "You mean besides the earthquake?"

"Chicago *has* experienced seismic activity before, you know." The silken ends of his wavy hair whispered across his shoulders as the second man shook his head. "I swear to God, I will never get used to how those people jump back and forth through that mirror."

Those people? Apparently, these two men were acquainted with her mother and father, and had witnessed such an unceremonious tumble through the veil before.

She squinted as the faint recollection of a bedtime story her father had oft told her whispered across the tableau of her mind. Could it truly be…?

Awareness swooped in like the wings of a dove and she dropped to her knees in display of reverence and devotion. At the time, she'd believed her father's tale a mere fable, a moral founded on friendship and the strength of unselfish love. How mistaken her assumptions. Quite certainly, these men had foreseen her arrival. She'd abandoned her realm for the province of gods.

"Forgive me. I was uninformed the veil would deliver me to your presence, Wizard Oliver, Sir Jon the Brave." She clasped her hands before her chest. "I beg for clemency in this hour of my kingdom's need."

Remaining abeyant in the long moments that stretched above the heavy beat of her heart, she awaited their divine commands.

"Oh, my darling girl." Wizard Oliver cupped his narrow palm along her jaw and tipped her head back, and she was struck by the profound yearning in his azure gaze. "Who told you to call us that?"

Fearing their displeasure, she resisted the urge to frown. How could they not know? "My father, His Royal Majesty King Caedmon Austiere, commissioned the bard pen songs in your honor. Every soul in the far reaches is privy to the tale. The gallantry of your heroics is legendary."

Sir Jon hitched a breath, pressing three fingertips to his lips. "I always did love that man."

"Shush, Jon." Wizard Oliver gripped her upper arms and lifted her to her feet, and she held steady and firm under the scrutiny of his lengthy perusal. "My God," he whispered, his eyes awash with the sheen of unspent tears. "You're the spitting image of Rowena. What's your name, sweetheart?"

"Princess Faedrah Isadora Austie—"

He whisked her close and enveloped her in his arms, cradling her cheek against his chest. Sir Jon rounded the broken crockery and joined their embrace, and the two men swayed her back and forth as if reunited with a long-lost companion.

A smile tickled her lips as she basked in their heartfelt welcome, and she wound her arms around both their waists to hug them back as well. Their propensity for kindness was exactly as the bard had described it, and she sent a prayer of thanks heavenward for safe deliverance to their gracious home.

"We knew, of course." Wizard Oliver withdrew and skimmed both his palms down her arms. Lifting her hands to the sides, he absorbed the measure of her from head to foot. "Of course, we did. It's just that seeing you like this…"

"Having you here with us after so long…" Sir Jon fluttered a hand before his clean-shaven face as if to dry his watery gaze.

"It just means the world to us that we're finally able to meet you." A grand smile creased the skin near Wizard Oliver's eyes as he clutched her hands near his chest. "You must call us Uncle Jon and Uncle Oliver. We insist."

"You really must, you know. Princess Faedrah…" Sir Jon sighed her name, combing his fingers down the length of her hair. "And don't be shy about telling us exactly how we can help." He wrinkled his nose at his taller companion. "Isn't this exciting, Ollie? We finally get to participate in another quest."

Faedrah chuckled, yet she could not deny their enthusiasm to aid her cause was a welcomed relief. She glanced toward the armoire then snapped her head around, slipping her hands from those of Wizard Oliver as she crossed the rug to the open door.

The veil had dimmed to an obsidian sheet of glass. Gone were the shimmering light and hum of energy which had emanated from its surface. She placed her hand along the smooth plane and her stomach sank as the hard resistance of a solid barrier cooled her palm.

The magic surrounding the mysterious portal had locked her within the future. Perchance her impulsive leap had angered the Goddesses and they'd imprisoned her as penance. Or perchance this unforeseeable circumstance held a more dire warning, and a certain evil wizard employed his black magic to keep her escape at bay. Regardless, her choices had narrowed to the head of a pin. Whatever secrets she'd been entrusted to unearth, she must now do so without the luxury or guidance of her parents…and, in the process, determine the clues to regaining admittance to her realm.

She turned back to her honorary uncles, lowering her hand from the glass. "You stated my visit was expected. Can you tell me how such knowledge came into your possession?"

The two men traded a meaningful stare before facing her. "We can do better than that." Uncle Oliver folded her arm through his and steered her down a long narrow hall on their right. "We can show you."

A few steps down the corridor and he stopped her before a

closed door. A twist of the knob, a gentle push, and the hinges swung wide to reveal a small, private chamber.

The full volume of her lungs expanded as she violently inhaled what seemed all the air in the room.

Across the distance, propped against another set of beige drapes, awaited a large hand-painted portrait of...*her*.

The plush rug silenced her footsteps as she neared. Her heart thrummed a heady, erratic rhythm. Whomever had fashioned the piece had wrought the strokes with a bold hand. Slashes of black pigment offset the line of her shoulders, the curves of her breasts, the narrowing of her waist above the voluptuous contours of her hips. She'd been captured in her white leather fighting garb, and yet it was the absence of color which so clearly depicted the width of her stance, the bend in her knees and the tense muscles in her arms as she perched on the edge of attack. Silver buckles adorned the white leather straps crossed between her breasts. The hilts of her short swords jutted over each shoulder through the untamed mass of her hair. Fierce determination had been forged within the angle of her clenched jaw, the glint of anger in her eyes, the hint of challenge subtly masked by the seductive curl of her lips. Yet 'twas the golden chain depicted round her neck, the rounded edge of a key peeking from the low-cut seam of her bodice which demanded her full attention.

The artisan who had struck her image upon this canvas grasped the entirety of her existence down to the marrow of her bones.

A soul-wracking shudder wrenched her body. Only one enemy bore the wrath of the single-minded resolve etched across that girl's face. The one who had called her here and then left this summons as his invitation, so no doubt would remain she'd landed in the proper place.

"The moment we saw the piece, we assumed it was Rowena." Uncle Oliver joined her before the painting and twiddled his fingers in the air. "But there were too many inaccuracies to be sure. The dark strip of hair, the wrong weapons—"

"And those beautiful brown eyes belong to your father." Sir Jon stepped forward and stroked a fingertip along the arched eyebrow of her painted visage.

"Yep, the eye color was our first clue something wasn't right and, on second look, there was no mistaking that face belonged to Caedmon and Rowena's daughter." Balancing his elbow on the back of his hand, Wizard Oliver pinched the tip of his pointed chin. "The gallery had several others on display, but the artist refused to sell no matter what price I offered."

Her eyebrows shot up in surprise. "Why ever not?" In her realm, the commission of sold works ensured an artisan's distinction, not to mention food and clothing for their family.

"The owner said the artist was unusually attached to the pieces." Oliver studied her face as if awaiting the deliverance of some mysterious epiphany.

"Well, who could blame him?" Jon wound an arm around her shoulders and squeezed her to his side. "Just look at her. She's absolutely gorgeous."

Faedrah scowled at the strange rune slashed along the inside length of one leather boot, squatted and ran her fingertips over the sharp edges of the raised paint. "What is this odd demarcation?"

"The artist's signature." Oliver sank to his knees beside her, yet the weight of his gaze carried more than his simple willingness to join her on the floor. "Rhys McEleod."

She snatched her hand back. Ah, yes. Her uncles would be privy to Gaelloed's loathsome deeds through her parents, and had undoubtedly formulated her same suspicions upon learning the artist's name.

McEleod…Gaelleod. The similarities were too parallel to ignore.

Not that she dare refute the implications of such an obvious overture. The vile bastard had lured her to the future and then manipulated the keen attentiveness of her two most-trusted allies. He'd encroached upon their good graces and exploited their efforts on her behalf.

He longed for their union? Gaelloed dabbled with paints while she cowered in fear through the tangled web of his hauntings? Well, certainly not if she had anything to say in the matter.

She stood and offered her uncle a hand up when he grunted above the protesting creak of his knees. "I would see this Rhys McEleod." Her hands curled into fists as she glanced between the knowing smiles of her two, dear uncles. "And make known to him the exact particulars of my own dire warnings."

"Way ahead of you, Princess." Jon sauntered to a recessed panel in the wall and rolled the door aside. Facing her, he opened a flat hand toward a long bar hung with a myriad assortment of clothing—presumably, her new wardrobe. "Tonight we drink wine and bring you up to speed on all things twenty-first century." He crossed his arms. "Then first thing tomorrow morning, we drive straight to the gallery and confront the asshole once and for all."

* * *

Chains rattled overhead as he delivered a series of hard one-two jabs to the punching bag. Pain exploded through his taped fingers, radiating into the bones of his wrists. Good. Maybe he'd finally be able to beat some skill back into his worthless hands.

Fucking Nate.

Diaphragm, diaphragm, upper cut.

Rhys steadied the swing of the bag with one swollen hand, swiping a forearm over his brow to clear the sweat burning his eyes. A pivot on his foot, and his grunt punctuated the jolt of the bag as he delivered a violent kick to the side. How he'd let that pansy-assed weasel talk him into selling her picture, he'd never know.

"Give the interested party a price he'll never agree to," Nate had suggested. *Jab, cross-cross, hook.* "Shoot him the highest number you can think of and he'll lose interest, guaranteed."

Shit. Before his next blink, the deal had gone down and Rhys had been left staring at the blank spot on Nate's gallery wall, a check for more money than he'd earned off his art in ten years crumpled in his fist.

All because of her.

Cross, upper cut, jab-jab.

The bag leapt on it chains and his knuckles left the imprint of a dark stain on the brown leather. He stepped back, his lungs burning, and glared down at his hands. A deep red trickle crept through the frayed edges of the tape separating his fingers, but it wasn't like the damage mattered. He'd been on lockdown for a week and the time alone with his muse hadn't done him a damn bit of good.

His fingers curled in on themselves as he ground his back molars. Christ, he'd wanted to pummel Nate's face right then and there. Unfortunately, the sickening realization had come way too late. Rhys had already lost the most important piece in his collection, the one that perfectly captured her from his mind's eye. By comparison, none of the others he'd painted came remotely close, and ever since he'd been unable to recreate that same image no matter how many tubes of paint he wasted.

He bit at the end of the tape stuck to the inside of his wrist and unwound the length with his teeth. After repeating the process to the other hand, he balled up the sticky mess in his aching fists and tossed it aside.

Maybe he should count himself lucky. He stepped off the grungy gymnastics mats he'd rescued from a nearby dumpster and navigated the odd bent nail protruding from the floor to the industrial wash basin and horizontal planks of wood that passed as his kitchen. The money his muse had earned him had bought him all this.

A bitter laugh caught in his throat as he swung open the freezer door. The ancient appliance wheezed an emphysemic breath as he retrieved four ice trays, cracked the plastic against the sink and dumped the cubes into the basin. He plugged the drain with a rubber stopper and twisted the cold tap. Clunks echoed inside the walls and the pipes shuddered before water showered from the faucet. Still—a sigh eased from his lips as he submerged his hands in the icy bath—this ramshackle warehouse with its greasy windows and sporadic plumbing far exceeded the penthouse suite his father had funded.

He could breathe here.

Hitching his hip against the sink, he trailed his focus over the box spring and mattress lying on the floor, the brushes and oil paints scattered over the scarred round table, the mismatched chairs with their wobbly, duct taped legs. In the far corner, a dented metal table stood beside a propane tank, his welding mask hanging off the dolly and staring at him like some cheap Iron Man knock-off. Sure, the furnishings were crap, but they were his. Items he'd purchased with money he'd made instead of luxuries provided by a dad who never showed and didn't care.

The rumble of boxcars from the train yard shook the window-panes and a layer of dust sprinkled down from the rafters. Nate had called him bat-shit crazy for using the money from his first legitimate sale to trade in his Gold Coast lifestyle for the seedy segregation of Chicago's industrial south side. And maybe he was right. A good chunk of the funds had gone toward the purchase of the building. Most of the rest had been used to ensure the third floor had electric and heat.

Rhys shook the water from his numb hands and dried them down the front of his athletic shorts. Then again, it was pretty much guaranteed Nate's southern Baptist father never treated his son like a useless, pathetic whore. Nate wouldn't have a clue the suffocating shame that went along with being Leo McEleod's heir, the need to escape or the constant reminders that his opinions counted for less than zero.

After dipping a hand towel in the sink, Rhys wrung out the excess water and yanked the plug. A quick stop to check the barren landscape of his fridge and his hand fluctuated between the lone long-necked beer waiting in the back and three innocent bottles of water.

What time *was* it, anyway?

Fuck it. Who cared?

He snatched the beer, popped the top with the calloused edge of his thumb and guzzled several deep swallows. This was supposed to be his vacation, after all.

Frigid water trickled down his back as he slung the towel around his neck. He strode to the brick wall that doubled as the headboard of his bed and the rough surface combed down either side of his spine as he sank to the floor.

Propping his arms on his bent knees, he raised his chin.

There she was, larger than life, staring at him from the wide span of his north wall. He'd whitewashed the damn thing so many times he'd lost count of the layers, but his efforts had paid off in the end. This version was closer than he'd gotten in his previous attempts.

He squinted. Still, something wasn't right.

The rim of the bottle cooled his lips and a few droplets of condensation splattered his legs as he tipped the beer for another swallow. He'd hoped concentrating on her face, on her eyes, would do the trick and, for once, his instincts had hit the mark. Showing her from the center of her forehead to mid-chin had allowed him to focus on the problem—that god-damned haunting stare in her bottomless brown gaze.

He tipped his head. The strength was there. Same with the vulnerability and fear. The full curve of her lower lip and the slight arc in her brow handled the defiant, gut-fisting sex appeal. So what had he missed?

His cell vibrated on the wooden crate at his elbow, and he leaned over to check the caller ID. Nate. What the hell? He was the one who'd suggested this hiatus in the first place.

Another droning shimmy along the top of his makeshift night-stand, and Rhys snatched the phone. "Yeah."

"Man, you need to get down here. Like, right now."

Wrong. He thumbed the disconnect button and tossed the phone back onto the crate. Nate calling him to the gallery to face off against another potential buyer ranked immediately beneath ringing the old man for money. Rhys would rather be bound and stretched on a rack.

He rolled his eyes. And he was the one who supposedly needed the mental health break.

Pushing against the wall, he rose to his feet, the bottle neck dangling between two fingers as he strolled to the center of the mural. Everything Nate had asked of him, he'd done. Carting pieces to the gallery he had no intention of ever selling. Smiling and shaking hands, dressed like a goon in a tuxedo during the week-long string of openings.

The entire thing was moronic. Ever since that first—and most important—piece had walked out the door, it was like Nate had realized the work's earning potential and been bitten by the greed bug. The dam Rhys held so firmly in place had finally collapsed only to spill a pile of money at Nate's feet. In return, he'd hounded Rhys repeatedly to let the other pieces go…something he wasn't about to let happen until he uncovered the elusive element they were missing.

Over the next few weeks, the tension between them had stoked to a low burn, until Nate finally suggested Rhys take a break, get his head together, get laid, and for Christ's sake figure out his issues so Nate could do his damn job.

The phone buzzed another annoying jig along the crate and Rhys stormed across the room to answer it. Yeah, great, but how the hell was he supposed to concentrate when Nate refused to leave him alone? "What?"

"Listen to me, you miserable son of a bitch. You see that girl you're looking at? The one watching you from your wall? She's here, man. I swear to God. She just walked in off the street, easy as you please, and is standing in the center of my gallery."

Rhys snapped his head around to stare at her picture. Not cool.

43

"That's not even remotely funny. I don't know what the hell you're trying to pull, but—"

"You think I'm *joking*?" Nate's heavy sigh reverberated through the line. "I know how crazy you are, dumb ass. You think I would risk being the beneficiary of that Hail Mary shit storm? She's here, man. With that dude and his partner who bought her picture."

Oliver Forbes. The ease with which the multi-million-dollar antiques dealer had scrawled his signature and happily handed over a check for three hundred thousand mind-blowing dollars slammed into Rhys' brain. Forbes *knew* her? He jerked upright. Or, the more obvious choice, he knew someone who looked like her. "What the fu—"

"Sober up, get dressed, straddle that god-damned Indian you love more than life itself and get your ass down here. Now." The line went dead.

Rhys stared at the screen on his phone, blinked and shook his head. A second later, the phone beeped with an incoming text and he opened the message to find a blurry off-center picture of a woman dressed in white.

He scowled. What, exactly, was that supposed to prove? Either Nate wasn't the best with his camera phone or maybe he'd tried to snap the photo on the sly.

Or maybe he hoped the picture would help validate his claim he wasn't the cause of the bad joke. Okay fine, but what could a rich guy like Forbes possibly stand to gain by going to the trouble of finding a look-alike of Rhys' muse and bringing her to Nate's gallery? That made zero sense...unless this was Forbes' lame attempt at getting Rhys to paint him another portrait.

Scratching at the dried sweat near his temple, he eyed his beloved Chief Classic motorcycle, parked safely in the corner near the freight elevator. The cool ride was the one luxury he'd splurged on—hot off the showroom floor, sleek, black and chromed to the max.

If today's spring weather was anything like the sunny skies and calm lake breezes of yesterday, it wouldn't hurt to take his beauty for a spin. He could confront Forbes face to face and find out what the man was up to. Besides, the fresh air would probably do him good.

Tossing his phone to the bed, he headed for the shower.

Just another fucking day in paradise.

Hooking the heel of his boot along the kickstand, Rhys leaned his bike to the side and slipped the key from the ignition. During the entire trip weaving through the high speed curves of Chicago's lakefront traffic, he'd told himself whoever Forbes had brought to the gallery, she couldn't be real. What, did Forbes think he was an idiot? Rhys had done enough bed-bouncing research of his own to know girls like his muse didn't exist. Not in his world, anyway.

He tugged the helmet from his head and stowed it in his saddle-bags, checked the alley for any scalpers who might get the bright idea to hock the parts off his bike and strode for the back entrance to the gallery.

In his previous life, all the women he'd scored had been leggy, blonde and stacked. Being the only son of Chicago's highest-grossing real estate tycoon held several disadvantages, but a shortage of women wasn't one of them. Mention the last name McEleod and the difficulty of finding someone to fill his cold, empty sheets was suddenly no longer a problem.

Coupled with the funds at Forbes' disposal, his fashion sense and keen eye, he wouldn't have any difficulty recruiting a long list of women to audition for the scam. The only question remaining, was why?

The grime and stench of the alley gave way to the immaculate interior of the gallery as Rhys stepped inside, the overhead recessed lights shining a path of white spots along the marble tile of the narrow hall. Fortunately, once this was over, the joke would be on Forbes. No woman Rhys had encountered could hold a candle to the ideal aesthetic of his white-haired vixen. How could they when he'd dreamed her up and obsessed over every curve and contour of her body since he was old enough to hold a damn crayon?

He ducked his head inside Nate's office to find the chair empty, the spotless stretch of his glass-topped desk vacant except for a maroon leather blotter, laptop and phone. One of Rhys' welded sculptures stood in the corner, a tag marked SOLD hanging off one of the sharp metal spikes. His brows rose and he mentally slapped Nate on the back with a hearty "good job." He was the one who'd spotted the side project at the warehouse and suggested it would be the perfect complement to the show. Looked as if he'd been right and Rhys would be eating next month, after all.

"Hello! I'm here! Call in the reinforcements." The lazy clump of his untied boots echoed into the open gallery as Rhys spotted Nate on the far side of a free-standing partition, talking quietly with Forbes and his dark-haired lover, but where was the—

He stumbled to a stop. *Jesus H. Christ.*

She stood with her back to the room, staring at her picture on the wall—the one he'd painted with her black strip of hair caught in the wind and blowing across her eyes. Her wild mass of untamed waves tumbled down the shaggy fur coat she wore, the same ash blonde as her hair, the bottom edge stopping just short of her completely bitable ass. Her mile-long toned legs stood braced slightly apart, knees locked, tightly encased in white leather. And on her feet. Sweet Jesus, those white, stiletto knee-high boots were enough to drop any sane man to his knees.

She turned and met his gaze over her shoulder, and the breath whooshed from his lungs like he'd been slammed in the gut with a wrecking ball. That was it. The fleeting element he'd been missing.

Dark anger simmered in her gaze, one that simultaneously hitched his balls and zeroed his entire world into focus. How the hell had he forgotten something so obvious?

One of her arms lifted, and she aimed a sharp finger at her picture on the wall. "Would you care to explain the meaning of this…this *abomination*? And I caution you to speak plainly, or

I shall be compelled to extract the truth by more than simple query alone."

Holy mother of God, that voice. He slumped. The cutting British accent and old world dialect were so much better than he could've ever anticipated.

On leaden legs, he clomped forward a step...and then one more. Not a day had gone by he hadn't fantasized about running into her like this. Someplace unexpected. Where he would never predict she'd been waiting for him.

But she couldn't be real. No way, *no way* could he seriously be staring into the face of the one woman by whom he'd judged all others. The one who was so perfect she couldn't possibly exist.

His hand instinctively lifted. Just one touch. One light caress of her cheek and he would know for sure. Had she walked into his life straight off the canvas? Or was this a twisted trick cooked up by some guy who had more money than King Midas?

She leaned away the same distance his fingers closed in. The sides of her coat fell open and the wink of a golden chain trailing down between her breasts snagged his attention.

The key? His hand changed direction. How was it even feasible she wore an object straight out of his imagination? He'd never shown it entirely in any of his paintings.

Her eyes widened. Her mouth parted on gasp and, before he had the chance to reassure her, she snatched his wrist, spun and flipped him ass first to the ground. The back of his head smacked the hard marble. Stars showered through his vision above the pounding steps of running feet. Black shadows danced before his eyes, but still, he smiled.

Oh, but she *was* perfect.

The light above narrowed to a tiny pinprick. A weak chuckle shook his chest.

His hand to God, she was fucking perfect.

Chapter 4

Shit. Exactly how many beers did he drink last night?

Rhys winced and tossed his arm over his face, trying to block the harsh mid-day light from penetrating the ineffective shade of his closed eyelids. He hadn't gone on such a bender in years. Last thing he remembered was...

He sprang to sitting and immediately dropped his pounding head into his hands. She'd been at the gallery. A woman who looked like his muse. He hadn't been drunk, he'd tried to touch her. No, he'd tried to touch the key and she'd freaked. He swung his feet off the couch to the floor in Nate's office, propping his elbows on his knees. Christ, what had he done?

"Easy there, cowboy. That thick head of yours took quite the hit."

Nate's voice speared through the gonging pain, and Rhys glanced up to find his best friend of eight years sitting opposite his glass-topped desk, his round brown cheeks lifted in a cheery smile.

What did he have to be so god damned happy about? Rhys muttered a curse and swept his hand down the blunt clip of his recently buzzed hair, gingerly exploring the damage. No doubt Nate had enjoyed every second of his epic fail. Watching Rhys get tagged with a WWE smack-down by a woman half his size, sporting a pair of killer stiletto boots, no less, had to be the high-light of Nate's week.

The quarter-sized goose egg which had taken up residence on the back of his head was tender to the touch but, other than the residual headache, his skull seemed intact…which was the least of his worries. "Where is she? Is she still here?"

"No. Her two bodyguards rushed her out of here PDQ." Nate snatched a bottle of aspirin off his desk and tossed it in Rhys' direction. It landed with a rattle on the cushion next to Rhys' thigh. "Forbes asked me to call if you decide to press charges."

"What?" That idea was just plain stupid and, based on Nate's belly jiggling chuckle, he agreed. The woman had just been trying to protect herself—or rather, the key—and a fucking excellent job she'd done of it too. Rhys shook three pills into his hand, tossed them back and chewed them dry. "Hell no, I'm not pressing charges. Positioning myself as the enemy is the last thing I need."

"That's what I told him." Nate lobbed a bottle of water across his desk and it landed with a thud at Rhys' feet. "He also said to make sure I forward any medical bills which may result from your injuries."

Rhys huffed a laugh, which quickly morphed into a groan under Nate's high-pitched *hee-hee-hee*. He picked up the water and twisted off the cap, rinsed his mouth and swallowed. Nice of Forbes to offer, but he wasn't heading to the ER…or anywhere else, for that matter. Not until he saw her again. The gallery was the one place she knew where to find him, and here was where he planned to stay. "Any idea when she's coming back?"

Because she had to. Leaving him hanging like this wasn't an option.

"None." Nate crossed his arms and leaned back in his chair, his full upper lip curling in a sneer. "Pretty freaky, huh? Can't say I would've believed it had I not seen her with my own two eyes."

Water shot up Rhys' nose with his next choking swallow, and he jammed his forefinger and thumb into the corners of his eyes against the burn razing his nasal passages. "Is that your way of saying you actually believe she was her? My her is she?"

Shit, he wasn't making any sense, but the mere concept he'd stood in the same room with the one woman he'd been drawing since childhood ranked right up top with getting abducted by aliens. Everything had happened so fast. "Did she say anything? Do anything that might have given you a clue why she was here?"

"Nope. Not a one."

The chair squeaked an annoying tune as Nate rocked in his seat, and Rhys ground his molars against the urge to hop the desk and shake his friend by the lapels of his spotless, black, eight-hundred-dollar suit. How could the jackass have let her get away like that? Didn't he realize how important it was for Rhys to see her again? "For Christ's sake, Nate, did you at least get her name?"

"Look, man, I don't know what to tell you." He opened his large hands to either side of him, the perfect illustration to demonstrate his complete lack of information. "She showed up pissed at the world and demanded to see you. That's all I know."

Rhys' eyebrows jacked up in surprise. He grimaced at the dull throb the reflex caused and rubbed three fingers across his forehead. "Pissed at the world, huh? You forgot to mention that. A little heads up might have been nice."

"And miss out on watching you get your ass kicked?" Nate chuckled and shook his head. "Not a chance. Consider it payback for all those times I ran interference for you in art school."

"That's bullshit, and we both know it." Sure, Nate had acted as Rhys' wingman more often than not during their wilder, sexually charged college days, but it wasn't like he hadn't reaped the rewards. "Besides, Tasha would smack you upside the head if she heard that."

The fiery, raven-haired mother of Nate's two boisterous rug-rats would never stand for being categorized as "payback." The thought alone was enough to shrivel Rhys' balls to the size of prunes.

Nate narrowed his gaze, drumming his fingers atop his desk, and Rhys pinched the bridge of his nose against the grating rhythm. "You never get tired of reminding me how you introduced us,

50

do you?"

"No. I don't." But chances were good Nate didn't fully comprehend the reason why. Truth was, Rhys would have given anything to experience the kind of deep connection Nate and Tasha had shared since the first night they met. Unfortunately, life spent stuck in the cold isolation of boarding school, a mother's abandonment and the continued neglect of a distant father, damaged a person. Made them use whatever tools were at their disposal to retreat from reality. Well, that and an obsessive desire for a woman who, up until a few hours ago, Rhys believed didn't exist.

He lowered his head and laced his fingers along the nape of his neck. Still, even during his darkest hours, those mornings after a three-day binge when he'd reach the lowest of the low, Nate had been there for him. Shit, Rhys had lost count of the times his friend had ditched class to rescue him from whatever hellhole he'd gotten lost in. Nate was the one person who'd accepted him regardless of his eccentricities, and the one who'd stood by him and believed in his art when no one else would. Including his wealthy, influential father.

Nate deserved better. Something else they both knew. "Look, I'm sorry. This whole thing is just really fucked up, but that's no excuse for my acting like a dick."

"Save the pity party for someone who hasn't spent the four years since graduation begging you to get your shit together." The chair creaked and Rhys lifted his head as Nate stood. He rounded the desk, propped his ass on the glass edge and crossed his arms. "My momma didn't raise no fools, Rhys. Our friendship aside, there's only one reason I agreed to show your work in my gallery." He gripped the edge of his desk and leaned forward, lifting one thick, dark eyebrow. "Money, my friend. Plain and simple. You might be nuttier than a fruit cake, but you're one talented son of a bitch, and I plan to make a boatload of cash off every single one of your sales."

"Now." He smoothed a flat hand down the length of his gold

tie and rose to his feet. "Since my first priority is to protect my investment, my biggest concern is how we're going to get you through this. And keep in mind Tasha will have my ass in a sling if I come home drunk."

Rhys grunted. While that was without question, tying one on was the last item on his agenda. He'd never been able to paint under the influence and he needed a clear head. A visual of *her*— the white-haired minx who'd taught him more about keeping his hands to himself in three seconds than he'd learned in a lifetime—streaked into focus in his head. He smirked. Yep, that would be perfect.

Seeing how he wasn't leaving the gallery, he might as well use the time hoping…longing, aching…for her return to his advantage. Shit, he'd wait days if he had to.

He pinned Nate with a hard stare from under his brows. "I need paint, brushes and several large tarps."

The glide of bristles coated in rich color, the steady reassurance of the brush in his hand and his headache faded to a minor inconvenience. The resentment he carried dissolved like oil paint dipped into thinner. Nothing Rhys ever tried helped him work out his angst like bringing his muse to life on the canvas, and this session was shaping up to be better than all those before.

Now that he had a precise, life-sized, three-dimensional model to work from, and had been on the receiving end of her enthusiastic, uninhibited anger, he became like a man possessed. The elements he'd missed in his original renderings zeroed into focus with the ease of breathing, as if the sole reason he'd been put on this earth was to showcase her beauty to the world.

At some point during his concentrated fine-tuning of portrait after portrait—adding a stark line of fury to her jaw here, a spark of rage in her eyes there—the glaring lights of the gallery had covered him in a film of sweat and he'd kicked off his boots and socks, shrugged out of his button-down shirt and stripped to his dego tee. Soon after, Nate had mumbled a few words about heading home and tossed the keys to the front door on the speckled tarp at Rhys' feet.

Hours or days could've passed while he worked; he lost track. The star-studded sky outside the wide gallery windows might have signaled late evening or the middle of the night; he didn't care. All that mattered was capturing the clear visual of his inspiration before time and the fading of his memories shuffled her features back to a fleeting, insubstantial wisp he couldn't pinpoint.

He stepped back and squinted at his current work in progress, bit the handle of the brush between his teeth and leaned down to pick up another. A sweep of the clean bristles back and forth through a dab of red paint, the addition of a little white and he lifted the brush to her lips. He'd not done them justice in the first go-round. In real life, they were fuller, juicier, and no doubt tasted like manna from Heaven.

If he was careful, with just the right touch, maybe he could—

The bell above the door jingled and he glanced over his shoulder, and the subtle layering of sexuality he'd been working to recreate no longer counted for squat. Because she was back. He turned to fully face her. Exactly like he'd been hoping.

"You." She pointed at him from across the room, that same furious spark he'd just added to the canvas glinting like a diamond in her eyes. She'd ditched her fuzzy coat, and the sheer blouse she wore over a white lacy camisole shot every ounce of blood he owned straight into his groin.

Sweet God Almighty. Any doubts he might have harbored about her being the same woman decorating the walls of the gallery flew out the window.

"I am not shocked to discover you are still here, going about your immoral business as if you'd nary a thought to do elsewise."

Evidently, she didn't like the pictures. He spurted the brush from between his lips and paint splattered his toes as it clattered to the tarp. How she'd gotten here, he couldn't guess and didn't

53

care. But she was real. In fact, she seemed *more* real than anyone he'd met throughout the entire course of his life. "Well, yeah. I've been waiting a long time for you. I wasn't about to leave."

"Ha!" She tossed her head back and his focus slipped to the slender line of her throat. God, what he wouldn't give to lick that soft stretch of skin just once. Even though one time would never be enough. Even though that single taste would leave him jonesing like an addict for his next high.

"Indeed, you have." Her hands fisted at her sides and she shifted uneasily from boot to boot. A second later, she narrowed her eyes and stormed across the gallery on those leather-clad come-to-Jesus thighs. "Then let us be done with this one-sided arrangement. 'Tis high time we had out our differences once and for all."

"Whoa, whoa." He back-pedaled away from her, tripping over tubes of paint and discarded brushes until his shoulder blades connected with the wall. "Careful. Slow down. Wait, wet paint!"

"Do not tarry about such frivolities with me." The back of his head bounced off the space between two canvases and stars showered through his vision as she jammed her forearm under his chin. "I am long accustomed to the ruse of your insincere distractions."

He dropped the brush and pallet to slide the cushion of one hand behind his head, and grimaced when the paint landed sunny-side down. Nate was gonna fry his ass for making such a mess. "Um, ouch?"

"You shall release me from your devil's bargain." The pressure on his wind pipe increased, and he seized her hips. Jesus Christ, who had lit a fire under her? One hard kneecap rose between his thighs and lodged a threat to the underside of his balls. "Henceforth, you shall cease and desist in this madness to infiltrate my realm."

Infiltrate her *what*? The air thickened with her scent, a mouth-watering combination of sultry leather and the hint of a crisp, clean breeze rolling in off a high mountain. Damn, he wanted to bury his face in it. Let it soak into his skin like the sun on a hot summer day. "Shit, you smell good."

With a flip of her wrist and a wink of silver, a knife appeared in her fingers and the tip jabbed the thin skin below his jaw. Okay, she was officially pissed off. "Release me at once. Or you shall leave me no choice but to end your reign on the sharp edge of my dagger."

Release her? He scowled at her past the high angle of his chin. Release her from what? "Yeah, correct me if I'm wrong, but you're the one who seems hell bent on inflicting injury here." Besides, if either of them had the other by the briefs, it was *her* who had twisted *his* life into a proverbial wedgie.

"I shall not ask again." The tip of her knife poked deeper and he gritted his teeth. "Release me at once."

All right, enough nancy-footing around. He grabbed her wrists, reversed their positions and slammed her back to the wall. Restraining her hands at shoulder height, he locked those dangerous knees of hers between the clenched muscles of his thighs, trapping her body with his.

Obviously, she had confused him with someone else, but he wasn't about to get spanked like some scared little kid. Not again. He'd spent enough time on the streets to know a thing or two about digging his way out of a jam.

Her frustrated growl vibrated into his chest as she thrashed against him, but he tightened his grip and held on. Hell, he could play this game with her all damn day. The silky strands of her hair tickled his nose as he lowered his lips to her ear. "If anyone in this room needs to be released, it's me."

The tempting curves of her breasts bumped his pecs. He inhaled along the dizzying slant of her neck and she growled beneath him. Every muscle in his body hardened as her nipples tightened and poked his chest through the skimpy layers of her shirt. "Take a look around, sweetheart. I'm happy to paint your picture, but don't think a day hasn't gone by I haven't asked myself why."

Her hips ground against him and his eyes nearly rolled back in his head. If she didn't stop, this little tussle of theirs was apt to head in a different direction altogether. Like the one where he tossed her over his shoulder and carried her into Nate's office, stripped her down and stroked her until she shattered in his hands.

"And what of the key? I presume you are fully prepared to relinquish your claim on that which is not rightfully yours?"

"I couldn't give a good god damn about the key." Hell, he had some chemicals back at the warehouse that would dissolve it in about ten minutes if that's what she wanted. "Figuring out why you're here is the only thing that matters to me."

She slowly stopped squirming. He leaned back and she lifted her eyes to his, and he was jolted by the confusion darkening her angelic face. For fuck's sake, she was young. Younger than he'd ever imagined. Too innocent and unspoiled for the grubby intentions of an asshole like him.

A second or two later, defeat crumpled her brow, and her gaze shifted back and forth across his neck as if she were searching his shoulders for answers.

He braced for the waterworks. Any second now, tears would fill her gorgeous brown eyes and he would be left standing like a dick. Nothing to say, unsure how to comfort her.

His brow twitched when they never came, and the dread squeezing his windpipe slowly receded. He'd always envisioned her as strong, determined, a bit of a pain in the ass. A pulsing heaviness tightened his balls. It shouldn't have shocked him to learn she could hold her own in a fight.

The tip of her tongue appeared as she pulled her lower lip between her teeth and bit down. His shaft jerked so hard and fast, his knees almost gave out. Jesus Christ, didn't she have any idea how the heat of her tight little body pressed into his nearly drove him insane? How much he wanted to sweep her tongue aside with his and suck that luscious lower lip of hers deep into his mouth?

Being anywhere near her was like fighting a full-out war with his endurance. This close? Shit, this close, he was a goner.

"You are not the monster I believed you to be." Her fingers

relaxed and the knife tumbled to the floor with ricocheting clang. "If you would kindly unhand me, I swear on the nine I shall no longer threaten or harm you."

Nine what? He shook his jumbled head. Didn't matter. She'd finally accepted he wasn't gunning for her and that was their first step in the right direction…not to mention the best news he'd gotten all day.

He nodded, lips turned down in a frown. Trouble was, now that she'd worked through her suspicions, the thought of letting her go made him ache worse than the throbbing bruise at the back of his skull. "That's too bad. I kinda like it when you go all Xena Warrior Princess on me. Makes me hot under the collar."

She snapped her chin up and he smiled at the pretty blush tinting her cheeks. Hopefully, one day very soon, he'd be able to recreate that same pink for his next piece. He'd ask her to sit for him and then work out the perfect thing to say so he could capture the delicate tones with his brush.

Lowering her hands to her sides, he stepped back. The loss of contact made him crave her even more. Her focus darted past his right side and he turned, then crossed his arms as Forbes and his partner streaked past the window, pounding down the sidewalk like their asses were on fire. No cars lined the street but, then again, she could've hailed a cab. "How'd you get here, anyway?"

"My uncles' shop is a short distance from here." She stepped to his side and repeated his crossed arms. "I waited until their backs were turned and slipped through the door." A glance in his direction, and she shrugged. "They feared I might run off and do something rash."

He grunted and side-stepped slightly in front of her as the two men ratcheted the door open and tripped over the threshold in their rush to get inside. Whether or not she left the gallery was her decision, not theirs. Besides, if the call were his to make, she'd stay within arm's length of him all night. Or forever. Whichever came first.

"There you are!" Forbes slapped a hand to his chest, doubled over at the waist and wheezed a series of long-winded breaths. "My God, we thought we'd lost you."

Rhys scowled. *He'd* known she was coming back. *She'd* known she was coming back. Why was it so difficult for everyone else to get on the same page?

The shorter, dark-haired man—Jon something-or-other— stumbled to a low ottoman and collapsed on the seat, lifting the back of his wrist to his forehead. "I'm too old for this shit."

Good God. If he didn't already spend time on stage, the dude definitely belonged in the theater.

"You have my sincerest regrets." His muse rounded his shoulder, strode forward and knelt before the guy like he was some sort of high-powered, gay, super hero. "I beg your forgiveness, Uncle." She lifted her hand to Forbes and he clasped it in his. "I beg for mercy from both of you."

Rhys squinted, irritation tightening his jaw. If either one of them so much as wagged a finger at her, he'd lay them out flat.

"Oh, my darling girl, it's all right." Jon sat up and ran his palms down her hair, back and forth along her upper arms, cooing and fawning as if he'd found his long-lost pet. "Are you all right? You scared us half to *death*."

"Let's just take her home." Forbes stepped close and squeezed his lover's shoulder. "I think we've all had enough excitement for one night."

Speak for yourself. If Rhys had anything to say about it, the excitement had only just started.

"Yes, quite right." She nodded and stood, helping the seated dude to his feet. Rhys leaned down and snatched her knife off the floor, ran his thumb over the embellished hilt and raised his brows. Huh, looked like an antique.

He flipped the blade in the air and offered it to her handle-first. "You forgot something." As she reached for the weapon, he tipped the end up and waited for her to meet his gaze. "What time do I see you tomorrow?"

Whatever hour she agreed to, he'd be counting the seconds until she walked back through that door.

She glanced between the two men standing on either side of her and his stomach clenched. He swallowed past the awkward breath freezing his lungs. For Christ's sake, it wasn't like he'd never asked a woman on a date before. Then again, none of them ever had him by the balls like she did.

A quick straightening of her shoulders, and she seemed to make her decision. "Assuredly, I will return early on the morrow. There is much yet to discuss."

Yeah, like if she was seeing anyone, for how long and who the lucky asshole might be...amongst other things.

He lowered the hilt and she gripped the blade, but before he let go, he tugged her forward a step. "One last thing."

She widened her eyes and that god damned, groan-inducing blush returned to her cheeks. The one that made him want to pick her up and wrap her mile-long legs around his waist so he could bury himself balls deep inside her. "Will these tests of my patience be something I must daily endure in your presence?"

He grinned. God, she made his heart beat faster. She made him *feel*. "What's your name, princess?"

She jerked on the knife so fast, the thin blade slipped from between his fingers. Oh, shit. Now what had he done?

His muse and her "uncles" exchanged glances like they all belonged to some high-level government agency and weren't sure if he'd been granted clearance.

She frowned and fiddled with the key between her breasts. "You do not know?"

Why? Should he? He scrubbed a hand through his hair. "Not unless you decide to tell me, no."

Another round of curious glances, and he crossed his arms and sighed. Since when was asking someone their name breaking one of the ten social commandments?

Forbes slightly shook his head and she turned back to Rhys.

"Faedrah." Tipping her chin to the side, she studied him like some strange specimen she'd discovered under a microscope. "My name is Faedrah Austiere."

Chapter 5

Her knee bounced an impatient jig, and the answering click of her pointed heel rapped a sharp cadence upon the hardwood floor of her uncle's shop. Faedrah sighed and dug a finger into the thick twist of her hair, scratching at the metal pins Sir Jon had employed to secure the heavy knot at the nape of her neck. Her mother had never been one to insist she coif her long tresses in the elaborate styles favored by the court and, at long last, Faedrah fully comprehended the reason why. The persistent tugging on her scalp and heated weight only served to heighten her agitation. "Is it nearly time?"

Wizard Oliver glanced up from the glowing screen he'd opened atop the glass case to peer at the tall, ornately carved cabinet ticking away the moments like some damnable mechanical heartbeat. "Ten minutes, love."

Faedrah sighed. Ten minutes, ten days, ten seasons… She cleared the dampness from her palm along the thigh of her fitted blue breeches and brought her gaze back to the street. No matter how long, this wait imposed all the same nuisance to her.

Her knee resumed its anxious bounce where she perched at an angle upon the padded window seat. A glance at the cloudless blue sky, and she shook her head. Helios had traversed nearly half the distance toward Apex and still her uncles refused her permission

61

to return to the gallery. According to them, for her to arrive before dawn in search of the mysterious Rhys McEleod would merely emphasize her unrestrained tirades from their previous encounters.

A huff left her lips, coating the window in a patch of condensation, and she rolled her eyes over such a ridiculous code of etiquette. Apparently inflicting bodily harm and threatening another with a pilfered dagger was frowned upon in this realm.

Gritting her teeth, she jammed a finger under the tight pull of her hair to scratch at the unrelenting itch.

"Keep that up and we'll have to re-do your hair." Jon selected a large ruby from the padded box on the counter and added the ring to the other baubles adorning his left hand. Rainbow sprites danced along the floor as he wiggled his fingers in the pool of light Helios spilled through the window.

She dropped her fisted fingers onto her lap. "Apologies, Lord Uncle."

To complain of their efforts on her behalf would be the height of rudeness, regardless of whether her appearance pleased Sir McEleod or she fell far short of the beauty he'd wrought with his able hand.

The memory of how desire had darkened his jade gaze, the way he'd held her captive against the wall sparked a web of tingles along her nerve endings. That fragile moment his breath had warmed her ear as he'd molded the unyielding press of his body to hers seared a path of arousal through the unsettled churning in her belly.

Whatever bond they shared, whichever link had stretched its fervent tendrils across time and distance to intertwine their fates, it was dangerous. Like a charged current before a lightning strike or the ominous rumble of thunder proceeding a dark storm, the inherent possession crackling between them both alarmed and intrigued her. From the moment they'd breathed the same air, her desire to be near him had grown increasingly more potent. Perchance this fascination with him was the very cause behind her violent reaction to his appearance.

The first prickles of doubt had begun to needle their way under her skin the instant he'd entered the gallery and their gazes had locked. The profound astonishment slackening his jaw...the way he'd stared at her with such awe and reverence...

Rhys McEleod had been surprised by her arrival. The answer she had been unable to determine, was why? Was he not the black demon who had summoned her to this realm? And if not Gaelleod, then who was this man? Why paint her as if he'd caressed every curve and contour of her form?

'Twas not until he'd reached for the key, alarm and confusion had dictated her instinctive response to attack. Yet, no question remained. The simplicity with which she'd rendered Rhys McEleod unconscious validated his innocence. Gaelleod could have never been bested by a mere flip to the floor.

The unrelenting need to be near her mysterious artist did not ease once her uncles had ushered her from the gallery and, upon her second trip, Sir McEleod's initial shock had been replaced with something exceedingly more daunting.

The tick of the pendulum inside the tall wooden device was interrupted by the mellow tolling of its chime and Faedrah closed her eyes, suppressing the urge to leap to her feet.

Desperation had lingered behind the dark fringe of his lowered lashes. A reckless need to confirm the same fire coursed through her veins at their nearness. His full mouth had brushed her ear, the thick scruff of his beard had swept her cheek, and his whispered confession bespoke her same longing for a satisfying release.

Nary one beat of her heart had passed before certainty slammed home.

Rhys McEleod was no more Wizard Gaelleod than she was.

The tenth tolling of the chime lingered in the air and Faedrah shivered. The time had come. She blinked to find her uncles standing before her, Wizard Oliver's arms crossed, one eyebrow lifted in shrewd assessment of her wayward ponderings. Sir Jon firmed his lips as if to restrain a smile and tossed a funny little head covering onto her lap.

"On second thought, maybe we should go with her." Oliver shook his head and turned back toward the glass counter.

Alarm skittered over her heart as Faedrah gathered the hat and stood, but she would not lose herself in a fit of hysterics. They'd discussed the matter at length, and to do so would only confirm their misgivings she was too young to handle Rhys McEleod on her own.

Though, given the circumstances, admitting her undeniable attraction to the man may have been a bit unwise.

Wizard Oliver rummaged through a drawer and slammed it shut before retracing his steps around the counter. Nevertheless, their options were limited. Her parents were undoubtedly grief-stricken with worry by now, and McEleod's portraits were their only clues to her purpose in this place. Confronting him unaccompanied was the most prudent course. He would never speak candidly with her elsewhere.

"Here." Her uncle approached with a small shiny gadget and beckoned her near. "This is a cell phone. Unlock the screen like this," he swept his thumb across the surface, "press the number one and hit send." An other-worldly chime sounded from a similar device affixed to his belt and she mirrored his motions as he placed the contraption to his ear. "Then you can reach us whenever you need to."

Her brows sprang up in surprise as his voice echoed in her ear. Goddesses' tits, this realm held wonders far behind the limits of her imaginings. He instructed her how to terminate their communication and she deposited the magical device in the slash pocket of her thigh-length double-breasted surcoat. "You have my solemn vow, I shall summon you at the first sign of danger."

"Pffft." Jewels sparkled as Sir Jon fluttered his hand in the air. "Danger-schmanger. We all saw the protective way McEleod looked at you. What's he gonna do? Adore you to death? Fall down and worship at your feet?" Her cheeks heated as he tugged the hat from her hand and centered the rolled brim low on her brow. "Personally, I don't blame you one bit for crushing on him. The guy is a rock-solid tower of smoldering angst. For God's sake, he practically vibrates."

No, no, she didn't intend to crush him. Not anymore…at least, not in a harmful way. A giddy laugh pressed upon her chest and she busied her hands by tightening the belt at her waist.

"Hmmm…" Oliver withdrew a step and assessed her from hat to her ankle-high boots. "It's good, but is it enough?" He snapped his fingers and spun away, disappearing behind a velvet curtain at the far end of the room. A moment later, he reappeared and propped a set of dark-colored eye shades on her nose, and she started when the room was cast into shadow.

"There." Stepping aside, he turned her to face the large mirror spanning the wall behind the glass case. "Those sunglasses belonged to your mother, you know." He ran his hands across her shoulders and applied a slight squeeze. In the reflection of the glass, his eyes filled with a glistening sheen. "Seeing you like this? My God, I could swear not a day has gone by since Ro left."

She covered one of his hands with hers and held tight. The similarities between her appearance and a modern-day version of her mother were undeniable. Yet, with her hair bound and covered, half her face hidden behind the disguise of her mother's dark shades, if any luck stood with her, no one would recognize her as the woman in Rhys McEleod's paintings—the goal her uncles had endeavored to accomplish all along.

Though she held firm her gifted artist was not Gaelleod, proof of whether or not the black wizard inhabited this realm had yet to emerge. Risking discovery for the sake of appearance was a gamble none of them were willing to take.

For all their sakes, they must keep her identity secret until no other choice remained.

Jon stepped to her other side and, with a nod toward her uncles and a parting kiss to their cheeks, she left the safety of their shop for the blessing of Helios' rays shining down upon the street.

Chin to her chest, shoulders hunched against the cutting wind streaming off the inland sea, she kept her steps measured and even in her trek to the gallery. The solitary journey she'd conducted the previous evening seemed far removed from the bustling activity crowded before the shops, and the reasons behind why Gaelleod may have selected this port city as his hiding place became more apparent than ever before.

How easy for him to conceal his presence amid the masses teeming the streets. How ideal the convenience of their transportation, belching vile fumes into the air which personified the blackness of his heart.

The steady rhythm of her heels slowed as she neared the gallery, and her eyes widened in alarm as she peered through the windows to the stark white interior. Whilst, certainly, she had expected a few patrons to be present, not in all her seasons on earth had she imagined the attending throng milling about inside.

Her stomach sank as if filled with stone. 'Twould seem all of them had come to view the portraits of her.

Unease danced its icy fingers down her spine, and she tugged the hat lower on her brow before swinging the door wide. A blast of warm air coursed her cheeks, laden with the scent of imaginings keenly brought to life by the pristine bite of fresh paint. She instinctively drew a deep breath, and then jolted at her response. This place smelled like him. The essence of Rhys McEleod saturated her skin.

Pressing her back to the wall, she slowly exhaled and scanned the faces of those nearest the door. Any one of them could be Gaelleod, veiled in the guise of a devotee. A lover of art who wished to purchase her picture to adorn a blank spot upon his wall.

One half of her heart grew heavy at the notion. The other half lightened with glee. If she trod lightly…if she remained discreet and kept silent, perchance this occasion would allow her to flush him out, providing her a slight advantage in his game of cat and mouse.

The caress of a heated stare tingled the side of her face and she turned, lowering her chin to peer over the top of her eye shades. Her lips parted with a sharp gasp. Through the shifting bodies, Rhys McEleod scrutinized her from the far side of the room. The disheveled mess of his thick hair shined in the light as if he'd recently bathed, his scruffy beard neatly trimmed to accent the deep hollows of his cheeks. The same style jacket favored by her Uncle Oliver rested on his broad shoulders, pushed up his forearms and hanging open to expose the crisp white shirt beneath. A pair of blue canvas pants rested low on his hips, the pockets frayed above the snug fit encasing his thighs, his long legs ending where the material bunched atop his unlaced black boots.

She snapped her gaze back to his and amusement quirked one side of his generous mouth. The slightest narrowing of his gaze and all motion ceased; the distance between them dwindled to nonexistence. Not the mingling bodies, his scent in the air nor the threat of Gaelleod's discovery mattered in the least. Not anymore. Because, in his eyes, that she would be here with him, alive and in the flesh, far exceeded the colors he'd placed to canvas with the talented stroke of his brush.

She knew it. Believed in it. As surely as blood coursed warm and swift through her veins.

That he would gaze upon her as a creature of such unsurpassed beauty made her heart take flight. Sir Jon had spoken true. No harm would come to her whilst Rhys McEleod was near.

He stepped in her direction, but the dark-skinned gentleman who had initially welcomed her and her uncles to the gallery gripped his arm, waylaying his departure. Their gazes broke as he rejoined the conversation with a buxom woman draped in a foxtail trimmed coat. A moment later, the room sharpened back into focus.

Faedrah waited, scratching at the prickling hair at her nape, removed her glasses and hid them inside her pocket to more carefully scrutinize the faces about the room. The intensity of Rhys' gaze returned and, secure in the fact he watched over her, she left the wall to follow the red velvet ropes stationed around the perimeter of the gallery.

The shelter of his stare disappeared, and she stopped, poised on the brink of a step. A subtle shift of the people to her left, and the comfort of his steady reassurance returned. Like the needle of a compass, the magnetic draw of his presence was her lodestone, providing direction, gifting her strength, until she came to rest before the largest of three portraits centered on the western most wall.

'Twas the same picture he'd been working on prior to their intimate scuffle of the previous evening, and the same that had held her spellbound the moment she had cast her eyes in its direction. The black strip of hair currently hidden beneath her hat fluttered on the wisp of a breeze, trailing free and loose over the shrewd assessment of her narrowed eyes. Lips parted, the angle of her chin slightly lowered, the woman before her defined the spirit of resilience. She was enigmatic and beautiful...or perchance the enigma lay within the oddity that Sir McEleod had recreated her with such a sympathetic eye.

Goddesses wept, what she wouldn't give... She lifted the heavy knot of her hair to relieve the pressure on her neck. For just one moment, if she could truly be the formidable warrior staring back at her, then perchance she could defeat Gaelleod, safeguard her family and return worthy of her position within the realm.

Her gaze fell to the bottom left-hand corner and the strange rune Rhys employed as his signature. Something in its rendering seemed familiar, but her mind refused to supply on what occasion she may have seen another of its kind. She stepped over the rope for a better view and lifted her hand to trace the fierce strokes with her fingertip.

"Oh no, dear, you mustn't touch my painting."

Faedrah glanced over her shoulder to the fur-festooned woman who'd been speaking with Rhys and the gallery owner, and dropped her hand to her thigh with a slap.

Her painting? A scowl tightened her brow, though Faedrah kept the surly words on her tongue banked against a reply. 'Twas not as if the painting were hers to sell or give away.

"She can touch anything she wants."

She spun to fully face the room and returned Rhys McEleod's smile. That he would so quickly jump to her defense set her heart back to rights, as did the way he kept their gazes locked, ignoring the disgruntled huff of the painting's new owner.

"Here." He swung his legs over the rope to stand behind her and, as if her curiosity was as natural as petals on a daisy, clasped her hand in his and lifted her finger to the canvas, guiding it over each of the strokes. "R...M...E. There, do you see it?"

A strange tingling suffused her hand at the contact, though whether from the warmth of his palm, the heat of his breath in her ear or some other mystifying reason, she had not the clarity to garner the significance of its meaning. All her efforts were focused on wrestling the urge to lean against his chest, wrapping his arm around her so she could indulge in the power of his nearness.

"I'm glad you're finally here." He twined their fingers together and lowered them to her side. A tug on her hand and her lashes fluttered when his knees bumped the backs of her thighs. "In all honesty, I didn't sleep a wink. I hope you know you're to blame for that."

Two identically uniformed men approached and she arched a brow at the strange arrangement of their attire. Instead of a surcoat and breeches, one light blue garment covered them from nape to heels, sewn together at the waist and belted with an odd assortment of tools. They lifted the painting from the wall and she stiffened as their task became clear.

"What's the matter?" The artist's hand left hers, and his warm palms landed atop her shoulders.

Snapping her focus to the right, she carefully studied the woman who had purchased the painting. If one inkling of Gaelleod's evil sorcery glinted in her eyes, Faedrah would drop the beast to the floor and strangle the infected body with those foxtails so artfully draped around her neck.

The woman withdrew a step, her hand pressed to her chest, and stormed off across the room. Faedrah grunted. And good riddance, too.

"Hold up a second, guys." Rhys turned her to face him and tipped her head back, the curve of his bent knuckle pressed to the underside of her chin. Her knees involuntarily locked as he scrutinized her face. Whatever whim he desired...whatever folly, 'twas a certainty he could melt hearts or destroy souls with a simple blink of such a determined perusal.

"I don't need these pictures anymore. Not since I found you. But if you don't want me to sell them, just say the word and I'll call off this whole deal."

A whimper caught in her throat, tinged with a combination of longing and misfortune. Her uncles had cautioned her. If she spoke plainly, the inhabitants of this realm would undoubtedly think her mad. But oh, how she hungered to confess the horrors in her heart. To watch understanding fill his gaze when she spoke of the dangers she faced.

"What's seems to be the problem?" The dark-skinned gallery owner approached, the offended woman in tow slightly behind him, jowls swaying beneath the imperial angle of her chin.

Faedrah stepped away from Rhys and squinted at the set of the woman's shoulders, the tempo and gait of her pace. No hint of Gaelleod showed upon the lines of her face...or in her eyes... and Faedrah dropped her focus to the floor.

She had surrendered to paranoia. This was nothing more than an exchange for goods tendered. "Do what you will."

Rhys glanced at the gallery owner and his client before reclaiming the distance and clasping her upper arms. "Dammit,

Faedrah, what aren't you telling me? Do you know this woman?"

"I do not."

"Of course we don't know each other." The woman crossed her arms over her ample bosom. "And I'm not about to let her bat those long lashes just so she can get her hands on a painting you've already sold…to *me*."

Faedrah brought her attention back to Rhys, fearing he might believe the worst though his keen inspection never wavered from her face.

He smiled. "Now, lady, that's where you're wrong."

A flick of his finger and her hat toppled to the floor. Panic shot through her veins, and Faedrah clamped both hands on top of her head. Oh no, he mustn't. He couldn't!

His jaw firmed and he shackled her wrists in his fingers, lowering her hands to her sides. "Don't."

Several heads turned in their direction. A hushed silence descended about the room. Impatience sparkled amid the striations in his eyes, and she stood mesmerized by the streaks of deep emerald surrounded by rings of the purest cerulean blue.

"Twenty years, I've been waiting to show off your beautiful face." He plucked the pins from her hair and crammed them into the pockets of his jacket, over and again until her long tresses tumbled heavy and loose down her back. "Twenty years of everyone calling me crazy while I walked around with an image of you in my head." He thrust his fingers in under her hair and a sigh slipped from her throat as he fisted the strands. One step forward and he tipped her head back, lowering his lips the width of whisper to hers. "Don't ever hide yourself. Not from me and not from the people smart enough to buy your picture. Do I make myself clear?"

She searched the hard resolve etched upon his face, dropped her focus to his mouth and nodded. Not one soul in this entire realm would think him any less than the brilliant artist he was… not whilst she had the power to ensure as much.

He lingered a moment longer before slowly withdrawing, and

she fell forward a step at the loss of his solid embrace. Opening his hand toward her, he met the stunned gaze of his well-to-do client. "This woman doesn't need any of my paintings. All she has to do is look in a damn mirror."

Faedrah scanned the slack-jawed expressions decorating the patrons in the gallery, a knot of anxiety lodged in her throat. Her attention snapped to the owner as he smacked his palms together, repeating the noise until all those present joined in his hearty applause. Before she could gather her wits, the crowd surged forward, all of them reaching for her and Rhys with outstretched hands.

Sweet tits, what had he done? She grabbed his arm and jerked him back several steps. With these people swarming in on all sides and her devoid of any weapons, the two of them were left dangerously exposed.

"Oh, shit." He chuckled, captured her hand in his and raced for the far side of the gallery. "Come on, I think that's our cue."

Down a long hall, she sprinted at his side, yet her jaw dropped and she slowed when he momentarily ducked inside a sparsely appointed room and snatched a bottle of spirits off a glass-topped table. Had the man lost his reasoning? *Now* was not the appropriate time for a libation!

"Thanks, Nate." He winked, tucking the bottle under his arm, and she rolled her eyes as he hurried her along the corridor to a plain white door.

The silver bar bisecting the middle gave way under the press of his hand and, as he placed his palm on the small of her back, she led them into the bright blue canopy of Helios' warm rays.

Chapter 6

No matter how many times Rhys jacked the starter, that first ear-splitting growl erupting from the engine made him grin. Based on the way the angel standing beside him flinched and jumped back a step, she was just as impressed by the fine-tuned rumble shaking the chromed tailpipes of his motorcycle as everyone else.

A chuckle cinched the muscles of his stomach as he handed her his helmet, though the sound was lost under the sputtering exhaust bouncing against the brick walls of the alley. His laughter morphed into an amused frown as she held the helmet in both hands like a basketball, twisting it back and forth in her splayed fingers as if she didn't understand what it was for.

Weird. Maybe she was worried about the fit being too big.

He grabbed the helmet, smirking at her wide eyes as he carefully worked the padded interior down past her ears and secured the neck strap under her chin. Rapping his knuckles on top, he lifted his brows. "Okay?"

She nodded, though her astonished blink was more like *what the hell?*

He laughed again and shook his head, tipping the bike to the side to heel the kickstand. Apparently, his muse had never been offered such a cool ride before. Another glance at her and he jerked his chin toward the empty spot behind him on the bike.

"Climb aboard, princess."

The inside of his mouth went dry as sandpaper. Christ, just the thought of her toned thighs straddling his hips shot urgency straight into his cock. He gunned the throttle and waited for the snarl of the engine to subside. "Or would you rather go back inside and face the music?"

One of her brows lifted in a defiant glare and she flipped down the visor. Grasping his shoulder for leverage, she swung her leg over the seat as if she'd been born to ride. Huh. Maybe he was wrong and she *had* been on a bike before.

He shifted into first and eased them to the head of the alley, a quick check both ways for oncoming traffic and he peeled right onto the street.

Her arms flew around his waist and he pursed his lips against a sly smile. *That's right, princess. Hold on tight.* A bob of his foot, and he shifted into second and then third, revving the bike until the wind beat at his face. Her hold on him intensified. Heat throbbed through his groin as her breasts smashed his back, a persistent pulse that had nothing to do with the purring engine between his legs. The smallest wriggle of her ass, and she was plastered to him from nape to hips.

Shit. A peek down at her thighs pressed firmly along the length of his and he bit back a groan. Fuck, with her limbs draped around him like this, it was all he could do to think straight. He concentrated on the stop light before the expressway ramp winking from green, to yellow, to red, and shifted into a lower gear. The strain of keeping his hands off her was like a corrosive acid eating away every last ounce of his self-control.

The bike rolled to a stop and he placed his foot on the ground to wait out the light. She loosened her hold and shifted away from him, bouncing the seat.

No.

Every cell in his body mutinied as the order rang in his head. Christ, he'd completely lost it. Having her close was torture, but the thought of her tempting curves being less than an inch away was worse.

He reached down, wrapped his fingers behind her knee and jerked her right back to his hips.

She flinched, slapping her open palm to the middle of his chest, but she stayed put. A moment later, her fingers fisted the material of his shirt and satisfaction settled to a slow burn over his skin. Good. If he was reading her signals correctly, she felt it too. The constant need to be touching. The nearly sickening desperation that accompanied the thought of saying goodbye.

He unwound her fingers from his shirt and brought them to his lips, rubbing her knuckles back and forth across his mouth. The scent of her skin nearly made him topple the bike. Clean. Natural. Intoxicating. The exact opposite of all the grimy disappointments he'd faced up to this point.

God, he wanted to drink her in.

The light turned green and, as he hit the gas, she wrapped both arms around him like a vice and squeezed him snug between her thighs.

They moved as one, dodging and weaving through the traffic jamming the wide, four-lane tarmac of the crowded expressway, horns blaring and drivers flipping them the bird. The swivel of her hips, the way she leaned with him and anticipated each maneuver, was like they were linked. The tiniest adjustment of her hand over his stomach, and arousal slid like an errant drop of paint down the inside of his legs. If she was this in tune with him on a damn motorcycle, what kind of mind-blowing orgasm would detonate between them in bed?

By the time he swerved for the off ramp, changed gears and rounded the Christian Mission, he was keyed up, rock hard and aching like a horny teenager who'd just copped his first feel.

He slowed for the turn onto the back street behind his warehouse and squinted into the shadows for signs of any box-dwelling derelicts, the occasional strung-out hooker or the local pushers who invited his business with a gold-toothed grin. A slide of his foot along the ground, and swung the bike onto the freight elevator.

Lowering the kickstand, he killed the engine, and the immediate silence that followed pushed against his eardrums like weight. The only sign he hadn't lost his hearing was the heavy beat of his pulse—throbbing with the same thick tempo as his groin.

"Let me get the door." He climbed off the bike and a loud rumble shook the elevator as he lowered the gate. After jamming his key into the lock, he twisted it to the right, jabbed the button for the third floor, and turned to face her…and nearly swallowed his tongue.

Lowering his helmet to her thigh, she shook out her long white hair, the ends feathering the dark crease between the curve of her ass and the seat. He fisted his hands, teeth clenched and knees locked. Every synapse in his body screamed at him to go grab a handful of that unruly mass, wrench her head back and cram his tongue down her throat.

The elevator lurched into its snail-paced ascent and she startled, falling forward to brace her hands on the bike. That black strip of hair tumbled past her shoulder. Thighs tense, the toes of her sexy black boots perched on the footrests, she rotated her hips as if squirming on the edge of a cataclysmic release. One he'd brought to her with the rhythmic tap and stroke of his thumb.

Jesus Christ. He widened his stance to relieve the tight pressure in his jeans. Strip her down to a black lace thong, and he'd be staring at the completion of every erotic fantasy she'd starred in.

Blowing a steadying breath through his pursed lips, he tried and failed to find something else to concentrate on. Sure, he'd brought her here to have her all to himself, maybe talk her into sitting for him so he could achieve one of his lifelong dreams of painting her in real time, but the right thing to do—the *proper* thing to do—was to get to know her first. Spend some time talking with her until she was comfortable.

She walked her palms backward along the leather seat, the line of her back arched against the downward slope, breasts thrust forward, until her fingers bracketed the padding between her legs. A bead of sweat trickled down his spine. Sweet Christ in Heaven, he was never going to last. Tipping her head back, she stared at the ceiling, exposing the long cool length of her throat.

Her chest rose with a deep inhalation and the last scrap of his willpower went up in smoke. "Fuck proper."

He strode forward, tossed his helmet aside, straddled the bike facing her and yanked her legs onto his thighs. Her sharp gasp cut through the creaking gears of the elevator. One hand clenching her hip, the other spearing through the hair at her nape, he hauled her flat to his chest.

A demanding sweep of his lips across hers and she went rigid, her mouth firmed. Denial streaked through his head and he switched angles, tipping her chin to the left. Nipping little love bites along her jaw, he frowned as her palm pressed his shoulder. Didn't she understand how long he'd been waiting for her? Hadn't the same hunger he'd lived and breathed since she arrived at the gallery nearly driven her insane?

Come on, baby, where are you?

He clasped her fingers and shoved them to the back of his neck. Flicking his tongue, he licked and prodded the seam of her lips. He wasn't about to give up. He'd been caught in limbo too damn long to let her go.

She softened in his arms. Her mouth parted on a sigh. He inhaled the sweet, unspoiled warmth of her breath and dove deep.

Yes… Everything he'd ever wanted suddenly filled his arms. The eager swirl of her tongue gliding over his, the silky strands of her hair tangled in his fingers, the groan-inducing pressure of her spread legs balanced on his thighs. God, he'd never get enough. Kissing her was like living a wet dream. Her hips hitched and he moaned into her mouth when the cradle of her warm sex rode the side of his cock. Hell, reality was better.

The jolt of the ancient cables broke them apart and Faedrah

leaned away from him, placing three fingers to her lips. Her eyes sparkled with awareness. The blush he'd already come to crave pinked her cheeks, and he ground his teeth to keep from pushing her hand aside with his chin so he could devour her lips. They'd arrived at the third floor and, if he had anything to say about it, would continue this exploration of one another's bodies inside.

"My mother once told me 'twould seem as if the earth had moved." She lowered her focus to his mouth, flipped her hand and skimmed a light touch over his lips. "At the time, I did not believe her description to be literal."

God, she was cute. Though he had to admit, the way his head spun had nothing to do with bounce of the elevator. The seduction of their kiss, the promise of where it might lead, had made the ground shift for him too. Except...

His smile slowly faded as her words sank in. "Your mother's description of what?"

"Why, a kiss, of course."

Surprise rocked him back on the seat and he dropped his hands to her thighs. She'd never been kissed? How was that even possible? "Wait a second. Faedrah, how old are you?"

"I've just passed the twentieth season of my birth." She squinted. "Why do you ask?'

Her twentieth season? Jesus Christ, she was practically a kid! He dug his index finger and thumb into the tight squeeze of his eyes and pinched them together over the bridge of his nose. Not to mention the most obvious setback this never-locked-lips realization brought to light.

She was a virgin. She had to be. All he could think about was screwing her brains out and she'd never so much as been kissed? Shit, he was an asshole. Not that his body seemed to care. Based on the stretch and flex tugging at his boxers, his cock was only too happy to accept the challenge of being the first to bring her to orgasm. *God! What the fuck?*

"You are dissatisfied." Her statement was a fact not a question, and she shoved away from him and climbed off his lap. The sharp rap of her heels crossed the elevator and she lifted the gate. A few quick strides into the warehouse and she drew up short, and he couldn't begin to imagine the shock tripping through her head as she came face to face with the mural of her on his wall. Add in the numerous canvases propped in the corners, the ones stacked like decks of playing cards around the room, and he was bound to come off like a complete psycho.

She whirled to face him, eyes bright with resentment and her jaw clenched. "I demand you return me to my uncles' home at once."

He huffed. "You're not going anywhere." At least, not until they'd had the chance to talk this through. "Cool your jets, woman. I'm not dissatisfied, I'm…" He tossed a hand in the air. "Cock blocked." And he needed a drink. Like, right now.

He swung his leg over the bike and wheeled it off the elevator, rummaged through his saddle bags and rescued the bottle of champagne he'd lifted from Nate's office.

His muse scowled, crossing her arms. "Whatever *blockage* is currently plaguing your anatomy, I will not stand idly by while you toy with me as if I'm a child. Either state your intentions in transporting me here or leave me be on my way."

Tubes of paint rattled as he slammed the bottle on the table. "My intentions are the same as they were from the first moment I saw you." Though he wasn't about to pop her cherry with a "wham-bam thank you, ma'am." She deserved better.

"And yet you place judgment on that which you do not understand." Aiming a finger at the floor, she strode forward several steps. "You kiss me as if the next beat of your heart relies upon my surrender and then grow exasperated when I comply."

Yep. Confusing as hell, right? And the pent-up frustration simmering in her brown eyes wasn't helping. Apparently, several years of abstinence had left her teetering every bit near the edge as he was. All it would take is a few quick flicks of his tongue and she'd come in his mouth.

His hand shook as he tore the cellophane off the bottle neck and twisted the wire. Shit, that ball-busting brainstorm couldn't have come at a worse time.

"I like it that no one has touched you, Faedrah." In fact, if anything, her lack of experience made her more perfect. More... *his*, somehow. "But your innocence also complicates things." He pried his thumb under the cork and a loud *pop* echoed against the rafters. Champagne fizzed and spilled down his fingers, foaming over the table and floor.

Whether or not she gave him her virginity, once they had sex she would be his and *only* his. Exactly the way he'd always planned.

The thought detonated like an atomic bomb inside his head, and he tipped the bottle to guzzle several deep swallows. The aftershock leveled everything, leaving one huge mushroom cloud that expanded with a reality so intense, he nearly choked on the wine.

No one had made love to her. And no one ever would.

No one, but him.

He lowered the bottle to the table. Dammit, he was so screwed. She had him. By the scruff of the neck, she had him. Funny thing was, there didn't seem to be anything in the whole damn world that could've made him happier than knowing he would be the only man to have her in his bed...other than the trip to convincing her that's where she belonged.

A glance in her direction and his shoulders fell at the barely contained rage stretched across her face. Shit, now what?

"Well, far be it for me to present you such a troublesome *complication*." She marched toward the elevator, fists swinging at her sides. "You have my most vehement regrets."

Yeah, except that sounded more like, "*Go fuck yourself, buddy.*"

He stifled a chuckle and shackled her wrist in his fingers as she stormed past, swinging an arm under her legs to lift those wicked boots off the floor. Kicking her feet and batting his shoulders, she struggled to be set down, but he wasn't about to let her leave. Not for a second.

"Baby, stop." He sat on one of the wooden chairs, propping her sideways on his lap, and clamped her hands to her thighs even though she continued to wriggle. "Stop before I change my damn mind. You misunderstood me."

She jerked her hands out from under his and smacked his chest...and then smacked him again.

Okay, he probably deserved that for serving up the old bait and switch. "Feel better?"

"No." She buried her face in her hands and he tugged her forward, easing her head in under his chin. "My patience has thinned, Rhys McEleod. You have befuddled me, sound and true."

He chuckled at the funny way she talked. But God, where did he even start? Nate always said honesty was the best policy when it came to women. Sound advice from a guy happily married six years. "I know where I stand, Faedrah, but I'm worried about you."

She leaned away from him, frowning. A moment later, suspicion narrowed her eyes, exactly the same as when she'd sized up that woman at the gallery. And he didn't like it. The distrust brewing in her gaze made him want to punch the wall. "Speak plainly, sir. Why would your worry be for me?"

His brow twitched. Hell, why wouldn't it be for her? She was keeping secrets from him. Secrets that scared her, based on the critical way she'd analyzed his client and her tight-lipped responses when it came to selling her pictures. Good news was, this confirmed he'd made the right decision in holding off on taking their...whatever this was...to the next level. Until she trusted him enough to tell him the truth, she'd never be ready to trust him in bed. Not with all the ways he planned to coax a climax from her non-stop, take-her-against-the-wall body.

He shook off that mouth-watering visual and trailed a finger around the curve of her cheek. "I've been seeing you since I was eight years old. Did you know that? For two decades, I've been visualizing every line and angle of your face, working hard to make sure I drew them just right." Her breath caught as he traced the bridge of her nose, over her luscious mouth, down the center of her chin to her throat. "You met me yesterday. That's a twenty year difference, princess. You need some time to catch up, that's all."

And he'd give her as much as she needed. Just as long as she played by his rule that no one—*no one*—besides him ever touched her.

"Twenty years…" Her eyes darted back and forth as if she were lost in thought, and she grasped his hand as he reached the little dip between her collar bones. The one he wanted to fill with his tongue. "That is the exact extent of my age."

He snapped his chin up. Holy shit, she was right. He'd been so distracted by his mind-numbing attraction to her, he'd never made the connection.

"I would see these renderings from your childhood." She chewed her thumbnail and then wagged a finger in the air. "And begin my inquiry there."

Being right sucked. Or so said the persistent stiffy rocking his crotch for the elusive Faedrah Austiere. Getting a concrete answer from her was like trying to pin down a cloud.

"And this one?"

The scratch of his charcoal paused mid-stroke as he glanced up from his sketch pad to the bed. The angel he was drawing lay on her stomach, knees bent and ankles crossed, stocking feet swaying leisurely in the air. The extensive drafts of her he'd filed away over the years were spread like a patchwork quilt over his blankets, depicting the various stages of his life. Though, in all of them she was the same, just as she was now—young, vibrant and holy hell gorgeous.

Dropping his heels from the edge of the mattress to the floor, he leaned forward in the chair and plucked the sheet from her fingers. "This one I drew eight years ago, during my second semester at art school." He remembered it well. The picture was the first time he'd shown her wielding a set of swords and, as a business art major, Nate had taken an interest in the piece.

Their friendship was the one good thing that had come from that Still Life 101 class. "After I turned it in, the instructor tossed me out on my ass."

He handed the portrait back to her and resumed his work in progress, but couldn't help smiling when she frowned down at the image of her posed in a crouch, the determined squint on her face a testament to all things kicking ass and taking names. "Whatever for? I think it's quite brilliant. Exceptionally fierce."

"The assignment was to draw a bowl of fruit."

"Ah." She nodded, though the delicate skin between her brows remained creased as she studied the page. He sketched a few quick lines on the side of his pad, capturing her concentration for later use.

"Eight cycles of the seasons ago, I began my training with the Roy—" She bit her lip; cleared her throat. "Vaighn gifted me a set of similar weapons in celebration of my twelfth season."

Rhys blew a frustrated huff through his nose, dropped the charcoal in his lap and flexed his fingers before he accidentally snapped it in two. By his count, that little slip made a dozen times she'd stumbled over her words since they'd finished dinner. As if she kept forgetting she wasn't supposed to spill the beans about certain things or there'd be hell to pay. The constant backpedaling drove him nuts.

"Who's Vaighn?" And what kind of negligent jackass gave a twelve-year-old girl a set of swords for her birthday?

"My cousin by blood, though most in the kingdom consider us siblings." She set the picture aside and selected one of his earliest drawings—a colored-pencil rendering he'd done as a kid. "His present was my most favored that year."

Kingdom, huh? He left off smudging the thick tumble of her hair to capture the wistful smile curling her lips, the happiness shining in her beautiful brown eyes. Interesting…but he bit his tongue against pushing for more. If he did, she was liable to clam up, just like earlier when he'd apologized for the transitional state of his living conditions and she'd brushed off his apology, saying she was quite comfortable. That his place reminded her of Fandorn's laboratory.

The way she'd pronounced the word cracked him up—*la-bor-a-tory*—like they were extras in a Bela Lugosi film. He'd casually asked after the guy and she'd muttered something noncommittal about her father's many "advisors" before changing the subject. Didn't matter. By that time, he'd already received the message loud and clear.

Pick up what she was laying down and don't mess with the stress. Follow up questions were a no go for launch.

To break up the quiet while she'd checked the plumbing and surveyed the contents of his fridge, he docked his phone in the player and tuned in some music. Her reaction to the pulsing beat was one of childlike wonder, and she sat in front of the speakers for a full hour, dialing in various songs. Turns out they had the same taste in music. Rock, very hard and very loud.

Same with her reaction to the beer and pizza he'd ordered for dinner, which was downright bizarre, and conveyed the extent of just how sheltered her life had been. Especially when she patiently waited for him to take the first bite, and then wolfed down four pieces as if she'd never tasted anything so good.

If that wasn't enough, those few tense moments after a rumble from the rail yard shook the warehouse confirmed she was from out of town. Like, far, far outside of town. She'd nearly come unglued and he'd spent the next ten minutes trying to talk her down from whatever neurotic ledge the shaking had initiated, explaining how close he lived to the box car switch and she didn't have to worry about the roof caving in. He'd had the structural integrity of the building checked and rechecked.

In the end, the only thing that calmed her down was a secretive call to her uncles. A few tense whispers, and she'd finally relaxed...and then it was all smiles and sunshine, like nothing had ever happened.

Yes, indeed, a day with her and what little investigative skills he'd acquired had been put to the test. At some points she came across as relaxed, confident and even ribbed him with her sarcastic wit. Other times she seemed sketchy and unsure, as if she didn't understand how to answer his questions.

If he wasn't convinced the secrets hidden behind her soulful brown eyes had her scared shitless, he may have suggested she have her meds checked.

But his angel wasn't crazy. He believed that down to the soles of his worn, black leather boots. Nope, in reality, the truth was a lot less disturbing.

Faedrah Austiere simply stunk at telling a lie.

"I adore this one. Truly."

He glanced up from where he'd been working the folds of her red, over-sized sweater, the way the slouching collar had slipped off one of her bare shoulders, and smiled at the picture she held. His lack of technique showed in the mismatched shading, which meant the depth perception was all screwy, but the angle of the stable door was pretty good. The head of the black horse he'd added was to scale, as was the subtle layering of Faedrah's hair, tangled with the horse's mane as it nuzzled her cheek.

Still, his ability with a set of Crayola colored pencils really wasn't what the picture was about. At least, not according to Sister Mary Ignatius at Georgetown Prep. She'd said the drawing "exemplified love."

Faedrah tapped the paper, indicating the horse. "Excelsior."

"Oh, baby, say it ain't so." He grimaced. "That's a terrible name for a horse."

She whipped the drawing against his leg in response to his teasing and he chuckled, exchanging the black charcoal for gold. His body went on lock-down as he traced the chain hanging around her neck, disappearing inside the cleavage peeking just over the edge of her sweater.

85

So…a kingdom, a horse, sword training, and she'd never been kissed. Maybe she lived in a monastery? One of those weird convents in the Himalayan Mountains that trained girls to be virgin ninja warriors?

He shook off the idea. That couldn't be right. She'd mentioned family, let little things slip about her mom and dad. Hell, maybe that's where he needed to start. "What's your father do for a living, princess?"

She added the drawing to a special pile she'd started—most likely her favorites—and selected another from the disheveled mish-mash on her right. "Since you insist on using my proper title, it should not surprise you he's the king."

Her imperial tone made his lips twitch against a smile, and he studied her from under his brows. Oh, so that's the game they were playing? As if the nickname he'd given her was literal? Okay fine, he'd bite. "The king of…?"

"The Austiere Kingdom, of course."

Right. Dumb question. "And that would make your mother the queen?"

Her jaw firmed, and he got the distinct impression he'd just stepped onto thin ice. Tricky, tricky. Too bad his little minx didn't realize her faith in him was directly tied to his—and her—sexual gratification. And when it came to earning that tender prize, he'd keep on keeping on until she folded.

"The white queen is the most revered of all subjects in the realm." She flipped a drawing to the side and chose another. "Beautiful, compassionate, brilliant and without equal in the eyes of the king."

Jesus Christ. No pressure there. Then again, he was fully in touch with her pain. Not that his father had ever given two shits his son dropped out of art school, or the outcome of any other success-to-failure ratio in Rhys' life. Nope, the yardstick by which he ticked off his value in comparison to dear old dad had always been carried solely by him. "Those are some pretty high standards to measure yourself against, princess. Trust me when I tell you that battle is a lose-lose."

He scrawled his initials on the bottom corner of the sketch and turned it to face her. "Besides, I'm proof positive the woman in this picture isn't giving herself enough credit. She's perfect, and I've got a check for a cool eight thousand in my pocket which says so."

She grinned. "'Tis an unfortunate circumstance you are not the slightest bit biased."

A push onto her knees, and she reached for the sketch pad, but he jerked it over his shoulder, outside her reach. "Hands off. I'm planning to sell this masterpiece and buy myself some furniture."

"Whatever for?" One of her brows rose as she opened her hands to her sides. "When you already own such a comfortable place to rest your head?" She fell forward onto her arms, the key tumbling from the top of her sweater as she crawled to the edge of the bed. "In fact, I daresay you've not entirely thought this through. Perchance if you gift the picture to me, I shall compensate your good efforts in ways you can only imagine."

Holy shit. Every muscle in his body hardened. Just the thought of all the ways she could thank him with that luscious mouth made him ache.

He leapt from the chair and tackled her to the mattress, and she laughed and beat at his back as he buried his face in her neck. "Stop! You have not yet held up your part of the bargain."

Shit. He rolled off of her and rescued the sketch pad from the floor, set it in her hands and returned to the one spot he belonged—his legs tangled with hers, arms locked around her waist, the bare skin of her shoulder available to his lips and tongue.

Her palm met the back of his head and her nails combed his scalp as he explored the curves of her body with his hands. Unfortunately, she seemed too preoccupied by the drawing to notice.

"Set that damn thing down and kiss me." He brushed his lips over the shell of her ear, tugged on her earlobe with his teeth.

"A moment." She shoved at his shoulder and sat up, and he was suddenly holding nothing but air. What the hell?

He rose to his elbows as she shuffled the papers around, comparing a few here and there to the sketch in her hands. "No rush. I'll just wait until whenever you're ready."

"None of these earlier drawings contain the key." She whirled to face him and he frowned at the dismay in her eyes. "Why do they not contain the key? When did you initially detect its presence?"

"Hell, I don't know." He sat up and tossed a hand in the air, trying to remember the first time he'd gotten a visual of the necklace. "I've been seeing it forever, but I only added it to this last round I did for Nate. Seemed right, I guess." She stood from the bed and he squinted at her back as she crossed to her portrait on the wall. Based on the tense set of her shoulders, this little side trip of hers was headed in a bad direction. But it wasn't like this latest piece of news was some big shocker. They'd spent the past fifteen hours discovering the events she experienced in her life ultimately showed up in his. "Faedrah, get back here."

Her arms dropped to her sides, and the sketch pad fell to the floor with a stinging clap. The picture wafted to a stop at her feet. "Why can I not see the answer? What detail eludes me?"

Hell, she wasn't making any sense. Then again, if she'd spent last night lying awake in bed like him, she was probably exhausted. Not thinking straight.

"I have risked the entirety of my kingdom only to discover… nothing." She slowly turned to face him and his chest constricted at the tears welling in her eyes. "Why am I here?"

Well, shit, there could be any number of reasons, but only one came to mind. "You're here because I wished for you."

Her shoulders fell, and the gentle smile on her face said she was happy to let him indulge in his little fantasy. A second later, she sighed and broke their stare to search the night through the dirt-streaked windows.

God dammit, no. He pushed to his feet and stood at the end

of his bed, arms crossed. She was shutting down again, retreating inside her head. "You don't believe me?"

"That is not it. I…" She dropped her focus to the floor. "There simply must be another explanation."

Wrong. That was the only explanation. And if convincing her she was here because she belonged with him was gonna take another twenty years, then they'd damned well better get started.

He strode forward and scooped her into his arms, carried her back to the bed and reclined against the pillows so she could rest her cheek on his chest. This time he'd be the one to fix everything. No more private calls to her uncles. No more feeding him a line of bullshit neither of them believed.

She snuggled against him, twisting his shirt in her fingers like he was her last lifeline in a storm. Dammit, how the hell was he ever going to get her to trust him? He closed his eyes and palmed the back of her head, hoping she would understand he was there for her…and always would be…no matter what disappointments she faced.

But he wouldn't ask her any more tonight. Not with her tired and upset. No, tonight he would just hold her, keep her warm and watch over her to make sure she slept. Then, tomorrow, after they'd both gotten some rest, he would insist she tell him the truth—the *whole* truth—and find a way to make her realize she'd wished for him just as hard in return.

Chapter 7

A languid stretch of her arms and legs, and Faedrah smiled as a large, warm hand slid around her belly, tugging her back against the firm wall of Rhys McEleod's chest.

"Don't." The gravel-laden timbre of his voice sent a thrill skating over her skin, as did the soft press of his lips upon the ticklish spot beneath her ear. "Sleep."

She covered his hand with hers, twining their fingers together. His soft murmur of contentment fluttered her hair. His knees slid across the sleeping pallet, nestling behind hers as if the two of them were spoons in a drawer.

Indeed, she could have happily succumbed to his request to remain abed. The slumber she'd enjoyed wrapped within his arms had been that of such deep repose, not one hint of Gaelleod's hauntings had invaded her dreams. How extraordinary one night in Rhys' chambers, falling asleep with her cheek cradled upon his chest, had offered her such a long-awaited reprieve.

Unfortunately, whether she chose to leave his arms or linger a moment longer was not her decision to make. "I need to use the privy."

He grumbled his displeasure, curling his entire body around hers in a blanketing embrace. "Across the room by the sink. It's the only door in the place." A tender nibble of her ear, and he grudgingly released her. "Come right back."

Amusement quirked her lips as she crawled from beneath the blankets. The man spoke as if not only her, but the entirety of the Austiere Kingdom were his to command. He would be well advised to remember the only crown she'd sworn to obey decorated that of her father's dark brow…and fulfilling even *his* commands stretched the limits of her exasperation.

After making use of the facilities, she stopped at the basin to splash a few handfuls of water upon her cheeks and comb her fingers through the unruly mop of her hair. A peek at Rhys through a crack in the door, and she swung the handle wide, stealing across the floor to the end of his bed.

He was not asleep, though the way he'd tossed one muscled arm over his eyes and the deep rhythm of his breathing was undoubtedly meant for her to believe as much.

She tipped her head to better scrutinize the series of elaborate, black runes that had been etched into the underside of his arm. How odd he would mark his body in such a way, though perchance their meaning held some significance she could not determine. They were a language she'd not yet encountered in her studies.

Shaking her head, she propped her hands on her hips. Confidence radiated from the relaxed sprawl of his limbs—one leg bent, his left arm lying crosswise atop her pillow, as if waiting to pull her close the moment of her return…as if her desire to do as much was a foregone conclusion. The masculine scent of youth and virility wafted off his skin in a hypnotic appeal that nearly had her rushing to do his bidding.

She lifted a brow in shrewd deliberation of reclaiming her spot at his side. Certainly, his request had been innocuous enough. Quite right, joining him for a heated tousle beneath the sheets bespoke a temptation she was loathe to ignore. Yet 'twould be unwise to allow their relationship to commence as if one utterance from him and she would scurry to grant his every wish.

Whisking her red sweater over her head, she stripped to her

lacy chemise and fitted blue breeches, and spun from the end of his sleeping pallet for the training mats occupying the corner of his vaulted chambers.

Eight years had passed since she'd enlisted in the Royal Guard. Eight years of striving to fulfill her duty, obeying each order without hesitation in her quest to earn a small measure of respect.

She sat cross-legged on the training mats and closed her eyes. She was not a child to be ordered about. Her arrival in this realm confirmed she'd left those days behind her. And she had not disregarded her father's warnings…she would not bear the punishment for her insubordination by turning straight around and charging headlong into a coupling where she was not afforded her own sway.

Filling her lungs, she placed her hands on her knees and slowly exhaled.

If Rhys McEleod wanted her in his bed, he'd best just come and get her.

"What…are you doing?"

She peeked at him with one eye—propped on his elbow, head braced in his hand, the thin material of his sleeveless shirt stretched tight over the beveled planes of his chest. No effort was needed to imagine the resistance those hard muscles would demonstrate pressed against her breasts. He'd presented her the opportunity the moment he'd yanked her onto his lap and a thrill had left her breathless beneath his searing kiss.

A shiver stole through her body, and she gritted her teeth as an answering echo quivered her core. "I'm about my morning meditations, sir. Now shush."

Closing her eye, she struggled to clear her mind of his enticing distractions. Though how such a task was to be accomplished while the intensity of his gaze heated her skin remained a mystery.

She drew another deep breath and slowly exhaled, directing her thoughts to the dilemma at hand—the missing details behind her purpose in this place, her search for Gaelleod and the meaning hidden inside her fitful dreams. Pressing her hands to the floor, she upended into a handstand, her hair whispering down her back as she uncurled her legs into the air.

While beautiful, Rhys' portraits of her did not convey the answers she'd hoped to ascertain from her detailed examination. They supplied no clues to her next prudent course other than confirming that which she already knew.

He'd somehow honed into the facets of her life, only to recreate those same moments in his.

The question which plagued her still, was how? What connection had permitted him such a deep understanding of her existence? And, more importantly, why his unending compulsion to draw her at all? What purpose did such a thing serve? If not to lure her here in order to gain access to the key, why had the goddesses dispensed him such a curious fate?

Frustration prickled the ends of her nerves and she flipped to her feet, utilizing her momentum to perform a repeated back handspring toward the far corner of the mat. Thrusting the heel of one hand high at a forty-five degree angle, the other a hard fist near her breast, she lunged forward and held, breathing through the turbulent chaos of her thoughts.

Clearly, the fault lay with her. She was not astute enough to untangle the threads of such a perplexing web. The rustle of blankets disrupted the still morning air, and her chin instinctively tipped to the right. Or perchance the fault lay in her fascination with Rhys McEleod. 'Twas a labor in futility trying to concentrate with him near.

Each stroke of the kohl he'd wrought upon the page the previous evening had been like a caress to her skin. Every time he'd peered at her with his commanding eyes, she'd had to struggle to locate her breath.

And when he'd swept her into his arms...when he'd squeezed her close as if nothing or no one could ever part their souls, a glimmer of hope had flared in her heart that, at long last, she'd found her true home.

A spin on her toe and she raced for the opposite wall. Three steps up and she wrenched back, arms extended. Her hands met the mat and she pushed off, careening through the air in a high arc. A whirl as she landed, and she punched her fist forward... and connected with the firm barricade of Rhys McEleod's chest.

A smarting pain shot down her arm, but if that same sting reverberated through the unyielding tower of his body, the stubborn set of his jaw gave not the slightest indication she'd dispensed any harm.

He gripped her wrist, forcing her knuckles deeper into thick muscle as he strode forward. She retreated the same distance to reclaim some space. Matching her pace for pace, he held firm, the tempo of their steps a dangerous dance relaying a fierce contest of wills.

Her back slammed the wall and he closed in, smacking his palms to the wooden planks on either side of her head. "Where did you learn to move like that?" She lowered her lashes to avoid his inspection, but he dodged low, keeping their gazes locked. "And spare me the half-truths, Faedrah. You and I both know lying to me is a waste of time."

Dipping her knees, she tried to escape the prison of his arms yet he moved with her, trapping her in place with the rigid tension in his thighs. "I can't help you if you don't let me in. Dammit, I can't protect you unless you tell me what you're hiding."

Frustration tightened her jaw, and she fisted the fabric of his shirt. If she confessed, if she allowed the slightest indication of her leap through the veil, he would undoubtedly think her deranged.

Her uncles had warned her. Magic did not exist in this place. To risk that Rhys' admiration for her would disintegrate to disgust, to exchange the lust in his gaze for pity... Goddesses wept, she would rather disengage from her quest altogether than to have him peer upon her as if her wits had fled.

"Why won't you trust me?" His hands left the wall for her cheeks. The calloused tips of his thumbs swept the thin skin beneath her lashes. "I swear to God, whoever put that fear in your eyes is a dead man."

She could not reason with him so close. All thought except banishing the sharp fury from his gaze was lost beneath the heady musk of his skin, the invitation of his lips hovering a breath from hers.

A whimper scuffed her throat as she ran her palm up his biceps, along his shoulder to scrape her nails through the short hair at his nape. His brow twitched. Arousal darkened his jade irises to the mystery of a shadowed forest, and he squinted.

"Do not be angry with me." Rising on the tips of her toes, she urged him near. She needed him to believe in her. Despite the secrets she guarded. Regardless of the uncertainties between them. His faith she could truly embody the woman in his paintings was the one thing to hold her steady and sure amid the unforeseeable tempest she faced. "For all my duplicity, I do not think I could bear it."

"Oh, baby." He sighed, shook his head, and dropped his lips to hers.

His taste burst across her palate with the intensity of lightning strike. Potent, demanding, filled with longing and the sweet realization of dreams brought to life.

The tip of his tongue swept a daring swirl around hers. He angled her head and brushed the curves of his mouth over hers before delving deep, matching her needs, stroke for stroke.

A resonating shudder unfurled in the pit of her stomach, warm and inviting. Her sex spasmed and sparks ricocheted down her legs to the soles of her feet.

Her uncles had been wrong. Magic did exist in this place. It sizzled in the air around them. Tingled in the tips of her fingers and moistened the aching emptiness between her thighs.

Rhys' hold on her cheeks disappeared. He slid his hands along her ribcage and she gasped as he hoisted her onto his hips. The taut muscles of his waist heated her inner thighs. She crossed her ankles in the small of his back and a moan left her chest as the head of his erection prodded her tender folds. Flashpoints exploded behind her closed eyelids. He was hot against her. The bunched tension in his shoulders hard and strong. A tremor quaked through her limbs as he rolled his hips, adding sweet friction to the fiery licks of his kiss. Moisture surged. He growled and thrust deeper, easing his palms down to the backs of her thighs.

The straining tendons in his arms, the flutter of his fingers along the seam of her ass flooded her body with ecstasy, her mind with lust. No perfunctory readings from her biology tomes came close to the searing desire racing through her veins. The gentle explanations from her mother and giggling admissions of her handmaidens were but a grain of sand upon the shore of this bliss.

He broke from their kiss and she arched against him, elbows bent, fingers plying the back of his neck. A dip of his head and he flicked his tongue, wetting her nipple through her silky chemise. Arousal pooled in her belly. He drew her into the warm cavern of his mouth, the edges of his teeth grazed her sensitive flesh and her hips bucked. Goddesses wept, he nearly had her undone.

A mechanical buzz shimmied his cellular device across the table. She frowned and tightened her thighs about his waist. No, no, he could not leave her teetering so near the brink.

His muscles bunched as he pumped his arms. The ridge of his shaft slid along the cleft of her sex and she writhed, trembling, cinching her ankles to press him deeper.

The persistent drone abruptly ceased and she crushed her lips to his. His low groan coasted hot and moist over her skin. He hitched her higher on his hips, centered the head of his manhood against her and drove harder, fisting a hand in her hair, raining kisses along her shoulder and neck.

A hiss eased from between his clenched teeth and he shook his head, eyes squeezed tight. "Christ, woman, you're going to make me come."

Exhilaration shivered her belly. That she held such power over him made her confidence soar. She grabbed his cheeks and sucked his lower lip, exploring the smooth texture of his tongue, taking all that she craved and more. And if the way she rode him brought him to orgasm, so much the better. Let them fall and tumble together. Let the yearnings of their bodies fulfill that which the goddesses had blessed.

The hum of his phone resumed its bothersome chant and Rhys hastily withdrew from her, muttering a vicious curse. He wrenched her from the wall, his determined stride bouncing her on his hips, tossed her onto his sleeping pallet and aimed a sharp finger at her face. "Stay there. I'm not done with you."

She rolled her lips together to suppress a smile and aimed an assessing brow at the thick bulge straining the crotch of his breeches. 'Twould seem he was more than happy to come and get her after all.

He stormed to the table and slapped the gadget to his ear. "This had better be a god damned emergency."

His shoulders snapped to attention and she pushed to sitting as the passion drained from his face…to be replaced with the ashen pallor of enraged shock.

She froze. Something unseemly had just occurred.

"How did you get this number?"

An anger so cold laced his words, she shivered. Her fingers curled into the blankets, and she flinched as he jerked the full force of his attention to her.

"Yeah, well, I'm not sure that's gonna work. For either of us. I'll get back to you."

He lowered the cell phone from his cheek, his knuckles white with his grip as he thumbed the screen. Flicking his wrist, he chucked the shiny object aside. "That was my father." He refocused on her and her heart tripped a beat at the menacing thunder in his gaze. "He heard about what happened at the gallery and has invited us to his place for dinner."

An uneasy wariness prickled her nerves, yet she resisted the urge to leap to any foregone conclusions. Twice now, she'd assumed the worst only to end looking the fool.

Rhys was not Gaelleod. From the start, he'd displayed no interest in stealing the key. Due their familial tie, 'twould seem unlikely his father bore the traits of such malevolence as well.

Still, she would have been blind to miss the forbidding tension simmering between them. Mayhap a rift had occurred. One which had never been healed between father and son. "And you prefer to decline?"

Rhys' shoulders fell and he raked a hand through is hair. "Yes. I do. My dad has never paid any attention to me or my work, and now suddenly you show up and he wants us all to be pals?" He shook his head. "No. I don't like it. You can bet your sweet ass that means Leo's up to no good."

Her brows lifted in surprise, yet she could not deny the relief which slowed her pulse to a more normal rate. Rhys had been depicting her portrait since childhood. Surely, if the slightest taint of Gaelleod's evil lingered within his father, Leo McEleod would have taken an instant fascination in his son's renderings of her. The similarities she bore to her mother would have ensured as much.

No, a more perplexing dilemma was at play. She stood and approached her seething artist. A mystifying riddle in which she held a significant role. Placing one hand on his chest, she cupped the other to the rough, dark stubble covering his strong jaw. An opportunity, perchance, to be the divining force to mend past hurts between them. And, in fulfilling her duty, the goddesses would grant her grace, and finally reveal the clues to her purpose in this place. "I suspect we should attend."

The warmth of his calloused palm covered the back of her hand and he turned his head to bestow a heated kiss to her palm. "I don't trust him, Faedrah. My God, if he ever hurt you…if he does or says anything to make you hate me, I'll never forgive myself."

She smiled. She and her talented artist were alike in so many ways. Their strengths…their fears… A chuckle warmed her chest as she swept her thumb along the generous curve of his lower lip. Their propensity for keeping secrets. "I could not be so easily persuaded to depart your side." Yet, Rhys had been wise to insist she ascertain all she could about him before their connection deepened. Learning the difficulties he shared with his father seemed a sensible place to start. "I presume this is but the first of many steps we shall take toward unraveling the mysteries of one another's hearts."

Stepping inside the shelter of his arms, she lowered her cheek to his chest. He understood much about her life, had drawn the scenes with his own able hand. She longed for that same indulgence. To determine all she could about him, inside and out.

"Now breathe easy, Sir McEleod, and speak with an apt tongue. You have my solemn vow, I shall not waver." Tipping her head back, she smiled into the troubled light filling his gaze. "Let us start at the beginning. 'Tis time for you to catch me up."

* * *

How the hell his little white-haired vixen had talked him into seeing his dad, he'd never know.

Rhys eased his motorcycle into an empty parking spot in front of her uncles' building, killed the engine and slipped the key from the ignition. Faedrah shifted behind him, crinkling the cellophane covering his dry-cleaned suit, and grasped his shoulder as she swung her leg to the ground. The disappearance of her warm curves in exchange for the cool breeze hitting his back pushed his sour mood from the safety of DEFCON four to the bright orange alert of DEFCON two.

She handed over his helmet, flipped the hanger onto her shoulder with one finger and smiled. The cellophane twirled and twisted behind her, riding the same draft that toyed with the ends of her hair. The late afternoon sun cast the shadowy fringe of her long lashes onto her cheeks, but nothing on God's green Earth could've shaded the playful twinkle in her eyes. "Sulking is an unattractive quality in a man, don't you agree?"

He cocked a brow, snaked an arm around her hips and jerked her close. Okay fine, he'd agreed to take her to meet the old man, but that didn't mean he had to be happy about it. "You've got a sassy mouth, you know that?"

Batting her lashes, she gasped and placed a hand on her chest. "You offend me, sir. Never before has my character been slighted to such a degree."

Yeah, right. He chuckled. More like she heard the same thing from everyone she knew on a daily basis.

He swept in for a kiss, and a hum of satisfaction vibrated his throat as she settled an arm around his shoulders. Her lips parted and he dove in full throttle, her breezy taste the perfect antidote to the frustration that had been tightening like a noose around his neck ever since he'd hung up on his father. He thrust his fingers under her hair and tugged her closer, angling her head to drink her in.

And if anyone watched them, they could just go ahead soak up an eyeful. If his father's lackeys recorded his activities from behind a set of tinted car windows, he really didn't give a good god damn. Let them see how much he craved her. Let them report back how she'd shown up in his life and he'd fallen for her like a ton of bricks. Whatever details they wrote down didn't matter. Because the moment his father had mentioned her name, the split second that rat bastard had expressed an interest in meeting his muse, Rhys had made a decision.

From now on, Faedrah went nowhere alone.

She pulled back from him and inhaled a shaky breath, her fingertips unsteady as she placed them on her lips. "I fear you have left me quite undone, Sir McEleod. My uncles are sure to look upon my face and immediately conclude the two of us have been about the pursuit of some illicit behavior."

"Good." She was his, and the quicker everyone understood

that, the better.

He pressed a kiss to her forehead and climbed off the bike, glancing up and down the street as he tugged his backpack from one of his saddle bags. None of the vehicles seemed out of place, but he tucked her to his side anyway and walked her to the front door of her uncles' building.

The minute the elevator slid closed, the sickening apprehension he'd been fighting all afternoon slammed into his stomach like he'd eaten a bad meal. Even though she was right. He swung the backpack onto his shoulder, the overhead numbers blinking their ascent to the seventeenth floor. Even though this was his chance to be the bigger man, accept the opportunity for what it was and try to salvage a relationship with his dad that had long since fizzled and died.

His cheeks expanded as he exhaled a deep breath. God knew, it wasn't Faedrah's fault the idea of being the bigger man, especially in comparison to his father, held all the appeal of sticking his hand in a meat grinder. Or how, deep down, there wasn't a snowball's chance in hell he would have agreed to this sham of a dinner if she hadn't insisted.

He captured her hand and lifted her fingers to his lips. Christ, what a mess. Why in the hell hadn't he kept his big trap shut? He should have never admitted the truth behind his painful childhood. His top priority should've been keeping her separate from the anger and hate.

Then again, a lie of omission was still a lie, and a good chance existed she would have seen straight through his excuses. Besides, side-stepping her questions would have only named him the biggest hypocrite in the world. How could he insist she tell him everything she was hiding, only to hand her a big ol' pile of bullshit the second she asked him the same?

The elevator binged and the doors slid open, and he followed her lead down the hall.

Shit. He couldn't even blame Nate for supplying his cell number.

The guy had been after him for years to call the old man, to try and reconcile their differences. Knowing Nate, he probably thought Leo showing an interest in Rhys' work offered them the perfect opportunity to reopen a line of dialogue.

Too bad Nate had never understood Rhys' reluctance in showing, much less agreeing to sell, Faedrah's pictures. Besides the obvious loss to him personally, doing so had put both of them on Leo's radar, and that was the last place Rhys wanted them to be.

She stopped at the front door of her uncles' condo and slipped her key into the lock. At least he'd had the brains to keep his mouth shut about that. Once he'd confessed all the gory details—moving out of the penthouse his father paid for the moment he could afford it, the frustration that accompanied a lifetime of being overlooked and how today's call was the first time they'd spoken in years—Faedrah had latched onto the details like a tick. Afterward, admitting the only way Leo could've known about her arrival was because he was having Rhys watched had seemed like a bad idea, especially once she adopted the whole fucked up mess as her personal crusade. For some screwy reason, she decided mending those broken fences was her responsibility, and said her help in rekindling the relationship could lead toward her "purpose"... though why that took precedence over the fact they belonged together, she refused to say.

Swinging the door wide, she entered and called a greeting to her uncles. Bottom line was, he couldn't bring himself to ruin her excitement. She hadn't smiled as much in the past two days. Even though meeting the old man was bound to end in disappointment, he'd reluctantly agreed, but only on the condition he drive her to home to get ready. As long as Leo was sniffing around, Rhys wasn't letting her out of his sight.

"We're in here, love!"

Faedrah grabbed his hand and tugged him down the hall, backed into a swinging door and surprised him with a quick peck on the lips as they stepped into the kitchen.

"At long last, the fair princess returns." Forbes' dark-haired lover turned away from stirring a pot on the stove, his eyes shifting from Faedrah to Rhys over a set of half-glasses. "And she's brought her new beau. How nice."

The aroma of simmering garlic and red sauce made Rhys' stomach grumble. He internally cursed, his focus pinned on Faedrah. He'd been so distracted by his father's call and their ensuing discussion, he'd totally forgotten she was probably starved.

"Good evening, my Lord Uncles." She placed a kiss on Forbes' cheek, rounded the table and offered the same greeting to Jon.

"We assumed you'd be alone." Forbes glanced at Rhys and twisted the stem of his wineglass, disrupting the red liquid against the sides. He cleared this throat. "You know, so you could bring us up to speed on everything?"

Uh-uh. No way. Rhys crossed his arms. Whatever happened between him and Faedrah was private, and if Forbes didn't like it that was just too damn bad. "Everything meaning what, exactly?"

"Unfortunately, I've not much to convey." She slid a chair back from the table and sat, plucking a cheese cube off the silver tray in the center. "While I was given ample opportunity to examine Rhys' portraits, they did not provide any answers other than that which I'd already suspected." She popped the cheddar into her mouth.

Rhys squinted. Wait, what were they talking about? "Answers to what?"

Another glance at him, and Forbes twirled a hand, motioning Faedrah to continue. "Which is?"

What the hell? Rhys scrubbed a hand along his five o'clock shadow. He *was* speaking, right? He was standing in the room? "That we belong together."

Everyone jerked their attention to him and he cocked a brow. There. That seemed to do the trick. He set his jaw as the seconds ticked by, daring any of them to contradict what he'd just said. Faedrah's pink cheeks showed her surprise, but she didn't look away from him. Even as Forbes and Jon shifted their focus to her, she kept their gazes locked. The same possession flowing through his veins emanated across the room from her, and the pressure in his chest gradually receded.

Thank God. Of all the opinions present, hers mattered most, and the fact she didn't outright contradict his claim gave him hope. With any luck, the hold he had on her, was steadily growing every bit as strong as the tight grip she had on him.

"Told you." Jon peeked at Forbes over his glasses before sinking his ladle back into the pot. He sighed and shook his head. "Ah, the power of love."

Fan-fucking-tastic. Now they were quoting *Huey Lewis and The News.*

"Be that as it may…" Faedrah held Rhys' stare a second or two longer before facing Forbes. "'Twould seem Rhys' portraits detail a chronicling of my life."

"Really?" He propped his elbow on the table and tapped out a rhythm with this fingertips. "That *is* odd."

Rhys grunted. Odd didn't begin to cover it…*or* this conversation. Like an object just outside his reach, their discussion seemed to be anything but what it really was. As if they were all talking about something different, something they preferred not to specify as long as he stood within hearing range.

"But, I've good news." She nodded and smiled around the room. "Rhys' father has asked us to attend him this evening at dinner."

"Meeting the in-laws already?" Jon swung open the oven door, waved a potholder to disperse the heat and reached inside to remove a metal pan. "Isn't that a little quick on the uptake? It's only been two days, love."

Uh-h-h try twenty years, bucko. Still, for Faedrah, the guy was right, and two days didn't seem nearly long enough before bringing her within a hundred miles of Leo. "I tried to talk her out of it but, seeing as how Faedrah wants to go, we're going."

"I do think this is the proper course, Uncle." She stared hard at Forbes as if trying to psychically embed a message in his brain.

"Given the circumstances, my aid in reestablishing Rhys' relationship with his father seems quite sound."

"What circumstances are those?" No one even glanced his way. Rhys gritted his teeth and dropped his focus to his jeans, scanned his unzipped leather jacket, his white dego tee. Okay, he was definitely *in* the moment. He was living the now. Why was everyone ignoring him? God, they were driving him bat-shit crazy.

"If I stay the course and follow my instincts, perchance our next steps will then be made clear." Faedrah smiled, opening her palms to her sides.

Rhys tossed a hand in the air. Fuck it. They weren't going to answer his questions anyway. He snagged a piece of cheese off the tray and crammed it into his mouth.

"All right." Forbes nodded, the corners of his mouth turned down in a shrewd frown. "That makes sense." He sat back and slid a calculating gaze up and down Faedrah's body. "But you're certainly not going to meet Chicago's premiere real estate tycoon dressed like that." He stood and flicked a hand toward Rhys. "Jon, be a lamb and show Rhys to the guest bedroom so he can change. The eggplant parmesan will just have to wait."

This sham was ridiculous. As if Leo had no clue of their location.

Rhys thumbed Forbes' address into his cell, sent the return text to his father and pocketed his phone inside his suit coat. Shit, at some point, McEleod Industries probably had a hand in developing this building.

A sarcastic huff blurted from his lips. Not that arguing the point would do any good. And, hell, if dear old dad insisted on sending a car to pick them up, Rhys might as well play along. Besides, a chauffeur driven limo was better than a cab. It would save him doling out cash for the fare and spoil his girl the way she deserved.

Pushing to his feet, he crooked a finger inside the collar of his white dress shirt and tugged at the choking stiffness of his tie. A monkey suit, of all things. Shit. If the call had been his to make, he'd have shown up at Leo's in jeans, his rattiest t-shirt and his comfortable black boots. Dressing to impress had never worked with his father—which was the icing on the cake, considering he was such a pretentious son of a bitch. Regardless of what they wore, the asshole would make assumptions, which was just fine by Rhys. Because he wasn't doing this for Leo. Fuck, no. Tonight's dinner was for Faedrah. To make her happy.

He'd try his damndest to remember that during the meal.

He paced the living room, hands resting in his pants pockets, fingers fiddling with his keys. Dwelling wasn't his style. In the past, stewing over his circumstances had never done him any good. But the day he'd moved into the warehouse, he'd also given up lying to himself, and he wasn't about to start that bad habit up again now.

A line of leather bound books filled one shelf of the entertainment center, and he tipped his head to scan the spines. The hard truth was, Faedrah's lack of trust in him had bruised his pride. And after that conversation in the kitchen, discovering she'd shared her secrets with her uncles all while keeping him in the dark, his irritation had shot straight to the teeth-gnashing level of downright pissed.

For Christ's sake, she kissed him like her life depended on it. He turned and strolled toward the antique armoire stationed along the western wall. She'd not denied the fact they belonged together or corrected Jon when he'd used the word "love." Rhys frowned. This piece of furniture was just plain weird. So what was the problem? What had he done or not done to make her so sketchy?

He swiveled his shoulders to scan the rest of the room, all the furniture articulating the expensive quality of Forbes' refined taste, and swung back to the armoire with a scowl. Hell, with its worn hinges, bowed sides and fire-charred edges, the thing stuck out like a sore thumb. It would've looked more at home at his place…or the city dump.

The mirror hanging on the inside of the door was all fucked up. He lifted his hand and rapped a knuckle against the glass.

His reflection was murky and dull, though Forbes had probably dropped a wad for the gilded frame.

"Oh God, no." Forbes strode up beside him, slammed the door and leaned against it with his back, crossing his arms. Faking a smile, he nodded over Rhys' shoulder. "She's ready."

He pivoted toward the hall, and all the blood in his body roared through his ears in its stampede to his groin.

The sultry, cherry-red halter dress hugging Faedrah's curves left little to the imagination, and the high slit showcasing her left thigh took care of the rest. Red stilettos sparkled on her feet like some sexed-up version of Dorothy's shoes in her trip through Oz. Forbes had left her hair loose, the strands glossy and sleek, falling like a white waterfall past her bare shoulders.

Rhys smiled and lifted his eyes to her face…and the bottom fell out of his god damn world.

Panic danced through her eyes. Her red lips were parted in horror. She wrung her hands and glanced between Forbes and his lover. "Perchance 'twould be best if we departed?"

"Right! Right!" The two men sprang into action, buzzing like bees around their queen, slapping a beaded bag into her hands and wrapping her in a red shawl. They spun her from the room and scooted Rhys out behind her, waving and flinging air kisses before slamming the front door.

A second later, the deadbolt clicked into the latch.

Rhys pinned Faedrah with an arched brow and she smiled weakly, fluttering a hand down the back of her hair. His phone buzzed and he pulled it from his breast pocket to check the text. "Our ride's downstairs."

"Excellent." She bolted for the elevator without a backward glance.

The trip to the bottom floor was quiet, and the yawning silence continued once he'd helped her into the car. He pinched the bridge of his nose and inhaled deeply to get a grip on his temper. That entire scene had been complete bullshit. For Christ's sake, the three of them had treated him like a full-blown idiot.

"You are angry with me."

Damn straight, he was angry. He dropped his palm to his thigh and peered through the window, the soft light of the setting sun adding a surreal afterglow to the buildings and window shoppers strolling hand in hand down the street.

He'd confided in her. Dammit, he'd told her things about his life he'd never shared with anyone...not even Nate. "I'm having a hard time reconciling the fact that you don't trust me."

She reached across the seat for him, but he laced his fingers together between his thighs. With the way she was dressed, he had a hard enough time keeping his hands to himself. Getting lost in her kisses, exploring the temptations beneath that dress, wouldn't solve anything.

Tossing her shawl and bag aside, she slid closer, and the clean scent of her skin wrapped around him like a fucking caress. The effect she had on him set his entire libido on hyper-drive.

"Neither would I have accompanied you this evening, nor would my uncles have permitted such a thing if our trust in you was not sound."

He grunted. "My ego doesn't need to be stroked, Faedrah. I'm not your pet. You can't ignore me and expect me to be happy about it. My father used to treat me like that and I'll be god damned if I'm going to accept the same behavior from you."

She eased her warm hand between his, unlocked his fingers and lifted them to her mouth. The tip of her tongue wet the end of his thumb as she nipped and rubbed it along her bottom lip.

A thick pulse tightened his shaft. Sweat beaded along the nape of his neck, and he clenched his jaw. Christ, she was like a drug. One he would never get enough of no matter how high she made him.

"'Tis not lack of trust which stays my tongue." She released his hand and climbed onto his lap. The material of her dress inched up her thighs, and a groan eked from his throat as she straddled his legs.

He jammed his heels into the floorboards, fisting his hands to keep from grabbing her ass and forcing her back and forth over the side of his cock.

"'Tis not disbelief in your character or a misguided conviction regarding the connection we share." Cupping his cheeks in her palms, she lowered her forehead to his and stared him straight in the eye. "'Tis the circumstances behind my arrival, the fear you may think me daft which delays my explanation." Her lips swept his in a kiss. "The fault lies *not* with you. 'Tis my weakness, the worry you may cast me aside once told. For all that your wrath wounds my heart, I would rather suffer the slings a thousand times over than to bear the torture of losing you to a tale you will surely not believe."

Je-sus *Christ*. Is that really what she thought? "Faedrah." He tipped his head and flicked his tongue along her upper lip. "Nothing you could ever say would make me let go. Nothing." He wrapped his hands around her knees and wrenched her higher up his thighs, centering them, seating her right where she belonged, where she ended and he began. She bit her bottom lip and whimpered, closing her eyes.

The heat of her sex was both pleasure and pain. Torture and paradise. He jerked his hips and she seized his shoulders, her eyes wide. Curling his fingers in her hair, he tipped her head back, brought her forward and buried his cheeks in the addictive curves between her breasts. "Promise me something?"

"You have but to ask."

No one or nothing would stop him from making her his. Not even her. "Once this dinner is over, you'll tell me everything."

"No more secrets, my heart."

He licked a path up her chest toward her throat, circling the little dip between her collar bones. Her thighs cinched his hips and he swooped in, devouring her lips until her taste washed all the filth from his mind.

Before he'd gotten his fill, before he'd coaxed them both to the edge like he'd planned, the car rolled to a stop and the driver's side door slammed, signaling the end of their ride.

He muttered a curse as she broke away from him and sat back, her breathy chuckle warming the air between them. She straightened the lapels of his jacket. "Do this for me and, once accomplished, I swear on the nine you may lay claim to my body in whatever ways you desire."

Fuck. How the hell did she expect him to last through dessert with that visual seared into his head?

The car door swung open and she slipped off his lap. Arousal sparkled in her eyes as she shimmied the hem of her skirt to her ankles, grabbed her shawl and purse and exited the car.

Rhys joined her on the sidewalk, the muted glow of the globed lights framing the front door of his father's north shore estate casting shimmers through her hair. He snagged her hand and led her up the three steps of the concrete stoop. A couple raps of the brass knocker hanging from the gargoyle's mouth and, a second or two later, Grady swung back the hinges and smiled at Rhys from the opposite side of the threshold.

"Nice to see you again, Rhys." His eyes flicked to Faedrah and back again. "You look well."

Good old Grady. His dad's butler never missed a trick. In fact, in many ways, his steady, unwavering presence had provided more warmth and comfort to Rhys than anything else as a kid. "Her name's Faedrah and, thanks to her, I'm better than I've been in years."

His angel sized up Grady before a thousand watt smile lit up her face. Jutting her hand forward, she stepped close and pumped his arm as if the greeting were something she'd rehearsed. "'Tis my utmost pleasure to meet you, Sir McEleod."

A spider-web of crows' feet crinkled the corners of Grady's eyes as he and Rhys exchanged a chuckle. "Oh, my dear, I'm not Rhys' father." He covered her hand with his. "But do come in. Make yourself at home." He withdrew a step, opening a flat hand toward the tiled foyer.

Rhys followed her inside, the creak of hinges and a resounding slam echoing against the high ceilings as Grady closed the door and slipped the lock behind them. A draft of musty air washed Rhys' face. Shadows leapt from beneath the row of small shaded sconces decorating the dark oak wainscoting.

Good God, the place resembled a tomb. "What kind of mood is he in today?"

Grady clasped his wrist in one hand, lips pursed. "Contemplative, but he did express his anticipation over tonight's dinner. He's waiting for you in the study." He turned away and then hesitated. "I feel I should warn you. He's not been well, Rhys. His health has recently taken a turn for the worse."

"How terrible." Faedrah grasped Rhys' forearm. "Thank Helios, we've come in the nick of time."

The butler nodded, his thick-soled shoes silent as he started down the narrow corridor, his shoulders slightly more stooped beneath his black suit since the last time Rhys had seen him.

He set his palm on the small of Faedrah's back as they followed, but she pulled up short as they neared the wide stairwell.

A variety of hand-painted portraits notched up the wall, hung at the same intervals as the runner-covered stairs, all of them depicting the McEleod moguls who'd ruled the empire over the years. An empty frame filled a spot near the landing, and Rhys bit back frustrated curse. At one time, he would've given anything to be the next in line, but Leo had made it clear in more ways than one he hadn't inherited the right DNA to earn his place on the wall.

Only now, after he'd become sick, was his father ready to hand over the reins. If that's what this dinner was about, Rhys would make sure the deal stayed unaccepted on the table. Any offers to join the family business came way too late.

He turned toward Faedrah, and a fist of anxiety punched him hard in the gut. For God's sake, she was as white as a ghost. "What is it?"

She snapped her attention to him. "Nothing, I…" A nervous laugh slipped from her throat. "I've just had the strangest sensation I've been here before."

A shiver wove down her back, dislodging his hand, and he gritted his teeth. He should've insisted they have a snack before leaving Forbes' condo. She needed to eat or she was liable to take a header for the floor.

Grady cleared his throat, waiting in front of the closed study door. Rhys wound an arm around Faedrah's waist and pulled her against him for support as he guided her down the hall. "Come on. Let's get you a drink."

Her steps were unsteady. She trembled in his arms. Grady swung the door wide and nodded a smile as they entered.

A soft fire crackled in the hearth, but the burning logs added zero ambiance to the room. In fact, the overdone heat made the atmosphere stuffy, and the stale air stunk like the drapes and windows hadn't been opened in months.

The green-shaded lamp on his father's double pedestal oak desk cast light along the stacks of papers, several sets of rolled blueprints and the antique phone, but the padded desk chair sat empty.

A rustle of movement caught the corner of his eye, and Rhys pivoted toward the fireplace as his father stood from his leather winged-backed chair. A toothy grin nearly split his face in two, and Faedrah snapped straight as a board inside his arm. Rhys couldn't blame her. The bloodshot ring of his father's eyes and sunken complexion was spine-tingling creepy. Time had not been kind to Leo McEleod. The guy looked half dead.

He rounded the chair, the end of his black silk smoking jacket whispering over the thick pile of the Asian rug, and extended his hand. "I'm so glad you've come, Faedrah. It's been far too long, don't you think?"

What the fuck? Rhys scowled. The two of them knew each other?

He glanced at his angel and his arm dropped like lead weight. The terror etched on her face said it all. But when? *How?*

"Gaelleod," she whispered, shrinking toward the door. Her gaze skipped to Rhys and back again and she gripped a shaking white hand around her throat. "No. This cannot be."

The amusement that shook his father's shoulders raised the hair on the nape of Rhys' neck. "Oh my darling child, no one has called me that in ages. But, I must say, I'm so pleased you've taken the time to know my son."

She choked, stutter stepped for the exit. Tears flooded her eyes, and she shook her head. A last glance at Rhys, and she whirled, dropping her purse and shawl as she raced from the room.

The Sacrifice

Chapter 1

I'm going to fucking kill him.

Rhys stormed down the hall, each swing of his fist flicking Faedrah's red shawl like a road flare in the corner of his eye. If his father had so much as *touched* her, he would beat the asshole to a bloody pulp.

Grady stood beside the open front door, his hand on the knob. "She's in the car."

Rhys nodded his thanks as he exited and ratcheted his feet down the front stoop, aiming a hard finger at the limousine driver. "In the car. Now. We're going to my place." Without missing a beat, he swung the car door open and dove inside.

A sparkly red missile spun toward his head, and he deflected the sharp tip of Faedrah's stiletto with his forearm. "Stop it." She launched the second shoe and he snagged it mid-twirl. "I said stop."

Pain exploded through his right eye. The back of his head bounced off the seat with the force of her punch. He pressed the heel of his palm to his eye socket, the other hand wrestling her arms as she volleyed a series of blows over his torso and chest. "Dammit, Faedrah, I'm not going to hurt you, I love you. God dammit, I'm in love with you!"

A stinging smack broke the dim interior of the car, and his face snapped to the right. Shit, the woman had a wicked right cross.

She gasped as if the slap had surprised even her and he ground his teeth until the smarting subsided. Slumping to her knees, she clamped her hands over her mouth, eyes wide in horror. She turned away and crawled to the corner near the backward-facing seat, covered her head with both arms and curled into a tight ball.

Jesus Christ. Note to self. Moving forward, remember to never piss her off. He ran his fingers along the side of his face, working out the kinks in his jaw, but the ache was nothing compared to the space she'd driven between them. Having her so far away, both physically and emotionally, tore his heart out. Regardless, he wasn't about to apologize. He'd waited twenty damn years to tell her how he felt. Fucked up timing aside, she'd be waiting another twenty if she expected him to take the words back now.

"Come here." He lowered his hand, wincing, but no matter how much he blinked the vision in his right eye refused to focus.

"I do not deserve your forgiveness or your love." Her hair shimmered down her back like a blanket of stars as she shook her head. "I have failed."

Her whisper was so soft, he thought at first he'd misheard her, and the thump of tires over potholes and blare of horns from congested lakefront traffic didn't help. He needed her closer. To figure out a way to reassure her. Whatever "failure" had happened between her and Leo, Rhys would bet the keys to his bike she wasn't to blame. She had no clue she'd be running into him tonight and, in typical Leo fashion, the asshole had enjoyed every second of his little stunt. "It's not your fault. Leo set you up. Hell, he set us both up."

"The fault most certainly lies with me." A soggy breath hitched in her chest. "I am a weak-minded fool. I scurried from his presence like a frightened rabbit. I consorted with the enemy and willingly revealed that which I should have protected above all cost."

Yep. That was classic Leo. He'd no doubt backed her into some intractable corner. Rhys had witnessed this same bullshit time and again.

Nothing got Leo's rocks off like pulling the old bait and switch. The way he loved cooking up some slip-shod investment scheme, secretly buying up shares in a company, targeting his competition and tearing businesses apart just so he could earn another notch in his belt. For Christ's sake, his mob-like tactics had ruined so many families, Rhys had lost count.

Free enterprise had never been part of the McEleod business strategy. *Survival of the fittest* was Leo's manifesto, and in whatever small way the opposition threatened his empire, he eliminated them without batting an eye.

Rhys huffed. God, he was an idiot. He should have seen this fist fuck coming from miles away, should've known he could never ditch the McEleod name and all the baggage that went along with it just by packing up and moving out of the penthouse. But the real icing on the cake? The final nail in the coffin Leo had used to hammer his point home? Chances were good he'd learned of Faedrah's family a long time ago. No way could he have heard about her showing up at the gallery just two days ago. Since they'd obviously run into each other before, he'd probably been planning this little surprise party for months. Once Rhys and Faedrah had met, the rest had been easy, and so what if Leo manipulated his son and asked to meet Rhys' girl after he'd bankrupted her family? Who cared if Rhys delivering her to dear old dad like a god damned cherry on a hot fudge sundae destroyed their relationship?

A growl grated the back of his throat, and he fisted his hands. This time Leo had pushed the envelope too far, even for him. The real boner being, he'd probably talked himself into believing he'd done Rhys a favor. What better way to secure his son's future than exploiting whatever tactics he could to force Faedrah's family under McEleod jurisdiction? With her "kingdom" all wrapped up in a tidy little package, he could hand over the reins to the company without worrying Rhys would fuck up and lose operating control of the assets.

He leaned forward, elbows propped on his knees. "Did you

hear me? He set us both up, Faedrah, but it's important to me you understand. I'm not like him. Never have been. Leo McEleod may have had a hand in bringing me into this world, but he's not my father. Not by a long shot." He reached for her a second time. "Now come here."

Unlocking her arms, she slowly lifted her head, and the uncertainty etched on her face nearly cracked his chest in two.

Shit. He dropped his hand and slumped back in the seat. They were right back to square one. So help him God, whatever illness was eating away at Leo's body, the disease wasn't doing its job fast enough. One more *fucking* word from him, and Rhys would make it his life's ambition to take down everything the rat bastard had built.

Faedrah sighed and looked toward the window, worrying her bottom lip, and frustration knotted in Rhys' gut as he studied her face. Most likely, this was the spot where she'd demand he drive her back to Forbes' condo. He shook his head; raked a hand through his hair. Once inside, she'd disappear from his life as easily as she'd entered.

He braced for the head-on collision screaming at him like a jack-knifed semi freewheeling an icy highway. There wasn't a chance in hell he was letting that happen. Not with Leo on her scent and not with the way their relationship dangled by a thread. She could fight him all damn night if she wanted. One or two knocks wouldn't change his mind.

She was staying with him. End of story.

"The sins of the father shall not be visited upon the son."

He squinted at the far-away tone in her whisper, the way her eyes followed the streetlights streaking past the window. "What did you say?"

Glancing at him, she tipped her head. "'Tis the first edict my father proclaimed as king."

Huh. Well, chalk one up for the CEO of the Austiere Kingdom. The dude had just slipped Rhys the ace he needed. "Your dad sounds like smart man."

A small smile surfed her lips…there and gone so fast it became a memory almost before it happened. She turned and locked her gorgeous brown eyes onto his, and his fingertips dug into his thighs as that same cold skepticism slammed into her gaze like god damn brick wall. "Did you speak true?"

About what? Loving her? All the fantastic bullshit that went along with being Leo McEleod's son or how he was damn sure whatever had happened wasn't her fault? Shit, that was a no-brainer. "Yes, Faedrah. Every word."

One of her arms fell forward, her hand hanging limp from her wrist, elbow extended across her knee.

His eyes flicked down to her fingers and back up again. An apology? Maybe. Or maybe she expected him to lean forward and kiss her knuckles.

Yeah, that wasn't happening.

He stared at her, waiting. A simple kiss of her hand wouldn't seal the crack between them. It wouldn't rub out the filthy reminder of who he was or be enough to convince her she was exactly where she belonged.

His jaw firmed. She knew that as well as he did.

She flipped her palm up. The slightest wiggle of her fingers, and he sat forward, shoved his hands under her arms and hauled her sideways onto his lap. He needed to taste her, to show her that, no matter what, the two of them together was what mattered most.

Thumb braced under her chin, fingers secure around her neck, he tipped her into the crook of his arm and crushed his lips to hers.

Her arms tightened across the back of his shoulders. She softened beneath him, her mouth parting to invite him in, and the temptation of her bare skin made him hard in three seconds flat. He coasted his palm up the outside of her thigh, jamming his hand under the mile-high slit in her dress.

Christ, everything about her made him ache. A shove of her hips and she whimpered into his mouth as he angled her higher on his lap. From the cushion of her perfect ass cradling his cock, to the enthusiastic swirl of her tongue, to the ball-busting fear stamped across her face the second they'd stepped into Leo's study.

He'd do whatever it took to protect her. A promise Leo could take to the bank.

"I'm not going to let him get away with this." He nipped the edge of her jaw, breathing her in; swept an open-mouthed kiss along her neck and tongued her earlobe so the euphoric high he got off her skin would coat the inside of his mouth. "Leo crossed the line, and you can bet your sweet ass, whatever he did to your family, this time, he's going to pay. You have my word."

She jerked back from him, cold terror glittering in her eyes, her face as white as the cuffs of his sleeves. "You cannot fight him."

He cocked a brow. "The hell I can't. In fact, nothing would make me happier than putting that asshole in his place." Except for however his muse might choose to thank him once this bullshit was over and done.

"No, no." She fisted the lapels of his jacket and sat up, hanging on as if his life tipped in the balance of her next words. "Swear to me now, you will not return to his chambers in search of some ill-advised revenge."

He narrowed his eyes. If asked, he would've easily torched every portrait of her in his collection for one glimpse inside her beautiful blonde head. "What, exactly, did Leo do to you? What threats did he use to blackmail your family? And, god dammit, who died and left *you* in charge of fixing the problem?"

"You misunderstand." She shook her head. "Defeating Gaelleod is a task for which I volunteered. Yet 'twas not the call of his heart which summoned me here. 'Twas not the yearning of his body or the unholy union of our souls." Releasing his jacket, she cupped his cheeks in her palms. "I regret that terrible privilege belongs to you, and I would not so foolishly risk all the goddesses have granted me in exchange for any sentence, be it the whole of my disgrace or the unwelcomed reinstatement of time and distance

122

which separates our lives."

She wrapped her arms around his neck and held tight, the silky strands of her hair tangling in his fingers as he palmed her back. "You must pledge to me, on your honor, you shall not return to your father's side until we've been given more time to ferret out our next course. He is too powerful for us to face him unawares."

God dammit. Rhys closed his eyes. She had a point. Tonight they'd stumbled into Leo's trap like two innocent babes lost in the woods. Before going back to face him, the more information they had about what he was up to, the better. A little internet research should do the trick.

"Okay." He hugged her to his chest, then chuckled into her hair as her sigh of relief heated his neck. Hell, if avoiding Leo was all it took to make her happy, that shit was done and done. And if his father got in their way, if he showed up and tried to drive a wedge between them, Rhys would happily break the fucker's nose.

Not that it mattered. Not anymore. Because his angel finally believed they belonged together, exactly like he always had. She'd used the word "we" and, moving forward, that meant they faced whatever odds Leo stacked against them, together.

Rhys sat back from his laptop, rotated his shoulders and tipped his head back and forth to work out the stiffness in his neck. Off to his left, Faedrah mumbled in her sleep. He leaned to the side, stretching in the seat to check she was still asleep. She rolled over under the blankets and flopped a hand across his empty side of the bed, but only a second passed before her deep breathing settled into its normal pattern.

Good. He relaxed against the chair and cocked a brow at the search image on the screen. Google was one condescending bitch. No, he did not mean "austere," dammit. He snatched his pen off the table and slashed several hard lines through the words "Austiere company name" he'd jotted on his list. Just like he hadn't meant "Galileo" when he'd tried searching out Leo's fraudulent investment firm, or those obscure references to some fairytale wizard who'd supposedly lived in the fourteenth century.

He jammed his thumb and forefinger into his tired eyes and then winced as the left one watered. Christ, this was like trying to find one specific grain of sand on the entire stretch of Chicago's lakefront beaches.

Shoving the pad aside, he stood and strolled the quiet loneliness that typically accompanied midnight in the train yard. Leave it to Leo to name his company after an imaginary jackass from history. Unfortunately, that little tidbit didn't do Rhys a damn bit of good. The information he needed had to be current. A corporation that had popped up within recent months.

He tapped the end of the pen against the center of his palm, stopping before the mural of Faedrah spanning his north wall. By the time they'd arrived back at the warehouse, she'd relaxed enough in his arms he'd gotten the sneaking suspicion she'd dozed off. And once the driver opened the door and she squinted into the overhead light, rubbing her eyes and mumbling an apology, his assumptions had been confirmed.

Not that he blamed her. Shock did strange things to the body, and witnessing the deterioration of his father's condition, that toothy grin coupled with those sunken, anorexic cheeks, had been enough to make even Rhys gag on his tongue. Asking the driver's help with the gate, he'd carried her into the elevator, up the three levels to his floor and tucked her into his bed.

The heat of her soft curves molded against his side made his hands impatient to stroke every arc and dip. The unending questions and constant replay of that sickening scene at Leo's, had all combined into a fucking assault on his brain. It took every ounce of his willpower not to roll on top of her and kiss her awake so he could sink deep, make her shudder around him over and over until they'd worked out some angst.

Muttering a frustrated curse, he'd snuck from the bed and opened his laptop to see what, if anything, he could find.

He crossed his arms, squinting at her picture. By no stretch of the imagination would he describe himself as a whiz at navigating governmental websites, but not locating her birth records at all? What was up with that? In fact, he'd found not one stitch of proof her family existed. No references to any kingdoms had popped up. Same with searching out corporations using the name Gaelleod, either solely or under the McEleod umbrella or its subsidiaries.

Raking both hands through his hair, he laced his fingers along the back of his neck. Four hours later, and he had nothing to show for his efforts but a big, fat dead end. He strolled to the side, his focus pinned to Faedrah's brown eyes. Maybe that was the problem. He'd been thinking too big.

Or maybe the problem was that he'd been thinking at all.

He pivoted back to the table, grabbed his sketch pad and flipped to a clean page. He'd always trusted his gut, especially when it came to drawing Faedrah's picture. Hell, back in the day, his instincts had been the only thing to guide his hand over the page. If he could somehow recreate that same intuitive style, lapse back into what he'd always known, maybe his subconscious would provide some hints about what he'd been missing.

It was either that or he was apt to blow a gasket.

Lowering onto the chair, he slid back the wooden cover on his box of charcoals, propped his heels on the edge of the table and settled into work.

Striving for perfection quickly became a waste of time. If the lines he sketched refused to focus, he tore the sheet aside and began again. He left off shading as the bowed sides of the armoire converged on the paper. Same with the gilded mirror and Faedrah's golden key. His hand circled each of the objects, jotted a quick arrow from piece to piece and he tore the sheet off to start fresh.

The high turrets of a white castle were next, and his brows lifted in surprise as the addition of a king, queen and princess came into view. The caricature of an evil wizard worked the muscles of his stomach, but he couldn't help chuckling at the dark eyes and freak show sneer. Before sliding the drawing to the table, he smirked and added Leo's name to the bottom, and then laughed again as the prank brought back memories from his days as a rebellious kid.

He didn't bother counting the pages. If the heel of his hand smudged the charcoal, he swiped it along the thigh of his jeans and kept drawing. Faedrah floating, tumbling naked to the floor with a thump. One where she appeared lost in a hallway with several doors. Asleep in bed, hands fisting the covers while she fought the terrors of a nightmare. The day she showed up at the gallery and flipped him on his ass to the ground.

Whatever image came to mind, he didn't fight it. No more second-guessing or removing an element just because it didn't seem right.

As the sky outside his windows pinked with the incoming dawn, he ripped the last sheet from his pad, tossed the final sketch to the table and released the charcoal to flex his sore fingers. He dropped his heels to the floor and stood, stretching his arms overhead, his jaw cracking with a deep yawn. A glance at the jumbled mess he'd made and he shifted the pages here and there, trying to rearrange the pictures into some sort of chronological order.

An errant sheet wafted off the table, and he stooped to rescue it from the ground. A scowl tightened his forehead as he scanned the image. Wait, hold on. When the fuck had he drawn this? His knees gave out and his butt slammed back onto the chair.

The sketch showed Faedrah coming *through* the mirror, her hair a tangled mass whipping around her head, arms forward, fingers splayed, the key dangling between her two luscious, naked breasts.

He dropped his hand to his thigh. Well, that couldn't be right. A second passed before he wrenched forward and sorted through the other pictures littering the table.

Sweet Jesus.

The air eked from his lungs like a deflating balloon. It was all there. A step by step illustration of the past week, every action she'd taken right up to the day they'd met. And he'd drawn *every—single—fucking—picture* as if they'd been stashed away in his brain.

Each moment following, every split second they'd spent together since, screamed a complete one-eighty and he shoved to his feet, his ears ringing like a struck tuning fork.

That was it. The way she talked, her references to those damn goddesses. Her hesitation over the music and food. The way she fought.

Jesus Christ, even her virginity fit the bill!

He strode to the end of the bed and stared at the woman who was the epitome of everything he'd ever wanted. Her limbs lay tangled in his blankets, the hint of one bare shoulder peeking through her black strip of hair, thick eyelashes spread like two dark fans on her cheeks.

He fisted his hands against the urge to shake her until she woke up, so he could tell her exactly how crazy, horny, fucking over the moon she made him.

He scanned the length of her body, his focus lingering on the patch of morning light hitting her lower back. His cock stretched and flexed against his button fly as he imagined running his tongue along that soft stretch of skin.

Or better yet…

Lowering his chin, he bit back an evil chuckle. His sneaky little muse thought she could keep him in the dark? She twisted him in knots all while side-stepping his questions?

Pivoting away from the bed, he grabbed his dress shirt and leather jacket off the back of the chair, stepped into his boots and clomped toward the elevator.

He would let her sleep. For now. But once he got back?

Stealing one last glance at the vixen in his bed, he stepped onto the elevator and closed the gate. All this time, he had everything backward. And she'd been only too happy to keep him guessing.

Her being here didn't have anything to do with *where* she came from. The answer he'd spend all day coaxing from her, was *when*.

Chapter 2

The distant roar of Rhys' mechanical horse pulled Faedrah from the shadows of slumber, and her eyes popped open to find his side of the sleeping pallet unattended. As the rumble increased, she rolled to the center of the bed, yawned and stretched her arms across the pillows.

'Twas of no surprise he had arisen early to retrieve their transport from her uncles' quarters. Regardless of the events they might face this day, the expediency of such a conveyance was a luxury they could not afford to dismiss.

The snarling abruptly ceased and, a moment later, the creaking gears of the building's rickety trestle took up their baleful song. Faedrah smiled and shimmied lower beneath the blankets, closing her eyes to feign the continuance of sleep. If luck stood with her, perchance she could catch her captivating artist unawares. She would creep up behind him and pounce, and then demand he use the morning to instruct her how to cast him into the throes of utmost pleasure.

The rigid strength in his arms as he'd carried her into his chambers the previous evening, the tender assurances whilst he'd removed her shoes and tucked her snugly abed, proved he'd spoken true. Yet his love for her had never been in question. The depth of his devotion had all but arrowed into her heart from the first moment he'd glanced upon her face.

'Twas his masculine pheromones lingering on the pillows which had sharpened her desires to the point of an unrelenting itch. The dim glimpses she'd stolen of him in the gloaming of deepest night. He'd been bound by a trance, feverously working the kohl over parchment, and she'd been too mesmerized by the energy sizzling off his skin to interrupt.

Yet this fascination had not stopped her from delighting in every curve of taut muscle, the broad span of his chest, his corded forearms or the raised web of veins that trailed down the insides of his arms. The profound concentration furrowing his brow had not staunched the heady pulse between her thighs as she envisioned capturing his lips for a kiss, flicking her tongue along the generous bow of his mouth whilst saddling the tension in his thighs.

Only Rhys, and no other, could lessen the persistent ache which had wound a tight desire through her body. And if he cut short their fulfillment, if he solicited the details of her quest, she would speak any truth, she would soothe his unkempt worries and endure whatever action necessary to verify he'd more than earned her trust.

If that did not snare his full attention, she would strip off her confining gown and walk bare-assed around his chambers as if she hadn't a care in her head.

A rumble shuddered the floorboards with the lift of the gate, and a waft of fresh air coursed her cheeks; a hint of spring mingled with the sultry scent of warm leather and the gear-gnashing taint of worn oil.

Crinkling broke the still silence, and she peeked through the fringe of her lashes. Rhys pulled several white bundles from his saddle bags, flinched and muttered a curse. A juggle of the packages to one hand, and he reached inside the flap of his leather jacket to retrieve his cellular device.

"Hello." He spoke softly, toeing off his boots and leaving them a pace apart as he strode toward the table. "Yeah, I kinda figured you'd call. Not to worry. She's here with me, safe and sound."

Wizard Oliver…or perchance the speaker was Sir Jon. None other in this realm would be allowed the ease of such a confidence.

"Not great." Rhys set his burdens upon the table and shrugged his jacket down his arms. "We left before dinner even started."

Wrinkles creased the sleeves of his formal white shirt, the unbuttoned cuffs flopping around his wrists, the sides hanging open to reveal the form-fitting undershirt beneath. Black smears marred one thigh of his faded blue breeches, the pockets frayed and a threadbare tear near his right knee.

"Hey listen, Forbes, does the name Gaelleod mean anything to you?"

Great tits above, no! Faedrah sprang to sitting and slashed her hand back and forth across her neck. Whilst she had every intention of relaying the details of Gaelleod's appearance to her uncles, announcing the news so unexpectedly was liable to propel them into to fits of apoplexy!

Jerking his head aside, Rhys grimaced as Oliver's squawk reverberated through the earpiece. Faedrah slumped and rolled her eyes. So much for her devious scheming.

Rhys turned toward her with a smile, and she gasped and slapped that same hand over her mouth. A dark purple bruise hung beneath his left eye, the surrounding skin slightly raised and undoubtedly tender to the touch. Sweet tears of the nine, what had she done?

"No, no, she's fine. She's still asleep, but I'll tell her to call once she's up." He winked and strolled toward the sleeping pallet, lowered to the edge and cupped his large hand along the back of her head. The soft press of his lips warmed the center of her brow. "'Kay. Talk to you later."

He thumbed the screen and set the gadget on the crate to their right, and the rasp of his shortly trimmed beard prickled the inside of her palm as she turned his cheek to better inspect the damage she'd wrought upon his lovely face.

"I am fully prepared to forfeit any ransom you may deem

necessary to gain your forgiveness." She smoothed her thumb along the bottom curve of the wound. "Does it cause you much distress? Helios wept, I am an addle-brained fool."

"What, this?" He squeezed the eye closed, shrugged and shook his head. "Nah, it doesn't hurt that much. But I could name a few other body parts that are aching for your attention." His brows bounced a suggestive wag.

Delight cascaded through her belly over his tempting invitation, and she cleared her throat to disguise a breathy laugh. Thank the nine, his desires matched hers. The anticipation tingling her skin had her close to snapping. "As are mine, to be sure."

A chuckle rumbled in his chest, the mischief in his eyes sparkling more than Helios bright rays spilling through the windows, and Faedrah dropped her hand to more carefully read the measure of his gaze. How odd that, after last night's fearful events…his impassioned pleas to share in her secrets…instead of being angry with her, this morning he seemed quite playful.

Hesitation plucked her nerves, and she squinted. Something in his demeanor had changed, yet she could not fathom the cause of his good humor any more than she could unravel the clues to the devilish smirk upon his face.

The slightest tip of his chin, and she received the distinct impression he played the stalking cat to her caged canary.

Heat blossomed in her chest, yet she shivered under his dark perusal. Any uncertainties she might have held about the wicked curl of his lips vanished like a puff of smoke.

The man meant to claim her, body and soul.

She exhaled a steadying lungful of air. Though to allow such a thing before she'd confessed seemed an ill-advised path to trod. Placing her hands upon his shoulders, she stared him hard in the eye. "I have not forgotten my vow. Ask me what you would, and I swear on the nine to satisfy your queries to the best of my ability."

"Yeah, about that." He dropped his focus to her mouth and leaned in until his breath warmed the moisture on her lips. "I'm not really in the mood to talk."

Her heart leapt, and she tightened her grasp on his shoulders.

Sliding a hand under her hair, he clasped her nape and lightly swept his mouth across hers, over and again until sparks shimmered at the edges of her vision. A whimper scuffed the back of her throat. A warm coil unfurled in her belly as he nipped little love bites along her jaw. Her eyelids fluttered and she rolled her head back, allowing him to bury his cheeks in her neck.

The curve of his lips brushed lower, the gruff texture of his beard shivered her skin, and a sigh escaped as he nibbled and sucked on her earlobe. "I say we table all discussions until later. That is, unless you're planning to disappear once I've had my way with you."

She nearly laughed. Helios wept, did the man not have any idea the influence he had upon her body? "I fear my knees shall be too weak to vacate your chambers."

Besides as much, even if the notion did not cause panic to race through her veins, she'd nowhere to go. The veil remained closed to her.

Misery wound its indifferent thorns amid the heated chuckle he grazed down her throat, the hot swirl of his tongue along the crest of her shoulder. Eventually, she must return to her realm but, for all the goddesses in paradise, how would she ever deal them both such a cruel blow? The mere thought cast a dim pall over the entirety of her heart.

"Hey." He eased back from her and she blinked as the back of his finger caressed her cheek. "Where'd you go?"

Despite her worthwhile obligations, she did not want to leave him. Neither once the portal reopened nor in this fragile moment they shared. She skimmed a light touch over his full lower lip. Not whilst he lingered so close, longing for her just as she longed for him. "I am here."

Desire shimmered in his gaze, and a smile came unbidden to her lips. "Perchance you should describe the exact location of these unsettling aches you mentioned, and I shall set about my most enthusiastic attempts in relieving your discomfort." His pupils dilated. The sharp edge of his teeth nipped her fingers and she shivered. "Or would it better serve your schemes to seek out the bothersome throb currently plaguing my form?"

Tension sated with desperate hunger swelled between them, as forbidden as it was thick. A muscle ticked in his jaw a moment before he tackled her to the bed. "You know, one of these days that sassy mouth of yours is going to get you into deep shit."

"Hmm…" She wrapped her arms around his shoulders, twining her legs through his. The weight of his chest and hips, the dense muscle in his thighs pressing her into the blankets, were like a lover's armor shielding her from the worries she faced. "Then perchance we should ascertain which abilities best suit my tongue."

He groaned…shuddered against her. A torturous glide of his hands up her sides, and his nimble fingers released the hook of her dress behind her neck.

Faedrah closed her eyes, sighing as his calloused palms grazed her shoulders. *Yes…* At long last, she would become a true woman. Rhys would brand her, guide her…make her his.

The material hugging her breasts sagged. His hand swept her ribcage, and he tugged the tab of the metal seam down to her waist. The constraining fit of her gown went slack around her torso. He slipped his fingers inside, tickling her skin as he dragged the tips back and forth over her belly. She pressed the collar of his shirt off his shoulders, longing to experience her lover skin to skin, so she could drown in his scent and satisfy her curiosity about every part and parcel of his riveting male form.

The mattress dipped as he shoved to his knees. He stripped the garment down his arms, fisted the back of his sleeveless shirt and yanked it over his head. Longing coiled in the pit of her stomach at the ripple of tendon, the stark definition of each ridge and muscle flexing along his torso and chest. Arousal surged and moistened her inner thighs. Anything he asked of her, any demand

133

he made, she would readily give in exchange for the taste of him upon her tongue.

Her hand shook as she reached for the downy line of hair below his bellybutton, the tension in his abdomen so tight, she yearned to test the resistance with her fingers.

He seized her wrist before she made contact. Apprehension spiked in her belly and she snapped her gaze to his.

A perilous storm stirred within his eyes. A craving so fierce, she daren't look away. "Do you trust me?" His words were clipped, honed by the tight set of his jaw.

Yet it was anticipation which had tautened his body. The same incisive awareness which heated her skin and crackled in the air between them. "With every breath of my being."

He searched her face. "And you'll do whatever I tell you? For however long I decide?"

A thrill coursed her veins, pulsing hard and fast between her legs. Proof enough that, in matters of pleasure, she was the student… and he was the master. "You have my solemn vow."

One of his brows rose. "Something tells me I'm going to pay for that at a later date." He released her wrist as she chuckled, thrust both his hands under her arms and his biceps bulged as he lifted her to her feet.

Her dress slithered down her body, a pool of red silk at her feet. Her skin pebbled and she shivered in the cool air, crossing her arms over her chest to hide how her nipples had peaked like the buds of rose.

A growl issued from the base of his throat and he pinned her with a stern glare. "No. Hands at your sides."

"But—"

"Hands at your sides and keep them there. I need to see you. All of you."

Just as she wished to crest a wave beneath the pitch and roll of his thrusts.

Lowering her arms, she did as he asked, wavering on unsteady knees.

Tendrils of light sparked through her body as he skimmed his hands up her thighs, over her hips, until his fingers snagged upon the thin bands of the diminutive bit of red lace her uncles insisted she wear to hide her cunny.

A pop of this thumb and the strap on her left snapped with a slight sting, recoiling along her ass. She stifled her gasp of surprise, her lashes fluttering.

Others had described the extravagance which awaited her. His fingers curled, the short nails scraping, and he gathered the slack, sliding the ball of fabric to her ankle. Her core spasmed and she swallowed past the dryness in her throat. Yet if she was to crash upon the shores of ecstasy, what man more deserving to lead her there than the one who'd sworn to protect her? He ran his palms along the backs of her thighs and tugged, widening her stance. If she was to be tossed into the abyss of rapture, what better tongue to propel her from the ledge than the one upon which he'd confessed his love?

She gazed down at the man kneeling before her, the smooth expanse of his brow, the strong set of his jaw, the rigid tension in his shoulders all displaying his rapt devotion.

He licked his lips, glanced at her face, and a second shiver wrenched her shoulders as his warm exhalation feathered her lower belly. "Don't move."

Not one doubt in her heart lingered. In gifting Rhys her innocence, she'd made her destined choice.

The first stroke of his warm tongue along her slit and starlight ricocheted down her inner thighs. She tossed her head back, her spine bowed. Embers ignited in the soles of her feet. The tips of her fingers tingled. His hum vibrated slick and deep, fingers digging into her ass as he latched onto her clit and drew her hard between his lips. She gasped and seized his shoulders. The bristle on his cheeks teased and rasped. Heat unfurled in her belly as he flicked his tongue, strumming her higher. The walls of his chambers wavered out of focus. Her knees gave and he caught her in his arms as she crumpled, guiding her down to the bed.

Nothing in all her imaginings had prepared her for the all-consuming stimulation, the quivering of her core or the desperate longing to be filled and stretched.

He propped one of her legs and then the other over his shoulders, parted her with his thumbs and blew a steady stream of air along her folds. She squeezed her eyes tight, a breath lodged in her throat. Her hips jerked, and he darted the tip of his tongue low. A flat swipe across her sex, and nothing else existed. He became the center of her world. The coaxing swirls ebbed and flowed like the tide, raising her higher then easing back to whet her need. She twisted the blankets in her fingers, writhing in pleasure as he nipped and sucked. A furious tap back and forth along her clit and a drone roared in her ears; she thrust her hand in his hair to fist the thick strands.

"That's it, baby. I got you."

The lust in his voice, the flex of his fingers kneading her ass and, with his next prodding sweep, the ground split. Her body convulsed as an eruption burst and stars cascaded through her vision. Surge after surge of warmth washed her skin. At once, she chilled and trembled.

Like a man driven by greed, Rhys increased the pressure. He lapped and sipped, extending her orgasm until he'd wrung every last shudder from her form.

As her trembling subsided, he dotted soft kisses down one thigh, up the inside of the other. "Well? How was it?"

"Give me a moment to regain my bearings and I shall tell you."

His knowing chuckle wafted through her nest of dense curls and a thrill trickled along her nerve-endings. "Not a chance. I need you nice and loose or I'll never fit."

She closed her eyes and moaned. The man was sure to be her undoing.

The tip of his tongue prodded her over-sensitive clit and her eyes snapped open. She squirmed as the ball of his thumb rubbed and tapped. "Wait—"

The firm pull of his lips drew her in and she was pitched head-first into another soul-shattering orgasm. Her hips rose from the bed. She thrashed as he wrapped his arms around her thighs and held on, jabbing her with tongue, feasting and humming as if the taste of her beheld some savory delight.

The light pouring through the windows took on an ethereal quality as she coasted back to earth. Dust motes danced on the beams like miniature sprites. Her limbs were languid, as if she floated in warm water. Sweet honey flowed through her veins.

Rhys kissed her slit in parting and crawled from between her legs, and her hips rolled side to side with the press of his hands against the sleeping pallet. Each touch of his lips on her stomach and torso sent a network of shimmers racing outward like ripples on a summer lake.

He pressed his lips to the underside of her breast, dragged the bristled side of his face across her nipple and she arched into the teasing rasp. The sting was soothed by the supple brush of his mouth, and she clamped a hand on the back of his head as he scraped the tight peak with his teeth.

His scalp was damp. A thin sheen of sweat coated his skin. For all the pleasures he'd gifted her, the delay of his fulfillment had not been easy for him to bear. She smoothed her palm down the defined planes of his stomach to his waist and popped the row of buttons on his breeches. He hunched, closing the distance, licking a searing path up to her ear as she eased her hand inside.

Her eyes widened at the length and width cradled in her palm, the sheer weight of him. She wrapped her fingers around the raised veins, lifted him out of his breeches and took the measure of the head with a sweep of her thumb.

A groan rolled up from deep inside him and he pumped against her grip thrice. His concerns had not been unwarranted. The fit would be exceptionally tight. "I've been hard for you so long, I may have to take you twice." His whisper was coarse, bathing her skin like the heat of a banked fire. Her core spasmed, dousing her folds with arousal, and she bit her bottom lip against the ache to have him fully seated inside. He would fill her, mold her to receive him and only him.

He pushed up on his arms, the extended muscles straining, and squeezed his eyes closed as she stroked down to the base of his shaft. "God help me, I want you bareback, Faedrah. Nothing between us so we both feel everything." A shudder dislodged the set of his shoulders. "But you should also know I've been tested, gotten a clean bill of health."

She frowned. Most assuredly, he had. He was hale and hearty, a man in the prime of his life. "All right."

He gritted his teeth as she applied a series of squeezes back up his manhood to the bulbous head, the texture a fascinating combination of rock-hard inflexibility covered in satiny skin. "When is the last time you got your period?"

One of her brows rose as a clear bead wept from the slit. She wiggled her thumb, smearing the liquid along the tip. "My period of what?"

A breathy moan blurted from his lips, and he shook his head. "Your monthly…bleeding."

Ah. He spoke of the risks of embedding his seed in her womb. Her mother had cautioned her regarding the timing of such things. Indeed, the king and queen had used this same method to thwart the result of an additional heir. For all the love they shared, they'd oft stated being blessed with Faedrah as their child and future queen achieved the pinnacle of their creations.

Yet her lover worried unnecessarily. She shoved her other hand down the back of his breeches, using the space between them to aid the roll of his hips as he worked his legs and kicked the last of his garments to the floor. The beauty of his naked body, the muscles fixed and trembling, the way his cock jutted proud and flushed into the air, set the floor spinning. She trailed her focus up the edgy tension in each perfectly formed ridge and locked her gaze to his. "The completion of my womanly course came two days past."

"Thank God." He collapsed on top of her and devoured her lips, the surge of his clever tongue mimicking the way his erection nudged and prodded for entrance. The sweep of his mouth soothed the stretching sting as he eased the head inside. Her body involuntarily stiffened at the invasion, and she breathed deep as the massage of his hands along her hips and bottom aided her relaxation.

The end of his shaft bumped the wall of her maidenhead and he eased back, his elbows bracketing her head. His large hands cupped her cheeks, and he nibbled the corners of her mouth. "You ready?"

Her internal walls quivered. She slid her hands past his hips and dug her nails into the sweet curves of his unyielding backside. Never before had preparedness been so securely ingrained in her heart. "Goddesses' tits, yes."

He huffed, rocked forward and pain tore through her body. Her spine arced off the bed. He hissed, shifting from side to side as he withdrew, snuck a hand between them and pressed his thumb hard against her clit. The hair at her nape tingled. Pleasure sparked alive and anew.

With his next slow drive he penetrated a fraction deeper, held firm while she squirmed and adjusted to his width. A growl rumbled in his chest. He stroked and teased her swollen bud as he retreated. The absence of him made her heart rebel, and she clenched his ass as he sheathed himself a third time, her silent consent she longed for him to be fully seated. Their bodies met, the base of his shaft bearing down upon her sex, and the pressure initiated a rippling tremor through her core.

He sharply inhaled, shaking his head. "Jesus fucking Christ, you feel good…so god damned tight, I can't…" The tendons in his neck popped and he bowed into her, roaring his release as the warm spurt of his essence melded and heated her from within. He seized her hips and joined them again and again, and with each of his movements, her comfort increased, he slid more easily inside her.

At the last, he fell on top of her and tended her with soft kisses, her lips, neck, eyelids and even the tip of her nose and chin. "I didn't hurt you, did I? There at the end?"

"Not the least bit." She enveloped him in her arms and urged his cheek to the slope between her shoulder and neck, enjoying the delicious heat of his skin, how the rise and fall of his chest and the beat of his heart pounded in perfect harmony to hers. The comfort and ease with which he nestled inside her made her curious where his attentive love-making might lead them next.

Had he spoken true? She'd been privy to rumors some men exaggerated their stamina in regards to reaching the apex twice. Especially so soon after a long-anticipated release.

The slightest wriggle of her hips and his cock twitched and flexed. He moaned against her neck. Answering flickers of arousal reignited where they remained joined and she smiled, cupping the back of his head. "'Twould be an unfortunate waste, do you not think? To so carelessly ignore the conditions of such a pleasant circumstance?"

He laughed, happiness shining in his gaze as he lifted his head. She swept her thumb over his injured eye, brought him down to tend the wound with a gentle kiss.

"Princess, there will always be one thing you can count on." He ground against her and she gasped as his lengthening shaft nudged a wondrous place high inside. "When it comes to you, *ignore* is not part of my vocabulary."

Chapter 3

As the second only woman in Austiere history to have ever trained with the Royal Guard, Faedrah had believed she held a firm grasp of every muscle and its function contained within the human body.

Oh, how wrong she'd been.

Rolling onto her side, she slipped her hands beneath the pillows, casting her gaze over the tapered expanse of Rhys' back. Metal clinked against glass from where he stood on the opposite side of his chambers. Helios' afternoon rays streamed through the windows to blanket one of his shoulders, the bulging bicep in his right arm and the delicious tiers stepping down his ribcage as he whisked eggs in a bowl. The dark-blue drawstring trousers he'd donned were tied low on his hips, exposing the mouth-watering dimples perched above his perfectly squeezable ass.

He pivoted and poured the egg mixture into a pan he'd placed atop a singular coil glowing orange with heat, and the sizzle and snap of melted butter spattered onto the wooden planks doubling as his kitchen counter. A pause with a flat utensil in hand and, as if sensing her lazy perusal, he glanced at her with a knowing wink.

A swarm of butterflies flipped and twirled their whimsical flight through her stomach. Her artistic lover had not merely followed through on his promise to take her once, but twice after their initial joining, and subsequently finalized the enthralling achievement of her first dalliance with a massage of his lips and hands from the top of her head, to the tips of her ticklish toes. Every measure of her skin tingled and buzzed as if she'd been struck by a lightning bolt…and, indeed, she had. Enough times, she'd lost count.

The edge of a sharp blade rapped the cutting board in rapid succession, and he scraped some diced vegetables into his palm before tossing them into the pan. His lips pursed, and a merry tune echoed inside the cooling box as he swung the door wide to retrieve a vessel filled with the juice squeezed from several oranges.

Faedrah grinned, shaking her head at his buoyant disposition, and yet the moment he hefted a stack of plates and silverware and conveyed the finery to his wobbly table, her smile faded, and bleak despondency crept in like long shadows leaching the ground on a summer's day.

Their intimate repast was sure to be ruined once she recounted the details of her arrival in this realm. Rhys would undoubtedly gaze upon her as if she were a bewildered child or, perchance, with his spirits so light, he would become bound by fits of laughter. Nevertheless, the passion in his gaze would fade; the connection between them would be severed. And she'd be left no choice but to either argue a lost cause or leave his chambers, abandoning him to the conclusion she was a witless dope who suffered bouts of lunacy.

The spring-loaded recoil of a mechanical device ejected two browned pieces of bread, and he snatched them from their slots and dropped them atop the stack he'd previously prepared. The rasp of a knife edge scraped a layer of creamy butter over each of the slices, he wiped his hands on a small towel and slung it over his shoulder.

Lifting a platter of fluffy griddle cakes, he transported his burdens to the table. "Breakfast is almost ready, though I'm not sure it's technically breakfast at two in the afternoon." He rounded the counter to re-attend the eggs. "Are you hungry?"

"Quite," she lied. A boulder of dread occupied most of her

stomach, and the needles of anxiety plaguing her nerves had done the rest to displace her appetite. Yet a firm resolve remained embedded in her heart. Until she'd convinced him of the impossible or he'd outright asked her to vacate his presence, she would do her best to make the last of their moments as congenial as possible.

She glanced toward his narrow metal closet and her red evening gown he'd draped over the top of the open door. It expressed a more formal attitude than necessary, particularly in lieu of the detailed familiarity he since possessed of her body. Yet to sit naked during their meal—or wrapped amid the linens in which they'd slated their lust—would surely distract them both.

Her gaze fell to his white shirt lying crumpled beside the sleeping pallet, and she snaked her hand from under the pillows to shake out the wrinkles.

The cuffs hung well past her fingertips and, as she stood to secure the buttons, the bottom half amply covered her rump, falling to mid-thigh. She rolled the sleeves up her forearms and crossed his chambers to claim a chair just as he delivered the hissing pan of eggs to the table.

He pushed a stack of drawings aside to create some additional space, glanced at her with a smile and snapped his head around. Her skin warmed under the smoldering perusal he trailed from the base of her throat to the top button fastened between her breasts. Her nipples peaked and hardened as if they'd a will of their own—one that begged for his gifted attentions—and his eyes flicked to her naked thighs before he locked his gaze to hers.

That calculating brow she'd come to adore inched toward his mussed hairline. "Just for the record, those goddesses and their sweet tits got nothing on you."

She rolled her lips to contain a smile and, at the same time, a profound sadness threatened in the skip of her pulse. A sheen of bitter tears blurred her vision. Clearing her throat, she dropped her focus to the table. "Thank you for preparing the meal. Everything looks quite delicious."

That a man of his means and abilities would go to such trouble spoke volumes about his willingness to care for her, and she would not ruin his efforts by falling into fits of despair.

"I wasn't sure if you'd ever tried scrambled eggs before." The chair legs scuffed the floor as he tugged his seat close and joined her, reached for the juice-filled pitcher and decanted a measure into each of their glasses. "Or pancakes, for that matter." He paused, frowning, the pitcher suspended in mid-air. "What *do* you normally eat for breakfast?"

Her back hit the chair with such force, the breath was propelled from her lungs. The way he'd formed his query, 'twas as if he'd already determined she was not of this realm.

That same smile of wicked delight teased one corner of his talented mouth. The mischief returned to his eyes, and she squinted. Surely, she'd misread his meaning. "My father prefers a light meal of salted fish and fruit to break our fast."

"Salted fish?" Rhys tipped his head side to side. "I guess that's doable."

Her jaw dropped, and she planted her elbow on the table, leaning forward to better survey his face. "Meaning what, if I may so brazenly inquire?"

"Isn't it obvious?" He scooped a portion of the eggs onto her plate. "I've decided to meet your parents." A second scoop and he deposited a slightly larger mound on the plate before him, glancing in her direction. "Couldn't go any worse than last night."

Oh, but it could. Her hand dropped with a lifeless thud upon the table, rattling the silver, and she closed her eyes to stem the reoccurrence of her tears. As if the achievement of such a task would be as simple as climbing aboard his mechanical horse for a quick sojourn to the Austiere Kingdom. The man had no comprehension the dangers of which he spoke. "'Tis an impossibility, I'm afraid."

"Why's that?" He speared two of the griddle cakes upon the tines of his fork and plopped them beside her eggs, his words tainted with sarcasm. "You ashamed of me? Think I might embarrass

144

myself?"

"Goddesses wept, no." That he would suspect such a limitation on her part shot an arrow of regret into her heart. And yet, the notion of transporting the son of Gaelleod inside Austiere castle walls made every hair on her body tingle with grisly foreboding. Before she'd had the opportunity to explain his appearance, he would surely be charged with crimes beyond his ken and imprisoned...or worse. "My concerns are for your safety."

Furthermore, the point was moot. For reasons unbeknownst to her, the veil remained closed. She could not return home even if the decision was of her choosing.

"Oh, so you think I can't take care of myself?" Loading a bite of eggs onto his fork, he shot her another roguish glance. He lifted the utensil to his lips and then hesitated, his brows drawing together in suspicion. "Or is there something else you're not telling me besides the fact you're from another time?"

The chair legs screeched across the floor as she leapt to her feet. Shock iced her veins with such intensity, her body went stiff as a board.

He'd uncovered the truth. Without her ever having to utter a word. What's more, he accepted it. Sweet tits, he accepted *her*. Mayhap more than any other. Certainly, more than she'd ever accepted herself.

Despite all her deceptions, regardless of her faults, he believed her incredible circumstances without a speck of proof.

A clink broke the still silence as he dropped his fork to his plate, the food uneaten. "Sit down, Faedrah."

How could he *do* such a thing? She held her empty palms to either side of her, fingers splayed. What depth of devotion resided in his noble heart? What unwavering conviction?

A gasp rushed her lungs; her heart splintered. She squeezed her eyes tight, pressing a hard fist to her forehead. Oh, no. No...no!

Love swirled the delicate shards in her chest. They coalesced in a brilliant vortex and reformed—larger, brighter, piercing her soul with the purest white light. Awareness capsized her in frigid swells though she struggled to deny the terrible realization.

She couldn't fall in love with him. She pounded the center of her forehead. She *could not fall in love with him*! If she succumbed, everything between them would be lost. In returning his affections the veil would reopen. Her parents would insist she tell them all she'd learned and demand she immediately remove herself from his side.

Her thigh bumped the edge as she spun away from the table. The glasses teetered; juice splashed. She clutched the front of his shirt, wanting to rip it from her worthless form. He unselfishly offered her a love throughout the ages and, in return, she would deal him a parcel of horrors the likes of which would destroy the very fabric of his life. He was Gaelleod's son. For them to share one heart, meant his certain doom!

"What is it?"

His fingers clasped her shoulder, and she twirled, backing away from him, a flat hand held firmly in air to keep him at bay. Eliminating the threat was her only course. "I must remove myself from these chambers. Immediately."

He crossed his arms, jaw clenched in gritty determination. "Well, since you're not going anywhere without me, where are we headed? Into the past or some dystopian future?"

Dis-*what*? She shook her head, rallying her resolve. Whatever future or past he referred to did not matter. To declare her love for him would be the worst of betrayals. She withdrew another step, battling the longing of her traitorous heart. "I do not love you."

"Yes, you do." One lunging stride forward and he grabbed her upper arms, applying a vigorous shake. "You love me and I love you. We belong together, dammit. And no one or nothing is going to keep us apart."

"I do not!" The ground rumbled a warning. The windowpanes rattled in their frames. She sharply inhaled and darted a panicked glance around his chambers. No! Not the veil! If it opened, she'd be left no alternative but to abandon him…or barter his safety— perchance his very life—in exchange for that which they shared.

She clenched his forearms, squeezing her eyes tight. "I do not love him. I do not love him. I do not love him." The mantra fell from her lips. Tossing her head back, she railed at the heavens. "I do not love him, do you hear me?"

Yet to speak thus was their very undoing! A sacrifice of unselfish love. She shoved out of his grasp, her heart like a heavy boulder in her chest. To the bowels of hell with Helios and his nine daughters. They had left her no escape from this adulterous cage.

The floor pitched, and she and Rhys stumbled to the side. He lurched forward and whisked her close, one hand protecting the top of her head, his arm cinched tight about her waist. Dusty particles sprinkled down from the ceiling. A glass skittered to the edge of the table, and he spun her away as juice sprayed and jagged shards exploded across the floor. She pounded a fist against his chest, yet he held firm, his thighs two immovable buttresses, shoulders hunched to safeguard her within the shelter of his body.

A sob of misery scored the back of her throat. Her understanding had come too late. Sweet goddesses wept, it had come too late. She wrapped her arms about him and hung tight. How could she let him go? For all that it would lead them to the tortures of heartbreak and ruin, she *did* love him. More than she would ever love another. Regardless of the years or distance or dangers which would war to keep them apart.

The earth gradually shrugged off the last of its grumblings, yet she and Rhys remained linked, chest to chest, heart to heart, the top of her head tucked snugly beneath the haven of his chin.

"Holy shit." His rigid hold on her relaxed, and he pressed a fierce kiss to the black strip which marred her blonde hair. "That was no boxcar, but two earthquakes hitting Chicago in less than a week? What are the odds?"

She expelled a muted sigh into the delicious skin of his neck. "'Twas no quake of the earth, my love. 'Twas the opening of the veil."

He seized her shoulders to bring her away from him, the glittering striations in his gaze sharp and alive with a hope that nearly re-fractured her heart. "What did you just call me?"

A gentle huff left her lips, yet she smiled. "Only through the sacrifice of unselfish love shall the veil be opened. I had forgotten, you see. 'Twas many seasons past my father related the story, when I was but a child."

"The veil…" He squinted, searching her face. A snap of his fingers and he pivoted toward the table, shuffled the stack of drawings hither and yon until he came upon the one he sought. He scanned the page before flipping it round to face her. "It's the mirror isn't it?" The sheet wavered as he tapped a rendering of the armoire. "The veil is the mirror. That's why Forbes freaked out when I touched it."

The strength left her knees and she stutter stepped forward to pluck the drawing from his fingers. Her other hand rose to cover her mouth, her focus riveted to the sketch of her, tumbling through the veil, her hair a tangled disarray of white streaks, naked breasts displayed for all the world to see.

She snapped her chin up. Whilst certainly, he'd honed in on her the same as a divining rod veered toward water, for Rhys to have drawn her arrival with such accuracy defined an omnipotence worthy of Fandorn. Her pulse deepened with dread. Or the clairvoyance of Wizard Gaelleod. "How? How has this come to pass?"

He stared at her, the potential power inherent in his father's legacy brewing deep within his gaze. "I keep telling you, Faedrah. We belong together. That picture you're holding proves it." Without breaking from her face, he reached down and crumpled the remaining sketches in his fist. "Do you believe me now? Or do you need to see the rest?"

One imbalanced stride forward, and she placed her hand over his. She harbored not one doubt their lives were destined for each other, yet to ignore he may hold the clues to where her purpose might lead would be a terrible risk.

Cupping her other hand along his bristled jaw, she skimmed her thumb along the dark strip of hair beneath his lower lip. He could not ask her to abandon her duty to her kingdom. For all that she longed elsewise, too many lives were at stake. "Rhys. You must show me."

His nostrils flared and he shook his head, but the tension in his fingers eased under her palm and he lifted the pages the between them.

A musical chime sounded from her beaded bag and they froze, each of them clasping one edge of the drawings like some suspended tug of war.

Rhys slowly lifted his eyes to hers. "Forbes?"

Goddesses' tits. The veil. Darting to the wooden crate beside the bed, she flung the pages to the rumpled coverlet, tugged open the cinched string on her purse and slapped the device to her ear. "Uncle?"

"Ah, yeah. I'm not sure what's going on over there, but over here we've got one extremely pissed off king and queen demanding to see you. Like, right now."

Blessed tears of the nine. Squeezing her eyes tight, she pinched the bridge of her nose. 'Twas exactly as she had feared. Her parents would most assuredly command she return to the castle, and she had neither the desire nor fortitude to trade quips with them regarding her actions.

Straightening her shoulders, she dropped her hand and glanced toward the man who had captured her heart. No. She would not scurry to do her parents' bidding like some disobedient child. For better or worse, Rhys was her future now, and she would not be persuaded to desert him until every other path before her had been explored to its fullest extent.

Her gaze fell to the sketches strewn across the blankets and she bent at the waist, selecting a sheet that had wafted toward the pillows. A shudder wrenched her shoulders. Those ghoulish eyes…the sunken cheeks…the hard slash of Rhys' hand across the bottom, naming the portrait as that of his father.

Regret capsized her heart in such anguish, she lowered to the edge of his sleeping pallet.

"Sweetie, are you there?"

"Yes, Uncle, I am here." And here is where she planned to stay. In Rhys' chambers, safely ensconced within his love, until she'd conveyed to him everything he must know about his father's place in Austiere history. The unending evil, the torture her father and king had suffered by Gaelleod's hand, the blight which threatened her realm and how Rhys must make a choice. Every soul throughout the ages depended on his compliance to rid their worlds of Gaelleod's malicious presence. Hers and his most of all. "Please express my sincerest apologies. My return to your chambers shall be regrettably delayed."

* * *

This was complete bullshit. What had started as the best day in all-time history, had deteriorated into a clusterfuck of epic proportions.

Rhys jammed his key into the lock on the freight elevator, twisted it to the right and punched the button for the bottom floor. He might as well have strapped on a pair of concrete boots and waded straight into Lake Michigan.

The elevator lurched into its creaking descent, and Faedrah stepped close to curl her index finger around his pinky. An affectionate tug, and he tried to reassure her with a smile but, based on the wide-eyed blink she offered in return, the tight stretch of his lips came off more like the odd-toothed leer of a jack o'lantern.

Shit. After everything she'd told him, the last thing he wanted was her carrying the responsibility for the sucking black hole of his existence. She was the one bright star he had left. Besides, if anyone had wedged him between a rock and a hard place, that blame rested solely on Leo's shoulders.

Once she'd hung up with Forbes, Faedrah had calmly sat both of them down and laid out her entire story. Yippee and fucking yahoo. In the frigid silence that followed, Rhys had received an up close and personal understanding of the phrase "ignorance is bliss."

Christ, what a mess.

He lifted the back of her hand to his lips, deeply inhaling as he brushed a kiss across her knuckles. Most of her life sounded like something straight out of Brother's Grimm, and though every answer she'd given him was reasonably logical, a lot of what she'd said tested the limits of his imagination. Not that it mattered. Regardless of the details, he wasn't about to hand her a big old pile of doubt in exchange for doing exactly what he'd been asking for since the day they'd met. Jesus Christ, if what she told him was actually real, it was a miracle in its own right she still trusted him. No way was he going to fuck that up by arguing her points or saying he didn't believe her.

His brain might be struggling to assimilate, but he wasn't stupid.

The elevator shuddered and his knees bounced as they hit the ground. He slid his hand from hers to lift the gate, wheeled his bike onto the street and plugged the key into the ignition. "Oh shit, I almost forgot. I got you something."

He flipped back the buckles on one of his saddlebags and pulled out a small helmet— brand-spanking new and glossy white with a black stripe painted down the center. The play on her hair had been his sarcastic slant toward a joke, but with the underlying tension so thick between them, most likely his attempt at humor would fall flat on its face.

"Oh!" She clasped her hands together under her chin, bouncing on her toes. "How wonderful. Rhys, I adore it. You have my utmost thanks."

The glacier creeping across his heart receded under her sunny grin. The shame squeezing his chest slacked off, and he fully filled his lungs for the first time in over an hour. God dammit, he was over the moon for her. One fucking smile…knowing he was the cause for putting it on her pretty face…and everything got better, easier somehow.

The only thing that really mattered anymore was making her happy. How fucking ironic his presence was bound to bring her nothing but pain.

She slipped the helmet past her ears and an unexpected chuckle cinched the muscles of his stomach. With the ends of his sleeping pants rolled around her ankles, those sparkly red stilettos and his dress shirt and suit jacket hanging off her shoulders, the striped headgear completed her look as the most adorable—and hands down, the sexiest—circus clown he'd ever seen.

A frown creased the smooth skin between her brows and she left off fiddling with the chin strap to prop her hands on her hips. "Care to impart what you find so amusing?"

Uh oh… If history was any indicator, that flash of anger in her eyes proceeded a sharp crack on the back of the skull…or maybe a hard jab to the eye. But if there was *any* good news to come out of her story, at least now he understood why.

She'd spent years trying to prove herself an able contender, fighting for respect. Where she was from, being the strongest, the smartest, the quickest on the draw counted for everything, and mockery was the worst kind of offense.

That was cool. He got it, but he also wasn't about to stand here and let her group her in with those men who'd ridden her ass for no good reason except to tease her through training. Or those wheeling-dealing nobles she'd described from the court. By the same count, he wasn't one of her subjects to grovel for forgiveness at the first slip of the tongue, either. In this world they were equal. That was a done deal. And, for fuck's sake, they had enough on their plate without retreading ground they'd already covered.

She had his respect. Shit, she'd had it the second she showed up in the gallery. The sooner she got that through her stubborn blonde head, the better.

He snaked an arm around her waist and jerked her against his hips, and satisfaction heated to a low burn as she blinked in surprise. Her spitfire attitude hadn't butted heads with arousal before. Good.

"I'm laughing at you. Is that so bad?" He slid a hand over her perky round ass and shoved her hips forward, grinding his cock into her belly. Her tough-as-nails exterior didn't scare him. In fact, it made him horny as hell. Another thing she'd be wise to remember.

A gasp parted her lips and she slapped both hands to his chest. "I do not take kindly to your impertinence, sir."

"Which is exactly why you need to understand a little good-natured ribbing doesn't change how I feel." He grabbed the mouth vent of her helmet and pried it off her head. When it came to Faedrah, there was only one way to show her where he stood.

She shook out her hair and the tips tickled his fingers. His shaft pulsed as he gathered the heavy mass along her back and dragged her lips to his.

The resistance on his chest firmed before she relaxed beneath him. Her lips parted and he accepted the cue to dip his tongue inside. She ran her palms under the unzipped sides of his leather jacket and fisted his shirt, tugging him closer, opening wider.

Christ, she drove him crazy. It was impossible he could ever get enough. He dropped the helmet and a hollow clunk echoed down the alley as he clasped her neck, devouring her lips again and again, nipping and sucking. The silky glide of her tongue, the hungry way she matched him stroke for stroke. Her flavor was like bathing in a breath of fresh air. Everything about her cooled his raw nerves and, at the same time, they were so alike—defiant, tough and persistently itching for a fight.

He scooped her up by the thighs, wrapped her long legs around his waist and strode forward, slamming her against the side of his building. She shuddered in his arms, shoved a hand under his dego-t and raked her nails down his spine. Shit, the way she responded to him, how she seemed to know exactly what he needed made him harder than the brick at her back. If it wasn't for the fucked-up mess they were in, he'd carry her back upstairs and bury himself inside her until all this bullshit about wizards and kingdoms and alternate realms was nothing but a bad memory.

"Fuck, Faedrah." He broke away from her lips, balancing his forehead against hers, their bodies swaying. "When I'm near you, I can't think straight."

Her heavy breaths matched his, but her brow twitched like he'd just admitted where Hoffa was buried. "I shall do my best to use that information to my fullest advantage."

He chuckled. One thing was for sure. Life with her would never be boring. "You got any leftover doubts about whose side I'm on?"

"None whatsoever."

"Good. Remember that moving forward."

With a parting peck to her lips, he released her to the ground. Two steps back, and he retrieved her helmet, flipped it in the air and resettled it on her head. Desire sparkled in her eyes. Her cheeks had rosied to the pretty pink he loved, and his kiss had left her mouth pleasantly plump.

If he had anything to say about it, those two qualities would be the first thing people noticed about her whenever they were together. So everyone would know he'd marked her as his.

He secured the strap under her chin and tapped the end of her nose. "And if anyone besides me gives you a hard time, just say the word and I guaran-damn-tee they'll never know what hit 'em." Including his father, her parents and any other hassles that got in his way.

She grinned and nodded, trailing him toward the bike. Her hand met his shoulder as she climbed aboard behind him. He jacked the starter and the snarl of fine-tuned gears ruptured against the vacant buildings. After adjusting his chin strap and flicking down the visor, he eased them to the head of the alley and veered onto the street.

The hint of her curves along his back kept him rooted in the present. The clamp of her arms around his waist and the heat from her inner thighs reminded him he wasn't alone. Not anymore.

He kept the bike in first gear, puttering through his ramshackle neighborhood. Once they arrived at her uncles all that could change. According to her, his father was the Austiere version of Satan…which basically made him the anti-Christ. Fucking great. The minute her parents discovered who he was, it was pretty much a given they'd demand she get as far away from him as possible. And who could blame them? If he had one ounce of common sense, he'd drop her off at Forbes' condo and head straight over to Leo's to confront the asshole himself.

Stopping at the corner mission, he put his foot to the ground and checked for oncoming traffic. Faedrah ran her palm up the center of his stomach and fingered the dip between his pecs. Her arms cinched as she wriggled closer, and he lowered his hand to squeeze her knee.

Maybe he'd been a full-blown idiot to second-guess everything she'd told him. He ran his fingers down her calf to stroke her bare ankle. For Christ's sake, he was the one who'd sketched Gaelleod's picture and then jokingly signed Leo's name to the bottom. There was no arguing with that…or Leo's disturbing appearance and the fact both he and Faedrah had recognized each other on sight. Besides, if it was fine and dandy to accept she was from another dimension, what was so fucking hard about admitting Leo had somehow taken that same leap?

Couldn't be that the details were just a tad too far-fetched now, could it?

Rhys expelled a frustrated breath, juiced the engine and leaned into a soft left-hand turn. If there was one thing Leo was proud of, the McEleod lineage could be traced back to the Mayflower. Shit, Rhys had passed the portraits of each mogul who'd run the empire over the centuries every time he went up and down his father's god damn stairs.

Each of them had birth records, had lived to old age and then died. So what explained that inconsistency? Reincarnation? Leo was an evil succubus who stole the lives of his victims in order to extend his own?

Faedrah had confessed right away she wasn't sure how Gaelleod had shown up in this time. Apparently, the dude never had access to the mirror. He'd never gotten his hands on the key or convinced Faedrah's mom to help him make the trip. She didn't have a clue how he'd done it, but that didn't lessen her certainty one fucking bit. She was proof positive Leo and this Gaelleod person were one in the same.

Her aggravation…the desperate way she'd wrung her hands and paced his floor over being unable to give him an answer had been the icing on the cake. When she could have easily lied, made up a bunch of bullshit to cover her ass, Faedrah had opted for the truth. She'd acknowledged her ignorance—a decision which no doubt nearly killed her—and been honest with him, and that had sealed the deal.

He would follow her. He would fight for her. He would love her until the end of forever. But none of that meant Leo's judgment day was over and done. That fucker owed both of them an explanation. Rhys would beat it out of him if he had to, the minute her parents were done ripping him a new one.

He changed gears into second and then third, following the ramp to the expressway, north.

Chapter 4

Faedrah shoved her key into the lock and twisted the knob, and Rhys followed on her heels as she stepped inside the tiled entryway of Forbes' condo. Mingled voices drifted in from the direction of the living room and she turned, locking her eyes on his as she quietly pushed the door closed over his shoulder.

A reassuring smile settled on her pretty face, but he wasn't buying it. No matter how much she tried to fake an outer confidence, there was no hiding the inner worry. Not from him.

He slipped his hand around her neck and tugged her forehead to his lips. Where the line had been drawn between what she believed…what he believed…he couldn't make that call. But if his muse still wasn't convinced her being here had anything to do with him, at least he could console himself there was one thing they'd agreed on.

Their time together wasn't over. No way, no how. And he'd be damned sure he used every single second they had left persuading her *this*—with his hands on her body, his lips on her skin—is where she belonged.

"Hey." He pulled back from her. "It's gonna be okay. As long as we stay on the same page, everything should be fine."

"Most assuredly." She clasped his wrist, fingers holding tight, but something in her voice, or maybe the way she kept her lashes lowered, made him hesitate.

Dragging his thumb across her throat, he angled her chin up and waited until she met his gaze. "We *are* in this together, Faedrah."

"Of course."

Nope. She was hiding something. Something she worried might piss him off, based on the way she trembled.

She jerked away and Rhys pivoted toward the living room as Forbes' chuckle coasted in beneath the higher register of a female laugh. According to Faedrah, Oliver and her mom had been close prior to the day she'd jumped through the mirror and into the arms of Faedrah's dad. Evidently, the two of them had been using the time to catch up.

"I most certainly did *not* eat an entire cake!"

"Oh yes, you did," Forbes insisted. "And then you complained about your stomach for a week. I didn't care, though. At least it stopped your kvetching about that idiot who broke your heart."

Another round of hilarity echoed down the hall, and Faedrah sighed, shaking her head. "'Twould seem I owe my uncle a debt of immense gratitude. If nothing else, his efforts to waylay the queen's anger have apparently been successful."

Rhys tangled their fingers together, leading Faedrah toward the noise. "Good. Then let's get this over with before your parents have the chance to remember what ticked them off in the first place."

It was a lame attempt at using whatever advantage they could to land on top, but it wasn't like he and Faedrah had a choice. As it was, their odds at being heard were about the same as standing in front of a firing squad.

The scent of melted candle wax grew stronger as they closed in on the living room. Same with the smarting tang of a smoldering fire. Rhys frowned. He could've sworn Forbes' fireplace was powered by gas.

The two of them stepped through the archway and Jon glanced over from where he and Forbes had placed two chairs before the open armoire. His focus dropped to their joined hands, and one of his eyebrows rose. He lifted his eyes to search each of their faces shook his head.

Shit. Evidently, Rhys and Faedrah's afternoon jam session hung off both of them like a cheap suit.

Forbes' attention never left the armoire. Seemed he was too wrapped up in his conversation with the queen to notice the guests of honor had arrived. A killed bottle of wine sat on the coffee table along with a picked-over platter of fruit and cheese. Leftover swills of burgundy discolored the sides and very bottoms of two thin-stemmed glasses, and Rhys smirked. Or maybe Forbes just had a good buzz going and was too busy reminiscing with an old friend.

The armoire stood against the same wall as the doorway, the mirror hidden from view…that was, until Faedrah filled her lungs like she was about to take a header into the deep end and stepped inside the room. Rhys' arm stretched, but he tightened his hold and followed her inside.

Not one damn thing in her world or his was coming between them. He'd smash the damn glass before he let that happen.

The conversation screeched to a halt. He turned to face the mirror and his knees gave as the floor tilted off-kilter beneath his boots. What. The. *Hell.* Sure, he'd believed Faedrah when she'd told him the mirror led to an alternate world, but this… Mumbling a string of obscenities, he dragged his hand down the five o'clock shadow on his face. No description could've prepared him for the clarity of the picture, the energy buzzing around the edge of the frame. He squinted and leaned to the side as a tendril of smoke drifted off the candelabra to the left of Faedrah's mom and crossed into Forbes' living room.

Jesus Christ. He darted a glance at Faedrah. Criss Angel had nothing on this mind freak.

The smiles on the king and queen slowly faded, and Forbes swiveled in his chair as the tension in the room spiked like the pulse on a heart rate monitor.

"Faedrah..." the queen whispered.

The seconds ticked by as Rhys sized up their opposition. The king or queen weren't anywhere near what he'd expected, though their notch-above-the-rest good looks made it clear where Faedrah had inherited her super model body and traffic-stopping beauty. Not that he was surprised. It'd been clear from the day one his muse descended from an enhanced gene pool.

Instead of fur robes and gaudy costumes, their clothing was pretty plain, though the king's puffy sleeves and black leather vest could've easily doubled as a pirate for Halloween. A gray leather cat suit hugged the queen like a second skin, her white hair pulled back in a long, thick braid. And Rhys had to hand it her, for a woman who had to be in her forties, she was in damn good shape.

The concern creasing their brows made them seem more real... more normal somehow. In fact, it if wasn't for the renaissance decor in the room behind them, he would've assumed they were one of those weird couples dressed to attend Comic-Con.

Faedrah dropped to her knees and his jaw firmed as her hand slipped from his. He frowned at her bowed head, lifted his scowl to her parents and crossed his arms. They'd get no such respect from him. Not until they'd earned it. If he'd learned anything as Leo McEleod's kid, people who demanded obedience were usually the ones who least deserved it.

"I beg your forgiveness, mother...father." She folded her hands under her chin and he fought to keep from grabbing her upper arms and hauling her to back her feet. This was such bullshit. What the hell did she have to apologize for? Being the bravest person he'd ever met? Risking everything to save their kingdom? "I swear to you now, the actions I took were my own. Neither Vaighn nor any subject in the realm should be made to bear the punishment for my insubordination."

"On your feet, Faedrah." The king slid a sidelong glance at Rhys before refocusing on his daughter. The queen's attention, however, stayed glued to Rhys' face, and he planted his heels against the impulse to shuffle his boots. Jesus Christ, the knowing glint in her sharp green gaze demoted him to a specimen under a microscope, as if she'd already figured out the exact role he played in this game of thrones.

"The court is not in attendance, and your mother and I have never demanded you kneel whilst alone in our presence." Faedrah's dad crossed his arms and muscle corded on either side of his thick neck. Excellent. The dude was a fucking Titan. "Do not attempt supplication to our sympathetic sides now. That time is long spent."

She rose, lifting her chin, and pride rushed to the surface over the determination concreted on her face. She wasn't about to grovel, which meant she planned on sticking to her guns. *There's my girl.* "Nevertheless, I disobeyed a direct decree handed down from my king. As a member of the Royal Guard, I am fully prepared to suffer the consequences of my sedition."

Like *hell.* Rhys unlocked his arms, hands balled into fists. So help him God, it was every man for himself if they so much as slapped her wrist.

The queen's brow twitched and a soft chuckle shook her shoulders, but she didn't leave off staring at him like some bizarre tropical fish. Blindly placing her hand on the King's arm, she tipped her head in Rhys' direction. "I like him, Caedmon. He's extremely protective of her. Do you not feel it? Goddesses wept, his frustration over these proceedings has nearly singed my ass in the chair."

Forbes grunted. "Try standing in the same room with him. He's liable to lop a person's head off if they so much as breathe at your daughter the wrong way."

A dreamy sigh issued from Jon, his hand wafting to his chest. "Sorta reminds me of another young man I once met who'd been smitten by an ethereal blonde beauty."

Oh, for God's sake. Rhys rolled his eyes.

The king's attention landed on him, but he didn't so much as flinch. Big as the guy was, he was about to be disappointed if he expected Rhys to tuck tail and run. It cranked his knob to know everyone recognized his obsession for Faedrah, and to shrug off something so important would only make him out to be a cocky prick.

"So, you are the one to whom our daughter has pledged her heart?"

"Yep. And I'm in love with her too."

King Caedmon narrowed his gaze. "How did you sustain the injury to your right eye?"

Rhys gritted his teeth, but no good would come from lying. Besides, if nothing else, the shiner proved Faedrah could hold her own in a fight. He nodded in her direction. "Your daughter took a jab and I forgot to duck."

"Outstanding. I've no qualms her vengeance was rightly deserved." The king's brown eyes hardened with the same fiery anger that had sparked in Faedrah's gaze the day she'd shown up at the gallery. "And who are you to lay claim to that which I and her mother hold most dear? By what right or title do you petition our consent to court the future queen of the Austiere Kingdom?"

Fuck. The shit was about to hit the fan. *I'm just the son of Gaelleod. No big deal. Oh, and by the way, I'm having sex with your daughter.* "My name is Rhys Mc—"

"He is a gifted seer of this realm." Faedrah stepped forward.

Rhys jerked his attention to her. Seer? Since when was he a seer?

"'Twas his heart which beckoned me here." Her gaze darted back and forth between her parents. "Do you not recall my persistent fascination with the armoire? The unrelenting splintering of my soul? 'Twas Rhys' summons which called to me across the ages, and 'tis by his knowledge and with his aid, I was able to uncover the whereabouts of Wizard Gaelleod."

"Oh, crap." Oliver slapped a hand to his forehead. Jon sprang forward in his chair, a gasp shaping his mouth into a perfect round "oh." The queen paled, and apparently all her blood flowed straight into the king because his face flooded an artery popping red.

Crossing his arms, Rhys cocked a brow at his white-haired

minx. Yeah, okay, she'd told them the truth, but not the *whole* truth. Still, after the smooth way she'd moved the discussion off of him and onto his father, he wasn't about to throw her under the bus…and neither were Forbes and his lover.

He nailed them to their seats with a warning glare. Whatever Faedrah's reasons for delaying the inevitable, he trusted her gut. Since Oliver and Jon were the only other two who knew about dinner at Leo's, if they planned to see the light of tomorrow they'd keep their big traps shut.

Jon clapped his hand over his mouth, elbowed Oliver and shook his head.

"Are you stating this rebellious soothsayer purposely led to you straight into the arms of our most vile enemy?" The king's voice built in volume until he roared like a caged guerilla.

Faedrah flinched, but she didn't look away, and Rhys flexed his fingers against the urge to punch his fist through the mirror and see if he could dent the guy's grizzled square jaw.

"She didn't know," he snapped. "Neither of us knew who he was until she met him face to face."

"Is this true, Faedrah?" Her mom moved her hand to her chest. "Moreover, are you quite certain the entity you encountered and the black wizard are one in the same?"

"His appearance was somewhat altered, and yet I am thoroughly convinced Leo McEleod is the same dark lord who haunts my dreams."

Really? Rhys shot her a frown. That was news to him. He'd assumed the Leo in this time and the one in hers looked exactly the same. Not that it mattered. The damage was done.

He refocused on her parents. "Bad news is, he recognized her too."

The king wrenched forward in his seat, a rigid finger aimed at his daughter. "You shall return to the Austiere Kingdom at once." He sized up Rhys from under his brows. "And you shall return to this realm *alone*. Now come." He waved her forward. "The decision has been made."

Over my dead body. Rhys inched in front of her, staring down her dad through the glass. It was time they got a few things straight. "Sorry, but that ain't happenin'. Faedrah's not going anywhere without me."

Jon *tsked* three times, shooting him the stink eye. Oliver looked Rhys up and down, lips smacking like he'd just eaten a dog turd.

King Caedmon froze. A second or two passed before the corner of his mouth twitched and he tossed his head back with a hearty laugh, pounding his fist against the arm of his chair. "I do believe your affections have left you somewhat addled, my boy. You do not decide how and with what decree I rule my kingdom. No entitlement in either realm presents you such privilege over my daughter."

"I love her." Rhys gritted through his teeth. "And she loves me."

"Drivel." The king fell back in his seat. "You've known each other but the span of three days."

The queen slowly turned. She pinned her husband with a deadly stare and Rhys grimaced over being the beneficiary of that loaded weapon. Hopefully, it wasn't hereditary.

The king's shoulders fell, and he muttered a curse. "Our three days were different, my love. 'Twas the Gleaning, pre-ordained by prophecy and under celestial providence of The Nine."

She huffed. "And as a product of that same destiny, is it not our duty to hear out our daughter's petition? Have the goddesses not opened the veil as divine blessing of her choice?" Lifting her hand, she cupped the king's cheek. "Perchance our best course would be to allow Rhys safe haven in our kingdom. Given time, mayhap this will grant us the opportunity to learn the true nature of his heart."

"No." Faedrah rounded Rhys' side and stood with him shoulder to shoulder. A squeeze of his hand, and he bit his tongue before he had the chance to stick his foot in his mouth. Her mom's suggestion had sounded like a damn fine idea to him. "Rhys and I will do neither."

Aw, fuck. As sure as shit was slick, the woman was headed

straight down a rabbit hole. His nostrils flared as he peeked at her from the corner of his eye.

"I caution you to bide your words carefully, Faedrah." Propping his elbow on the arm of his chair, her father leaned toward the mirror. "My patience over this discussion is threadbare, at best."

"And what of my entitlement, father? As future queen, am I not afforded the same courtesy to speak you've so steadfastly professed to grant every subject in the realm?"

The queen dipped her head in consent. "Of course you are, dove."

King Caedmon opened his mouth like he was about to rain down a bunch of objections, but another sharp glance from the queen and he snapped his jaw shut. Rolling his eyes, he tossed his hand in the air.

Faedrah squared her shoulders like she was prepping to bungee jump off a cliff. "What news of the black infestation?"

The two royals exchange a long stare before facing their daughter, and the king raked a hand through his hippy-length hair. "Despite our best efforts, the source remains a mystery, and the northern most forest has all but succumbed."

Faedrah stiffened beside him, and Rhys lifted her hand to his lips. What this "infestation" had to do with Leo, he wasn't sure, but if she believed the two were somehow connected, that was good enough for him. "And, to this course, have you yet determined whether or not Gaelleod retains a foothold in our realm?"

"No." A frown wrinkled the king's forehead, dislodging the gold band resting an inch above his thick eyebrows. "Where does this line of questioning lead, Faedrah?"

She sighed and shook her head. "I do not yet know. However, 'twould seem a misspent error of profound neglect to not confront the bastard whilst the opportunity presents itself."

Gotcha!

Rhys rolled his head back on his shoulders, cheeks expanding as he blew a breath toward the ceiling. A small laugh cinched his stomach as chaos erupted, both in her world and his. Oliver and Jon leapt to their feet, squawking like hens. The king and queen shouted a jumble of complaints he couldn't even try to understand.

But the real kicker? Faedrah had already made her decision. Even before they got here, she'd come up with this plan. She meant to go after the asshole and nothing anyone said would change her mind.

Tipping his head forward, he laughed again. Christ, he was an idiot.

He pivoted toward the girl of his dreams and his chest constricted at the bloated tears balanced on her lower lashes. She worried her bottom lip. Disappointment shaded her beautiful brown eyes as they flicked from face to face.

Her parents, Oliver and Jon, were only upset because they cared, wanted to protect her just like he did. But, to her, their knee-jerk reaction meant something different. Rhys had lived the same rejection enough to know.

In her eyes, none of them truly believed in her. They didn't think she was strong enough, smart enough. They called her out for being a failure without even giving her the chance to try.

He'd squared off against those odds before, and whenever his father had told him his efforts were useless, hearing those words had been like sucking warm piss through a straw.

Regardless of the risks involved, he couldn't do that to her. He loved her, and would be the last guy to let her down. "I'll go with you."

Her eyes snapped to his. Relief, gratitude…hell, even love flooded her gaze. He smiled, huffing. Shit, she had him wrapped around her little finger, but no one had ever looked at him the way she did. Like he was more, better…good.

"Shhh…" Oliver flapped his arms in the air like he was trying to corral a swarm of bees. "Be quiet!"

The shouting cut off mid-stream, and the sudden silence was louder than the uproar that had filled the room a second ago.

"Now." Forbes tossed his head. "What did you say?"

Gathering both of Faedrah's hands, Rhys tugged her a step closer and brought her knuckles to his chest. "I said…I would go with her."

She smiled; nodded. A single tear tumbled and left a clear, shiny trail down her cheek.

"She has not yet been granted the sanction of her king and queen!"

"Caedmon." Queen Rowena's harsh whisper carried more emphasis than her husband's ear-clanging shout. "Our daughter is a grown woman, wise in reasoning and brave beyond measure. We have taught her all that we know and raised her well. 'Tis time we trust she knows how best to seek her fate. Though worry pains my heart as it does yours, the day has come to let her fly."

Tremors shook the king's body. He clamped both hands on the arms of his chair. "So that she can soar straight into the arms of death? I cannot…I *shall* not ever willingly consent to such an abhorrent revelation."

"What other choice do we have?" The queen placed her palm on her husband's wrist, pried open his fingers and cinched their hands together. "We have always known Faedrah was special, and now we have unparalleled proof. The goddesses have granted her passage to the future to fulfill a higher cause. We must be strong, my love. Stronger than ever before. For all the dire circumstances of her path, Faedrah may be our kingdom's only hope."

A long moment of stress-filled tension hung in the air.

"Yeah, that might not be entirely true."

Rhys swiveled his shoulders to find Forbes' elbow balanced on the back of his hand, thumb and forefinger plucking his bottom lip. He wagged that same finger in the air. "There's one thing we've all forgotten. A person we should definitely consult before these two kids charge off into the unknown."

He raised a brow at the king and queen, shifted his attention to Jon and smirked.

Rhys frowned around the room as the strain disappeared from

each of their faces. Wait…what or *who* was Forbes talking about?

A grin split the guy's face, and he chuckled as all four of them spoke at once. "Violet."

Chapter 5

"Okay. Sounds good. We'll see you then."

Forbes thumbed the screen on his cell and slipped it into the pocket of his creased, black slacks. "Violet asked we give her the night to research. We're supposed to meet at her place tomorrow morning at ten."

Relief dropped Faedrah's shoulders a solid inch, and Rhys lowered his chin, jaw clamped tight against weighing in with his two cents about their decision. The second Violet's name had come up in the living room, Oliver and Jon, Faedrah's mom and dad had all breathed a little easier…and bucky for them. Apparently those four had been on the receiving end of this Violet person's internet savvy skills before, and the answers she'd provided twenty years ago regarding some or another important event had elevated her status to an oracle-like prophet. If Faedrah believed following in her parents' footsteps and asking Violet's advice was their next best move, he was happy to go along. Still, when it came to their future together, trusting some computer geek he'd never met— especially one who called herself a witch—didn't sit that well in his gut. Whether the kooky old bat was more phone psychic than *Girl with the Dragon Tattoo* remained to be seen. She so much as mentioned the words "Ouija Board" and they were out of there.

Oliver strolled to the side in the guest bedroom and propped his ass on the edge of the desk. Crossing his arms, he sized up Faedrah from under his brows. A protective streak sliced through Rhys like a set of halogen high beams, and he slipped an arm around her waist, tugging her against his hip.

Forbes' focus shifted to him and Rhys narrowed his eyes. Based on the frustration simmering in her uncle's light-blue orbs, this conversation could only be headed in one direction, but he would be damned before he let anyone criticize Faedrah's decisions. She'd done the best she could. Shit, the only reason she'd lied was to protect him.

"I don't like this one bit." Oliver sighed, shaking his head. "The two of you have put me and Jon in a terrible spot."

Ha! The guy should spend ten minutes in Rhys' shoes. Try having his dad be the reincarnation of Charles-fucking-Manson and then he could talk. "It would have only freaked her parents out more to find out I'm Leo's son." His fingers tightened on Faedrah's waist. "Their faith in her would have been flushed straight down the shitter and we all know that's the last thing she needs."

"Rowena and Caedmon are our friends," Oliver snapped. "They trust us, and purposely keeping them in the dark goes against everything Jon and I believe in."

"Uncle…" Faedrah left Rhys' side and approached Forbes, placing her hand on his crossed arms. "Had there been another way, I swear to you, I would have pursued a more honest course." She searched his face, fingertips whitening as she tightened her grip. "Please. I beg your understanding. Surely, you must have endured a time whence subterfuge was employed to safeguard the yearnings of your heart."

"Pffft." Jon walked through the door, a stack of folded clothes in his arms. "That's putting it mildly." He set the garments on the bed, selected a white t-shirt and held it open in front of Rhys's chest. "You've just described every gay man's adolescence."

Tossing the shirt aside, he picked up the next and stretched it end-to-end across Rhys' shoulders. "Good God, you're nearly as beefy as Caedmon, aren't you?" He smiled up at Rhys, backed away a step and glanced around the tense faces in the room. "Should I go pour us a round of nightcaps?"

Rhys shook his head. It had to be after midnight, and the only thing he needed was Faedrah, alone. Just the two of them like they'd been earlier today, followed by a solid block of uninterrupted shut-eye. After last night's drawing jag, followed by the stress of meeting her parents, blind exhaustion had been the only thing to make him agree to sleeping at Forbes' instead of heading home. Navigating Chicago's dark streets with her on the back of his bike was a bad idea. "It's time we call it a night. Both Faedrah and I need some sleep."

Jon's smile returned. "All right, then. Leave your clothes outside the door and I'll be sure they get laundered before we head to Violet's in the morning."

"I vow to relay the full details of Rhys' lineage to my parents the moment the most reasonable opportunity presents itself." Cupping Forbes' cheeks, Faedrah brought him down to peck each side of his face—one, two, three—back and forth like some *avant-garde* movie. Oliver pursed his lips, his gaze following as she crossed the room and gave the same goodnight kiss to Jon.

"And I shall explain the deep frustrations you endured at our expense." She squeezed Jon's hand. "The anger of the king and queen shall not be placed upon your brow, I swear it."

"Eh?" Forbes' dark-haired lover shrugged. "Wouldn't be the first time your dad was peeved at me. He likes to growl a bit to make sure he's heard. You should've seen him the day your mother insisted they go back to his realm. Good grief, I thought steam was going to hiss out of the big guy's ears."

Rhys grunted. Good one.

"Jon." Oliver warned.

"What?" He propped his hands on his hips. "It's not my fault Faedrah's just like her mother." Narrowing his eyes, he wagged a finger. "Had Rowena been given this opportunity to save their kingdom, she would have made the exact same decision and you know it."

Oh, really? Rhys cocked a brow. That was interesting...

Forbes rolled his eyes and stood from the dresser, pressing his lover's shoulder to go in front of him out the door. "Come on. Let's let these two get some rest."

"Rest, my lily white ass. We both know that's the last thing on their agenda." Jon gasped and slapped a hand to his chest, stopping in the threshold. "Oh, Ollie, just think. Grandkids! Did you ever imagine? The two of us as grandparents?"

Oliver slumped. "The only thing I'm thinking is you need to slow down." He grabbed the handle and, with a wink in Rhys and Faedrah's direction, swung the door closed. Jon's excited chatter grew muffled as their footsteps faded down the hall.

Rhys smirked. Kids? Yeah, he really didn't qualify as dad material. Especially since he'd grown up with the worst possible role model. Then again, he'd never been loved before. Never shared a connection with someone the way he did with Faedrah. He turned toward his muse.

"Apologies." Her attention left the door and landed on him. "Sir Jon employs a tendency to speak out of tu—"

"Don't."

Her lips parted, and the anticipation that had been percolating along the periphery ever since her parents had signed off from their mystical Skype chat tensed every muscle in his body. The heated glances she shot his way, the constant touching had him geared up and aching.

Silence stretched between them, weighted with meaning...and though her smile was as enigmatic as the Mona Lisa, the sharp glitter of desire in her eyes clanged like a five alarm fire in his head.

She loved him.

She needed him.

Just as fucking much as he needed her.

One stride forward, and he caught her as she jumped into his arms, her lips seeking his, loose hair creased in his fingers like bolts of silk. He got lost in the cool supple curves of her mouth, flicked his tongue in time with hers and dove in for more.

Her warm moan vibrated his lips. Seizing her ribcage, he hitched her onto his waist and lurched for the wall. He needed her closer. To have every dip and curve naked for his greedy hands.

The edge of the desk bumped his thighs. Trinkets rattled and clinked along the surface. He propped her sweet ass on top and buried his face in the unspoiled slope of her neck. Shit, ten seconds alone with her and he was hard, hot and craving her with an urgency that obliterated any concerns for where they were or what tomorrow might bring.

"I yearn for you, my love." She gasped, shivering as he nipped little love bites down the side of her throat. He wound his hands up the sides of his dress shirt, the baggy fit roomy on her tight little body, and cradled her breasts between his forefingers and thumbs. "That you would have such faith in me has left me completely undone."

A sweep of his thumbs over her stiff nipples, and she tossed her head back. A repeating swirl over those pointed tips and a shudder wrenched her shoulders. *Yes...* He wanted her trembling, wet and warm around him. Until he'd rocked her to the brink of orgasm and she'd forgotten everything but him.

Lifting his elbows, he urged the shirt higher until she tugged the unbuttoned collar over her head. His mouth watered at her flawless skin—the faint blue vein pulsing in her neck, the angles of her shoulders as she worked her arms from the sleeves and chucked the shirt aside.

He lowered his head and sucked the first ripe berry into his mouth. Her hand clamped the back of his neck and he chuckled as her nails scraped, her fingers fisting his hair. Fuck, the way she gave in to him was better than any adrenaline rush, more mind-blowing than any success he'd ever achieved. "There's no way in hell I'm letting you face off against Leo alone."

173

"And yet not one amongst all the kingdom has ever shown such confidence in my abilities." She twisted the tight fit his of dego-t near his stomach and jerked the bottom edge from his jeans. Her nimble fingers slipped the buttons on his fly, and she eased him into her hand.

Jesus! Her breast left his mouth with an audible *pop* as he hunched forward, bracing his palm on the wall over her shoulder. The firm band of her fingers stroked down to the base of his cock. The blood roared in his ears, throbbing in time with the heavy pulse in his balls. She kept the pressure tight back up to the head, wiggling her ass back across the desk toward the wall, and with her next downward stroke, she leaned forward and flicked her tongue across the slit.

More… Christ, he wanted more. To hold on and never let go until nothing and no one would ever come between them.

"I once overheard my handmaidens discussing in great detail, the proper way to express gratitude for a man's generous deeds is to bestow upon him the kiss of coaxing." The soles of her feet braced the backs of his calves as she lowered her lips to his throbbing dick.

Shit, he was never going to last. How many times had he lain alone in bed, imagining this very scene? A bead of sweat trickled down his back. She'd reached inside his head and plucked out his greatest sexual fantasy.

"After discovering my presence, they instructed me in the delicate nature of such things, though, as of yet, I am unschooled in practice." Tingles shot down his shaft, tightening his groin as she rubbed the head along her lips in a slow circle. Smooth…smooth and slippery. "You must convey your thoughts if my performance does not merit your satisfaction."

His heel repeatedly hit the floor as her tongue wet the fleshy rim in that same painstaking pace. "Princess," he croaked. "I'm pretty sure there isn't much you could do wrong at this point."

Her lips parted, and he braced for the warm cavern of her mouth as she took him inside. So soft…so wet and soft, her tongue

174

cradled him as she slid down. He fisted his fingers, hitting the side of his thigh to keep from driving all the way in to the base. The leisurely rhythm she set nearly killed him and, at the same time, he wanted to enjoy every second. Make it last. Slide in and out until he'd hit the edge of control.

A hiss dried his teeth as she withdrew, her curled fingers following her lips to the pulsing rim. A quick kiss to the tip and she eased him in a second time, pushing him a step closer with the tension in her legs. He closed his eyes and sank deep, squeezed his lids tight while she cupped and fondled his balls. Her throat constricted as she swallowed, and her warm hum shot up his cock and straight into the nerves at the base of his spine. His hips jerked, and he pumped twice, trapping a moan in his chest. If he ever ran into those handmaidens, he would happily hand over the keys to his bike.

Another sucking pull as she withdrew, the firm squeeze of her fingers and he arched his back as she took him in again, all the way down until he bumped the wall of her throat. An undulating roll of her tongue and the force of his orgasm threatened to flood her mouth.

A spurt shot and he grabbed the back of her head. "Don't move." The urge to come was so strong, he silently counted to ten, imagined adjusting the carburetor on his bike, anything to beat back the firestorm raging through his system.

As good as this was, nothing compared to the two of them climaxing together. The way she quivered around him while calling his name was better than any solitary fulfillment. He'd done that enough on his own, and satisfying her newfound sexual awareness was important. If he had anything to say about it, she'd never leave his side unless all her cravings had been met.

Every cell in his body rioted has he pulled out. A small whimper left her throat, and he gritted his teeth against her assumption she'd done something wrong.

"No." He wrenched her head back and kissed his salty taste from

175

her lips, dipped his tongue inside and washed it from her mouth. "I want us to come together." Smoothing a hand up her stomach, he palmed the weight of her breast, plucked and tweaked the nipple. "You'll never disappoint me, Faedrah. Do you understand?" Her skin cooled his lips as he dotted kisses over her forehead, her eyelids, cheeks and the center of her beautiful stubborn chin. "Not ever."

Lashes fluttering, she breathed his name.

Something inside him fractured.

He lifted her off the desk, turned and tossed her to the center of the bed. The mattress bounced as he jumped on top of her and, working together, they stripped off the rest of their clothes. Rolling onto his side, he scooped her against his body, their limbs a tangle of arms and legs. The scent of her arousal flower-bombed his nose and his mouth dried in anticipation. There was no better aphrodisiac than discovering she was just as turned on as he was. Then again, why wouldn't she be? They were in tune in a way that defied explanation.

Still, after this afternoon's marathon tri fecta, coming at her like a bull in heat might do more harm than good. He tongued the little dip at the base of her throat, skimmed an opened-mouth kiss up to her chin and nibbled the corners of her mouth. "Are you sore?"

She narrowed her eyes, lips pursed. "I would say pleasantly so."

Adrenaline spiked in his gut. Shit, her words were like an erotic assault on his senses. He rolled on top of her, nesting his cock in her tight damp curls. Her thighs parted and she ground against him as he nuzzled her ear. "You want it fast or slow?"

"Both."

God dammit! His cock flexed, the skin straining over the challenge of bringing her to orgasm twice. She shuddered and writhed, dragging her sex along the side of his shaft. A loud buzzing droned in his ears. The pressure built. Shit, she was going to make him come before he was ready. "Good, because fast is what you're gonna get."

He eased the head inside and the tight band inside her massaged him like a fist as her hips rose, bringing them together all the way to the base. A groan eked from his throat. He pressed a hard thumb to her clit and tingles detonated down his spine as her internal walls clamped down tight.

She wrapped her arms around his neck and brought him to her lips, riding the length of him, thrashing and shivering. His control snapped and he let it fly, driving into her, meeting her stroke for stroke. His orgasm hit like a freight train and his back arched as he erupted inside her, every muscle tense, a roar caught behind his clenched teeth.

Breaths coming in short bursts, he collapsed on top of her and drank in the top of her shoulder, rolling his hips and chuckling into her hair while she squirmed and panted in his ear.

Based on the way she continued wriggling, she was still as hungry as he was, still ready for more, and now that they'd gotten fast out of the way, he planned to show her just how fucking awesome slow could be.

* * *

Firelight winked off the ceremonial blade, and terror iced the blood in Faedrah's veins. She struggled against the gripping hands of Gaelleod's henchman, a growl rasping her throat as his thick digits plied her upper arms.

From across the underground level of his father's dimly lit chambers, Rhys locked his gaze with hers, his scowl a combination of regret and blistering rage. The span of his bare chest corded and tensed. The muscles of his arms strained as he swayed to and fro, wrists shackled and chained by overhead restraints. "Let her go and I'll do anything you say."

Gaelleod's quiet laugh raised the hair on her nape, oozing down her spine like an oily serpent. "Take heart, my son. The princess shall be released from our bargain long before you join her in paradise."

His empty eyes darted toward her and the whisper of his black robes caressed the floor as he drew near. Her pulse leapt. A shudder stole through her body as his fetid breath lingered before her lips. She stifled a gag, twisting her head for a lungful of air. He lifted the golden key from between her breasts and wrenched her against his body by the neck. "Just as soon as her duty is fulfilled in providing my heir."

No! Tears flooded her eyes. A wail of despair lodged in her throat.

A bellow ricocheted against the stone walls and Rhys thrashed, seeking purchase on the toes of his boots. "Don't touch her, you fucking asshole!" His biceps bulged as he hefted himself off the floor, his face a terrifying red. "Do you hear me! I will kill you if you hurt one hair on her head!"

The sinuous tendons of Gaelleod's throat worked as he tossed his head back, the dual quality of his protracted laugh needling her eardrums like the call of a Dregg. "And yet, that is the most glorious part." He pivoted toward her love and raised the curved edge of the razor-sharp blade. "This body you wear shall impregnate her for me."

A sob broke from Faedrah's throat. Glee danced in Gaelleod's obsidian eyes as he lifted his weapon high. The dour tones of a malicious incantation tumbled from his lips and the dagger glowed. Faedrah thrashed against the grip of her oppressor. His hands slipped, but the slack in his hold came too late. Air sliced as the knife plunged toward Rhys' chest, and she screamed...

"Stop! Faedrah, it's me!"

She flailed against the thick muscle pressing down upon her body, her legs tangled in the voluminous layers of her skirt.

"You were dreaming, dammit! It's me!"

A sharp crack echoed in the room, and her palm stung from the force of her slap.

"Shit!" The weight disappeared and she sprang from the bed, scanning the room for any tool she could use as a weapon.

The door burst open and her uncles raced into the room.

Faedrah frowned, tipping her head at their unlikely appearance.

Her gaze shifted to Rhys, sitting wide-eyed on the side of the sleeping pallet, not a stitch of clothing masking his frame and his cheek ablaze with evidence of her abuse. She clamped a hand over her mouth, closing her eyes, but nothing could contain the sob of relief which broke through her fingers.

A dream. She shook her head. It had just been a horrifying dream.

Oliver strode forward as if to gather her in his arms and then pulled up short, taking the measure of her nakedness from head to foot. "Sweetie, are you okay?" He spun to face the door. "From the way you screamed, I thought someone had died."

Yet therein lay the crux of her anguish. Someone *had* died. Her very heart. Her reason for being.

"I'm all right, Uncle." She lowered her hand, meeting Rhys' troubled frown from across the room. And yet, why now? Why was she made to suffer Gaelleod's visitation here, in the safe haven of her uncles' home, while slumbering peacefully in the presence of her heart's desire?

A dangerous glint sparked in Rhys' eyes, and he curled a finger, beckoning her near. She stumbled forward, crawled into his lap and snuck her arms about his waist, burying her face in his chest. Her fear dimmed as he slung the blankets across her back and cocooned her snugly within his warmth. His strength seeped into her skin, and she released a sigh of gratitude he'd read in her gaze the exact remedy she'd craved.

Him. To bask in the rhythm of his heart beating in tempo with hers. To have him hold her close and banish all the dark evil from her mind.

"It was just a dream, baby. A bad dream." Rhys' murmur in her ear was a comfort beyond his ken. For this moment, he was safe, alive and rocking her in his arms. She snuggled closer, breathing in the sultry scent of his skin. "It's over. I got you."

His voice rumbled against her cheek. The stubble of his beard combed through her hair as he turned with her on his lap. "She's

179

okay. I'll watch her. You guys head back to bed."

A moment later, the door clicked into the latch and Rhys laid them back abed, the wall of his chest nestling her from nape to hip, the soft press of his lips tending her ear. "Get some sleep, Princess. I'm not going anywhere."

Yet she would find no more respite this night. What portend her nightmare contained, she did not know, nor did she care. The sharp tang of grief was still too bitter upon her tongue. The horrifying visuals too vibrant to dissect their meaning.

Only one thing, above all, was certain. Rhys' life was in danger, and she must do her utmost to ensure he never gained the attention of his father's cruelty again.

For her purpose had become clear.

Once their meeting with the witch Violet had concluded, she must break her promise to remain at her lover's side, and set off to face Gaelleod, alone.

Chapter 6

Oliver rapped his knuckles upon the wooden door of the witch's quaint two-story abode and Faedrah darted a nervous smile over her shoulder. Her heart lurched at the detached unrest staring back at her through Rhys' gaze. She bit her lip to stem a rueful sigh and dropped her focus to her feet.

'Twas the same since Helios' bright rays had broken through the curtains of her uncles' guest chambers and her beloved had stirred at her side. Wrapping her in his arms, Rhys had urged her close, welcoming the golden sunrise with a gentle kiss. Yet her hope of succumbing to the blissful tide of his lovemaking had vanished the moment he inquired after the details of her dream.

An uncontrollable trembling had consumed her form at the cruel remembrance of her one true love dying on the point of Gaelleod's glowing blade. Her throat had closed as the dark lord's horrific promise whispered she'd one day sire his heir. Reliving her nighttime terrors had been no less frightening than when they'd initially invaded her slumber. Gaelleod's stench was still just as strong, her desperation as tragically rich, and the disquiet hardening Rhys' eyes over her condition merely served to heighten her worries.

How was she to look upon the man she loved and describe to him the appalling circumstances of her visions? What words could she use to detail his murder by his father's own villainous hand? Rhys had stood by her side when no one else would. He'd believed in her with a conviction beyond any she'd ever known. The thought of bestowing him such torment in return for all he'd gifted her had cast her into misery and, unable to answer his queries, she'd left the bed to dress

Throughout the breaking of their fast, their preparations to meet Violet and the trip to her home, he had remained silent, ever avoiding her gaze. Yet Faedrah refused to allow his anger to sway her decision. Until the witch had foretold their future, she would do all she could to protect him. Their future had not yet been cast, and perchance such facts would be revealed to either disprove or alter her worst fears.

The door swung open and she frowned at the sprite-like woman who grinned at their entourage from the opposite side of the stoop. Goddesses wept, Violet was more pixie than witch.

An airy floral-print dress hung nearly to her ankles, belted at the waist and accented by a series of musical bangles stacked along each slender wrist. The purple spikes tipping her short white hair defined her penchant for mischievous pranks and spells. Black boots laced up her calves, though the thick heel added little to her diminutive height. Indeed, if her ears had been pointed and tufted with hair, Faedrah would not have been the least bit surprised.

"Ollie!" The witch tossed one arm around the neck of Wizard Oliver, wrapping the other about the shoulders of Sir Jon. "And Jon! I'm so glad you're here. God, it's been forever."

Amusement tickled Faedrah's belly as the three of them shared a lopsided embrace, yet her smile slowly faded as a man thrice Violet's size tromped his massive bulk into the frame of the doorway behind her.

Mountainous shoulders squared off either side of his wiry gray beard. His black leather waistcoat, the skull and crossbones scarf tied low on his brow bespoke the pirates that oft lie in wait off the Austiere shoreline in search of her merchant ships. Myriad silver rings adorned his sausage-sized fingers, his legs braced wide and thick as the trunk of a tree. The colorful runes encasing his forearms were much the same as those etched into the skin above Rhys' wrists.

Yet 'twas the menacing glint in his coppery eyes which set Faedrah's nerves to fraying. Had she to guess, she would've sworn the man was the cross-bred progeny of an ogre and female Dregg.

Rhys' hands landed on her hips and urged her back a step. Apparently, he'd tuned in to the gruff mannerisms emanating from this monstrous man as well.

Violet released Oliver and Jon, searched Faedrah's face and glanced over her shoulder. "Todd." She slapped the back of her hand against the man's chest. "Stop scaring our guests. I already told you, Oliver said he's cool."

By "he" Faedrah could only assume the witch spoke of Rhys, which meant her uncle had offered these two strangers full disclosure regarding her beloved's ties to Gaelleod.

Her muscles tensed as the moment stretched. Trouncing a man so large would require a feat of epic strength, yet if one of his eyelids scarcely twitched, she would be left no choice but to try.

Sir Todd focused his attention past their shoulders and Faedrah followed his gaze toward the street. The metal pipes of Rhys' mechanical horse winked in the morning sunlight, parked behind the glossy red encasement of Oliver's motorized carriage. As a group, they'd agreed to travel separately to Violet's chambers on the possibility her counsel best be followed by departing in opposite directions. Perchance this colossal man took issue with their mode of transportation.

He crossed his massive arms, sizing up Rhys from the top of his head to the toes of his black leather boots, and jerked his chin in the steel horse's direction. "That your sweet ride?"

His gravel-laden voice was a flawless match to the weather worn creases bracketing his eyes, and Faedrah held firm as Rhys' fingers tightened about her waist another degree. "The seat behind me belongs to Faedrah, but my name's on the title."

He shifted his perusal to her and nodded, swinging his shoulder aside. "You can come in."

Or perchance he'd sworn allegiance to some modern-day guard which patrolled this witch's domain upon their own iron steeds. 'Twas a fortuitous stroke of luck Rhys' penchant for danger and speed designated him an equal to Sir Todd's *gens d'armes*.

Faedrah followed her uncles into the entryway, stopping to blink several times within the shaded interior. Yet before she'd been given proper time to absorb her surroundings, Violet's palms clasped her cheeks and the witch lowered Faedrah's forehead to her lips.

"Just let me look at you." Tears threatened atop the lower lashes trimming the petite woman's eyes. A small smile bandied about the corners of her mouth. "My God. I swear it's like the past twenty years never happened." She squinted. "I only met your father once, briefly, but you have his eyes." Her hand stroked the side of Faedrah's head, and she instinctively leaned into Violet's touch. "And this black strip of hair, no doubt, came from him."

She ran her palms the length of Faedrah's arms, grasped both hands and hung tight. "You have no idea how happy I am to see you, sweetie. The last time I talked to your mom, I didn't give her very good news." Concern darkened the older woman's azure gaze. "How is she?"

Faedrah smiled. Her mother's friend was a faithful ally, to be sure. "The queen is…happy. Still and always, desperately in love with her king."

Violet nodded, dropping her focus to the tiled floor, though the relief Faedrah expected to smooth her wrinkled brow never came. "And now it's your turn. Now you stand in front of me, looking for answers." The witch sighed. "Some days, I really hate my job."

Alarm skittered through Faedrah's belly and she glanced at Rhys. He crossed his arms, eyes narrowed. "What'd you find out?"

"Right. Where are my manners?" Violet squeezed Faedrah's fingers before releasing her, and opened a flat hand toward an open archway on their left. "Let's have a seat. I'm sure you're all anxious to hear what I've learned."

Rhys grunted, skepticism set within the angle of his shadowed jaw.

Faedrah paused to allow her uncles precedence into the room, in addition to stealing a moment of privacy with her beloved. She turned her back to Sir Todd, voice lowered as he lumbered after their troupe. "You do not trust this witch to speak plainly?"

"I believe she'll give us the truth according to her." Rhys' eyes glittered like faceted emeralds, and she marveled at the captivating shimmers in the muted light. "Just remember, not everything this woman is about to tell us is necessarily fact."

Her faith these proceedings may remedy the riddle of their plight vanished like a wisp of smoke. More than any other, she trusted Rhys' instincts. If he harbored qualms regarding the information they were to receive, she would be wise to heed his advice.

"Listen." He slid his calloused palm against her throat, brushed the ball of his thumb along her bottom lip. "This distance between us is making me crazy. God Faedrah, ever since this morning, I feel like I've been losing you and I don't know how to stop it."

And rightly so. Her inability to share her dream had kept him unawares. "My heart is yours. *I* am yours."

"Just promise me, no matter what happens here, you'll remember that."

She encircled his shoulders in her arms, the rasp of his beard tickling her neck as she cradled the back of his head. "I could no easier forget how to breathe."

With a crushing squeeze of her ribs, he released her, linking their fingers as he led them into the room.

The interior was a shade or two darker than the foyer, though the blue haze emanating from the three glowing squares placed atop a semi-circular desk provided ample light by which to navigate the furnishings. Each of the panels cast an eerie pall over the faces assembled, their inner workings humming like the surface of the

185

veil, and Faedrah wavered in her decision to draw too close. Strange magics were afoot. This witch controlled a keen malevolence far beyond her understandings.

"It's okay." Rhys tugged her hand to step beside him, and Faedrah assumed the vacant spot between his shoulder and that of her uncle Oliver, completing the opposite side of the circle to match the curvature of the desk.

Violet had already acquired the oversized chair in the center, the base a strange five-pointed star set upon tiny wheels that pivoted and rolled with her movements. She spun to the first window on her left and her fingers flew over a series of letters and symbols set within an elongated, flat, black box. "I started at the beginning, back where I had left off when your parents last came to see me."

The screen flashed and Faedrah withdrew a pace, a breath lodged in her throat. A quick survey of the picture, and her apprehension vanished. As sure as she lived and breathed, this witch had stolen inside the armory and plucked a charted survey of the Austiere Kingdom off Denmar's desk. "Sweet tits. That is my homeland."

"Right." Employing the use of her index finger, Violet rotated an elevated fragment of a palm-shaped device and the picture enlarged to a detailed rendering of the castle and its surrounding villages. Faedrah slapped a palm to her chest. Helios wept, if their enemies ever discovered such mysterious enchantments, her kingdom was doomed.

The witch pivoted toward the center panel and a series of documents shuffled past the window. "The last mention of Gaelleod I could find happened the Night of Silver Knives, during the battle he fought with Rowena and Fandorn." A blur of her fingers over the board, a furious series of clicks, and the parchments scrambled and rearranged. "Except for here." An arrowhead danced along the verbiage, encasing several of the lines in a bright yellow block. "A small footnote about twenty years later reports a Crystal Cave where Gaelleod's tomb was found."

Faedrah stiffened. "Twenty passings of the seasons? That would put the discovery precisely during this timeframe."

"Yep, and I can do you one better." Violet swerved back to the map, scooted the picture to the right and hemmed a section of the Austiere Kingdom's northern most coastline within the lines of a box. A click and that same region enlarged to encompass the entire pane. "That asshole buried himself in the cliffs." She cleared her throat, glancing at Rhys. "No offense."

He huffed. "None taken."

"From what I could gather, I'm guessing the entrance is located somewhere in this area here." She wagged a finger at a small section centered in the screen. "Bad news is, the actual crypt where he's hidden will be a lot harder to find. There's a labyrinth of tunnels and dead ends leading inside, and the supposed spells he cast over the area make for a dangerous minefield. If a person would ever decide to try their luck at finding him, they could easily get disorientated and lost…or walk straight off a ledge into an abyss."

Faedrah clutched at the last strands of her quickly diminishing hope. "Do you know the proper course?"

"Nope." The chair twirled and Violet faced their group, one delicate white eyebrow lifted in firm regard. "If the secret route through the tunnels ever did get recorded, I couldn't find it. Which means it was either destroyed or left uncharted to begin with."

Pinching her bottom lip, Faedrah frowned as another, more devious, alternative occurred. "Or Gaelleod had the diagram entombed along with him, thus awaiting the day of his resurrection and ensuring he could furrow his way out."

"Holy hell."

She snapped her gaze to Rhys and her hand dropped lifeless at her side. The ashen pallor of his cheeks nearly cast her into a tailspin.

"I've seen it." He raked both sets of fingers through his hair and threaded them together along the back of his neck, elbows forward. "God dammit, at least I think I saw it. It was a long time ago, when I was a kid. I went into my dad's study looking for a

187

sketchpad and ended up picking the lock on his desk. When I stumbled across a secret compartment filled with what I assumed was a treasure map, I thought I'd hit the Lotto." He released his hands, shaking his head, the laugh tumbling from his lips rife with scorn. "Leo found me soon after, got all bent out of shape over what I'd done, as usual."

Faedrah clasped Rhys' arm and a chill whispered over her skin. Reliving the memory had wound him so tight, his muscles vibrated beneath her grip. "Can you recall the path?"

"No way." He glanced at her from under his brows. "But I remember how he whipped me with a leather belt until I could barely walk."

Jon clucked his tongue, pressing a cloth hankie to his nose.

"And I know where the map is hidden. If he's still keeping it in the same place, that is."

"Yeah, well, I wouldn't advise going anywhere near him if you can help it." Violet spun back to her mystical portals, faced the one in the center and her fingers plucked a tuneless song along the lettered board. "When I reached a dead end moving forward, I decided to start in the present and go back. See what else I could discover about Gaelleod's history."

A black and white image of a young Leo McEleod filled the screen and Faedrah's pulse skittered with dread. He was debarking a motorized carriage, though the lines were more cumbersome than those of her uncle's sleek coach, a wide-brimmed hat sat low on his brow and a satisfied grin creased his cheeks.

"Here's an article from the *Chicago Tribune* dated May 12, 1966, the day Leo inherited the reins to McEleod Industries, three days after his father's death." A tap of the witch's finger and another image appeared, blanketing the first, a portrait of the man Faedrah assumed was Rhys' grandfather, slightly blurred and tattered near the edges. "Rayburn McEleod took over on January 24, 1910, also three days after his father's death." She tapped in rapid succession, the pages altering from white to yellow, exact depictions changing to those sketched by hand. "Same with every single McEleod who ran the business from the time the company first appeared back in the seventeen hundreds. Always the only son born, always three days."

"Yeah, so?" Rhys crossed his arms. "We have a predisposition for birthing sons and like to follow tradition. What's so weird about that?"

"The weird thing is that prior to their inaugurations, each heir had absolutely nothing to do with the business." Her hand bounced with a final click and she rotated the chair back around to face him. "This is Leo a week before Rayburn died. Look familiar?"

Alarm washed the entirety of Faedrah's being. She slowly lifted her focus to Rhys...as did Oliver, followed by Jon. A low growl issued from Todd's chest and he swung his leg around to stand beside the witch, a towering wall of flesh bent on protecting her at all costs.

"Fuck me." The whisper falling from Rhys' lips bore such anguish, Faedrah clenched her jaw to stifle a moan, yet none could deny the resemblance of a young Leo McEleod to that of his natural born son.

The smile dimpling Leo's cheeks, the dark scruff offsetting the square line of his jaw...even Leo's hairline was a flawless match to her beloved. But of all the details defining them as father and son, the one which most cast her heart into the throes of despair, was the beautiful blonde woman Leo McEleod clasped in his arms. Rhys' mother, and the love shining outward from their joyous gazes was as tangible as the devotion Faedrah shared with the man at her side.

Violet locked her attention onto Faedrah. "You need to sit down?"

"No." She wound a hand around Rhys' bicep and held tight. "I do not regret, nor do I fear my decision in offering the son of Gaelleod my heart. We were destined, our union blessed by the Goddesses."

"Yeah?" Violet's eyebrows rose. "Well then, I suggest you hold onto your ass." She twirled back to her desk and commenced another string of infuriating clicks. The window to their right blinked repeatedly, presenting the fair guise of one young maiden after the next, the final, topmost scene a representation of Rhys' mother adorned in a white, lace-trimmed gown. Her arm was linked with Leo's bent elbow, his formal attire, a black well-appointed suit. "Grace McEleod married Leo three months after he became chairman of the board. A year later, Rhys was born and, a week after that, she disappears off the radar. It's like the woman never existed."

Violet slid their likeness to the left and it reappeared in the center window, alongside the depiction of a young Leo and Grace caught in a loving embrace. "Do you remember her, Rhys?"

"No." The word croaked from his throat and Faedrah released his arm to slide her hand about his waist. He gathered her to his chest, pressing a fierce kiss to the top of her head.

Violet pivoted back to the right screen and the remaining image of another blonde beauty, her smiling face shown beside the tangled remains of a pile of charred wreckage. "Henrietta McEleod, married to Rayburn two weeks after he was sworn in as chairman, gave birth to Leo ten months later and died in a car crash three weeks after that." Another tap and a third woman filled the screen. "Jane McEleod married Oscar two months after he gained control of McEleod Industries, mothered Rayburn a year later and died shortly thereafter of tuberculosis." The fourth beauty appeared. "Margaret McEleod, wife of Lucas. Shot to death in a robbery gone wrong six days after giving birth to Oscar."

Rhys' arms tightened around her shoulders and Faedrah closed her eyes, her mounting horror too poignant to bear.

"Annette, died in childbirth, leaving a son, Ulmer."

This witch spoke of too much death.

"Camille, found dead in bed two months after Louis was born."

Struggling for air, Faedrah clung to Rhys' shirt, each name

arrowing home the dire similarities to her dream.

"Francesca didn't survive the trip to the Americas, but her infant son—"

"Stop!" Rhys' sharp retort rebounded in her ear. "Just stop. This is killing Faedrah, can't you see that?" His warm hand covered the back of her head. "For Christ's sake, it's killing us both."

"Killing her is exactly what I'm trying to prevent." A squeak of the wheels and Faedrah lifted her eyes to find Violet facing the room. "All of them died, you guys. *All* of them. The life expectancy of a McEleod wife is three months, tops. Her survival rate? Shit, it's less than zero."

"This is completely ridiculous." Rhys' voice shook with unrestrained anger. "All those deaths can be explained."

"Which is most likely why they were never investigated."

"Please." Faedrah broke from Rhys' embrace, fisting her hands. "I compel you to speak plainly. Are you stating a consent to matrimony condemns all McEleod women to some inescapable curse?"

"Sure." Violet shrugged one slender shoulder. "If you can call murder a curse."

"That's bullshit!" Rhys stutter-stepped forward.

Sir Todd leapt into his path and seized her love by the collar of his black leather coat. "Hold it right there, cowboy." The burly man hauled Rhys to the tips of his boots, leveling them eye for eye. "Last time I checked, you showed up at my house with a truckload of questions. What kind of husband would I be if I let you bust the messenger's balls just because you don't like the answers?"

"And let her accuse me of premeditated murder?" Rhys thrashed against the man, his feet searching for purchase. "Fat chance in hell!" He grasped both of Todd's wrists and sparks sizzled and cracked at the contact. "Now let *go!*"

Faedrah gasped as the air compressed and a silent percussion whipped her hair about her shoulders. Sir Todd's arms flew wide, pin-wheeling in the air as he stumbled back. A squeak issued from Violet and she shrank in the seat, using her heels to propel her out of harm's way.

Sir Todd careened to the ground with a harrowing slam, lay prone on his back and stared at the ceiling. "What the hell?" A loud groan filled the stunned silence as he pushed to sitting, rubbing his hand along the back of his head. "I swear to God, Violet, I'm too *old* for this shit."

She scooted forward and cupped her husband's cheeks in both palms. "Oh, sweetie, are you okay? I'm so sorry." A coo issued from her throat as she rained a series of kisses over his forehead, down his nose and lips.

"Jesus." Rhys held his splayed fingers before his face, eyes wide and disbelieving. He shifted his gaze to her and Faedrah started at the panic etched on his face. "Faedrah, what's happening to m—?"

"You are Gaelleod's son, my heart." Stepping close, she grasped his hands and lowered them to his sides. What that she could remedy the bristling fury of all such an honor entailed. "I have long since suspected you inherited a parcel of his powers."

"Oh my sweet Lord." Jon's lashes fluttered and he grabbed Oliver's arm as if his wavering legs necessitated additional support.

"*What?*" Rhys' grip tightened around hers before he shoved her hands away. "Aw, *hell* no." He withdrew a step, his red-rimmed eyes filled with dismay. "This can't be happening." He shook his head, shoulders tight, and thrust his fingers through his thick hair. "This can*not* be happening. I mean…for Christ's sake, Faedrah, what if I hurt you?"

Her heart rent in two as he battled the agony of his worst fears. "You will not." She believed as much down to the marrow of her bones; drew near lest Rhys assume the responsibility of such appalling horrors. "Have I not belief in you above all others? Have I not dared to seek the mysteries of your heart?" She placed a hand on her chest, standing tall and proud, her love for him ringing loud and true as the tolling of a thousand silver bells. "Keep faith, love. I trust in your noble heart. You merely need time to determine the breadth of your abilities." Opening her hands to her sides, she beckoned him back to her arms. "Ours is a love throughout the ages. You would no more harm me than you would yourself."

"How do you know that?" He aimed a finger at Violet, blanched and clenched his hand into a trembling fist. "She just said I was apt to lose it and—"

"That's not at *all* what I said!" Every head in the room spun toward the witch as she helped her husband to his feet. "You misunderstood me. God, give a girl the chance to explain."

Oliver and Jon rushed forward to brace Sir Todd with their shoulders and aid him to the nearest seat. They slid an ottoman before the settee and the injured man moaned, propping his heels along the cushioned top.

"Now, if everyone would just calm down and try to focus, maybe we can get through the rest of this." She plopped into her chair and, straightening her shoulders, whirled back to the center screen. "Look here." The little white arrowhead wriggled back and forth between the two images she'd previously shuttled to the surface—Leo with his darling Grace prior to Rayburn McEleod's death, the one beside it those same two lovers during their marriage rite a scant season later. "Is it just me or do these men seem like two totally different people?"

Faedrah frowned and closed in on the window with the rest of the group to better study the likeness of Leo's face. Her knees locked and she flinched away from the desk, a million icy shivers racing down her spine.

Whilst, unquestionably, the Leo represented in the first view was a near reflection of her beloved Rhys, the cocked head of the man in the second scene, the arrogant slant of his shoulders and knowing curl of his lips called to her through the dark shadows of her dreams. Only one decrepit soul she'd had the ill fortune to meet beheld the haunted mien of the evil entity standing at Grace McEleod's side.

Awareness rippled through her soul, impressing the clear cold reality of the dark lord's insidious plan.

"Helios save us," she whispered. "Rhys is marked to be possessed by Gaelleod."

Chapter 7

Possessed? Rhys wrenched upright, scowling at the row of backs hunched over Violet's desk. Did the girl of his dreams just say, *possessed*? "Hold up. Just wait a damn second. Are you now telling me Leo is like one of those pod people from *Invasion of the Body Snatchers*?"

His hands tingled like they'd fallen asleep, and he flexed his fingers before cramming them in the back pockets of his jeans. The string of deaths, the jolt of electricity that had come out of left field and exploded through his body... Jesus H. Christ, what was next?

Faedrah straightened, her chin elevated as if she were hatching a plan to take on the entire alien force. "I am unfamiliar with the history of this invasion. Exactly how many bodies were snatched?"

He slumped. "No, it was a made-up story, but that's kinda my point. People just don't go around getting possessed. At least not in this era."

"Nor in mine." She squinted, tapping a finger against her lips, the far-off stare she aimed at the wall a sure sign the spring loaded coils in her head were cocking back to face plant him in a big ol' pile of shit.

Violet swung to the left-hand monitor networked on her desk like a CIA operative and pulled up a fresh browser. A few clicks of the keyboard, and she leaned toward the screen. "Too bad the Catholic Church never got the memo." Spinning away, jerked her thumb at the search results. "Last year alone, they recorded over one thousand cases of demonic possession."

Jon shuddered. "As of tomorrow, I'm hanging a crucifix in every room in our condo."

"And we can stop at the store for garlic on the way home." Oliver nodded.

Rhys rolled his eyes. This entire conversation had morphed into an episode of *The Twilight Zone*. Though he had to admit, Leo being possessed by an evil entity described his father's personality to a T. His focus landed on Leo's picture, and Rhys ground his back teeth. How many times had he stared into that face as a kid? How many hours had he wasted cowering in fear?

"Faedrah's suggestion does hold weight, Rhys." Violet returned to her computers and tapped a folder on the right-hand screen. "Check this out." Two side-by-side photos of Rhys' grandfather filled the monitor, one a young Rayburn presumably before he stepped in as chairman of McEleod Industries, the other supposedly taken sometime after. "I got the same hinky feeling from these two pictures of Rayburn as I did from the ones of Leo. Like the men were different, somehow. Not the same guy." She slid the mouse to the left and the split image raced across the center monitor's divided view of Leo before and after he took control of the company, to resettle on the screen on her far left. A double picture of Oscar remained on the right, again half the screen apparently before he took control, the other half sometime after. "Same here. Something's just not right on Oscar's face."

A click and all three screens flashed, shuffling the "after" pictures of Leo, Rayburn and Oscar to the center so they were displayed like a tri-fold brochure. "If anything, *these* are the three faces that look the most similar to me."

Rhys stepped close and his stomach dove for his boots. No. It just couldn't be. But there was no denying those three men had the exact same smile…if that greasy leer qualified as a smile.

God *dammit*. He turned away, digging his thumb and forefinger into his eyes. As if doing so could erase the visual. As if the motion could somehow rewind time to before they'd arrived at Violet's so he could forget this whole fucked up mess.

He dropped his hand and exhaled a long, slow breath. "Okay. For the sake of argument, let's forget reality for a second and say this is all true." He faced the group. "How the hell does he do it? How does Gaelleod jump from one body to the next?" Realization knocked him upside the head, shooting the coffee and toast he'd eaten for breakfast up the back of his throat. "And even better, what the hell happened to those men? Where are their souls? Are they still in there with him?"

"Gads." The color drained from Oliver's face. "I never thought of that. Talk about a living hell."

Yeah, no shit. *Welcome to my world*. Sharp prickles flooded his fingers and Rhys shook his head, stowing his fists under his crossed arms.

"I fear those lights were extinguished long ago." Faedrah's whisper drew his attention, and he squinted at the sadness softening her eyes. It was the same damn misery she'd been fighting all morning. Ever since she woke up thrashing in his arms, screaming over…

He froze.

That fucking nightmare.

A sardonic huff blurted from his lips. Faedrah knew exactly what had happened. Yet, here they were again. Always keeping secrets.

Well, not any more. It was high time she learned pulling that shit on him was useless.

He strolled forward, his body buzzing, jaw cranked tight enough to chew glass. He leaned in liked he was about to kiss her, and stopped just short of her lips. "So, Princess. You ready to share your dream with the rest of the class?"

One of her eyebrows rose. Her gaze flicked to his mouth and back before she squinted. "This ability you have to ramble about inside my head has become quite distressing."

Good. She'd received the message loud and clear. He closed the distance and pecked her lips. No more holding back. About anything.

She smoothed her palm down her stomach, tossed her hair over her shoulder with a flick of her hand, and he smirked. Shit, she was sexy when she got flustered. He could spend the rest of his life ruffling her feathers.

"Nevertheless, *yes*." Her eyes widened to with her sarcastic jab. "Rhys is correct. The visions which burrowed into my sleep provided glimpses of how Gaelleod may have achieved such a transformation."

"Ohhh…" Oliver and Jon crooned in understanding, nodding their heads.

"That's why you were so upset last night." Oliver grimaced. "What did you see?"

Just like that, her breathing grew shaky. She side-stepped and glanced around the room like she would've rather phoned in an exit. A weak smile came and went before she cleared her throat. "'Tis hard to find the proper words."

Shit. Not good.

"Hey." Rhys clasped her hands and brought them to his chest. For Christ's sake, what had happened to the confident girl who stared him down just a few seconds ago? "It's okay. I'm right here."

She nodded, filled her lungs and, exhaling, closed her eyes. "Gaelleod had secreted us within the lower level of his dank chambers. You were bound by your wrists, suspended from the ceiling by thick iron chains. A man stood behind me, gripping my arms to deter my escape."

Above the fringe of her long lashes, her eyeballs skipped back and forth. Mentally, she'd gone back to Leo's basement. She was reliving every fucking moment the bastard had pumped into her sleep. Rhys released one of her hands and cupped the back of her head, lowering the soft skin between her eyebrows to his lips. "I got you. You're with me."

A shiver wracked her shoulders. "He promised my freedom, yet also maintained I must first bear his heir."

Something violent twisted inside him. The loud whine of speaker feedback filled his ears. If that asshole got anywhere near her, Rhys would rip his fucking head off.

"You thrashed against your restraints, demanding he release me." Her eyelids squeezed tight. "Gaelleod lifted a blade. Recited an incantation. Magic glowed as he plunged the jagged knife toward your chest." She shoved out of his arms and reeled back, tripping over her feet.

"*This body you wear shall impregnate her for me…*"

Her whisper coated the room in a layer of silence. The only sound; Faedrah choking back a sob, the back of her hand pressed against her lips.

Sweet Jesus. No wonder she didn't want to tell him. Two strides forward and he wrapped her in his arms, rubbing her back. Had their positions been reversed and he'd watched her get stabbed to death while being able to do nothing about it, he'd have worked damn hard at keeping that imagery to himself. "Shhh…it's over. It was just a dream."

"No." She pushed against him a second time and aimed a sharp finger at the center monitor on Violet's desk. "'Twas not just a dream. Gaelleod means to possess you, just as he has every male heir since the dawn of his resurrection."

No. That was impossible. They'd taken a bunch of ridiculous ideas and strung them together with facts that overlooked common sense. He wasn't anything like Leo. And he never would be.

"Well…" Violet sat up and slapped her hands on her knees. "At the very least, I think we can all agree Faedrah's dream perfectly matches the M.O. For what it's worth, Gaelleod has apparently tapped into some arcane energy source which allows him to transfer his soul into his dying son."

Rhys almost laughed, and probably would have had the sour

199

churning in his stomach not told him he was up a crick named shit without a paddle. "Now hold on. There is something seriously wrong with this picture."

Violet crossed her arms. "Like what?"

"Well…" Rhys tossed his hands in the air. "For starters, I've never once witnessed Leo using any kind of magic." All his father ever cared about was the family business, how to best cheat someone out of their next buck. They might be estranged, but Rhys liked to think that, as a kid, he would've noticed if Leo had been boiling a cauldron of bat wings in the kitchen.

"Maybe he can't." The leather couch cushion farted like a whoopie cushion as Todd sat forward and shoved a throw pillow behind his back. "Maybe once this Gaelleod fucker does his ritual, all his energy is drained, enough that it takes several years for him to get ready for the next go-round." He dipped his head to the side, the corners of his mouth turned down. "Maybe even, say, a lifetime?"

Oliver's eyebrows jacked toward his hairline and he exchanged a nod with Jon.

Rhys slumped. God dammit, they had an answer for *everything*.

"That would suggest Gaelleod's powers are once again at an all-time high." Faedrah wagged a finger. "A dire circumstance, to be sure." She frowned at her feet, chewing her bottom lip. "I must be crafty. Sneak in to pilfer the map whilst his attention is otherwise engaged."

His shoulders ratcheted back. Wait…*what?*

"Whoa, whoa, whoa." He slashed a hand through the air. "You're not going anywhere near him. In fact, if anyone's going after the map, it's me. I'm the only one who knows where it's hidden." And if he just so happened to run into the bastard, even better.

In fact, maybe a little father-son time was exactly what the doctor had ordered. Rhys could stare his dad dead in the eye and see for himself how Leo handled these accusations.

She slowly lifted her head and locked onto his face. "Should he be able to detain you, all would be lost. My presence is not required for Gaelleod to perform the ceremony and inhabit your form. And 'tis my realm which suffers the consequences of his diabolical plague."

Desperation shaded her eyes as she walked toward him. "You cannot enter his domain, Rhys. I beg you. If such an opportunity arose, he would gain the exact arrangement of his ultimate scheme."

No. She misunderstood. "I don't give a flying fuck about his scheme. It's mine I care about, Faedrah. Mine." His body hummed, fingers tingling. A strange pressure expanded in his gut. "I need to hear him say it. I need to see Leo's face when he confesses the truth. Don't you get it? He owes me that. After everything he's put me through, it's the least I deserve."

Her eyes slipped closed and she placed a hand on his chest, sighing. A second passed before she blinked and offered him a gentle smile; nodded. "Then we go together. Always and forever together."

"Oh, good God." Oliver clamped a hand on top of his head. "Caedmon and Rowena are going to kill me. Isn't there any way we can just call the police and have Leo arrested?"

"On what grounds?" Violet opened her palms over the arms of her chair. "As far as the City of Chicago is concerned, Leo McEleod hasn't committed any crime."

Right. Not to mention, Rhys wouldn't be surprised if Leo had a few of the higher-ups in his back pocket. He released Faedrah and paced a couple steps away. Forbes definitely had a point, though. Going in without backup was just plain dumb. On the other hand, it wasn't like they had a lot of options. The people they could trust made up a very short list.

He snapped his fingers. "Got it. I know exactly who we can call. A guy who's made it a habit of watching my back." Tugging his cell from his pocket, he hit speed dial and put the phone to his ear. "Hey, Nate. I need a favor."

Muted light slivered the darkness from between the drawn drapes of Leo's study. Rhys squinted, muscles stiff, crouched beside Faedrah in the shrubbery bordering his dad's backyard. "Shit. I can't tell if anyone's inside. Looks like we might just have to risk it."

"What that I would give to have the reassurance of my short swords at my back." Her frustrated sigh cut short as a light flicked on in a second floor bedroom. "Thank the nine. Perhaps we've dallied long enough and Gaelleod is finally preparing for his nightly slumber."

"Or Grady's up there turning down the bed." Rhys pulled his cell from his pocket. "Either way, I'm sick of waiting. The sooner we get in, the quicker we can get the hell out."

He winced at the glare of the LED screen, thumbed the text app and typed in a message.

At Leo's. Headin in.

A second later, his phone buzzed with Nate's return text.

Check. Twenty minutes.

It had taken some arm-twisting, followed by a firm handshake to surrender every portrait of Faedrah Rhys had in his collection but, in the end, Nate agreeing to wait down the block while he and Faedrah snuck inside was a huge shot in the arm. Especially since Nate had promised to run interference if he hadn't heard from Rhys in twenty minutes. Given Nate's street smarts, his business acumen and ability to keep a tight lid on his mouth, if the shit hit the fan there was no one Rhys trusted more to assess the situation and decide which steps came next.

And if this unauthorized stopover went according to plan, no harm done. Rhys could snap a picture of the map with his phone and Nate would be none the wiser. He could crawl into bed at night believing the half-truth Rhys had told him—he simply wanted to get his hands on a piece of memorabilia from his childhood, and preferred to do it without explaining his reasons to dear old dad.

"Okay, let's go. The clock's ticking." He grabbed Faedrah's arm and they hunched across the yard to the back door.

A smile threatened as he ran his fingertips along the top of the jamb and rescued the key from its hiding spot. Evidently, some things never changed. Or maybe Grady simply forgot he'd stashed it there after the last time Rhys had liberated himself for a night out as a teen. Regardless, that his father's butler had left the key undisturbed all these years offered Rhys a sense of continuity, a belonging Leo had never once seen fit to give him.

Making a mental note to thank his old caregiver in some way, Rhys slipped the key into the lock, twisted the knob and led Faedrah into the dark kitchen.

The stench of rot drilled into his head like a jackhammer. His eyes watered and saliva coated the inside of his mouth as he tapped the keypad to disengage the alarm. He swallowed repeatedly and blinked to find Faedrah's hand clamped over her mouth, her thumb and forefinger pinching her nostrils. Sweet Jesus, what had Grady served up for dinner? Road kill? The entire place reeked of death.

Filling his lungs with a breath of fresh air, he slowly pushed the hasp into the latch and snuck past the island to the opposite side of the kitchen. Faedrah stayed on his heels, silent as his shadow on a summer day. Their eyes locked and her jaw firmed as he placed his hand on the swinging door to the front hall. His pulse pumped loud and fast in his ears, hands prickling like they'd been zapped by an exposed wire. His lungs burned and he silently exhaled, pushing back the hinges to peek through the small crack and check the front hall.

Empty. Though muffled footsteps wore the floorboards overhead.

He jerked his head toward Leo's study and Faedrah slipped through. Her chest rose and fell in labored breaths as she pressed her back to the wall, her focus riveted to the stairwell. He guided the kitchen door back to center and sheltered her in his arm, directing her toward the first room on their left. A twist of the knob, and they entered.

Sweat broke and itched along his skin from the stifling

temperature. His stomach heaved as the putrid odor thickened in the air. God dammit! Was it asking too much to open a fucking window? The entire place was like diving headfirst into a crematorium.

A dying fire sputtered in the hearth, the orange coals providing just enough light to make out the back of Leo's leather winged-back chair, the two couches on either side of the mantel and the low coffee table in the center.

Rhys pointed at the door, aimed two fingers at his eyes and swiveled them to Faedrah. She nodded and kept the handle ajar to monitor the hall.

He crossed to the shadow of his father's desk and skirted the side, a tap of his cell and he used the light from the screen to scan the front. The little brass keyhole centered in the middle drawer winked at him and, if luck for once was on his side, the map would be waiting in the false bottom underneath. He set the phone on the seat of the chair, rolled it back a few feet and knelt, tugging a set of lock picks from his pocket.

Left, right and right again, he shook out his numb hand and twisted the tool until the tumblers released with a slight click. He expelled a breath and silently slid the drawer open. A glance at Faedrah to make sure no one had gotten wise to their break-in, and he emptied the contents onto the blotter.

Curling his hands around the sides of the drawer, he depressed the front corners with both thumbs. The bottom sprang open and he mentally prayed to Faedrah's nine virgins as he inched his hand inside.

A folded corner of paper bumped his fingertips. *Bingo!*

He withdrew the map, the yellowed paper crackling with age as he spread it open across the desk. Faedrah snapped her head around and the relief on her face sent his heart into overdrive. He retrieved his phone and snapped a picture…and then snapped one more just to be safe.

Ten seconds later, the map was securely back where he'd found it, the items returned to the drawer and the chair rolled in place. He grinned at his angel as he rounded the desk and neared the door. Now to just retrace their steps and they were golden.

The rolling tumble of a spine-chilling chuckle broke the silence, and Rhys froze with his hand on the door. "You think that will save you?"

Shit!

He spun to face the room and searched one murky corner after the next. Where the hell was he?

See me...

The whisper attached to his brain like a leech, and he stumbled back, forcing Faedrah into the hallway behind him. A dark fog bled from the shadows, creeping along the floor to merge before the fireplace. The mass swirled, taking shape.

Faedrah gasped and seized his arm. Rhys' jaw unhinged as the man he'd once called his dad stepped from the void, his skeletal smile filled with triumph...and the promise of pain.

"You're early." He waved his hand and the black cloud faded into the floor. "Not that it causes me undue distress. I'm quite anxious to be rid of this decomposing carcass."

A thick bank of decay drifted across the room, and Rhys jammed the back of his hand under his nose. Fuck, that smell came from Leo? He retreated another step, his body twitching, chest cramping like it was being hacked with a dull axe.

No, not Leo. The whites of his eyes had hemorrhaged; filled with blood. This rank piece of shit was Gaelleod.

The floor dipped under his boots and Rhys seized the jamb. Everything Faedrah had said was true. It was as obvious as the evil that danced in the fucker's empty black eyes. How could he have been so stupid? His hand to God, no matter what bizarre explanations came out of her mouth, he would never doubt her again.

"My one regret is how the princess provided you the finer points surrounding our history. Pity that. I've always found the shock in their eyes as the last of their lives fade away most gratifying."

A disappointed sigh left his cracked lips, and Gaelleod shook his head. "Yet, I suppose, such is the sacrifice I must bear to gain possession of the key." The edge of his black silk smoking jacket trailed along the floor as he crossed to the desk. He picked up the phone and hesitated, locking his dead eyes on the space over Rhys' shoulder. "You know the location of the mirror, yes? The two of us have several realms to conquer before you've outlived your usefulness." He jabbed a button and put the receiver to his ear. "Come. It's time."

Faedrah whimpered behind him and a dangerous heat built across Rhys' shoulders, his hands burning like he held them over a roaring fire. Rage blow torched his gut, and he welcomed it, let the hatred and disgust consume him. If he and Faedrah stood once at getting out of here alive, he would gladly let whatever poison he'd inherited rip him apart.

"You *son of a bitch*!" He stomped forward and stared the rat bastard straight in his soulless empty eyes. "You will never touch her, do you hear me? Never!"

Gaelleod tossed his head back, a prolonged laugh working the Adam's apple in his scrawny throat. "Oh, Rhys." He chuckled, dropping the phone to the desk. "I do so enjoy your anger. It will serve me well in the years to come."

Someone cleared their throat and Rhys pivoted toward the door. Relief dropped his shoulders a solid inch at the sight of Grady, standing beside Faedrah in the hall. "Thank God. Grady, get Faedrah out of here and go call the police. Right now."

The butler frowned. "Rhys, what are you doing here?" He entered the room; glanced between Rhys and the entity he'd once believed was his father. Sadness washed over Grady's face, his brown eyes softening with a misery Rhys had never once witnessed in all their years together. "I'm sorry, son. You shouldn't have come."

He scowled. Good God, was it possible Grady already suspected what Leo had become? Did he understand the danger they were in?

"Ah, yes, the loyal Grady." Gaelleod smiled. "More father to my son than any other he's been privileged to know." His smile transformed into a sneer. "Your services are no longer required." He flicked a finger and Grady crumpled to the ground at Rhys' feet.

"No!" Faedrah raced forward and fell to her knees, running her hands over Grady's face and shoulders, his neck and arms. "No, no, this cannot be." Fisting the lapels of his suit, she turned toward Rhys. As tears filled her eyes, she shook her head.

Grief tightened around Rhys' neck like a fist. The fucker had just killed his only childhood friend. The one man who'd offered him family when no one else would.

Gritting his teeth, he leveled a glare at Gaelleod from under his brows. Sparks sizzled along his fingers. A growl built to match the blinding fury detonating in his chest. He snarled, raised both fists and shot them forward, releasing a roar of outrage and the pain of the past twenty-eight years.

Glass exploded as the windows shattered. Faedrah dove atop Grady and covered her head with both arms. The curtains billowed and twisted, the ends shredding under the force of Rhys' rage.

Gaelleod lifted a palm toward the ceiling and Rhys hesitated as the shards hung suspended in the air, twinkling like bloated raindrops on a spring day. He refocused on the demon and a sinking horror slithered through his stomach.

Jesus Christ. They were fucked.

Gaelleod chuckled, the source of his humor no doubt the shock on Rhys' face. "Excellent, my son. Your powers exceed even my expectations." He dropped his hand and the broken glass hit the ground, scattering in an out-of-tune song.

A door banged open down the hall at the same second exhaustion slammed into Rhys' body.

He staggered sideways, the entire room tilting to the right. "I'm-m-m not your s-s-son!" The words refused to form right. He blinked and tried to focus as several sets of heavy footsteps pounded toward the room.

Shit, where was Nate? The floor pitched to the left and pain sliced through his legs as he thumped to his knees. If his friend had been hurt or worse, Tasha would never forgive him.

"Rhys!" Faedrah scooted in front of him, lifted his face in her hands. Sweet Jesus, she was beautiful. He loved her more than any man had a right to.

He tipped forward into her arms. Fuck, what was wrong with him? He couldn't even raise his arms to hold her.

A deep moan formed in his chest and leaked up his throat. Christ, he would never forgive himself if anything happened to her. He should have trusted his girl from the very beginning. Coming here had been a huge mistake.

Five large men filed into the room. "Hold it." The first aimed the barrel of his gun at Rhys. "Don't move, asshole."

Ha! Jokes on you, buddy.

A second thug grabbed Faedrah by the arm and Rhys' ass dropped to his heels as the dickwad hauled her to her feet. He growled in frustration as she struggled and fought against the fucker, his meaty paws pinning her arms behind her back. For Christ's sake, he was liable to yank her arms right out of the sockets!

A stomp of her heel and a grunt of satisfaction bounced his chin as the asshat's face contorted in pain. The dude let loose an ear-splitting howl, wrenching forward as she elbowed him in the gut.

'Atta girl! She would show them what it meant to go down swinging.

"Do not touch me!" A fast spin and the goon's head snapped to the right as the side of her boot connected with his jaw. *Hit 'im again!* Another suit closed in, and she jabbed his larynx with her knuckles. He stuttered backward, clawing at his throat.

She pivoted and raced for the wall. Three steps up and she back flipped, hair flying, landed on a third dude's shoulders and swung her entire weight in a circle, throttling his neck in the crook of her knee. He crashed to the ground with a grunt and Rhys grinned. If his body wasn't so god damned numb, he would've jumped to his feet and applauded.

"Yield!"

Alarm paled her cheeks and her arms dropped like lead weights to her sides.

Gaelleod nodded and two more of his goons came forward, and Faedrah flinched as the first wrenched her head back to whisper something unintelligible in her ear.

Rhys ground his back teeth. That asshole would be the first to die...right after he'd strangled the last breath from Gaelleod's maggot-infested throat.

"Thank you, gentlemen. Your timing is perfect." The carcass of his father circled the desk. Sweat beaded and trickled down Rhys' back as he tried and failed to lever to his feet. If he could just muster a few seconds of strength, he'd beat that leering smile with his fists until nothing was left but a bloody stump.

"Breaking you will be such an enjoyable challenge." His boney finger skimmed down the front of Faedrah's throat, lower to the top edge of her sweater. He plucked the key from between her breasts and she shuddered. "Only a few short hours and everything you are will be mine."

She wound up a pitch and Gaelleod's eyelids fluttered as her wad of spit splattered his face. "Never!"

A weak laugh hitched Rhys' chest. Maybe Gaelleod was right. That look of total surprise *was* kinda funny.

"Secure them in the basement." The wizard turned and started for the door, Faedrah's spittle dripping off his chin. "Keep them guarded until you hear from me. Now that we have them, I've much to prepare."

To be continued...

A Wizard Rises

Chapter 1

Far off in the distance, an eerie wail wound to a high-pitched shriek.

Faedrah jerked her focus to the narrow windows set about the dank, lower level of Gaelleod's chambers. The metered pulse of several red lights flickered upon the panes, and she sprang forward, wincing against the wrist-biting sting of her restraints. Such forbidding harbingers could only mean one thing. This realm's armed guard had been alerted all was not well at the McEleod estate.

"I thought I told you to stop squirmin." Gaelleod's thick-necked minion left his post before the door and clomped toward where he'd thrust her upon her ass in the corner. His hunched shoulders spanned the width of an ox. His meaty paws clutched his deadly weapon; the strap cutting into the folded collar of his black surcoat as he advanced.

Faedrah braced and awaited the wrath of his retribution. 'Twould be a small price to pay in exchange for his nearness. If she struck with her bound feet at precisely the right moment, mayhap she could trip him up, send him careening to the floor and turn the tide of this imprisonment by delivering a sharp kick to his jaw.

"Uh, oh…" Rhys smirked, shackled and strung up by heavy chains before a dark curtain shrouding the opposite wall, his teasing banter at complete odds with the unadulterated hatred in his eyes. "Sounds like the neighbors called the cops. You sure you want them busting in here to find you beating a defenseless woman?"

Faedrah widened her eyes, her jaw set to curtail an exasperated huff. What in all the sane reasoning was the bullheaded man doing? In his weakened state, any punishment he received could harm him thrice fold what she could endure.

Exactly as she'd feared, Gaelleod's henchman altered his course, bore down upon Rhys and a loud *crack* tensed her muscles as he delivered a backhanded blow to her lover's cheek. "Shut your fucking hole before I do it for you."

Rhys slowly turned his head to face the man, a droplet of blood beading on his bottom lip, and though his wrists remained bound overhead, his arms stretched to the limit of their extent, the man stumbled back from the weight of her beloved's lethal gaze. "Hit me again, asshole. I dare you."

Muffled shouts proceeded a repeated thumping from above. A guttural chuckle worked the drawn muscles of Rhys' chest. Wicked satisfaction curled his lips into a sneer, and shivers born of awe and fascination scuttled the length of Faedrah's spine to the floor. Though he'd been nearly dismantled by drawing upon his magic in Gaelleod's study, abilities such as his could not be perpetually subdued.

Even as they remained imprisoned, Rhys' power gathered in strength, awaiting his summons to return.

"Sounds to me like you need to make a decision. Let's count down how this is going to play out, shall we?" He squinted as if conjuring the events about to unfold. "The cops discover the broken glass in Leo's study... Grady's dead body... and next thing you know they're conducting a floor by floor search of the premises."

The man paled. Shaking his head, he retreated another tentative step. A moment later, the index finger of his right hand curled around the weapon's discharge apparatus and his jaw firmed. "I should pop one off in your gut right now."

Rhys laughed. "Go ahead. I'm sure Leo wouldn't give two shits if you killed me. Hell, he'd probably only skin you alive." A loud bang shook the floorboards, and he glanced toward the ceiling. "Oops. That can't be good." Tipping his head, he frowned. "Speaking of which, where *is* Leo, anyway? Funny how that guy always seems to disappear right before the shit hits the fan."

Faedrah's focus slid back to the armed guard, and she lowered her chin to conceal a smile. Sweat glistened along his protruding brow; his eyes darted around the chamber in panic. For all his bluster, he displayed the conviction of a mouse. Rhys nearly had the dim-witted buffoon scurrying for the safety of a darkened corner.

Footsteps thundered amid the chaos of raucous calls and slamming doors. The ruffian pulled a shiny, black mechanism from his breast pocket, slightly larger and thicker than a cellular device, and lifted it to his lips. "What the hell's going on up there? Respond. Over."

A crackling much like sausages frying in a pan echoed into the tense silence, but nary a voice heeded his call.

"What's it like, listening to the inevitable?" Sympathy softened the corners of Rhys' eyes and he *tsked*. "It's gotta suck, standing here while your future is shrinking to the size of a prison cell. I hope to God Leo's paying you enough."

A frustrated growl built in the man's chest, and he spun for the door. "Fuck this shit." He seized the handle and shouldered through, quietly pulling the latch closed behind him.

Faedrah's chest fell with a breath of relief. She met the tortured gaze of her beloved, all hints of anger replaced by the steadfast light of his undying devotion.

"Are you hurt?" He ran his focus down the length of her body and back up again. "So help me God, if that fucker harmed one hair on your—"

"Calm yourself, my heart. I am not a fragile flower." She thrust her back against the wall, employing the leverage of her thighs to push to her feet. "Indeed, if I correctly recall, at last count, 'twas

I who had inflicted the most damage between us."

Rhys chuckled… then groaned. Undoubtedly, his shoulders were all but dislocated from bearing his weight for so long. She hopped toward Gaelleod's altar and scanned the accoutrements of his necromancy for any tool she might employ to sever the thin white band cutting into the skin of her wrists. Black candles stood perched at intervals inside their silver holders. Several leather tomes branded with inverted pentagrams or hands centered with the all-seeing eye awaited the blasphemy of the dark lord's pitiless touch. Two silver chalices cast with writhing, goat-headed forms sat empty upon the ebony cloth…but no blade.

The squeak of rusty hinges made her spin for the windows. A gloved hand gently lowered the center pane to the wall, and Faedrah's jaw firmed in aggravation. Sweet goddesses wept. Could she not get one moment's respite to make good their escape?

A shoulder emerged from the darkness, a tawny head covered in shorn black hair, and a breath of thanksgiving parted her lips. Rhys' loyal companion Nate had come to their rescue.

Placing his hand against the wall, he slithered through the narrow opening and dropped his feet to the ground. Disgust pleated his face into a scowl as he swiped his hands down the front of his suit. He glanced at Rhys and then snapped his head up, alarm bulging his eyes so wide Faedrah feared they may pop.

"What the *fuck* is going on?" Flinging a hand toward the door, he advanced. "I heard an explosion and I show up here to find cops crawling all—" His eyes darted toward Faedrah and his shoulders wrenched. "Oh, sweet Jesus." Running a palm down the front of his face, he shook his head. "Please don't be telling me I just climbed through a goddamned window into some kinky episode of *Bondage Gone Bad*."

She narrowed her eyes at him. What meaning did he infer? She and Rhys were about the frippery of some titillating sexual game?

"Do I *look* like I'm having a good time, asshole?" Chains rattled and swayed as Rhys shoved forward on his toes, trying and failing to lunge at his friend. "Not to mention, the one person who's supposed to be torturing me with pleasure has her hands fastened with a plastic rip-tie behind her back!"

Faedrah aimed a withering eyebrow at Rhys. Perchance this issue warranted further discussion during a later, more clandestine, engagement.

"I tell you what." Nate strode toward her, slipped a small red object from his trouser pocket and pried a tiny blade from the center. "I've hauled you out of some fucked up shit, but this... damn, man, this takes the cake."

A jerk of his hand and the pressure about her wrists gave. He knelt and cut the bindings around her ankles as she massaged her upper arms with numb fingers, rotating her shoulders to increase the blood flow to her tingling hands.

"Just hurry up and get me down from here." Rhys rolled his head back and the muscles in his neck corded from the strain. "Christ, my arms are killing me."

Stumbling forward, Faedrah scooped up Rhys' jacket from where it had been discarded near his feet and ransacked the pockets for his lock-foiling device. She offered it to Nate and, once given, propped her shoulder beneath her beloved's arm, holding tight to Rhys about his waist. "My hands are too dulled to be of much use, I'm afraid."

Nate nodded and set straight to work on the first shackle, the tip of his tongue peeking through the corner of his full lips.

The noise above had gone eerily silent, and unease prickled the hair along the nape of Faedrah's neck. For all the safety the protectors of this realm could offer them, if discovered locked in this foul chamber, she and Rhys were bound to be presented a list of queries they would be wise to avoid. May the goddesses grant the *gens d'armes* of this realm had chosen to explore the topmost floors of the manor first.

"Shit, Faedrah, I'm so sorry." Rhys leaned down and bestowed a gentle kiss to the top of her head. "I was a fucking idiot to not believe everything you told me. I should have insisted you wait outside. I wish to God—"

"Shhh..." Her knees wavered unsteadily as his left arm fell and landed across her shoulders like a heavy sack of grain. "I would have never allowed you to confront Gaelleod alone and you know it as well as I." She turned her head and rewarded his concerns by meeting his lips for another kiss. "Be still now, love, and let Nate finish."

His second arm dropped, and the groan of relief issuing from Rhys' chest incited a swell of grateful tears which blurred her vision. She blinked as he found his feet, his balance and legs steady despite the way he swiveled and shrugged the sore muscles in his shoulders and arms. "Damn, it's good to be back on solid ground."

"Great, now let's get the hell outta here." Nate tipped his head toward the window.

"You read my mind." Cramming his arms into his leather jacket, Rhys approached the wall and, with a nod toward his friend, Nate lowered his linked hands and glanced at Faedrah.

"You're first, Princess. Let's go."

Faedrah smirked at their attempt of chivalrous aid, retreating a few measured steps to size up the distance. "While your offer is kind, 'tis not the slightest bit necessary." She launched toward the wall at a dead sprint. The floor cooled her palms, her hair flying as she flipped head over heels and slipped through the high opening, easy as a secret missive slid under a lover's chamber door.

Cool grass skimmed her cheek, chest and the front of her legs, and she turned her nose to the ground to breathe in the scent of fertile soil and freedom. A moment later, Rhys' warm hand met her back and she pressed into a low squat. The ebony sky glittered with starlight. The pulsing red lights beyond the front of the house had transformed Helios' white diamonds into a canopy of rich rubies.

Rhys pointed to the window and she nodded, scurried to the side opposite him and dangled her arm through the opening. Nate clasped her hand and, amid some huffing and puffing, she and

Rhys eased him up and out onto the ground.

A beam of white light scoured the bushes to their right. Nearby voices exchanged information, accented by an undercurrent of crackling distortion. Nate scrambled to his feet and the three of them remained crouched as he led them around the far side of a high hedge, down the property line and past three gated courtyards to his horseless carriage.

'Twas not until he'd awoken the beast, however, steered them out of the vicinity and onto the road leading away from further danger, Faedrah was able to fully fill her lungs and give thought to their next course.

"We must immediately make for my uncles' home." She sat forward from the center of the rear bench and placed her hand on Nate's shoulder. A peek to the side, and she grasped Rhys' shoulder as well, squeezing her fingers to emphasize her next words. "I fear there is only *one place* in which we shall be safe."

Rhys tugged his cellular device from his coat pocket then froze. He twisted in the seat and pinned her with a hard stare. A weighted moment of silence hung between them, the wheels of deduction spinning in his gaze. His brow twitched and the tension in his jaw went slack as her veiled message slammed home.

They could not remain in this realm. Not if they wished to evade Gaelleod's evil clutches. Furthermore, those they had relied upon to aid their cause must be warned.

Faedrah subtly tipped her head toward Nate. Once she and Rhys crossed into the Austiere Kingdom, Gaelleod may very well detain or even torture their friends in his ambition to gain possession of the veil.

A curt nod toward her, and Rhys cleared his throat. "Nate, when's the last time you took the wife and kids on vacation?"

"*Vacation?*" Nate slammed his hand against the steering aperture and Faedrah flinched, withdrawing her hands. "The last thing I'm discussing with you is the trip I took to Disney with Tasha and the kids last year. You owe me an explanation, man. What the hell happened back there?"

She eased away to settle in the seat, sending up a prayer to The Nine. May the goddesses grant Gaelleod never learned of Nate's children and wife.

"I can't tell you that." Rhys propped his elbow on the door, running a hand along the bristle on his cheek. "All I can do is ask that you trust me. Drop us at Forbes' condo, head straight home and pack up your family for parts unknown. Don't tell anyone where you're going. Close up shop and leave tonight."

"Have you lost your *damn mind*?" The carriage swerved precariously as Nate glanced at Rhys, and Faedrah sent up a second prayer this high-speed exodus would see them reach their destination alive. "People are practically killing themselves to get at your work. We're in the middle of the most successful show in the gallery's history and you want me to *leave*?"

A weary sigh lifted Rhys' chest and he dropped his hand to his knee. "All right, what if you think of it this way. If you leave without notice, everyone who's been itching to get their hands on a piece will go crazy. They'll be like a bunch of junkyard dogs, snarling and trying to outbid each other for even the tiniest scraps." He shifted against the seat to better face his dark-skinned friend. "Once you get back, you'll be able to name any price and they'll gladly pay it."

Nate mumbled something non-committal and veered toward a divided lane on their right.

Rhys grinned and satisfaction lowered Faedrah's shoulders to a more natural position. If she was reading this tête-à-tête correctly, her beloved had just won their verbal joust with a well-aimed thrust. He nodded firmly and faced forward. "Especially once they learn the artist and his beautiful muse have mysteriously vanished."

Tires squealed and she slid to her knees on the floor. A glance toward the front window, how Nate had brought them to a dead stop before the red light stationed near the intersection, and a breath lodged in Faedrah's throat.

He slowly turned and glared at Rhys as if he'd lost every last bit of his reasoning. "Man, what kind of shit mess are you in?"

Rhys' jaw firmed. "I already told you. You're just gonna have to trust me. Besides, it's all around better you not know."

Faedrah slowly exhaled.

"So let me get this straight." Nate lifted his hand and ticked off his points on each blunt finger. "I'm supposed to close up shop, pack Tasha and the kids and indefinitely leave town, only so I can come back some time later and tell everyone you and Miss Marvel Comic here have disappeared off the face of the earth?"

Squeezing one eye closed, Rhys hissed a breath between his teeth. "Yep. I would say that about sums it up." He swiveled to face her. "Unless you've got anything to add?"

Faedrah shook her head, climbing back onto the seat. Her love had assessed the situation perfectly, and done so in a way that ensured the utmost secrecy.

"Well…" Nate tossed his hands in the air and they dropped to his thighs with a slap. "Can you at least tell me where you're going?"

"Oh. Well, yeah." Rhys waved off the question as if it contained no value. As if accompanying her through time and space to another dimension warranted not the slightest consideration. "Faedrah's taking me home to meet her parents." He met her gaze a second time, eyebrows raised. "Isn't that right, sweetie?"

Sweetie? She glanced between the two men. At this point, 'twould seem diplomacy was the most prudent course. "Quite."

"You…" Nate blinked and pointed at Rhys as if this latest bit of news stunned him more than the request he vacate his home. "Are going to meet Faedrah's parents."

"If they'll have me." Swiping his thumb across the front of his cellular device, Rhys shrugged. "They're bound to be sketchy, all things considered." He tapped a small picture and Faedrah gasped as a replica of the map from Gaelleod's study appeared on the screen.

"Well… all right then." Nate chuckled, the light flashed to green, and he turned the wheel, starting them down the street. "That's the first thing you've said that makes a lick of sense." Another soft laugh jiggled his belly and he shook his head. "All righty. Yes, sir, it's about damn time. Ten years, I've known you, man. Ten long years and never once since the day we met have you agreed to meet some girl's family."

Faedrah's pulse stuttered over such a fascinating confession, and she crossed her arms, a secret smile gracing her lips.

"Watch your mouth. Faedrah's not *some* girl, she's *the* girl." Rhys spread his thumb and index finger over the map and the picture enlarged, almost as if he'd magically brought it closer to the device. "Now shut up and let me study this thing."

"Hmmm…going to meet his lady's parents. Now isn't that a fine how d'ya do? Yes, indeed-y, the man's officially been snagged, tagged and bagged." Nate grinned at her in the reflection of the small mirror attached to the forward facing window. "Just so you know, Rhys isn't the only one who's been waiting to meet you, lovely lady. You take him off my hands and I may just have to book *two* vacations."

Take him off Nate's hands, indeed. Faedrah returned his cheery smile, her cheeks warm with happiness and a flutter of excitement tickling her belly. She was only too pleased to have any part of Rhys firmly clutched in her fingers.

They turned onto a wide boulevard and, beyond the span of the windows, the city's vast structures grew closer together. Bastions of industry topped with iron needles pointed straight toward Selene's diamond-littered kingdom.

Faedrah twirled in her seat to check the path behind them. Though a few denizens roamed the streets, the pre-dawn hour ensured minimum foot traffic. No motorized carriages followed their course.

For now, 'twould seem Gaelleod's minions had either scattered to the four winds or been detained, but this did not staunch the urgency bearing down upon her shoulders. Only a matter of time remained before the dark lord would gather another horde to seek out his most coveted prize.

Nate pulled alongside the front of her uncles' building and set the brake. She and Rhys must act quickly, inform her uncles of the impending dangers and make straight for the realm of Austiere.

"My kingdom owes you an immense debt of gratitude." She sat forward, pecked Nate's cheek and swung the door wide. "A knighthood, I should think, with a parcel of lands and a heavy purse."

"I'm a knight?" Nate wrenched his head around as she debarked to the raised walkway. "Well, hell's bells. Fancy that."

"Don't get cocky." Rhys climbed from the carriage, rounded the front and, as the window slowly disappeared inside the door, shared a hearty handshake with his friend. "I'm supposedly a seer." He tossed a set of keys through the opening and they landed on Nate's lap with a metal *chink*. "For the rest of Faedrah's pictures. That should make us square."

He stepped away, but was pulled up short when Nate refused to release his hold on Rhys' hand. "When you comin' back?"

Rhys turned toward her, his brows lifted, and a wave of sorrow capsized Faedrah's heart. Dropping her focus to the ground, she shook her head. "I know not."

Indeed, whether or not they would ever return was only one of many unknowns… unknowns which teetered solely on their next decisions, and could easily bring the fate of both worlds to its knees.

The golden chain hung heavy around her neck and she tugged the key from between her breasts to study its mellow hue in the dim light. Perchance she'd been too hasty in her decisions. Whilst, certainly, Rhys faced a treacherous peril in this realm, to insist he renounce the entirety of his life in exchange for her kingdom's survival was not their only choice. Mayhap for him to remain was the better alternative. At least then, he would be facing a foe he fully understood, instead of leaping headlong into the one place in which his name alone would condemn him.

"I guess I'll see you when I see you, then." Nate withdrew his hand, glancing between them. "Watch out for each other, okay?" He disengaged the wheel brake and then paused, his lips parting as if he meant to continue. A shake of his head and he smiled, speeding off into the night... and perchance that was best.

Perchance his belief they would certainly meet again was the most generous parting gift she could give him.

Rhys turned to her and his gentle smile increased the pressure in her chest. Yet, as he offered his hand, she clasped it in hers and placed the rough texture of his knuckles to her cheek.

To be parted from him would surely destroy her heart. It would destroy both their hearts. "You do not need to accompany me. The likelihood you will be accused of crimes against the crown still remains." Though she would rage against them until every last breath left her being.

"Hey." Flipping his hand, he cupped her jaw and tipped her head back until she met his gaze. "There's something you need to get through that beautiful blonde head of yours. Whatever else happens, I'm not letting you out of my sight."

She smiled, though tears threatened, her throat constricted to an aching knot. He did not understand. How could she ask him to reject all the comforts of this world only to risk a trip to the gallows? "Nothing from this world shall pass through the veil. We emerge on the other side stripped of all possessions save the key."

"Stripped, huh?" The straight edge of his teeth appeared as he pulled his full lower lip into his mouth and bit down. One arm snaked about her waist and he yanked her to his hips. "That sounds promising."

Compressing her mouth in a firm line, she placed her hands against the hard planes of his chest to reinstate some distance. He was not taking her seriously and, before advancing, must fully comprehend the stakes at hand. "The king and queen shall undoubtedly be present, as will several members of the court. Our first steps in earning their good graces... in securing you an equal place among them, are paramount."

"They've already met me, Faedrah." Her elbows gave as he drew her close to nibble the edge of her jaw. "They know keeping you safe is more important to me than anything." His supple lips dotted a moist trail along her throat to her ear and her knees trembled. "You really think they'll toss me in jail the second I get there?"

She wrapped her arms around his neck and held him close. A long internment in the dungeons could be the least of his punishments. "I cannot state for certain, but I fear the worst once they learn the true nature of your lineage."

A deep inhalation heaved his shoulders and he drew back to study her face. "Okay, fair enough. Besides, they're right. As future queen, your security should be their biggest concern."

He released her and paced a few steps away, tapping one end of his cellular device against the center of his palm, the creases between his brows relaying his deep concentration.

His focus fell to his hands, and he slowly stopped tapping. A smile spread, and he simultaneously lifted the front of the device—and his lively green gaze—to hers.

The map to Gaelleod's crystal crypt.

She gasped. Of course! 'Twas the one lot the goddesses had cast in their favor. With his artistic abilities, none other than Rhys could ensure its safe deliverance to her realm.

Grinning in unison, they rushed toward each other and clasped hands, hurrying for the front entrance of her uncles' home.

* * *

Finishing the picture with the habitual scrawl of his signature near the bottom, Rhys slid the paper off Forbes' desk and glanced between the sketch and his cell phone, comparing his drawing of the map to the picture he'd snapped of the original in Leo's study. He'd nailed it—his focus darted to the time display on the top right corner of the screen—and with not a second to spare.

He stood and fished the lighter from his pocket, lit the corner and held the sheet upside down until the flames caught. One hour he'd been quarantined inside Forbes' guest bedroom. One hour while Faedrah gave her uncles the four-one-one about what had happened at Leo's, helped them pack and then pow-wowed with her parents regarding her and Rhys' upcoming visit to her world.

It was anyone's guess what kind of payback Leo had cooked up in that time, whether the cops were still at his house or his goons were seconds away from breaking down the door to Forbes' condo.

Grady's face flashed in his head, and Rhys ground his molars against the misery clawing at his gut. A simple flick of Leo's finger... no more than an afterthought, as if Grady's life had meant nothing... and the only person who had ever given two shits about him had died at Rhys' feet.

He dropped the burning sheet into the metal garbage can, tossed in the wadded pages of his previous attempts and stepped back as the entire works crackled and smoked. But what dear old dad failed to realize is how in killing Grady, he'd upped the stakes. The next time they stood in the same room, Rhys would be packing heat, and the split second the asshole was within range, he wouldn't hesitate. Whether in this world or Faedrah's, the fucker was going down.

A soft knock pushed the door ajar and Faedrah poked her head inside the room. "Everything has been prepared, love. How does your mission fare?"

"Good. There's a pattern to the route I didn't see until after I spent some time studying the map." He shrugged. "Evidently, when it comes to cartography, there's a method to Leo's madness."

Orange flames leapt up the sides of the can, blackening and charring the metal. A parting glance at his cell, and Rhys chucked that in as well. Once they got back, he could always buy another one, and nothing was more important than covering their tracks, making sure if and when Leo tried to find them, he'd hit nothing but a solid brick wall.

Faedrah joined him at the desk and placed her hand on his arm, staring down at the bubbling plastic and warping screen. "Seems an appalling waste of such powerful magic. Are you quite certain of your decision? 'Tis not too late to join Sir Jon and Wizard Oliver as they depart for their island."

Their *island*? Rhys gaped at Faedrah. Then again, nothing should shock him anymore. Besides, Forbes had enough money to buy and sell whatever the hell he wanted three times over. A lesson Rhys had learned only too well the day Forbes had purchased Faedrah's picture, and Rhys' life had taken a sharp right turn straight toward a magic mirror and all the mind-numbing concepts that entailed. He frowned. "What's their plan for the armoire?"

"They vowed it shall never leave their sight." Sighing, she dropped her hand and paced a few steps away. "As too did Violet and Sir Todd. 'Twould seem the four of them will best feel safest together, surrounded by water on all sides. Should Gaelleod petition for entrance, they will be alerted to his arrival and can outright refuse him access to their lands."

Yep. After learning about Faedrah's history, how her friends on this side of the mirror had been involved twenty years ago, for Forbes to use a portion of his wealth and buy them all some peace of mind in the form of an island retreat made perfect sense. And who knew? If they got extremely lucky, maybe Rhys and Faedrah could visit one day.

He grabbed his water bottle off the desk, dumped the leftover swill over the flames and his phone sizzled and snapped. Pitching the empty bottle in with the cinders, he wrapped the cuff of his sleeve around the lip of the can and pivoted for the door. "You ready?"

Her chin jutted in the stubborn way that heated his blood and made every muscle in his body flex. "Do you presume to offer me any other choice?"

Christ, the challenge in her eyes made him want to dive inside her and never come up for air. What sucked is how that would never fly unless he proved to her parents he was head over heels in love with their daughter. Faedrah was too loyal to stay with him without their blessing—so, by God, that's exactly what he aimed to get. "No. I want you home."

Her grumbling followed behind him, out the door and down the hall to the living room. Rhys shook his head, muttering a curse against the impulse to slam her against the wall and kiss the sass right off her mouth. They were better together than they were apart. She *knew* that, and her being worried over what might happen once they got there was a complete pile of bullshit from top to bottom.

The whole thing stank up the joint… exactly like Leo. The asshole had fucked with her head; made her second-guess herself. Fine. If that's the game they were playing, until Faedrah got back to square one, Rhys would just pick up the slack.

She would be safer at her parents' house. According to her, an entire posse of royal guards were dedicated to nothing other than her survival. And if drawing the map for her parents didn't work… if giving them the one thing they needed to save their kingdom still landed him in a cell, so fucking what? At least Faedrah would be the hell away from Leo. Rhys could fall asleep at night knowing he'd done everything he could to make sure he'd put as much space between them as possible.

No. They were going. End of discussion.

Oliver and Jon stood from the couch as he and Faedrah entered. The armoire door hung open, the mirror hummed, sparks dancing along the surface just like when he'd met Faedrah's parents. But, instead of the king and queen occupying two chairs in the center, a navy velvet curtain hung a few feet opposite the glass. Huh. Maybe her mom and dad had cleared out the room. Or maybe they put up a screen to allow Faedrah and Rhys some privacy once they landed on the other side. Especially since they'd be bare-ass naked.

Forbes' cheeks were drawn and pale, his hand resting on the top edge of a large picture balanced beside his leg, wrapped in brown paper and tied with twine. Jon clutched a copper bottomed skillet to his chest.

Rhys frowned as he set the garbage can by his feet. The picture he got. More than likely, it was the same portrait of Faedrah Forbes had purchased from the gallery. Good idea to take it with them, but the skillet made zero sense. "They don't have frying pans where you're headed?"

Jon sniffed, elevating his chin. "I paid nearly a thousand dollars for this pan. It makes the perfect omelet and I'm not leaving without it."

Rhys nodded, sliding his fingers through Faedrah's as she stopped beside him. Whatever the dude needed to bubble wrap himself in a sense of normalcy was A-Okay with Rhys. Both Forbes and Jon… hell, they'd become just as much a part of Faedrah's family as her mom and dad. Even better, considering Rhys could count on one hand the times he'd been accepted at face value so quickly. Their understanding when anything could—and generally did—happen, had been a huge ace in the hole for Faedrah. Shit, it had been huge for them both. "Thank you for… well, everything. You both earned a solid 'I owe ya' in my book."

Jon heaved a soggy breath and placed three fingertips to his lips. "Why does it seem as if we're always saying goodbye, Ollie? Why is everyone always leaving?"

Forbes hooked an arm around his lover's shoulders and pulled Jon to his side. "This isn't goodbye. It's… until next time." He extended his manicured hand toward Faedrah. "Whenever that might be, sweetie, we'll be waiting for you."

Brushing Forbes' arm aside, she stepped close and hugged both her uncles, burying her face between their chests. "I have not the words to convey my gratitude. Please swear to me you will keep yourselves safe."

The three of them hung on to each other and bawled like life-long friends departing summer camp.

Sighing, Rhys crossed his arms, rolling his eyes toward the ceiling. He'd never been one for soppy goodbyes. The thought of exchanging his first with a pair of gay men? Not on the top of his bucket list.

"I spent some time talking with your mother." Forbes rubbed and patted Faedrah's back. "Without giving her all the details, I got her promise to hear you out before making any decisions about Rhys."

Aw, shit. His shoulders fell, and he dropped his arms, striding forward to sling a hug around the sniffling trio. Jon grabbed his belt loop and hung on like Rhys was his personal life preserver pitched off the Titanic.

Okay, okay, enough with the togetherness. He eased back and tipped his head toward the armoire. "I hate to be a buzz kill, but we should probably get going. Leo could show at any time and I've got a map that's itching to be drawn inside my head."

"Of course." Faedrah ran a hand down each of her uncles' arms as she withdrew. "Our duty awaits."

"Give your parents our love." Oliver clutched her fingers, arms stretching until the distance split their hands and she stepped away to join Rhys in front of the mirror.

"Especially your father." A tear left Jon's chin and splashed the handle of his pan.

Rhys scowled and faced the armoire. He'd bet his last dime the story regarding that bizarre relationship was one for the log books. Just the thought of Jon approaching Faedrah's dad... He huffed. He'd have to make a mental note to ask Faedrah about what happened someday.

She tangled her fingers with his, locked her bottomless brown eyes onto his and nodded. "Are you quite ready?"

He cocked a brow. "For the record, you never need to ask me that, Princess. Whatever you're flinging my way, I'll catch."

She smiled, lifting his knuckles to her lips. He followed her lead when she backed a few steps away and, filling his lungs, he hung onto her hand as they hauled ass for the mirror and leapt.

Chapter 2

Pain exploded through his left shoulder and ribcage. A groan eked from his throat and Rhys fell to his back, arms locked around Faedrah in a death grip.

Shit, dodging his bike through the side mirrors of Chicago's clogged expressways had nothing on that trip. He'd officially become the ball in some warped, cosmic game of keep away. If it hadn't been for Faedrah's curves pressed along his body, the scent of her skin and the way she kept her arms fastened around his neck, he would've tripped the light fantastic straight into a psychotic break.

He pressed the heel of one hand against his throbbing forehead. Christ, the inside of his mouth tasted like it'd been scrubbed with a dirty rag. His skin crawled and every synapse in his body jittered as if he'd been jolted with a hundred volts. How in the name of all things holy had she ever survived the jump alone?

Peeling back his eyelids, he blinked and squinted into the dim light. Three stories overhead, pre-dawn rays of orange and pink streamed through a series of long skinny windows. The bottom of a dark-blue velvet curtain was crumpled against his left shoulder, an iron pole threaded through the top and suspended from the ceiling by a thick rope to create a privacy screen in front of the armoire.

An image of the map slammed into his brain like a sledgehammer and he grimaced. Christ, what the hell? As if the sucking vortex of swirling lights and trailing rainbows hadn't been enough, now his memories had to show up late to the party and flatten him on his ass?

Easing Faedrah aside, he sat up and gripped both sides of his head. Dammit. God *dammit*, the pressure was like a vice. The twists and turns of the route to Gaelleod's crypt harsher and sharper than when he'd memorized them in his world. Fuck, if he didn't get the picture down on paper he was liable to burst an artery. Either that, or his head was going to crack like a walnut.

Faedrah moaned and shifted beside him, pushing her black strip of hair from her eyes. Her focus landed on him, and she sprang to sitting, her cool palm meeting his blistering cheek. "Are you ill? Shall I send for the medicant?"

No, he wasn't sick. Pain leached up the back of his head. His stomach flipped. Other than coating his sheets in the sweat of a hellish hangover, he hadn't spent a day in bed since... Shit, he didn't know when. "It's the map. I need to draw it or, I swear to God, my skull is going to explode."

She scrambled to her feet, glanced left then right before yanking a bunch of clothes off the open door of the armoire and tossing half the wadded fabric his way. "Parchment and quills! Bring them, quickly!"

For Christ's sake, did she have to scream? Rhys struggled to his feet, the floor pitching like high a speed rollercoaster, and shoved his arm into the silky mess. More than likely, whoever she shouted at was just on the other side of the curtain, and he'd be damned before he met her family bare-assed and cock dangling in the breeze.

A row of gold tassels skimmed his arm and the material slithered off his shoulder to the ground. What the fuck? The world reeled as he snatched the garment from around his ankles and tried again, only to repeat his performance. What the hell had she given him? The sheet off a bed?

Footsteps neared and he jerked the material around his lower half as the velvet curtain was yanked aside. An entire entourage stood in what he guessed was the throne room—based on the towering pillars and raised dais along the far wall—the first among them Faedrah's mom and dad, some skinny dude with a long gray beard, a bald guy sporting a nasty scar and an eye patch, and a dark-haired pro football player who'd traded in his jersey for a leather pants and black knee-high boots... and a really long mother-fucking sword.

Rhys huffed. That weapon had Napoleon complex written all over it. The guy had to be compensating for the size of his dick.

Faedrah cleared her throat. "Allow me." She gathered the ends of the silk and Rhys held his elbows to the sides as she tied them around his waist like a bath towel. Great. Was there a specific reason he hadn't been given an actual robe like her? So he could avoid standing here like an idiot who didn't know how to dress himself while making the mother of all first impressions?

Silver jangled and he hissed as the sound clanged in his head, vibrating his jaw and jabbing the backs of his eyes like a drunken game of darts. Faedrah grabbed his upper arms and his gut bottomed out at the panic in her eyes. "Hold on, my love. They are coming."

Jesus Christ. He must look like shit.

Two men rounded the crowd, carrying a solid oak desk between them, the stamped sheet metal covering their chests and arms like something straight out of King Arthur's court. They set the table near the armoire and the thud of wooden legs against the stone floor nearly dropped Rhys to his knees. His hands prickled, fingers buzzing like he'd jammed them in an electric socket. Sweat broke over his skin and he locked his knees against a loop-de-loop of disorientation. So help him God, the *last* thing he would do was face-plant the floor. Not here. Not now.

A third guard came forward and Rhys fisted his hands, prepped and ready for the crackling pain shooting down his spine as the asshole dropped the chair. The feet shrieked, sliding over slate as the soldier positioned the seat before the desk. He gave Rhys the once-over and smacked down a stack of papers, followed by the plunk of an ink bottle and several quills.

"Sit." Faedrah prodded him toward the desk and he stumbled on the tasseled edge of his bed sheet. A growl lodged in his throat, he gathered the slack and marched straight for the damn chair. "Draw." She pointed at the desktop, pushed the pages close and kissed his cheek. "Quiet." The room stilled as if everyone present was waiting for him to pull a rabbit out of his ass.

He picked up one of the quills and tipped it back and forth. Seriously? A feather? He sighed and slid over the stack of thick yellow sheets. At this point, he wasn't about to be choosy.

Dipping the hollow end in the ink, he braced his aching forehead in one hand and prayed to God whatever "adjustment" his body needed to make, getting the map on paper was his first step back to being a contributing member of the human race.

The first few lines scraping the parchment shivered his scalp like fingernails on a chalkboard. His cheeks expanded as he blew a hard breath. Jesus Christ, what was *wrong* with him? Even after losing his shit in Leo's study, he hadn't gotten the willies like this. It was almost as if he'd shown up in Faedrah's world inhabiting a different body, or like an alien life force had somehow latched on and infected him during the trip.

He squeezed his eyes tight, blinked and tried for some semblance of concentration. The tremors in his hands slowly subsided as a rhythmic scratching took shape. The cliff walls came easy. Same with the surrounding landscape and trees. He turned the sheet and the pounding in his head eased up as he sketched the castle and grounds in relation to the entrance of Gaelleod's tomb.

The ink flowed almost on its own, as if he were nothing but the conduit to getting it on paper. He swiveled the page, dipped and kept drawing. The knotted muscles in his neck went slack as the path leading through the caves bled from the tip of the quill.

Right for Rhys, left for Leo, right again for Rayburn, then his hand dipped and he drew the deep pit of a yawning chasm, the obstacle they would have to go *over* for Oscar. Lucas—go left, Ulmer—under the sharp overhang of a narrow crevice they would have to shimmy through on their stomachs before turning left for Louis.

Down through the generations, Rhys counted off each McEleod mogul. Men who'd lost their lives, the women they loved and sons in exchange for Leo's greed.

His shoulders loosened, dropping from around his ears, and he smirked. Satisfaction warmed the center of his chest, a revenge so sweet, he almost chuckled. He drew a five-pointed star and circled the location of Gaelleod's crypt. *Yes!* The fucker could cram that up his ass and then suck it.

Scrawling his name along the bottom, he sat back from the desk and reviewed each line, every shadow. In a word, his copy of the map was... perfect. And even better, his headache had dulled. The constant twitching in his muscles had toned to a light buzz. He faced the room. And if his efforts didn't win him the respect of every person in this highfalutin castle, they could kiss his hairy, white—

He frowned. The entire group had backed away several feet, including Faedrah, her waist pressed against the king's outstretched arm as if she wanted to cross the distance but her dad refused to let her get too close. A variety of emotions played across their faces—alarm, fear, hostility... desperation from his lovely muse. All, except for the gray-haired geezer, who stared at Rhys with a calculating fascination that reduced him to a cut of prime USDA choice.

God dammit, now what? He locked eyes with Faedrah's dad, the same deep brown as the woman he loved, flipped the map around and offered it to him. Hopefully, the king would view it as the peace offering Rhys intended. If not, well then... His jaw firmed. He'd just have to find another way to convince them.

Even if admitting his connection to Gaelleod did nothing but

235

land him in a cell. Even if he offended the entire kingdom with his bad language or completely fucked up any chance at earning their trust, he would make damn sure they heard him out. He wasn't about to give Faedrah up. Not without a fight. Anything less would only confirm their suspicions he was incapable of loving her as much as he did.

He stood. The two of them belonged together. The quicker everyone in this room got on that same page, the better. A few steps forward, and silver rang through the air as the dark-haired buccaneer drew his sword. The row of guards behind the queen followed his lead, sunlight winking off their weapons like paparazzi flashbulbs at a movie premiere.

Rhys ignored the warning and kept moving. They could threaten him all they wanted. This was no schoolyard, and it would take more than a few scrapes to make him back down. Because being with Faedrah wasn't just about wanting to share his life with someone. Not anymore. For him, loving her was about survival.

Now that he'd tasted her, now that he'd experienced everything good and pure she held in her soul, to give her up would wipe out what little decency he had left.

If he let her go, his life would never be the same, and it would be only a matter of time before the blackness returned and consumed him.

Stopping a few steps short of the king, he extended the sheet. "This is for you. Or rather, for your kingdom. It's the secret path to Gaelleod's crystal crypt."

The queen's eyes widened, and she glanced at the king. Faedrah smiled, dipping her chin in a slight nod. No one else moved, and Rhys sighed and impatiently waved the sheet in the air. What, did they think it was going to reach out and bite them?

"With your permission, Sire?" The bearded fogy in the gray robes tipped his head toward the king.

"Aye, but tread lightly, Fandorn." The king narrowed his eyes at Rhys. "Strange magics are afoot."

Magic? What magic?

Rhys resisted the urge to lunge at the dude as he took the sheet and held it in a shaft of sunlight. So this was Fandorn, huh? The advisor Faedrah had mentioned. The one whose laboratory resembled Rhys' warehouse space. His face was so wrinkled and weathered, any quick movements and he'd probably drop dead of a heart attack. But, for Christ's sake, it was a fucking picture. Since when did sketching a map make anyone a magician?

"Hmmm…" The guy stroked his beard, his bushy eyebrows crumpled together like a caterpillar. "'Tis certainly something which bears our full consideration. The lad has perfectly depicted the kingdom and its surrounding lands, presumably without ever setting foot upon our soil." His watery gaze lifted, and Rhys was jolted by the sharp awareness lingering in those ageless orbs. As decrepit as he was, apparently the stinky old coot was still playing with a full deck. "Which leads one to contemplate where the boy may have come upon such valued information."

Shit. Let the games begin. "I stole it, if you must know." Rhys crossed his arms. "Is there gonna be a problem with that?"

"Guard your tongue, laddie." Black leather eye patch mirrored Rhys' crossed arms, jerking his pointed goatee toward the bearded wonder. "You address a wizard of the first order. Show the proper respect."

Wonderful. Apparently, Gandalf the Gray was cut from the same cloth as Leo. Or maybe this was a case of good cop-bad cop. Fandorn was more like Glinda the floating soap bubble from the *Wizard of Oz*. "Yeah, right off the top, I gotta tell ya that's not gonna happen. In my book, respect needs to be earned."

"Smart."

Rhys' attention skipped to the queen and back again. While her compliment was slicker than shit, he wasn't about to get side-tracked from this showdown he had going with the scrappy one-eyed warrior. Based on the jagged scar crawling down one side of his face, today wasn't the guy's first rodeo, and the way he sized up Rhys like he was itching to tear him a new one held more weight than the dozen or so blades at the queen's back.

Still, there was no denying the smirk that tugged at Rhys' mouth as the king swiveled his head and peered past their daughter so he could aim a hard glare at his wife.

Waving his hand in the air as if he wished they'd all shut the hell up, Fandorn strolled a few feet away, muttering to himself, his focus pinned to the map. His shoulders straightened and he scowled, turning the sheet back and forth as if he wasn't sure which way faced north.

"This symbol here." He strode toward Rhys and tapped the page. "Where did you come to learn the sigil of such a powerful incantation?"

Uh-h-h…come again? Rhys raised his hands as if Fandorn had just cocked the barrel of a shotgun instead of asking a simple question. "Sorry. I think you got me confused with someone else." Drawing sigils and casting spells was more Leo's ballgame.

Holding his breath against the overall stank floating off the old guy, Rhys leaned in and smiled over how Fandorn pointed at his signature. Okay, good. No harm done. "That's my signature. It's just this stupid habit I have. I sign every piece."

Fandorn blinked. His arm dropped like a dead weight, the map fluttering against the side of his robes. "Helios wept, my boy. Have you not a clue what you are? Your mark invokes a ward of the utmost protection."

Rhys snapped his gaze to Faedrah. His hands fisted and he ground his back molars at the certainty in her eyes. Shit. If he'd learned anything in his time with her, snubbing his nose at things he would've generally considered impossible was a mistake of epic stupidity. These were her people. This was her domain. And if she trusted this Fandorn guy to lay down the truth, well then, so did he.

Expelling a frustrated breath, he raked both hands through his hair and laced his fingers across the back of his neck. What was he? Christ, fuck if he knew. He'd always defined himself as an artist but, admittedly, ever since Faedrah had walked into his life, that description had fogged a little around the edges.

He reviewed the events the past forty-eight hours—all the shit that had happened since he met her mom and dad—and his chin dropped to his chest as the undeniable slammed home.

Well, son of a bitch.

A cynical chuckle blurted from his lips. That god damned mother fucker. He rolled his head back and his bark of laughter shot toward the ceiling. That lowlife piece of *shit*. Faedrah had hit the nail on the head when they were at Violet's, right after he'd knocked Todd on his ass with the blast of energy that had shot from his hands.

Even though Gaelleod hadn't gained the chance to possess his body, Rhys had still inherited a portion of his genetics. Of course. Why wouldn't he? It wasn't until *after* the possession ritual took place, the McEleod women got pregnant. No doubt, a critical piece in Gaelleod making damn sure he held a physical connection to each new-born son.

Which meant somewhere, buried deep inside him, Gaelleod's DNA lurked like a dormant virus. Not only had Rhys honed in on it the day he'd designed his signature, the cellular glitch also explained the constant prickling in his hands and the way he'd been able to blow out the windows in Leo's study.

Jesus Christ. If that were true, maybe the latent Gaelleod gene he carried also explained why he stood here vibrating like an exposed wire plugged into a thousand watt amp. As much as this was Faedrah's world, it was also Gaelleod's. A time before his power had been diluted by passing his traits from one generation to the next. When his strength had been at an all-time high and he'd initiated a war that had nearly taken down two kingdoms.

Well, fuck a duck. Talk about the pot calling the kettle black. Seems Fandorn wasn't the only one to have his picture framed in the wizard hall of fame.

"The runes etched along your arms."

Rhys' eyes slid to the right as Fandorn turned to face him, squinting at the identical tattoos he'd gotten years ago after he'd lost a bet with Nate. "Their language is familiar to me." Lowering his chin, the wizard pinned Rhys with a stare that said the jig was up. "Are you privy to their meaning or is this also something of which you are unaware?"

God dammit. Rhys dropped his arms, a growl of aggravation grating the back of his throat. This was a test. One he was about to fail. But how the hell was he supposed to deny something so obvious? "Of course I know what *veneficus* means. I purposely had them done in Latin so no one *else* would know, as a joke, to piss off my friend because he said when it came to painting Faedrah's picture I was a fucking…" he gritted his teeth against the word, seeking her beauty in the long line of faces, "wizard."

Understanding softened the corners of her eyes, but she didn't look away. Even as the uncomfortable shuffling started behind her, several of her family members trading whispers that no doubt make him out to be the reincarnation of Genghis Khan, she kept her focus solely on him.

"So the princess misled us in her assessment." Fandorn passed in front of him, tapping a bony finger against his lips. He spun and pointed that same finger in the air. "You are not a seer, but a wizard."

Oh, fuck no. This crafty old geezer may have pieced the facts together like Sherlock Holmes, but no way in hell was he about to make Faedrah his scapegoat.

"None of this is her fault." Sure, she'd lied, but she'd done it to protect him. To stop this trial by jury from happening so their relationship would stand a chance in hell of surviving. "And if you plan on seeing tomorrow in the same shape as today, I suggest you leave her out of it."

The prickling in his fingers intensified. Tingles sputtered and sizzled up the insides of his arms. He hunched his shoulders, wrestling the fucked up blood in his veins, before he lost control and this god damned legacy his father had handed him fried his organs from the inside out.

"The princess' testimony is but a minor aspect in these proceedings." Fandorn flapped his hand in the air. "The truth is evidenced as much by the aura which overtook you during the creation of the map, as well as your own admittance."

"What are you talking about?" Rhys squinted. Maybe he'd been wrong and the dude *was* off his rocker. "What aura?"

Fandorn smiled, opening his palm toward Rhys. "The one which consumes you even now."

The king spread his arms, pushing his wife and daughter back several steps. At the same time, the bald-headed warrior, the sword-toting line-backer and a bunch of the guards stomped forward.

Rhys dropped his focus to his hands, fingers splayed, and lifted them in front of his face. Sparks zigged and zagged along the surface of his skin, crackling through a thin iridescent layer of what looked like stardust. A winking speck disappeared under his skin and he flipped his wrist, brows jacking toward his hairline as the spark re-emerged through the center of his palm.

Or, better yet, like he'd dunked his hands inside a nebula and brought some of it back with him from outer space.

"The goddesses do not allow one to simply pluck such abilities out of thin air. The magic contained within you is gifted through blood." The reek surrounding the wizard set Rhys' gag reflex on high alert as Fandorn pivoted and returned to his spot beside the king. He smacked the bottom of his wooden staff against the floor and it resonated around the room like the crack of a gavel. "What is your name, my boy? And, more importantly, what is the surname of your father?"

Son of a bitch. Rhys balled his hands in the air. Eyes glistening, Faedrah proudly boosted her chin, the love she held for him as bright and beautiful as the summer sun on her face.

Jesus Christ. Everything about her was what he wanted, needed… had wished for every god damn day for the past twenty years. Even now, after being caught in a lie, she stood here like a champ ready to defend him.

But, dammit. She'd never agreed to all this.

Neither of them could've imagined the second he landed in her world, the darkness he'd inherited would slam into his body and turn it into a foreign entity he couldn't control.

Now that it had, maybe her dad was right to keep her away. Hell, if he knew what was good for his family, he'd keep them all away. Rhys being here put everyone she loved in danger. Jesus Christ, it put *her* in danger. Not that the realization should've come as a shocker.

From the very beginning, he'd known he wasn't good enough for her. Too bad all it had taken was a trip through time to get that through his thick skull.

Possessed or not, in her world or his, he was still his father's son, and no matter how far he ran there was no escaping the bullshit that wonderful relationship entailed.

He dropped his hands, surrendering to God, Fate… whatever supreme being ruled in this place. The only consolation was at least they were all in agreement. Every person in this room had Faedrah's best interests at heart, and if locking him away or, shit, even stringing him up by the neck is what they believed would keep her safe, then he would happily take one for the team.

"My name is Rhys McEleod." Funny how those four words epitomized everything he'd always hated. Now more than ever, everything he wanted to deny. "And, in your world, my father goes by the name of Wizard Gaelleod."

Shouts mingled with gasps, echoing like a hailstorm against the ceiling. Armor clanged over heavy footsteps as a line of soldiers burst past the king.

The dark-haired quarterback was the first to reach him, leveling the point of his sword at Rhys' chest. "Say the word, father, and I shall run the bastard through to the hilt of my sword."

Yep. Rhys grunted. That sounded about right.

"No!" Faedrah smacked her dad's arm, batting at his hands as he cinched her waist and held her a foot off the ground, her back bouncing off his chest. "Vaighn, lower your weapon. Rhys means us no harm."

Vaighn, huh? Oh right, the older cousin. Like he had the first clue about what Faedrah did or didn't need. "If memory serves, you're the jackass who gave my girlfriend a set of short swords for her twelfth birthday."

The end of Vaighn's weapon scratched a line up to Rhys' jugular, but he didn't flinch. What for? Everyone had already cast him as the enemy, and a good chance existed they were right. Besides, he wasn't about to play the victim. Running scared wouldn't change a damn thing. In fact, that would probably only make things worse.

The dude got all up in Rhys' grill, nostrils flared and hatred burning in his eyes. "What I fail to recognize is why my sister hesitated in removing your head from your shoulders."

Maybe she should have. It would have saved her a boatload of pain.

"Fine." Rhys tipped his head to the side. "Do it. Just don't miss."

"No, Vaighn, stand down. I love him!"

"Your impudence will be your undoing." Vaighn swung the sword high over his left shoulder, fisting the hilt like a baseball bat.

"Vaighn, stop!" Faedrah squirmed against her dad, slithered out from under his arm. Tripping over the end of her robe, she lurched and ran at them in a dead heat. "He's my heart! Do not touch him!"

Sunlight glinted. A silver arc whizzed through the air. Faedrah shoved between them and Rhys swore a blue streak as she leapt into his arms. Fuck! No!

He spun her away and thrust a hand toward the incoming blade. Eyes squeezed tight, he braced for the pain. The hit would likely take off his arm, but at least it would deflect Vaighn's aim.

A hollow vibration pulsed through his wrist, down the bones to settle in Rhys' shoulder. He waited, counting three heartbeats, and… nothing. He blinked. Maybe he was in shock.

Turning his head, he held Faedrah tight to his chest. She didn't need to see this. The amount of blood, the sight of a hacked off arm would be enough to make anyone sick.

He slowly lifted his eyes.

His hand was curled around the middle of the sword, the edge balanced between his thumb and forefinger like Vaighn had carefully placed it there instead of hauling ass with a life-threatening blow. Sparks sizzled and winked where the two connected, encasing Rhys' hand and forearm, glinting down the weapon to the hilt of the blade.

Holy shit. Rhys tipped his head, a sound somewhere between a laugh and a huff of disbelief caught in this throat. *Rock on, motherfucker.*

The asshole had the balls to growl in frustration and try to jerk the blade out of Rhys' grip.

He didn't let go. "I'm only gonna tell you this once. You ever lose your shit like that again when Faedrah is around, and I promise to make it so you will never lift another sword so long as you live."

Her quiet sob warmed his ear, and he held her tighter still. She'd just given her life for his. Thank God, he'd been able to return the favor by putting his inheritance to good use.

The queen rushed forward and grabbed Faedrah's shoulder, prying her from Rhys' chest. "Thank Helios, you're all right." She wrapped her daughter in a hug. "I feared the worst. My foolish, headstrong girl, I thought we'd lost…" Her voice cracked and she dissolved into tears, clamping a hand along the back of Faedrah's head.

Rhys uncurled his fingers and shoved the blade away. Vaighn stumbled back, the handle still lodged in his hand, but this little standoff they had going wasn't over. Not by a long shot.

"Denmar." The king jerked his head toward Rhys and he sighed as the bald guy marched forward, a set of iron handcuffs dangling from his meaty hand.

They weren't getting it. Rhys shook his head. A set of shackles? Come on, that was never gonna be enough.

"You as well, Fandorn." The king strode forward and placed one hand on his wife's back, the other circling Faedrah's waist so he could pull both women into his arms. "Pending the decision of his fate, the son of Gaelleod will be our guest in the dungeons. Fortify his cell with a spell."

Now they were talking. Relief lowered his shoulders and Rhys breathed a little easier. Until he could figure out what he was up against, they needed to beef up security around this joint.

"Then you imprison me as well, father." Faedrah pushed out of her parents' arms and held up her wrists at Rhys' side. "Rhys saved my life. He deserves your punishment no more than I."

Oh, for Christ's sake. He rolled his eyes. The last place she was going was the creepy underbelly of the castle. Especially with him. If her dad didn't make sure of it, he would.

"Aye, Faedrah." The king's eyes softened as he looked at his daughter. "Sparing you harm is the one thing which stays his execution."

Rhys lifted his hands, the thick metal cooled his skin, and Faedrah flinched as Denmar snapped the locks home. She spun and her arms flew around Rhys' neck, pulling him down until his cheeks were buried in the soft mass of her hair. "I will suffer every moment we are parted, my love. Your confinement will be swift, I swear it."

God, if only he could pull her close and get lost in her kisses, forget who he was for even a few brief seconds. But pretending the iron cuffs could hold him was best. Safest.

"It's all right," he whispered. "I'll figure this out." He kissed her ear. "I'm not going anywhere."

A pair of hands grabbed his shoulders and wrenched him out of her arms. Rhys turned, keeping their gazes locked as he was prodded toward the door.

He would go. He would be the ideal prisoner behind a set of

iron bars. But only because doing so was in Faedrah's best interest.

At least, for now...

Lowering his chin, he smiled.

Chapter 3

"The loyalty of Rhys McEleod lies fervent and ever-lasting with me!"

The king huffed at Faedrah's empathic declaration, perched upon the padded edge of his gilded throne. One of his long legs stretched to the floor, bracing his tense posture, the other bent and his heel rapping a discordant rhythm atop the throne's marble base. "He's volatile, Faedrah. Disrespectful. His very presence within these walls undermines the welfare and safekeeping of our entire kingdom."

Jaw agape, Faedrah spread her arms wide in amazement. "Was not the queen appraised with the same disfavor upon her arrival in this realm?" Their hypocrisy was ludicrous. "Was she not erroneously feared and judged far outside her ultimate result as our loyal champion and savior?"

Her father sprang forward in his seat, one rigid finger aimed directly at her face. "You will speak of your mother with none other than the utmost esteem and admiration. She sacrificed everything in the interest of this kingdom."

"As has Rhys!" Faedrah threw her fists down at her sides, striding forward a step. Over and again, she had relayed the details of their meeting—Rhys' portraits of her, his astonishment at learning the wickedness of his father's immortality and how his heart had called to her through the unending span of time and space. She'd conveyed her beloved's bravery—his persistence to defend her, his diligence to stand strong and fierce by her side no matter what the cost. Yet, despite her most ardent efforts, her parents simply refused to see reason. 'Twas as if she stood before them spouting nothing but hot air. "He denied the entirety of his existence to ensure my safe return home."

"Our daughter does present a valid point, Caedmon." The queen placed her hand atop the king's arm and eased him back in the seat. "Though the memories of my world are long lost to me, not a day goes by I do not recall the enmity I faced those two years prior to your escape from Seviere's dungeons."

Faedrah's shoulders fell and she shook her head. Though her mother's validation was welcomed, reminders of the long internment the king had languished under Gaelleod's pitiless cruelties would merely bolster her father's determination to forestall Rhys' release.

The king's jaw firmed to such a degree, Faedrah feared his teeth would crack. "Still and thus, I cannot allow the son of our nation's most perilous enemy to roam freely about the castle halls!" He flung a hand over his head as if to encompass the room. "The Council would unseat us in a thrice!"

"No worries of that happening, Majesty. We've got the bugger chained up nice and tight in the pit." Denmar refilled his wine goblet from the banquet table, plucked a wedge of cheese from a silver platter and used the slivered tip to point at the king. "The entire rank of the First Battalion volunteered to stand watch. On my honor as captain, should Gaelleod's heir think to make good his escape, he will not breach the lower levels alive."

Faedrah fisted her hands, her nostrils flaring. "So this is how you reward the man who forfeits his life to save your future queen? By shackling his limbs and tossing him into a dank hole reserved for our most callous criminals?"

The king sighed. "He *is* a criminal, Faedrah."

"Oh really, father?" Sarcasm dripped from her words, yet she was powerless to curtail her wheedling tone. "On what grounds do you convict? Freely presenting you the map to Gaelleod's Crystal Crypt? Or, perchance, the more bothersome transgression—stealing your daughter's heart."

His face flooded a deep red, and the tips of her mother's fingers whitened on his arm.

"That's enough, Faedrah." The queen's eyes hardened as if the king's anger had leached through his skin and into her hand. "No one here doubts Rhys' affections for you. The goddesses would have never allowed him safe passage through the veil was his love not true."

She blinked and 'twas as if the motion removed all traces of irritation from her gaze to replace them with empathy… and a passionate plea for understanding. "But yours is not the only fate we discuss this day. As the future sovereign of this kingdom, you must recognize our concerns stretch far and wide. We simply do not yet know if the man can be trusted."

A heavy door slammed behind her, and Faedrah glanced over her shoulder to find Vaighn crossing the throne room at a hurried pace. Her gaze fell on Fandorn as she turned back to her parents.

The wizard faced an open window, peering toward the pristine blue sky, one bony hand grasping his wooden staff. Of all those present, he'd yet to cast his lot regarding the outcome of Rhys' future. A shiver stole over Faedrah's skin. She could only deign to guess what thoughts might have been coursing across the ageless canvas of his mind.

Whilst, certainly, Fandorn had done his utmost to guarantee Rhys' arrest, ever since her love had been led away in chains, the wizard had remained silent… pensive, and his inattentiveness conveyed a grim pall which robed her in despondency and gloom.

"Thank the nine you've finally returned." Vaighn grabbed her shoulders and whisked her to his chest. "Your absence has weighed heavy on all those within the realm."

249

She stiffened in his arms, all at once bound in a war between falling into bouts of bitter tears and delivering a hard smack to his jaw. He was her brother. At a time, he'd once been her dearest, most-trusted ally.

"Why, Vaighn?" Balling her hands into fists, she pressed them against the hard wall of his back. He, above all, should have grasped the dire circumstances she and Rhys faced. "Why would you deliver me the hardship of such a cruel blow? Can you not see Rhys and I are of the same heart?"

He wrenched back from her, glancing toward the king and queen. "What madness is this she harbors to protect him?" Cupping her cheeks in his hands, he squinted into her eyes. "Has the vile demon ensnared her within a spell?"

A strangled laugh caught in her throat and Faedrah tore his hands from her face, withdrawing from the masquerade of his concern. Of course Vaighn would believe as much. He'd yet to experience the deep connection of unselfish love… the joy, the yearning… the anguished misery of being parted. "If standing in witness to the man who would willingly sacrifice his life for mine is an act of madness, then yes. I have fallen under his spell. I love him, Vaighn. He is the fated half of my soul."

"Then let us be rid of this foul infestation." He ground out his warning, facing the king and queen. "Allow me the honor of dispatching the fiend who threatens to defile the Austiere name."

Rich words from a man who, as a troubled boy, had all but suffered these exact same odds. "Rhys is *not* Gaelleod." The impending offense soured her tongue, but Vaighn had simply left her no choice. "Or do you also choose your loyalty be judged by the duplicity of your father's actions?"

Vaighn jerked his face back to her, his cheeks ruddy with indignation. "How dare you." Leaning in, he lowered his voice, heated and tight with a lifetime of unfulfilled frustration. "Not once, in all the days since my father's desertion, have I shown anything but fealty and devotion to my king."

Oh, that she could have spared him the wounds of such a terrible reminder. Tears filled her eyes and she placed a gentle hand on his shoulder. "That you have. Without fail, brother." She tightened her hold. "What I ask now is for you to give Rhys that same chance."

Lifting her chin, she stood proud and tall before her king and queen. "The sins of the father shall not be visited upon the son. Was that not your first edict as king, father? To remove the iniquities so unfairly placed at Vaighn's feet? To displace the yoke of injustice worn by him due the traitorous deeds of Braedric Austiere?"

Striding forward, she glanced between the intensity of her father's dark scowl to the bright, clear pride shining in her mother's gaze. "I beg you. Do not repeal a ruling that has served you so well. For all the blessings we have gained by embracing Vaighn into our fold, so too may we benefit from welcoming the son of our united enemy."

A long moment of silence hung suspended in the air.

"There is another choice."

Faedrah spun on her toes at Fandorn's soft summons. He slowly advanced, the heel of his staff aiding each measured step. "The boy displayed surprise over his abilities, did he not? Dare I say, even amazement?" Head tipping to the side, he waved one hand before him as if presenting his description as a gift. "Which leads one to ask if they had not before occurred."

"Only just." Faedrah frowned and then dropped her focus to floor, revisiting the events leading up to her and Rhys' tumble through the mirror. The wizard was correct. Rhys had been caught unawares at Violet's home, after he'd knocked Sir Todd to the ground. "'Twas as if the manifestation of his powers hinged upon the opening of the veil, deepening with each passing moment." She shook a finger. "That must be it. Beforehand, the only other indications of his legacy were through his drawings... the sigil, his portraits of me."

"Ah, yes." Fandorn nodded, coming to a stop at her side. "'Twould seem once the pathway was clear, the powers he inherited were allowed a direct route to inhabit his form." He pursed his lips, squinting. "And once landed in our kingdom, his transformation was made complete." One of his bushy brows lifted. "A shocking revelation, no doubt, to be gifted the throes of such an all-encompassing power, and yet the lad went willingly to his confinement."

Faedrah's eyes flew wide. Her heart stuttered then raced. Yes, yes, once again, Fandorn had narrowed their focus to the topic at hand. There was no telling the amount of magic coursing through Rhys' body upon their arrival, and yet he'd allowed himself to be led away in chains.

She smacked a trembling hand to her forehead. But of course he would. How else could he circumvent the risk of putting her in harm's way?

Helios wept, he'd gone to the dungeons on purpose!

The king sat forward, glancing at Faedrah. "What are you hedging at, Fandorn? The boy's compliance to be jailed dictates his willingness to conform to our rule?"

"Perchance. Perchance not." The wizard shook his head. "'Tis too soon to tell." The sleeve of his robe flapped as he waved a hand in the air. "Quite certainly, without assaying the limits of his strength."

Denmar slammed his goblet to the table. "I take no pleasure in where this is headed, you crafty old hobgoblin. The son of Gaelleod is no idle threat." He crossed his thick arms. "What happens if the laddie loses control, goes off half-cocked and destroys our legions? The castle would be left in ruins and nigh on defenseless."

Faedrah gritted her teeth. How could they not see? Rhys would rather languish and rot in the dungeons than to cause any of her loved ones such a grievous fate.

"Indeed, we would have to be cautious. Until his true nature reveals itself, perchance our best course is to ward him with a spell." The wizard stroked his long beard. "Nonetheless, every indication we've witnessed thus far points to one conclusion.

Control is precisely what the boy longs to achieve."

"Then do it." Faedrah clutched Fandorn's arm, hope sparking alive and anew in her heart. "Offer Rhys a chance to take your test. That is all I ask." She spun to her parents. "That is all I have ever asked."

The king exchanged a meaningful stare with the queen before refocusing on the aged wizard. "How shall such a thing be determined, Fandorn? Moreover, how can you ensure the safety of our kingdom?"

"'Tis a matter of great simplicity, Your Highness." The wizard smiled. "You give the boy to me."

* * *

Faedrah!

Rhys jolted awake, rattling the heavy chains at his ankles and wrists, and blinked into pitch black obscurity. Son of a bitch. The back of his head hit the dirt wall with a muffled thud. That had to be the worst fucking nightmare in all-time history. He raised both hands to his forehead and fumbled the sweat from his eyes. Not like sitting in this maggot-infested shit hole set the mood for visions of sugar plums but, god damn.

Filling his lungs, he balanced his elbows on his bent knees and slowly exhaled, hoping to steer clear of cardiac arrest. Shit, even being stuck alone in the darkness with nothing but his thoughts to keep him company was better than that fist fuck of a dream. Too bad the thick blank wall of nothingness made the perfect movie screen to replay the graphic images.

He closed his eyes and his bark of laughter fell flat against the damp dirt. *Good one, dumb ass.* Like that was supposed to help.

Faedrah had been sitting alone, in the study at Leo's, her loose hair a white waterfall sheeting over the back of the chair. His confusion over why she was there... why they were both there... had put fear in her eyes, and her reaction was so far off her usual, sexy stubborn sass, he'd almost laughed. For God's sake, she didn't need to be afraid of him. He was head over heels in love with her.

As he'd closed in, she stood, backing toward the mantel. The misery on her pretty face nearly killed him. She shook like a leaf, her cheeks were pale, but the way she crossed her arms was defensive, and from her constant glances around the room, she was looking to hightail it outta there.

He'd reached for her, wanted to reassure her, to pull her into his arms and kiss away whatever the hell was bothering her, but he'd gotten distracted by the weirdness of his hand. It wasn't his, and the sinking realization he'd somehow seriously fucked up had covered him in a layer of ice cold sweat.

The long, scraggly nails... the lines of dirt embedded in his skin... the scent of a freshly turned grave and sour stink of decomposition...

Something scurried along his shoulder and he swept it into the void. No doubt the smells in his nightmare were an offshoot of his pleasant accommodations. He turned his head and tried for a fresh breath but, as his chest lifted, it seemed to bump a compressed wall of air.

Jesus Christ. He was fucking losing it.

In the dream, Faedrah had pulled a kitchen knife from her sleeve. She'd jabbed in his direction, but he'd swept it aside with an easy wave of his hand. She didn't understand what had happened, and no matter how hard he tried, he couldn't come up with a single way to convince her everything was okay. Regardless of what he looked like on the outside, he was there, inside, and there wasn't a snowball's chance in hell he would ever hurt her.

Squeezing his eyelids tight, he growled as the body he'd been wearing grabbed her upper arms. He'd tried to let go, not be so damn rough, but his hands refused to listen, and he'd cursed a blue streak as they slammed her against the wall. She fought, kicking and scratching. Her head thrashed, hair tangling in a white mass as he'd stepped in.

254

Their struggle had caught in his peripheral vision, and he'd turned his head, and every hope for a future with Faedrah died on the spot as Leo's hungry leer stared back at him from his father's study mirror.

His throat closed, and Rhys dragged in a breath, holding it against the building panic. Oh fuck, he *was* going to hurt her, make her scream... and there wasn't a god damn thing he could do but watch her torture unfold through his father's black eyes.

The weight on his chest increased. His heart jack hammered in his chest and his skin grew clammy. Rhys shot to his feet, bracing both hands on the cool damp wall. God dammit, he'd never had trouble with confined spaces before, but his entire body had compressed like it was being squeezed by a blood pressure cuff.

He rolled his shoulders and blew a slow steady breath, counting to ten. Then again, he'd never loved anyone like he did Faedrah, and nothing twisted his nuts more than the gut-fisting dread of becoming just like his father. The combination of his two worst fears, of being unable to protect her all while being the architect of her horror, was enough to make what little god damn grip he had left on reality take a long hike off a short pier.

Heavy keys clinked and jangled overhead, and he shoved away from the wall as the trap door creaked open. Lifting a hand, he winced into a beam of light that burned straight into his corneas like a laser beam. Oh, shit. What were they doing?

A rope ladder tumbled down the wall, bouncing and swaying, and he frowned, crossing his arms against the impulse to grab hold and get the hell out of this fucking crater. For Christ's sake, had they lost their damn minds? Letting him out was about as smart as tossing gas on a fire.

His shoulders fell. Or maybe Faedrah was up there, thinking she'd help him escape. God dammit, the woman needed to stay as far away from him as possible!

"Son of Gaelleod, climb."

Wait, that sounded like Fandorn. Rhys scowled into the light. What the hell? "Nah, I'm good. I could use some food, though." And a fifth of vodka. "Maybe something to drink."

The air behind him grew thick, and he was shoved forward a step. "We have not the time to banter about your insecurities. I have you well in hand. Or do you not suffer the burden of my restrictive spell?"

Ah. So that's why it seemed like he breathed water. Rhys gripped the wooden rung at eye level, steadying the one near the bottom with his bare foot, then hesitated. As much as he wanted out, he wasn't about to make that dream a self-fulfilling prophecy. "You sure about this?"

"Quite."

A musty draft crawled up his legs and back, and his eyes flew wide as he was lifted off the ground. Holy shit. Fine, fine, message received.

The muscles in his arms and legs ached as he scaled to the top, all thanks to being crammed up the earth's ass for so long, but whether he'd been down there an hour or a week, he had not one fucking clue. He curled his fingers around the square metal frame encasing the hole, and his spine popped as he pushed up and out onto the floor of a barred cell.

A group of armed soldiers stood behind the hairy wizard, the entire crew eying him like a rotten dog turd. The one wearing the most disgusted scowl, Faedrah's adoptive brother, Vaighn.

"Well, I'm out." Rhys shoved to his feet, dusting off his hands. He propped them on the satin blanket tied around his hips and cocked a brow. "So? Whaddaya want?"

Vaighn lurched forward with a growl, but Fandorn smacked the back of his hand against the dude's chest. Sizing Rhys up from neck to knees, the wizard sighed and shook his head. "Have you slept?"

If he could call huddling in a ball while he watched his entire life circle the crapper "sleep," then sure. "A little."

Using two fingers, Fandorn waved a couple of the guards forward. "Take him to the lower keep and lock him in one of the royal guard's vacant chambers. Bring him food, a tub of warm water and..." his beard twitched as he sniffed, "a cake of our strongest soap. Once he's bathed and eaten, have him dress and deliver him to my laboratory."

Wait... what? No, no, that was the dumbest thing they could've done. Jesus H. Christ, what if someone got it in their head to take him down and he ended up killing them? They'd execute him on the spot. Then where would Faedrah be?

Rhys narrowed his eyes. "And if I decide not to go?"

"No one gave you permission to speak, ya filthy grubber." The end of a sharp spear nicked his side and Rhys swiveled his head, glaring at the guard. Armor clanked and shoulders bumped as the man stumbled back.

"Make it so." Fandorn turned for the iron door, the end of his robes snagging on the stone floor as he crossed the cell, but then paused before leaving. "I surmise 'tis not necessary to remind you, anything less than absolute obedience will land you back inside that pit."

Well thank God for small favors. Rhys grunted. "I'm counting on it."

A small smile quirked one side of the wizard's mouth before he disappeared down the dingy hall.

"Okay, you're gonna have to give me that again." Rhys propped his elbow on the table and dragged his thumb and index finger over his closed eyelids. Fuck, he couldn't remember the last time he'd been this tired. In fact, he hadn't just hit the wall of exhaustion, his entire body had slammed into it so hard, his mind had decided a few hallucinations were in order.

Faedrah's horror-struck face popped into his head and he balled his hand, dragging the front of his curled index finger down his nose and lips before dropping his fist to the table.

Christ, the constant visions were driving him bat-shit crazy. Sure, a good chance existed they were just a residual offshoot of that iconic nightmare, but it wasn't like the source mattered.

Regardless of how hard he tried to concentrate, he just couldn't ditch the needling suspicion something was wrong with her. That she was in trouble, somehow. So much, the second he'd entered Fandorn's laboratory for this midnight class in Wizardry 101, he insisted one of the guards go check she was safe and sound in bed. "Just start from the top. My power is what?"

"Kinetic, my boy. Objective." Fandorn stopped pacing the worn track in front of a long wall filled with multi-colored corked-topped bottles, tinted vials and a bunch of other preserved oddities Rhys preferred not to identify. Shit, Ripley's had nothing on the weirdness Fandorn kept in stock.

"'Tis revealed in the way you are able to manipulate the objects around you." He aimed a finger at the ceiling. "Allowing the magic to flow from your body and influence your specified target."

Huh. The dude was talking about telekinesis. Well, wasn't that a kick in the ass. "Is that how you were able to control the air density in the pit?"

"No, no, that is not even remotely similar." The sleeves of his robes flapped around as Fandorn waved his arms like a goose shedding water.

Rhys raked a hand through his damp hair and clamped down hard on the tension at the back of his neck. Even though he'd guessed wrong, at least he had one thing to be thankful for. No one had made him dress like a monk *or* given him grief about his wardrobe.

The low rise black leather pants the guards had handed him— fine. He'd been known to rock a pair of leathers in his day. The black, knee-high pirate boots—not great, but better than walking around barefoot on the fucking ice-cold floor. The lace-trimmed puffy-sleeved shirt was where he'd drawn the line. No way in hell was he wearing that thing and, when he'd pitched the doily into the fireplace in his cubicle-sized room, none of the guards who'd been ordered to watch him had argued.

Deciding to just leave his arms bare, he'd shrugged into the leather vest, flipped the sides closed over his stomach, buckled the leather belt and tugged the bottom edge near his cock to flatten the wrinkles.

"My abilities are *elemental*." Fandorn strode to an overstuffed bookshelf and lowered a thick leather-bound encyclopedia into his arms.

Rhys fell back in the chair, shaking his head. No fucking way. If Fandorn expected him to sit here and memorize that thing, the hairy dust rag was about to be disappointed. An image of Faedrah's white hair, the silky strands tangled in a dirty fist, screamed into his head, and Rhys gritted his teeth against the urge to fly out the door and go search every god damned nook and cranny in the castle for her, himself.

Strolling across the room, Fandorn flipped through the pages and dropped the open book on the table. "Every wizard has within himself the ability to hone in on the aspects in which his natural instincts are most prevalent." He spun the book around and tapped the page, and Rhys leaned in to skim the ink-smeared symbols and flowery text. Yeah, so? Looked like Greek to him.

"Mine center around the four elements. Earth, water, fire…" Fandorn clapped his hands and Rhys tipped to the side as a small ball of blue flames popped up out of nowhere to float above the wizard's palm. He lifted his focus to Fandorn's face. Okay…? What the hell was he supposed to do with that?

"And…?" Wagging his bushy brows, Fandorn nodded as if he expected Rhys to finish his sentence.

"Air?"

"Precisely!" A flip of Fandorn's wrist and the fireball crackled, the air around it sucked like a vacuum and the flames were shrink-wrapped back to wherever they'd come from. "'Tis not through the ability to control one's deeds, I am able to hold a body in place.

259

Rather, 'tis the influence I'm allowed over the air surrounding them which does the trick."

Right. That made sense, based on what had happened in the pit, but what the hell did all this talk of the four elements have to do with him? An echo of Faedrah's scream whispered in his ear and Rhys sat forward in the chair, glancing toward the door. Where the fuck was that guard? Jesus Christ, he'd been waiting over an hour.

A nervous sweat broke along his forehead. Numbing prickles flooded his fingers, the first since he'd blocked Vaighn's sword before he could hack off Rhys' arm. He shook his head, his heel tapping an anxious rhythm on the floor.

God dammit, it was happening again. A weird, multi-colored light spread around his hands and he shoved them beneath the table. His power was building, and it was anyone's guess what would happen if he blew his gasket in this room lined with chemicals, potions and spells. "So, what you're saying is, since I'm a kinetic, I should be able to control people's bodies? I can somehow keep everyone away?"

"No, no, my boy, you are not listening." Fandorn sighed and plopped into a chair at the end of the table. "No wizard should attempt such a thing. The human form is too complex a being. If an effort is made to influence it in any way, the results could be disastrous."

Grady's smiling face bobbed to the surface of his memories and the tingling intensified. Rhys jammed his clasped hands between his thighs. "But some do?"

"Indeed." Fandorn whispered, his watery, gray gaze shifting to the wall. "Quite certainly, and much to the goddesses' dismay." He tipped his head, squinting, and Rhys got the sneaking suspicion the dude had just taken a trip into la-la land. A second or two later, he refocused on Rhys. "As a kinetic, you must remember your gifts flow *through* an object, much like water through a sieve. They stem from an energy which is part and parcel of a larger force, the cosmos and all it contains. Tapping into such vast potential is not to be taken lightly, and also why 'tis paramount the expulsion of power remain consistent. To do elsewise could harm not only the item which you choose to manipulate, but also you, as the divining source."

Bingo! He'd just nailed exactly what had happened at Leo's, the way Rhys had been nearly catatonic following his balls-to-the-wall meltdown. He nodded. "Already been there. After I blew out the windows in my father's study."

"Ahhh…" Fandorn lifted a finger. "Glass. Another clue to the tendencies of your gift." He shoved to his feet, muttering incoherently, grabbed another book off the shelf and carried it back to the table. "From what I've observed thus far, the proclivities of your magic are mineral in nature. The silver in Vaighn's sword, for example, the sand in the glass, the iron used in making ink, etcetera, etcetera."

Rhys collapsed in his chair a second time. And that also included his portraits of Faedrah. Son of a bitch. There were any number of minerals in the pigments of oil-based paint.

Heat surged through his body and he shot to his feet, pacing the length of the long wooden table. Minerals were in food, water… the god dammed ground and pretty much every living thing. His heart raced like a jackhammer. The hair on his neck stood at attention, and he stumbled to a stop. Jesus H. Christ, the little fuckers were *everywhere*. What the hell? "So what, exactly, does that mean?"

"Hmmm?" Fandorn used his finger to hold his spot on the page and peered at Rhys from under his hairy brows. "What it means, my boy, is that you are a wizard of extraordinary resources." The binding crackled with age as he slowly flipped the book closed. "However, in order to manage such immense abilities, we must first determine the impetus behind their release. The…" he waved a hand in the air. "Flint to the kindling, if you will."

A grunt bounced through Rhys' chest. With his luck, his impetus, or whatever the hell Fandorn had called it, was most likely his asshole of a dad. Nothing came close to the hatred he had for that man.

Faedrah's tear-stained cheeks surged to the front of his brain and Rhys closed his eyes, pressing two fingers to the pulsing spot between his brows. That is… nothing except his connection with a certain white-haired woman who had shown up and flipped everything he'd ever known on its head.

He envisioned her smile, her deep brown eyes and the sexy curve of her full bottom lip. The prickling in his hands condensed, trickling into the ends of his fingers. The way she arched an eyebrow in challenge, that goofy striped helmet he bought her and the heat of her thighs when she straddled his hips on his bike. The fist of anxiety in his chest shrank. He filled his lungs, letting the magic flow smooth and easy through his veins.

Dropping his hand, he smirked. Hell, even the stubborn way she jutted her chin drove him crazy.

A warm chuckle pressed against his breast bone, and he shook his head. How the hell could he have been so stupid? His impetus? The spark to his fire? His light, his love and the only reason his life was worth living? Hell, that was a no-brainer.

Blinking, he nodded at Fandorn. "That would be Faedrah."

Chapter 4

Rhys flipped to the sparring mat with a back-stinging smack. Applause rained against the stone ceiling, mixed with jeering and laughing, and he pounded his fists on the floor to either side of his hips.

God dammit. He could thread a bead of mercury through the eye of a needle, but he couldn't flatten this skinny, sixteen-year-old kid?

Frustration growled up the lining of his throat. Fandorn had royally screwed him over. No physical contact, his ass. But the real icing on the cake? Rhys had willingly volunteered to take part in his own spanking humiliation.

Sitting up, he tapped two fingers against his forehead in a mock salute, but the smiles and nods around the crowded perimeter of the room didn't fool him. Not for a second. These men were loving every smack, jab and punch Rhys' pimply-faced opponent swung home.

The kid rocked forward on his toes, the end of his wooden lance planted between his bare feet, satisfaction glinting in his eyes and a smug smile in place. Perfect. Based on the ruddy enthusiasm in the red head's cheeks, this little victory jerked him off better than a wet dream.

The door swung open and two more soldiers entered, chatting

each other up, faces filled with anticipation and glee. Rhys sighed. Fucking awesome. Evidently, word the son of Gaelleod was in the sparring room, getting his head beat in by a teenager with a wooden stick was all the incentive they'd needed. More guards than Rhys cared to count had lined up to watch him get his ass kicked. Or maybe they'd come hoping for their own chance to dole out some payback in exchange for all the shit his father had put them through.

Either way, once this was over, he and Fandorn were gonna sit down and have a nice, long "come to Jesus." The scraggly old coot had purposely set him up to fail.

Rhys shoved to his feet and shook out his hands, tipping his head back and forth, bouncing on the balls of his feet to rework the kinks in his spine. The whole thing made zero sense. What in the hell had Fandorn been thinking? Or maybe, the more obvious choice, the hairy fleabag hadn't been thinking at all.

If taking the rap for dear old dad was supposed to earn him some respect, then fine. Rhys would happily stand here and get wacked upside the head all damn day. But letting some skinny kid smack the shit out of him didn't prove anything, especially after the phenomenal progress they'd made over the past three days.

Not only had Fandorn taught him how to hone in on the characteristics of his power, Rhys could now control it—summon or shut it down at will. Not only that, by exercising his gift, by allowing some of the magic to leave his body at regular intervals, the constant needling in his hands had cooled to a comfortable heat. Thanks to Fandorn, Rhys could lift a boulder with his mind if he wanted or melt a sword simply by concentrating on the silver forged in the steel.

So when Fandorn had suggested some hand to hand combat might be in order, Rhys had readily agreed. Testing his abilities against a real life challenger had seemed like the next logical step.

What he hadn't counted on was the sly old stink bomb warning the guards they should leave all metal objects at the door. Asshole.

Rhys fisted his fingers and shot the wizard a dark scowl. He'd started to believe they were friends but, evidently, the joke was on him. By ensuring no minerals entered the room, Fandorn had basically tied his wrists and tossed him into a tank of shark-infested water.

Rhys' scrawny opponent crouched low, holding his long wooden staff diagonally across his body, prepped and ready for however Rhys might attack.

A cynical laugh cinched the muscles in his stomach, and Rhys cleared his throat to keep his amusement in check. Fuck, in any other situation, this little boxing match would have lasted five minutes, tops. He would've easily sent the kid running home to his mommy with a fat lip.

The little asshole squinted, almost as if he'd read Rhys' mind, and jabbed Rhys' bare stomach with the pointed end of his stick. Shit. He batted the pole to the right and the kid stumbled side-ways; some general grumbling rippled down the ranks. This was stupid. If Fandorn would just let him use his fists, then maybe he could finally teach the kid a lesson and move on to someone less green, someone he wouldn't have to worry so much about hurting.

Too bad when it came to exercising his magic… hell, when it came to *breathing*, Fandorn refused to let Rhys sidestep the rules. Which sucked worse than being watched twenty-four-seven, since he hadn't been born with an obey-the-rules gene. But, when it came to their working relationship, above everything else, the wizard had made himself clear as crystal. If Rhys ever planned on seeing Faedrah again, he'd do whatever Fandorn told him to do—no questions asked and a pleasant smile concreted in place.

Air whirred as the kid rotated the pole in a wide circle over his head. Rhys widened his stance, bracing for impact, reflexes on high alert and his body tense. Every time he'd tried to dodge the end, the little shit somehow flipped him ass-first to the ground. Well, that was done and done. Just because he wasn't allowed to punch the kid's lights out, that didn't mean he had to stand here and be the brat's personal piñata.

A fast spin of the weapon and a loud *crack* filled the room. Pain exploded through his hip; the crowd cheered. Rhys gritted his teeth and slapped his arm against his side, trapping the pole in place with his elbow. Curling his other hand around the middle, he focused on the kid's face and jerked. His feet tangled as the recruit lurched forward, eyes flying wide with panic. Rhys dropped the pole, grabbed the kid's upper arms and hoisted the skinny fucker off his feet.

There. Finally.

Booing and some nasty cat calls erupted from the guards over how he'd used his hands, but Rhys didn't give two shits. He was done being the main attraction like some side-show circus freak.

"Big man has a big stick." He brought the kid close, staring him straight in the eye. Jaw flapping like beached fish, the recruit blinked… then blinked again… but other than shaking like wet dog, he didn't struggle or asked to be set down. Rhys slowly lowered him to the ground, keeping the kid's arms locked in a tight grip. "You 'bout done?"

"Unngh…" He swallowed; nodded.

"Good." Rhys spun the kid around and shoved his shoulders. "Now go home. And, on the way, be sure to tell everyone you beat the son of Gaelleod in a fair fight."

The grumbling got louder. Maybe because no one could find fault in his suggestion. Or maybe because Rhys had just doled out his first order—and the kid slouched out of the room without a backward glance to obey. He couldn't tell and, frankly, he didn't care.

"You are not applying yourself." Fandorn rapped the bottom of his staff against the floor and stood from a chair he'd placed along the side-lines. The muttering quieted to some general shuffling and whispers as everyone turned toward the walking carpet that doubled as their wizened wizard. "You have not taken full stock of your surroundings. Weapons are not merely composed of silver and stone. Should you encounter an enemy outside the castle walls, you must be prepared to use whatever tools are at your disposal."

Rhys slumped. Was he fucking kidding? "If I were outside, I could use a ton of different stuff." He spread his arms wide. "You stuck me in a room with nothing organic." For Christ's sake, there weren't even any windows he could shatter and use as a weapon. Sure, he could yank a couple blocks from the wall, but where would that get him? Convicted and hung for toppling the castle? "How the hell do you expect me to win when you've stacked the deck in my opponent's favor?"

Fandorn whipped down the head of his staff. A small bolt leap from the head and Rhys flinched as the air squeezed around his throat. God dammit. His eyes watered and he struggled for air. A few of the guards bumped elbows, chuckling at his expense. He should've known Fandorn would never let him off easy. The guy excelled at getting Rhys to test his powers in ways he could've never imagined.

"If I were to recant the numerous times the odds had been cast against me, we would be trapped in this room an eternity and a day." The wizard flicked his hand and the pressure around Rhys' larynx released.

Yeah, right. He ran a hand over the front of his throat, gritting his teeth. Easy words for a dude who could summon the god damned air to do his bidding.

A creak split the hushed silence as the door flew back on its hinges. Denmar and Vaighn entered and Rhys slammed his lids shut, mumbling a few choice words. Wonderful. Now he'd get to make an ass of himself in front of Faedrah's brother, the one guy who hated his guts more than anyone in the castle.

Fandorn swiveled his head back around to Rhys, his eyes narrowed, and dread performed a swan dive in Rhys' gut. Aw, fuck, *now* what was going on inside that pointed gray head of his?

"You lack concentration, my boy. You must widen your focus." Fandorn strolled over to Denmar and Vaighn and nodded a greeting before pivoting to face the mat. "Perchance the issue is your lack of a proper incentive."

Swell. As if the sleepless nights and constant visions of Faedrah facing off against his father weren't enough. As if he hadn't been constantly fighting his needs, using every fucking ounce of will-power to follow the rules just so he could ignore the gut-fisting urge to find her and make sure she was okay.

Nothing helped. Not the late-night drawing stints until he'd wallpapered his room with her picture. Not his time at the smithy spent banging on silver. Not a god damned thing.

No matter what he did, every second away from her left him empty, frustrated and horny as hell. It was anyone's guess how much longer he'd last.

"There is a gathering of the king's most-trusted advisors slated for this evening's repast." The end of Fandorn's staff struck the stone floor, matching the rhythm of his steps as he slowly came forward. "A few select members of the council and their wives will be in attendance to celebrate the safe return of our fair princess, after which the topics of discussion shall include the map of Gaelleod's Crystal Crypt, the incursion of the black infestation and our king's concerns over whether 'tis wise risking our trespass of Sievere's Kingdom to seek out the source."

He stopped at the edge of the sparring mat and frowned. "Talk amongst us has been heated regarding the issue of your attendance. Some, such as myself and the queen, feel it would behoove us to gain the knowledge of your advice before advancing. Others, such as the captain and our young Vaighn, maintain your counsel is not to be trusted."

Not surprising, but Rhys still nearly bit his tongue bloody to stop a long line of obscenities from exploding. So he couldn't be trusted, huh? Since the day he'd shown up in this god-forsaken place, he toed the line and kept his mouth shut, followed orders like a good little soldier. Maybe that's where he'd made a mistake, but that situation was easy enough to rectify.

"'Tis a conundrum, to be sure." Fandorn opened his palm toward Denmar and Vaighn. "While the captain has agreed to waylay his personal opinions in deference to the queen's predilections, Vaighn remains unconvinced your presence will be an asset to our cause."

Dropping his hand, Fandorn shook his head. "Unfortunately, this has created some difficulty for, you see, the king is loathe to extend you an invitation without the blessing of his adoptive son."

"Oh, really?" Rhys crossed his arms, sliding his gaze from Fandorn to Vaighn. In other words, the stubborn son of a bitch was the only one standing in Rhys' way.

Vaighn met Rhys' glare with an easy smile, crossing his arms right back, and a few snickers trickled around the room.

"Indeed." The wizard squinted at the wall, tapping an index finger against his lips. "If memory serves, Vaighn was quite insistent your mere presence, alone, would foul the food upon our plates."

What a dick. Heat surged into Rhys' hands and he carefully lowered them to his sides, clenching and releasing his fingers. Christ, what he wouldn't give for just five minutes alone with the cocky asshole. He'd make damn sure Vaighn shoved his opinions straight up his ass.

He filled his lungs and slowly exhaled past the anger simmering in his stomach. Losing his cool wouldn't get him anywhere, and threatening a royal prince with bodily harm would only earn him a nice long vacation back in that hellhole he'd once called home.

"'Tis quite regrettable the matter cannot be settled to a more satisfactory conclusion." Fandorn tipped his head. "Say, perchance, with a contest of skill?"

Rhys jerked his attention back to Fandorn. *Come again?* What, exactly, was the sneaky old coot suggesting? He should duke it out with Vaighn for a chance to attend the dinner?

A sarcastic huff blurted from his lips. *Yeah, right. If only...*

The wizard smiled, but Rhys didn't buy that fake disguise for one damn second. Fandorn was up to something. Something dangerous, something that would probably end with Rhys coughing up a fine for stepping outside the box.

"Yes, yes, quite regrettable, indeed." The wizard sighed. "Especially since your beloved Faedrah will be in attendance."

Every muscle in Rhys' body stiffened at the exact same second Vaighn tossed his head back with a full-throated laugh. Aw, fuck, was this a joke? Rhys resisted the urge to shake the damn wizard and force the truth out of his double-sided mouth.

Christ, to learn she was so close, only to have her fucking *brother* keeping her out of reach… He raked a hand through his hair. Shit, the idea alone literally made him ache.

Shifting his focus back to Vaighn, Rhys glowered at the one guy who held everything he wanted in his hands. If he could somehow knock the fucker out, he'd finally be able to see Faedrah, touch and smell her. Jesus Christ, what he wouldn't give to even stand in the same room with her, just to breathe the same air.

"You're reasoning has only one flaw, Fandorn." Vaighn shook his head, grinning. "The son of Gaelleod has nothing to offer me should I win out the day."

"I don't?" Rhys cocked a brow as the prince snapped his head over with a frown. Shit, maybe he'd gone off the deep end for even considering the idea, but it wasn't like all the shit he'd done so far had gotten him anywhere.

Besides, for the chance of being with Faedrah, for the smallest possibility he might be able to hold her in his arms and drink in her kisses, he would risk… fuck, he would risk *everything*.

He smiled—the first genuine smile he'd experienced in three days. Because no way in hell was he going to let Vaighn win. Even if he couldn't figure out some way to use his magic, even if he got his head bashed in with a wooden stick, there was just no fucking way. "Tell you what, Your Highness. You win, and I promise to never go near your sister again."

A mumbling hubbub circled the room. A few of the guards exchanged glances. Others bounced coin bags in their hands, brows lifted as if getting ready to place a bet.

Vaighn grunted. "I am not a fool. Do not suppose for one moment I believe the lies which slide so easily off your forked tongue."

Rhys tipped his head back and forth, bottom lip jutted forward like he was mulling over Vaighn's insult. "Okay, let's say I'm lying. You really think there's one guy in this room who would let me go back on my word?"

The muttering increased, accented by the clink of gold coins exchanging hands. Rhys glanced over and rolled his eyes. A second later, realization slammed into him like a truck. A breath stuck in his throat and he stumbled forward like he'd been shoved.

Holy shit, that was it! He relaxed his shoulders in lazy slouch as Denmar squinted and crossed his arms. Shit, he'd better watch it or Captain America was apt to get wise Rhys had just figured out Fandorn's plan.

"Of course there's always the other alternative." He chuckled, shaking his head. God, he'd been an idiot. Fandorn was right. While fighting the kid, he had lacked incentive. Good thing the wizard had locked on to the one thing... the one woman who'd always forced Rhys to upload his A game.

Strolling to the side of the mat, he shrugged at Vaighn. "Something tells me you're just plain chicken."

Deep, red anger crawled up Vaighn's neck. His jaw firmed. "To the bowels of hell with your vile impertinence." Leaning down, he tore off one of his boots. He tossed it aside and, hopping on one foot, quickly followed the first boot with the second. "'Tis with extreme pleasure, I shall render you speechless."

Ripping his shirt over his head, he marched to the center of the mat and kicked the pole into the air. The end whirred a fast circle as he caught the stick mid-flight. Balancing it along the top of his shoulders, one hand gripping the far end, he extended his other arm and bent his knees in a crouch. "I agree to the terms of your wager."

271

The guards jostled for position around the mat as Rhys squared off against Faedrah's brother. For a few brief seconds, he almost regretted how easy this was going to be. He ran a hand down his face to hide a smile. Almost.

Vaighn whipped the pole in a low arc and Rhys jumped to avoid being knocked off his feet. Zeroing in on a gold coin in the nearest dude's palm, he selected it with his mind and exerted a slight push. It zipped across the room and flicked off the back of Vaighn's head.

A muffled *tink*, and the prince's jaw dropped; he slapped his palm to the spot.

The coin hit the mat and wheeled a few feet away. The men standing in its flight plan retreated until it spun a whirly-gig then lay flat. The owner held up both arms to keep everyone back, glanced left then right before stomping forward and snatching his money off the ground.

Rhys compressed his lips, trapping the silent laugh cinching his stomach. Ah God, that was good. Like taking candy from a baby.

Vaighn turned back to the fight, focus narrowed and a vein pulsing in this neck. "It shall take more than a simple gold coin to defeat me, Wizard."

"Good." It was high time they got a few things straight. "In fact, I'm counting on it." Rhys pinpointed two dozen gold pieces with his mind. "Tally 'em up quick, fellas. This party's about to get messy."

Tension spiked in the room and musical jingles sang off the stone walls as the guards counted the money in their palms. Rhys would pay back every dime if he had to. The cost would be worth teaching this royal prick a thing or two.

Faedrah's brother flipped the wooden lance around and held it high over his right shoulder. Rhys sized him up from the opposite side of the mat, both of them walking a slow circle. Though maybe half an inch taller, Vaighn's arms weren't any thicker. His weight and muscle mass seemed equal to what Rhys carried. It really did suck Fandorn insisted on the hands off rule. Just the thought of pounding some flesh out of that smug fucker's face gave Rhys a buzz he hadn't enjoyed for a week.

Vaighn smirked, jabbing the end of the lance at Rhys' chest. Adrenaline surged, and Rhys levitated the coins he'd selected, drawing them closer, a swarm of gold bees funneling and winking in the air. Vaighn's knuckles whitened on the lance. He filled his lungs and, the split second he moved, Rhys let the fuckers fly.

Each piece zipped toward its intended target. Gold flashed and spun. Rhythmic clinks zinged through the room as Vaighn batted the coins away like a series of blinding, high-speed pitches. They flew in every direction. The guards ducked and scrambled, arms covering their heads to deflect the out of control missiles.

A sweep of his hand and Rhys gathered them up, plucking one after the next as they soared through the air. He pivoted toward Vaighn as the prince spun low. A stinging *smack* burst through Rhys' ankle and he stumbled sideways. God dammit, the fucker was fast. He tripped on the stick, hit the mat on his hands and the men cheered. Tucking his shoulder, he conserved his momentum and somersaulted, pushing to his feet. But no way was the asshole faster than thought.

Spreading both arms, Rhys collected every ounce of gold in the room and thrust his hands forward.

A whirling cloud of gold pummeled the prince's chest. Coins sprayed like pounding water, ricocheting in a stream to either side. Arms pin-wheeling, neck strained, Vaighn reeled back on his heels. *Not so fast, you royal motherfucker.* Rhys flicked his wrist and the wave of incoming coins changed direction, shoving Faedrah's brother forward like a rag doll. A clench of his fist and they stuck to Vaighn's skin, aligning down his outstretched arms, slapping in place like gold-plated armor until his torso was covered from shoulders to hips.

Rhys jerked his chin and the metal hoisted the prince off the mat, twirling him around like a loose kite, lifting him higher and higher. A loud grunt punched from his throat and a few coins rained down as Vaighn's spine slammed the ceiling.

Well, looky here. Propping his hands on his hips, Rhys squinted up at Faedrah's brother. Pinned. In less than five minutes flat. Maybe that would teach the asshole some manners.

Vaighn gnashed his teeth, head thrashing. "Release me at once, you black-hearted demon, or I shall order you shackled and strung up in chains."

Or maybe not. Snagging one of the loose coins near his foot, Rhys floated it in front of Vaighn's face, tipped the thin edge toward the prince and tapped it against his forehead.

Vaighn stopped squirming.

"See, now, this is the part where we find out the difference between you and me." Rhys shook his head, sighed and crossed his arms. "I'm sure by now everyone here understands it wouldn't take much for me to maim or even kill you."

Vaighn squinted, anger hissing through his teeth. "Make it so and you shall not take one step out of this chamber alive."

"Right, right, you'd like me dead and all that shit. I get it." Rhys nodded, dropped his focus to the mat and shrugged. "But let's be clear. That's not the reason I won't return the favor." He tipped his head back and stared up at the prince. "Whether or not I kill you doesn't have anything to do with you, or me, or anyone else in this room. It has to do with Faedrah. Because if I kill you, she hurts."

Rhys lowered his chin and turned in a circle, meeting the eyes of every man standing near the mat. "It's real simple, folks. I bring harm to any one of you and her heart breaks... and I swear to God, there's no way in *hell* I'm ever gonna let that happen. You got that? She's the only thing that matters to me. Her, and the safety of her future kingdom."

Spinning on his heel, Rhys released his hold and the gold pieces showered to the mat. Vaighn dropped to his chest with a thud.

The guards peeled off, giving him a wide berth as Rhys strode for the exit. Grabbing the handle, he glanced over his shoulder to find Vaighn shoving to his hands and knees. "Try to remember that when I see you tonight… *at dinner.*"

With a parting glare around the room, Rhys pushed through the doorway and left.

Chapter 5

The steady cadence of a determined stride echoed down the long corridor, and Faedrah lifted her gaze from the floor. Rhys. Though he had not yet entered the banquet hall, the strike of his boot heels were as familiar to her as the beat of her heart.

She smoothed down the folds of her deep red gown and then cursed her trembling fingers. 'Twas restlessness over the night's festivities… her desperate longing to ascertain her beloved remained sound in body and spirit, nothing more. If any concerns passed between them this eve, 'twould be for him. The pangs he surely endured chained within the castle dungeons far exceeded the terrors she'd suffered these past three nights. Though fatigued nearly beyond reason, she would do her utmost to convince him all was well.

Filling her lungs to their fullest extent, she straightened the delicate lace edging along her wrists, fidgeted with the ruby beads sewn across the top of her corset. She would not act the swooning maiden whilst Rhys was near.

"I daresay you're as skittish as a church mouse." Vaighn sauntered to a stop where she stood before the open terrace doors, shaking his head with a chuckle. "The man has lamented your absence for three days. Have faith, Princess. The fit of your gown will be the furthest thing from his mind."

Heat leached up her neck, yet she shot Vaighn an icy scowl. If only the mere impression of her attire encompassed the totality of her worries. "You do not know him." It had been a fool's errand trying to conceal the dark smudges below her eyes, the ashen pallor of her cheeks. She twirled the golden chain around her neck and the key flipped inside the safety of her cleavage. "Rhys is sure to take one look upon my face and determine with uncanny accuracy the severity of my exhaustion."

The footsteps ceased and Faedrah hesitated, forestalling the urge to turn lest her beloved take issue with her appearance. The heat of his gaze tingled along the side of her cheek, down her throat and the slope of her bare shoulder.

Yes... Her lashes fluttered, her heartbeat slowed as the potency of his stare traversed the distance and seeped into her form. At last, at last, he was here.

"Oh, I know him well enough." Her brother tipped his head toward the hall's wide double archway, a royal guard standing in full dress regalia to either side of the open doors. "Speak of the devil and he doth appear."

And still, she waited, her breath sliding easy and free through her lungs for the first in three days... basking in the strength of his presence, gathering the power of him from across the room and clasping it close to her heart. Goddesses wept. Simply occupying the same space with him made her terrors flee, as if everything she feared shrank and faded under the influence of his attendance, alone.

Denmar turned from his private discussion with the king and queen and crossed his thick arms, one eyebrow cocked in calculating assessment of her lover's appearance. Conversations trailed off as two council members followed the captain's steely stare toward the banquet hall entrance. Councilman D'Anthe pressed a lace-edged kerchief to his mouth and withdrew a step. Artemis Vlandross smacked a palm to his chest and paled.

Faedrah smirked, her hair whispering across her back with the subtle shake of her head. Had they assumed the son of Gaelleod would appear as a shy, reticent devotee? She turned to Rhys with a smile. What incompetent foo—

Her shoulders wrenched, and her brother grunted in amusement at her side. Sweet tits, the man all but kindled the atmosphere in the room. Energy crackled in the air about him, bolstered by the sheer magnitude of his confidence and wrath. For all her preparedness, 'twas as if a sunlit cloud had burst through the doors and a lightning bolt had struck the floor to announce Rhys' arrival.

Black leather encased his body from shoulder to boot, the sides of his waistcoat flipped closed and cinched with a plain silver buckle. The snug fit of his attire pulled taut across the span of his chest, his trim hips and the thick tension in his upper thighs. Yet 'twas the absence of a shirt which granted her full view of each defined curve in his arms, and made her palms greedy to bathe in the heat of his skin beneath the deep leather V arrowing down to his stomach.

Wide silver vambraces adorned his forearms, etched with the sigil of his signature, though how he'd managed to pry them on without a hinge and clasp remained an utter mystery.

A thrill coursed her skin as he set foot in her direction, the smoldering jade embers in his gaze holding her rapt to the floor. And yet, at once, the need to race across the room, to leap into his arms and experience the hard planes of his chest pressed against her breasts, grew to such intensity, she stepped forward to more quickly close the distance.

"No." Vaighn seized her elbow and pulled her back to his side. "Let him come to you. You are our kingdom's future queen, and too many meddling eyes would eagerly condemn your refusal to show the son of Gaelleod his proper place."

Faedrah scowled at such a ridiculous notion, yet a quick glance about the room confirmed her brother was correct. In the name of diplomacy, her father had insisted the senior most council members and their wives be present during the evening's festivities—an opportunity to provide the commonwealth a voice before any decisions had been made. Some of their expressions held candid fascination, others a hint of something more sinister should she falter in the slightest at upholding her duty to the crown.

Anger scored the inside of her chest, tainted by the sour bite of indignation. Whilst she craved the firm band of Rhys' arms, longed to meet his lips in a long-awaited kiss, the attendees inside this room held her to some lofty ideal she was hard-pressed to achieve.

She refocused on her beloved, fisting her hands as he neared. For all the goddesses in paradise, what woman *wouldn't* melt under the dark perusal of such a heated stare? What courtier of the female persuasion would deny a man of his mouth-watering temptations an invitation into her bed… if only to languish under the glorious control of his tormenting kiss?

He squinted, yet whether in response to the weariness etched upon her face or her aggravation over being detained by protocol, she had not a clue.

Vaighn released her and edged slightly in front as Rhys stopped but an arm's length away. Her jaw firmed as she fought to inquire what, in all of Helios' bright reign, her brother thought he was doing.

Everyone present fully understood protecting her was his sworn duty. As her elder sibling and the senior-most member of the royal guard, he had every right to determine the quality of any man who petitioned an audience with the woman who stood first in line to the Austiere throne. Still and thus, had the three of them been in the sparring room, she would have whacked him over the head with one of her short swords before shoving him out of the way.

With a slow tip of his head, Rhys shifted his attention to her brother. He edged his weight onto one hip and a raised vein bulged in his biceps as he crossed his arms. "You got something to say?"

As a way of reply, Vaighn offered his hand in greeting, and the surprise which shot Rhys' brows heavenward was an exact replica of the amazement skipping through her head. One did not… under the most dire of circumstances… freely clasp arms with a wizard. Especially one of Rhys' limitless abilities. Unless, of course, a bond of deepest trust thwarted the slightest indication of any harm.

Rhys lifted his gaze from Vaighn's open hand to his face. His eyes narrowed in suspicion, and Faedrah would have given her seat upon the throne to know what passed between them in the silence which ensued.

Three heartbeats pounded in her ears before Rhys unlocked his arms and grasped Vaighn's forearm in a hearty handshake, though he did not smile, and an uneasy friction thickened the air between them.

"This afternoon's match was well played, Wizard." Vaighn cleared his throat, placing his free hand on Rhys' shoulder.

Faedrah frowned. What match?

Her beloved's eyes locked on hers, a mischievous spark dancing in their depths as Vaighn urged him near. "Nevertheless, if you embarrass my sister…" he whispered, fingertips whitening against the black leather of Rhys' waistcoat. "If you take action which mars her reputation or your eye so much as twitches in another skirt's direction, I shall make it my life's ambition to ensure you never again ascend out of that hole. Do you fully comprehend my meaning?"

One corner of Rhys' lips curled in a sly smile. "I do."

And Faedrah did, as well. In stating as much, Vaighn had just granted them his blessing.

The gratitude which swelled for her adoptive brother brought a sheen of warm tears to her eyes, and she returned Rhys' smile, placing a hand on her brother's back. "Thank you, Vaighn."

He nodded, withdrawing a step as he removed his grip from Rhys' shoulder. A sidelong glance at her, and Vaighn tipped his head toward the open doors leading onto the terrace. "Perchance your reunion with the princess would be best accompanied by a breath of fresh air."

Turning toward the room, he was pulled up short when Rhys

delayed the release of Vaighn's arm. "For what it's worth, I owe you one. I won't forget this, Your Highness."

Her brother huffed. "Nor shall I, Wizard. Nor shall I."

He ambled off toward her parents, hands swinging with the easy gait of his stride. That was, until one of her handmaidens crossed before him, lips pursed in coy flirtation, and he veered after the girl at an increased pace.

Rhys swung back around to face her and Faedrah boosted her chin, squinting at him through the fringe of her lashes. "What match?"

"Later." He grabbed her arm and spun her toward the terrace.

Her feet tangled in her skirts at the quick rotation. Clumsy from lack of proper sleep, she stumbled and fell into the unyielding tower of Rhys' shoulder. He pivoted, scooped her into his arms and, amid a cascade of shocked gasps, strode through the open doors and carried her down the veranda, well out of earshot and devoid of curious stares in the hall.

The moment her feet touched ground, he captured her lips with his. His fingers dove into her hair with the same urgency he thrust his tongue into her mouth… as if his hunger for her could no longer wait to be sated. As if his desire to be inside her would tolerate not one more moment's delay.

She sighed as the magnetic taste of him flooded her senses, shuddered beneath him as the potency of his kiss slid hot and sleek through her veins. Banding one arm about her waist, he jerked her to his hips. A thrill burst in her stomach as the firm ridge of his arousal pressed her lower belly, coasting down her inner thighs into the soles of her feet. Swirling her tongue in time with his, she followed his lead as he angled her head, allowing him free reign to slake his thirst.

His low growl vibrated against her lips. She wrapped her arms about his broad shoulders, fisted her fingers in his glossy hair. At once, a portion of his strength suffused her skin, gifting her deliverance.

All her fears… all her weakness withered and died under the searing ecstasy of his kiss. She became lost in the flick of his tongue, the heat of his breath as it bathed her cheek, the force of his splayed hand pressing her back as he trailed opened-mouthed kisses down to the top of her corset.

"Jesus H. *Christ*, you smell good." The rasp of his beard cast an array of white, hot tingles into her breasts. She bit her bottom lip, squeezing her eyes tight as her nipples pebbled and ached against the unyielding constriction of her stays. "You taste like fucking Heaven."

Each spot his supple lips touched sparked and sizzled as if he somehow bathed her in his magic, the small dip between her collar bones, the side of her throat, the ticklish skin beneath the lobe of her ear.

He balanced his forehead against hers and peered into her eyes, keeping her close and locked tight to his hips about the waist. "I missed you."

Heart fluttering with giddy excitement, she smiled and smoothed her palms up and down the rigid tension in his arms. "You've conveyed your misery over our parting quite soundly."

One of his hands met her cheek, his fingers threaded through her hair, and he eased away to run the tip of his thumb along the thin skin beneath her lower lashes. "So, what's the plan for getting rid of your nightmares?"

Her eyelids slipped closed and she shook her head. Whilst she'd no doubts one glance and he would read the measure of weariness upon her face, for him to pinpoint the cause of her suffering with such surety confirmed their profound connection had not waned in the slightest, and he rightly bore the title of a wizard of unsurpassed renown. "How is it you always fully comprehend what transpires in my head?"

He chuckled, though his smile edged away almost as quickly as it had appeared. "I've been getting visions of you facing off against Gaelleod ever since Denmar tossed me in the pit. It just took me a couple days to figure out they always come at night, most likely while you're sleeping."

She dropped her arms from around his shoulders and sighed, turned away and strode toward the balcony. That he'd been made to share her nightly sojourns into the terrors of Gaelleod's cruelty settled on her shoulders like a yoke. Especially submerged in a place of such repulsiveness, a darkness so complete, Helios dared not show his face. "There is nothing to be done. The sleeping tonics only make matters worse, I'm afraid. Once taken, I'm unable to wake and escape the dark lord's relentless pursuit."

"Dammit. Yeah, I thought something like that might happen." He joined her at the railing and propped his hip against the side, standing close enough his left thigh heated the back of her leg through her skirts. His hand smoothed a weft of hair over her shoulder, down her side to her waist until he'd encircled her, once again, in his steady embrace. "All right, then what about the key? Have you tried taking it off to see if the two are connected?"

She shook her head and placed a gentle kiss on his arm, turning her cheek to his shoulder. If he held her just so, perchance she could glean a few precious moments of uninterrupted slumber. She could rest safe and protected in his arms. "My mother suggested as much, but I fear not. Last eve, I removed the key and, in doing so, the veil closed. 'Twas not a scant moment later, Gaelleod's hold on me amplified to a shriek of unending rage. Almost as if, in shuttering the veil's connection to your world, his strength in this realm multiplied thricefold, allowing him even more sway over my thoughts."

He flinched beside her and she lifted her head to find a thunderous tempest gathering in his gaze. "That son of a bitch." A sardonic chuckle worked the muscles of his throat. "That asshole is funneling his power through the veil. From this time to the future. That has to be it. That explains how he was able to infiltrate your dreams there and why he's so hell bent on getting the key. Here is where Leo's always been the strongest, and he got his boxers got

283

all wedged in a knot when you broke the connection."

She blinked as another, more terrifying, realization occurred. "And, perchance, this explains the black infestation invading our forest. Somehow, Gaelleod has found a way to leach the energy from the ground and send it back through time to aid in his quest for domination."

"Jesus Christ, Faedrah." Rhys' lips landed on the crown of her head and his deep exhalation warmed her hair. "Shit. That fucker's got us right where he wants us." He propped his chin atop her head and sighed. "Okay, let's think about this logically for a second. The only time you didn't have the nightmares was when you were at the warehouse. Maybe the answer is that you need to sleep with me."

She leaned away from him, searching his face, and then chuckled softly at the devilish way he bounced his brows. "I'd already considered as much… although it's highly improbable sleep would merit our agenda, and the guards stationed outside your chamber door would most assuredly wag their tongues to every willing ear regarding the shameless activities they'd overheard inside."

His hold on her tightened a degree. "And that would be bad?"

She huffed, turning her face toward the muted gold and pink streaks searing the evening sky. Were the answer that simple, she would have joined him two nights hence, the opinion of her parents and ensuing rumors be damned. "You're missing the point, my love. When at my uncles' home, abed with you in their chambers, Gaelleod was still able to invade my slumber." Her tired eyes fell closed for a brief moment. Sleep crept in along the periphery and she forced her lids open, her body jerking as she fought to remain awake. "As much as I would relish the security and… *exhilaration* found in your bed, I fear the answer is more complex than where, or in whose arms, I lay my head."

A rumble of discontent built in his chest and he curled his body around her, one hand cupping the side of her face, returning her cheek to his chest. "God dammit, it's killing me the bastard is

284

putting you through this. We've got to be missing a piece. There's got to be *something* I can do to stop this from happening."

The last shining curve of Helios' bright descent sparkled from between a deep crevasse in the surrounding mountainside and, with it, the horologist's mallet struck the setting bell. A melodious chime rang outward from the tower, reverberating through the air with a song as smooth and melancholy as the onset of night.

Not a heartbeat later, a lighter bell pealed through the open doors, announcing the commencement of the evening meal.

Of course, Rhys would take it upon himself to divine the answer. Not one doubt lingered, he would labor tirelessly until her suffering had ceased. She placed her hand upon his chest, slipping her fingertips beneath the edge of his leather tunic to bask in the heat emanating from his skin. "'Tis of no matter now that I've returned to your arms. Truly. Your presence this eve allows me more comfort than I've partaken of since the moment we parted."

A shadow appeared in the square of light from the banquet hall and she peeked over the slope of Rhys' shoulder to lock eyes with Vaighn.

"Our guests are taking their seats." He jerked his head toward the room, turned and disappeared inside.

"Come on." Rhys squeezed her tight before releasing her and, withdrawing a pace, slid both hands down her arms until their fingers were linked. "Let's get you something to eat, and then we're all having a nice long talk about how to guarantee you a solid night's sleep."

The mellow aroma of melted candle wax drifted over her as she entered the hall at Rhys' side. A pleasing compliment to the scents of crisply browned bread and rosemary-seasoned quail displayed upon the servants' silver platters. Yet Faedrah swallowed hard at the trials to come, her stomach rebelling at the thought of consuming food. Her appetite had left her long ago and, if offered the choice, she would've happily wrestled two of the high-backed chairs aside, crawled beneath the table and curled into a ball at Rhys' feet.

His hand on her back, he escorted her to her seat on the queen's right, nodded a greeting to her parents and scooted her chair toward the table as she sat. Silver bowls overflowing with periwinkle asters had been stationed at intervals along the elaborately appointed length. Water beaded upon flagons of etched crystal filled with the rich crimson of mulled wine. The place settings were porcelain china stamped with the royal blue insignia of the Austiere crest. Still and thus, the candlelight reflecting off the silver goblets, the cutlery and jewels adorning the guests, made her wince as the beginnings of a dull headache furrowed up the back of her neck.

Though slated, in part, to celebrate her homecoming, this evening was bound to challenge the limits of her over-taxed endurance.

Rhys tugged the chair beside hers from the table, but stalled as Vaighn deftly slipped in to occupy the seat. "Whoa, hold up. I'm sitting by—"

Fandorn loudly cleared his throat. He opened a hand toward the chair on his left, down the table past where Denmar sat beside her father, and Rhys sighed before stomping off to join the elder wizard.

Based on the enthusiasm those around her had for the meal, the food was undeniably delicious, though each bite Faedrah set upon her tongue contained the flavor of dry sand. The wine soothed the pounding in her temples, yet she daren't drink too much for fear she would succumb to inebriation and descend into the vortex of Gaelleod's maddening pursuit.

Nonetheless, above all, the one thing which grounded her in the present and bolstered her against collapsing into fits of despair, was the way Rhys kept watch over her from his seat on the far side of the king. Every morsel she lifted to her lips, if engaged in conversation or resting a moment to gather her wits, his steady gaze was there—heating her skin, calming her heart, soothing her fears.

'Twas an unfortunate twist of fate her attendance did not convey to him the same level of ease, and yet she could no more deny her horrid condition than she could force herself to eat.

Each time their gazes locked, she read his mounting irritation over the unending courses presented during the meal. If slightly distracted, her focus circled back to his at the heave of his impatient sigh, the way he consistently shifted as if a burr had found its way into his boot or the dark scowls he aimed at the guests seated nearest his plate.

The way tension all but crackled off his skin, 'twas of no surprise to her his was the first voice to cut through the frivolous chatter of the council members and their wives upon the servants' removal of the dessert plates.

"Okay, dinner's over." He swiped his linen napkin over his generous mouth and tossed it upon the table. "Now, are we ever going to talk about why we're really here?"

Vaighn choked on his wine, coughing into his fist. Jaws gaped in unison around the table and Faedrah lowered her chin to hide a smile. Though, apparently, she was alone in her lack of disbelief.

Her father held up his hand to still the uncomfortable shuffling of the guests. "Curtail your charge, Fandorn, or I shall order him removed from these proceedings."

"Apologies, Sire." Fandorn respectfully tipped his head. "Despite my most ardent efforts, the boy remains impetuous to a fault."

Impetuous? Faedrah curled an index finger over her lips to staunch a chuckle. The man was a white-hot spark sizzling down a wick toward an immeasurable detonation.

"Really?" Rhys planted his elbow on the table and leaned forward to peer at the king. "We're gonna sit here and dissect my personality when your daughter hasn't slept in three days?"

The women flinched as her father pounded a hard fist on the table, rattling the silver. "I am fully aware of the suffering Faedrah has endured since her return to this realm. Two nights, her mother and I have watched helpless while she paces the floor until the soles of her feet all but blister. Only to then succumb to exhaustion so

287

that she can thrash unresting upon her bed."

Faedrah dropped her forehead into her hand at her father's ill-timed admittance. Though true, Rhys would find no reassurance in such words. Indeed, news as this would merely add fuel to the blistering heat of his aggravation.

"And lest we forget." The king aimed a rigid finger at her beloved. "'Tis by your father's hand she is made to bear this arduous plight."

She closed her eyes, heart sinking like a stone tossed into the pit of her empty stomach. The ripples reverberated outward, and she braced as the first needles of anger prickled up her spine. 'Twould seem no matter how hard she argued his innocence, Rhys would forever be made to bear the insurrection of his father's evil deeds.

"Well, then, let's go get the bastard!" Rhys' silver vambraces glinted in the soft light as he tossed his arms wide. "Right now. Tonight. We've waited too long as it is!"

A smile came unbidden to her lips over his valiant defense of her. Goddesses wept, the love she held for this man outnumbered Helios' diamond offerings in the sky.

Denmar grunted his repugnance and she squinted at the captain of the royal guard. "One does not simply waltz into enemy territory without first determining the risks, lad." He bobbed his head toward the king. "His majesty has many factors to consider, not the least of which is incurring the gamble of war."

"Trade routes from the sea would all but cease." Councilman D'Anthe straightened the ruffles of his lace-edged cuffs. "Not one of our allied merchants from the east would endanger their ships should Seviere choose to retaliate in exchange for our encroaching on his lands."

Rhys crossed his arms. "Yeah, so?"

"Talk amongst the gentry is divided on the matter, Sire." Vlandross straightened from where he'd leaned into his wife's whisper, light winking off the single glass lens perched before his left eye. "While the woodworkers' guild is in upheaval over the threat of economic collapse, rumblings from the commonwealth state the aid which the guild has already received from the crown offers them an unfair advantage. Especially in lieu of the high cost for lumber."

Chair legs screeched across the floor as Rhys shoved to his feet, arms braced on the table and body tense. "Are you fucking kidding me? The woodworkers' guild?"

He jerked upright, shoulders tight. Faedrah sprang forward in her seat as his face flooded a deep red and his hands fisted at his sides. "Shit." He gritted his teeth. "I got it, Fandorn. Back off."

She glanced between the wizard and Rhys, her weary mind finally interpreting the clues to how Fandorn had employed the use of his restrictive spell. "Release him, Fandorn." Sweet tits, her beloved was the only one present to keep the conversation on point. Did they not see? His annoyance over Vlandross' wily political crusade was a direct reflection of the deep concern he harbored for her. "In fact, I demand you remove the spell altogether. Rhys shall do us no harm."

Her father pinned her with a scalding glare, yet Faedrah did not shrink or cower under his censure. Their true enemy was outside the castle walls, laying waste to the kingdom, and their energies would be much better served by standing united against the demon who rightfully deserved their retribution.

"Do as she asks, Fandorn." Her mother tapped a finger against her lips, elbow propped on the table. The king's head spun toward his wife, and she shrugged. "I'd like to hear what Rhys has to say."

Her father grumbled his discontent, yet he did not negate the queen's command.

"As you wish." The wizard nodded toward her parents and Rhys slumped, filling his lungs as he ran a hand along the nape of his neck.

"What you guys aren't getting is that, any second now, there could *be* no commonwealth." He flicked that same hand toward the table. "All this. Your servants, your castle and fancy clothes are all gonna disappear unless you *save—this—woman*." He emphasized

289

each word, pointing in her direction. "Faedrah is the only thing that matters. Don't you get it? Gaelleod has somehow connected himself to her, and unless we figure out a way to break that tie, he's gonna destroy her and everything you love right along with her." He glanced around the table before meeting her gaze. "The only thing we should be discussing is who's going after the bastard because, if we don't, you can bet your white, powdered asses, he's coming after her. And I don't know about the rest of you, but I'm not about to let that happen."

A long moment of silence descended as those present traded stares about the table.

"Perchance." Vlandross removed the lens from before his eye, heated the glass with a puff of air and rubbed both sides with his linen napkin. "Or perchance, you merely aim to lead us into ruin so you may possess the key for yourself."

What? Faedrah clamped down hard on the barbed retort perched upon her tongue. Her beloved stomped forward a step, his rage swooping in with such ferocity, a metallic taint literally coated the air.

"I cautioned you to proceed carefully, Councilman." She narrowed her gaze at the pompous courtier. He could not have found a nerve more raw to pluck. "Such an accusation is a lie of the foulest contempt."

Jaw tight, Rhys repeatedly clenched and released his hands. "Not to mention, you've got no right to accuse me of anything, least of all deceiving the woman I love."

His jowls wobbled as Vlandross silently laughed. "You are the son of Gaelleod. Come, now." He replaced his lens before his eye and opened his hands to encompass the guests at the table. "I think we can all agree your blackened heart holds no love for anyone but yourself."

The silver wine goblets nearest Rhys crumpled, the sides folding in on themselves as if crushed by an unseen fist. The crowd gasped and several guests pressed their chairs back from the table.

"I could not more vehemently disagree, Sir Vlandross." The queen lifted a withering brow. "Or does your lofty position in such matters also allow you to place judgment on the divine intervention of the nine?"

Faedrah squeezed her eyes tight, shaking her head against pounding in her temples. This in-fighting served no purpose. They must stand united in their cause. To do elsewise would surely condemn them to failure.

"You self-serving son of a bitch." Rhys hunched, lowering his chin to peer at the councilman from under his brows. Ethereal light glowed from his hands. The silver cutlery upon the table shook and vibrated, emitting a high-pitched whine. "If you think for one second, I'm gonna stand here and let you shit all over everything I care about, you'd better think again."

"Get yourself under control, laddie." Denmar waved the guards forward from their spots before the door. "Or I shall have you escorted from this room in chains."

Faedrah fisted her hands under the table. No! No! Such a threat was ludicrous beyond measure, and would accomplish nothing but to make Rhys even more irate.

He huffed. "I'd like to see you try."

"Be careful, Wizard." Vaighn stood. "You address the king's right arm. Insubordination will not be tolerated."

Goddesses wept, when would it end? She rubbed her fingers over the throbbing pressure in her brow. Seized the arm of her chair to steady her balance.

"Sit down and be quiet." Her father snapped. "All of you. This is an open dialogue and Vlandross has every right to his opinion."

Her mother crossed her arms, edging away from the king. "At the peril of blaspheming our goddesses?"

"We must address every angle before instigating a war."

"Or what?" Rhys tossed his arms wide. "You may actually save your kingdom?"

"I told you to *sit down*!"

"Enough!" Faedrah sprang to her feet, snagging the attention of all those in the room. "If and what is to be done, will be decided upon by *me*." She gripped the table edge to shore up the trembling in her legs, staring at the array of shocked faces, daring any of them to disagree. "This is *my* task, handed down from the goddesses and placed at *my* feet. Not one of you stands to lose all I risk in defense of our kingdom. There is not one soul in this room, save Rhys, who has yet to stand by my side and oppose the evil at our gates."

She slammed both fists on the table, her frustration too much to bear. "You ask I forfeit my life to save all that you have and think not of insulting me in the process. You sit and place judgment on that which you do not understand, yet compel me to sacrifice what little happiness I have known. You prepare me to lead and then question every word that falls from my lips, naming me a child unfit to rule.

"So hear this." She shoved up from the table, the force of her anger stoking a strength she had not known lay dormant within her. "I will not stand for dissension. Not when everything I love is to be weighed against the balance of your pride. You sit here and squabble like children and, in doing so, be sure to pick your side. Because I promise you this. I *shall* find this bastard, with or without you, and I shall rout him out to the very gates of hell. You have but to decide. You either stand and fight with me or I shall cut you down at my side."

A grin the likes of which she had never before encountered split Rhys' face nearly in two. He bobbed his chin in smug agreement and crossed his arms, peering at those present over the imperial slant of his nose.

No one else moved, and a breath lodged in Faedrah's throat over the outcome of her furious tirade, every set of eyes staring at her as if she'd suddenly sprouted a third eye.

She slowly exhaled as Vaighn bowed his head, dropping to one knee. "Forgive my impertinence, Your Highness. Of a certainty, you have my sword. I serve at the pleasure of the princess."

Thank the nine... The next chance she found alone with her brother, she would hug the breath right from his scarred, able chest.

Her mother stood. "As do I."

Faedrah smiled, tears born of relief blurring her vision as she nodded in thanks to her strong and noble queen.

"Aye, lassie." Casting a sidelong glance her father, Denmar pushed his chair back from the table and knelt. "Lead on and I shall follow."

Fandorn squinted, tapping a bony finger against his lips. "My verdict remains bound to the king."

Faedrah's gaze landed on her father, head bent, thumb and index finger stroking the neatly trimmed beard on his chin. He slowly lifted his eyes to hers, but he did not stand. "You have the support of the crown."

Meaning, as king, he stood with her. As her father, he did not.

'Twould have to do... for now.

"Then these proceedings have reached their end." Spinning on her heel, she beckoned Rhys with a wave of her hand and strode at his side from the room.

Chapter 6

The stars are different here...

Rhys shrugged off the chilly spring breeze blowing through the castle's high narrow window, a bizarre constellation in the shape of a sickle perfectly centered in the frame. If only his adjustment to being in Faedrah's world began and ended with a few misplaced stars. Maybe then his comments wouldn't have derailed that so-called homecoming celebration so far off the fucking track.

The long narrow rug muffled his boot heels as he strolled the quiet corridor outside his angel's bedroom, nodding a greeting to the two soldiers stationed on either side of the door. Regardless, he would have given anything to kick that pretentious asshole Vlandross in the ass. The woodworkers' guild, for fuck's sake. Rhys rolled his eyes and stopped before the next window to peer up at the night sky. More than a few donations had probably found their way into the councilman's pocket to guarantee he brought up that topic with the king. His back alley double-talk was the exact same kind of bullshit Leo loved to use in his smarmy business tactics, and the reminder had nearly made Rhys lose his shit. No telling what would've happened if Faedrah hadn't stepped in and put the jackass in his place.

He grunted. Hell, she'd put everyone in their place, and in that singular moment he'd never been more proud to be the man standing at her side. A few sharp words off her talented tongue, and everyone at that table had blushed like they'd gotten busted smoking in the bathroom at school.

A smile tugged at the corner of his mouth. He should've known getting her pissed would lead straight to the answer of what came next. No one with a brain in their head would be stupid enough to get in his angel's way once she was on a rampage. Not if they planned to be spit out the other side with their faculties intact.

Inhaling a deep breath, he closed his eyes and cleared his mind, searching for any hint Gaelleod might be trying to sneak his bony ass into Faedrah's dreams. The blackness on the back of his eyelids remained blank. The only sounds echoing against his eardrums, the beat of his heart and the far-off chirping of frogs.

Maybe she was still awake. He blinked and shook his head. It had only been a few minutes since he'd stepped into the hall, hoping that by removing himself the ball-busting tension in the room would drop several degrees so she could relax.

Shortly after they'd arrived at her bedroom door, her parents had shown up, hot on their heels. And the back-off scowls her dad had aimed at Rhys from the second they'd entered Faedrah's receiving room, had reallocated Leo's sneers to the welcoming cuddles of a fuzzy puppy. Apparently, the king was in lock-down mode, and the last thing he wanted was some cheese ball interloper sniffing around his daughter.

He'd strode straight for a chair near the fireplace and assigned himself guard duty, settling in for the duration. In response, Faedrah had paced, worrying the key around her neck, anxiety stretched across her pretty features and exhaustion hollowing out her eyes.

Seeing her so stressed while being unable to do anything about it had nearly killed him, and Rhys knew his next move without having to be told. Even though the thought of leaving her ranked somewhere in the vicinity of getting repeatedly run over by a cement truck, his first priority was to do everything in his power to make sure she was comfortable. Being locked in the same room with her dad didn't exactly create a tranquil atmosphere, and the continuous glares they traded like she was the all-or-nothing hand in a game of high-stakes poker were shared at her expense.

He couldn't do that to her. The last thing he wanted was to be just another fucked up problem for her to solve. Faedrah getting some honest-to-God sleep was all that mattered... and, besides, it wasn't like he had to go far. With a parting kiss to her cheek, he'd turned for the exit, reassuring her he'd be right outside the room the second she needed him.

A door softly closed behind him and he turned from the window to find Faedrah's mother coming toward him down the hall. She smiled in greeting and he nodded a hello as she stopped near his right side.

"She's resting easy." The queen sighed, crossing her arms. "At least, for now."

Thank God. Though how long that shaky condition might last was anyone's guess. "I appreciate you coming out to let me know." He squinted, pausing a second to scour the night for any inkling of Leo's laughter, the slightest hunch that bastard was getting ready to pounce.

"I fear it should be her father and I who are offering our gratitude to you."

He flinched, scowling at the queen like she'd lost her damn marbles as her warm chuckle echoed down the corridor. "Gratitude for what?"

"Your leaving the room was a difficult sacrifice, I'm sure, though I'm not surprised you put Faedrah's wellbeing ahead of your own." She faced him, a hint of empathy softening the corners of her eyes. "You have done so at every turn since your arrival, Rhys. A true testament to the strength of your undying devotion."

He tipped his head to acknowledge her compliment, and something about the way she held his gaze a second or two longer than necessary told him she'd been quietly cheering in his corner from the get-go… which was actually pretty damn cool. Her silent acceptance offered him a glimmer of hope that the shit mess Leo had dumped in his lap might one day change for the better. Everyone else in the castle always looked away whenever he came within range, as if terrified they might catch some contagious disease just by breathing his same air. And the one time Fandorn had called it quits and Rhys had left his training session early, the maid he'd found cleaning his room had keeled over in a dead faint right at his feet.

Not that he gave a rat's ass if everyone viewed him as a pariah. After all, none of those people were the one standing in his way. "Any idea if the king will ever see me as anything other than a leper?"

The queen wrinkled her nose, hissing in a breath. "What you must keep in mind is Faedrah's father has a tendency to be a spot overprotective."

Rhys cocked a brow. "A spot?"

"And I tend to understate the obvious."

A chuckle shook his shoulders as he carefully assessed Faedrah's mother. He'd be smart to be careful. The woman's wit was every bit as quick as her daughter's.

Slipping her arm through his, she turned him from the window and started them down the hallway at a slow stroll. Still, to him, Faedrah's family situation came across as just plain weird. On one hand, growing up in a stable, safe environment had most likely been nice for his muse. Based on his knowledge of Nate, good things happened when a person matured in a loving home, knowing their parents would always be there for them without fail. On the other, to have every move scrutinized, the constant strain of continuously being judged against some unachievable standard had to be like living in a pressure cooker.

Jesus H. Christ. He expelled a sharp breath through his nose. After spending a good portion of his life trying to live up to Leo's expectations, he could only imagine Faedrah's frustration… and his father was only one man. Carrying that same weight under the strain of an entire kingdom? No fucking way. By now, his room would've been lined with padded walls.

He rolled his eyes. Of course, this *was* Faedrah they were talking about. A woman who had jumped through time and space on the off-chance she'd get to bitch slap Satan, fully prepared to put her life on the line if need be. Given the choice, could he honestly say he'd have made that same leap?

His brow twitched and he lowered his gaze to his feet. Didn't matter, because Faedrah had already made the decision… for all of them. She'd willingly shouldered the back-breaking responsibility of saving not only her world, but his. He lifted his focus, jaw clenched as he stared at the far wall. And he'd happily go straight to hell before he let one god damn citizen in either realm deny his muse had been born with an iron-clad set of balls. "Faedrah's a lot stronger than her dad gives her credit for."

"Oh, to be sure." The queen smirked. "And after this evening's tirade, I've more than a smidgen of certainty Caedmon will twice consider his words before inviting his daughter's wrath, as well."

Well, then, what was the fucking problem? Only a complete idiot could've missed how the king refused to stand when Faedrah had asked for his consent to go after Gaelleod. Her dad obviously loved her… he believed in her… but he snubbed her request for support?

He stopped them in front of the last window and faced the queen. "I just don't get it. Then why is he so hell bent on disagreeing with Faedrah's decisions? Doesn't he see how doing that is like jamming a knife in her chest?"

"You misunderstand." The queen grasped his upper arms. "'Tis because of his profound love for her, Faedrah's father deters his endorsement of her perilous path. He would no more willingly sanction her confrontation of Gaelleod's evil than he would cast her into the fiery pits of hell."

Releasing her hold on him, she placed a hand on his chest. "You must believe here, in your heart, our king holds only the utmost

298

care and concern for his daughter. No doubt his boundless love for her… and for the future of our kingdom… is the one thing which also stays his consent you pursue Faedrah's hand in marriage."

Wait, what? He shook his head to rearrange the bearings. *Marriage?* His shoulders fell. Then again, it wasn't like he ever planned to let Faedr—

A creepy chill lifted the hair on his nape and Rhys hesitated, turning his head to search the night. "Hold on."

She backed away a step. "What is it?"

The sickening-sweet scent of rot blew in on the breeze, and he pinned Faedrah's mom with a frown. "Do you smell that?"

"No." She sniffed. "What—"

He took off like a shot down the hall. The fucker was back. God dammit, any second now, Gaelleod would infect Faedrah's dreams.

The guards scrambled out of his way as he flung the door back on its hinges. The knob slammed the wall and rebounded as he burst into the room. The king flinched, blinking and glancing around like he'd fallen asleep, dropping his heels from a padded ottoman to the floor. "Has something happened?"

A shrill scream drilled through Faedrah's bedroom door and Rhys sprinted past her dad, grabbed the handle and shouldered into the room.

Sheets tangled around her legs as if she'd been thrashing, she flailed her arms, fighting off an invisible enemy. Sweat dampened her hair near her scalp, the front of her nightgown glued to her chest.

That motherfucker! Three long strides, and Rhys scooped her into his arms, gritting his teeth to cap the roar of hatred lodged in his throat. He carried her to the nearest chair, spun and sat with her on his lap, cradling her head on his chest. "I got you, baby. I'm here, I'm here."

Her lashes fluttered. She gasped and clutched his shoulders, burying her face in his neck. "Thank you," she whispered. "Thank you, thank you for waking me."

Smoothing a hand down her back, he held on tight, rocking her as her frazzled breathing subsided. God dammit, this was literally a fucking nightmare. He'd never fought such a useless panic his entire life. He locked onto her parents, standing just inside the door. Somehow… some *way*… they had to do *something* to stop this never-ending bullshit from repeating.

"Thank the nine, you reached her in time." The queen placed a hand on her chest, exhaling a harsh breath.

"No, I didn't," Rhys snapped, but that was about to change. From here on in, he wasn't going anywhere. Not even into the god damn hall. He'd watch over her all fucking night if he had to, stay awake and hold her in his arms to make sure she stayed safe. "The asshole still got in. Most likely, because I was distracted."

Faedrah's body gradually went slack in his arms, her hold loosened on his shoulders. He gently lowered her from his chest to find her eyelids were closed. Thank God. At least his being here had offered her some security, however small.

"Yes, but look." The queen nodded toward her daughter. "For Faedrah to return to slumber so quickly is unheard of. These past three nights, her torment has been much, much worse."

Worse? Aw, Christ, he would never sleep again. His grip on her instinctively tightened. Not until he'd figured out a way to stop Leo dead in his tracks.

"Come, Caedmon." She wound her index finger around the king's pinkie and tugged. "Let us leave Faedrah to Rhys' safe-keeping. 'Twould seem he is the perfect remedy to soothe her aching heart."

"Alone and without chaperone in her chambers?" The king scowled, crossing his massive arms. "I think not."

No way had he just fucking said that. Rhys' heart rate spiked as the intentional jab hit right where it counted most. Obviously, the king believed his moral fiber ranked lower than a bottom feeder, but he wasn't about to let that insult slide. "If you're insinuating I plan to take advantage of your daughter while she's practically in a coma, you and I are about to have a serious problem."

"Of course he is implying no such thing." The queen stepped forward, a heated glare aimed at her husband. His jaw dropped like he was gearing up to disagree, but she shoved a big ol' *talk to the hand* in his face. "Propriety be damned, Caedmon. I care not what rumors trickle through the court over the outcome of Rhys occupying Faedrah's chambers. Our daughter has not slept in three nights." Her nostrils flared and she extended a rigid finger toward the receiving room. "You order one hundred guards to patrol the hall, you insist she take Fandorn's potions and rail against the heavens and, still, *she does not sleep*! Rhys and none other has been able to circumvent Gaelleod's cruel spell. Goddesses wept, he sensed the dark lord's appearance whilst standing in the hall!"

She propped her fists on her hips and Rhys' eased back in the seat, covering the side of Faedrah's head with his hand. Oh shit. If the dude knew what was good for him, he'd best get ready to tuck and roll. Rhys swallowed the chuckle pressing against his breastbone. And here, all this time, he'd assumed Faedrah inherited her scrappy spitfire attitude from her dad.

"The boy is staying. And you and I, my stubborn king, are off to find our own well-deserved sleep. Now come." She jerked her head toward the door. "Or I shall be compelled to use more than mere words to get your regal backside moving."

Rhys rolled his lips to curb a smile, dropping his focus to Faedrah. Throughout her mother's rant, she didn't so much as twitch but, even still, he didn't dare glance at Faedrah's dad. Not as his boots stomped toward the exit or the door swung closed behind them. If he did, not even a visual of Leo would keep his laughter from exploding. By God, the queen had her husband by the balls.

Yeah, right. He grunted. That comment sorta reminded him of another relationship, all up close and in his face. Shit, if they ever got the chance to work through their differences, maybe he and the king could commiserate over a couple of beers.

Faedrah shivered, shoving her toes between his thigh and the chair, curling her hands in a ball under her chin. Glancing around for something to cover her with, Rhys finally scooted to the edge of the seat and stood, carried her to bed and tucked her snug inside the covers. The dying embers in the fireplace pulsed orange and red, but they weren't emitting much heat. Kneeling before the grate, he stacked a few more logs on top, arranged them with a poker until the flames caught and then stood, brushing his hands down his leather pants.

Her low moan made him spin toward the bed. No way. For fuck's sake, it hadn't even been five minutes. He slumped as she writhed, disrupting the blankets. The way she moved was like that possessed kid in *The Exorcist*. Next, she'd be levitating off the fucking bed.

Hopping first on one foot and then the other, he tugged off his boots and tossed them aside, climbed onto the bed and spooned her with his body. Faedrah settled, going limp in his arms and, a few seconds later, her breathing deepened then slowed.

Huh. Weird. Earlier in the day when they'd been out on the balcony, she'd said sleeping with him wasn't the answer to protecting her dreams. As much as he wanted to believe the opposite, he had to admit, she was right. She would never have had that horrible nightmare at Oliver's condo if that were the case. So, then, what was the difference? Why no bad dreams when he held her now? And even more baffling, why none when she'd slept at the warehouse?

He sighed and flopped onto his back, tossing an arm over his face. Other than the obvious lack of fine furnishings and a slight difference in geography, the only discrepancy between his place and Forbes' were Faedrah's pictures. They covered every square inch of free space along his walls. So, was *she* somehow the answer?

The edge of his silver vambrace dug into his cheek and he grumbled at the distraction. Sitting up, he wrapped a hand around his wrist and forged a wide line down the inside of his forearm by focusing on the minerals in the metal. A repeat down his other arm, and he pried off both vambraces and set them on Faedrah's nightstand.

Her legs jerked beside his and she whimpered. One of her hands flew through the air and flopped onto his thigh. Frowning, he turned back to the nightstand. Okay, what had just changed? Not two seconds ago, she'd been fine.

He squinted at the metal, the orange firelight flickering in the polished silver. The swirl of his signature winked at him like some seductive invitation and his shoulders snapped to attention. A fast shuffle toward the edge of the mattress and he swung his legs over the side of the bed.

Shit, maybe that was the answer. He snatched up one of the vambraces and turned it toward the light. Faedrah's pictures all held his *signature*. Fuck, there were hundreds of them at the warehouse. What had Fandorn called it? A sigil of utmost… *protection*.

Son of a bitch!

Shoving to his feet, he lifted the silver arm band toward the ceiling, muscles tight as he shook both it and his fist in the air. God dammit, he finally had it! And, even better, he knew exactly what came next. In just a few short hours, that fucking asshole Gaelleod was about to meet up with the castle's solid stone wall.

Glancing left then right for something… *anything* he could use to draw, he strode straight for a desk in the corner and then pulled up short as Faedrah moaned. Oh, no. Not on his watch. This plan was a slam-dunk, but he wasn't about to sit here and paint while she suffered.

An evil smirk twisted his lips, and Rhys stared down at his hands. The vambrace liquefied at his command, floating upward in a glistening pool so he could bend and shape the metal. The links formed, a long silver thread fit for a princess. The pendant flattened and twisted, a shiny medallion styled in the firm hard lines of his signature.

Snagging the necklace from the air, he marched straight for the bed and, brushing her dark strip of hair aside, he placed a kiss on her cheek… and lowered the solution to Faedrah's nightmares around her neck.

* * *

A languid yawn cracked her jaw and Faedrah stretched beneath the comforting warmth of her blankets. Sweet goddesses wept. The last time she'd encountered such resplendent slumber, she'd awoken in Rhys' chambers and succumbed to the blissful talents of his artful love-mak—

Inhaling a breath past her dry throat, she sprang to sitting then froze. *What in all of Helios' bright reign…* She frowned. Had her soul joined the goddesses in paradise?

Myriad colors adorned her four walls, the ceiling and floor, merging and blending in a vast array of shimmers and swirls. Helios' bright diamonds twinkled in the shape of silvery stars, the heavens beyond a mingling wealth of rich hues rendered to embody the cosmos. Pillars of stardust, their towering height illuminated by glittering jewels, shone vast and deep over the posts of her bed. Nine glorious sun gods floated amid the roiling tempest, depicted in human form, their legs outstretched and bodies reclined in a posture of tranquil repose. A muscled physique defined each deities' appearance, long hair a wild maelstrom coiled in the wind, arms encircling the slender waists of nine naked goddesses and clasping them to their chests. Sun spots burst behind each fated pair, a symbol of their divine adoration, heads angled and lips parted as they perched on the edge of a kiss.

The quiet rasp of a brushstroke whispered past her ear, and she slowly faced the southern wall. High overhead, Rhys stood stripped to the waist, standing atop a strange contraption comprised of roughly hewn planks and a series of iron pulleys. The board swayed precariously as he stepped to the right, each end suspended by ropes that dangled down the wall to the floor. A variety of uncorked paints littered the tarp spread beneath him; gold and silver coins winked in the sunlight amongst a pile of assorted gems. Discarded brushes and stained rags awaited his use in a tangled heap.

Muscle rippled down his side as he swept the tip of his brush across his pallet. Her body tightened as he stretched his arm to blend a series of yellow rings around the glowing arc of a celestial orb. The same colors decorating her walls were smeared over his hands and the black etchings on his forearms, splattered atop his bare feet and the leather cords laced up the sides of his breeches. Speckles of gold dust highlighted the glossy thick strands of his hair. Yet 'twas the essence of magic which sparkled and danced along his skin that held her spellbound. The iridescent play of light coating his hands; the glint of uncapped power flowing down the brush from his fingers.

A gold coin rose into the air and she leaned back as it floated to a stop behind him. A gasp lifted her chest as the metal exploded and million tiny particles cascaded toward the wall.

She squinted at strange arrangement of the golden flecks as they layered upon the wet paint. Something in their configuration seemed familiar. A fleeting glance around her chambers, and she smacked a palm to her forehead. Blessed tears of the nine. Hidden within the framework of every star, the free-flowing tresses of each goddess and the infinite splendor of the heavens, the bold strokes of Rhys' signature affixed his intoxicating presence over the entirety of her room.

He peeked at her over his shoulder and then snapped his head around, meeting her amazement with a devilish lopsided grin. "Well, good morning, sleeping beauty."

Bending at the waist, he set the pallet and brush at his feet. Every tendon in his chest, the ladder of raised ridges encasing his ribs and the biceps in his arms flexed as he grabbed the wooden bar near his knees and swung off the plank to the floor.

"What…" She paused to clear the rasp from her voice. "Whatever are you doing, my heart?"

One long leg rose behind him as he leaned down to shake a clean strip of cloth from the jumbled pile. "My damndest to be a gigantic pain in Leo's ass."

Tossing a roguish smirk her way, he strode for the bureau near her window, leather sliding over trim hips, the dark scruff of his beard a tantalizing shadow surrounding the generous curves of his mouth.

She licked her dry lips against the enticing visual and more carefully studied the grand scene encompassing her chambers. Whatever grievous injury he hoped to bestow, 'twould seem her beloved had more than succeeded. But, tits of the nine, a task of such extensive effort had surely taken him several—

Her heart leapt as realization arrowed home, and she scrambled to her knees, shoving a lank of mussed hair over her shoulder. "How long have I been abed?" Whilst she'd needed her slumber, for her to miss several passings of Helios' face the exact moment Gaelleod nipped at the heels of her kingdom seemed a horrible waste.

"Relax." Rhys decanted a pitcher of water into her earthenware basin. "You've only lost a day." Water trickled as he washed the paint from his arms with a cake of soap, employed the use of a little brush to scrub at the stubborn stains under his nails. A tip of his head and he shrugged. "And two nights, if you wanna get technical."

Thank the nine. She slumped and yet, not a heartbeat later, the needling agitation returned to her chest. In such a short span, her artistic lover had accomplished all this? "You, however, have not spared yourself a moment's rest."

"Not true. I napped in the chair whenever I got tired." He jerked his chin toward the fireplace and her gaze fell to the crumpled blanket hanging upon the arm, the discarded trays of food stacked before the hearth and the steaming teapot hanging near the grate. Nonetheless, that he had gone to such trouble on her behalf displayed a devotion beyond any she'd encountered in her lifetime.

"But why, my love?" Palms opened at her sides, she tried and failed to absorb every detail wrought by his able hands. The limitless stretch of beauty made her mind reel, and she huffed and shook her head. A fortnight or more would be needed to discern all the facets buried within the design of this immense panorama.

Shaking the water from his hands, he tugged a towel from the bar and dried his arms, strode to the mantel and filled an empty mug with hot water from the teapot. "Do you see the pattern? The symbol hidden inside the scene?"

A smile hinted at his lips as she nodded. He referenced his signature, of course. Yet, for those who had not the occasion to study it as she had, the evidence would no doubt be lost. He'd secreted his sigil so well within the strokes of his brush, its depiction would remain concealed to the untrained eye.

He tipped a spoonful of tea leaves into the water and added a dollop of golden honey before walking the steaming beverage to the bed. The mattress dipped near her thigh as he sat and handed her the mug. "Do you remember what Fandorn said that first day I got here? About my signature and what it meant?"

The sweetened liquid soothed her parched throat… until understanding flashed like a flint striking kindling and she sputtered and coughed into her fist. But, of course! Rhys' mark was a sigil of the utmost protection!

She jostled the cup to her bedside table. The portraits of her at his chambers… the tingle of magic whenever she'd swept her fingertips along bold strokes he habitually used to sign his name. For all the goddesses in paradise, they were the exact solution to keeping Gaelleod at bay!

Rising on her knees, she threw her arms around her lover's neck and hung on tight. He was an absolute marvel. A contented sigh left her lips as his chuckle warmed the untamed mass of her hair. Without his keen wit and insightful talents, 'twas anyone's guess how many nights she may have lamented Gaelleod's vile pursuit. "So, as long as I remain within these chambers, the dark lord will be unable to infect my dreams?"

"Oh, I can do you one better." He settled her sideways on his lap, and her heart stuttered as he reached between her breasts and lifted a silver pendant she'd yet to notice hanging beside the key. "The minute I put this around your neck two nights ago, you slept like a baby. My guess is, as long as you wear it, you should be able to sleep anywhere… *go* anywhere you want."

She grinned as he dropped a large silver charm in the shape of his sigil into the center of her palm. What past good deeds ensured she be the recipient of such a noble lover's heart, she did not know nor did she care. Curling her fingers around the newfound treasure, she held it to her chest. The only thing which mattered was they were bound to each other, throughout the joys or despite the terrors they may face.

"Thank you, beloved." Cupping his cheek, she lowered his lips to hers. Yet one kiss was not enough to display her gratitude for his tireless endeavors. One taste of him was not sufficient to sate her hunger or unleash the fulfillment she craved from his clever hands.

Thrusting her fingers into his thick hair, she brought him down a second time, flicked her tongue along his lips and then swept her mouth over the supple curves to clear the moisture. His low grumble vibrated into her chest. The sharp edges of his teeth nipped her lower lip, and she sighed as he darted his tongue inside to dance and mate with hers.

Sliding a splayed hand up her back, he wound his fingers through her hair, gathering the strands into a tangled mass he clasped at the base of her neck. His other arm snaked around her legs. Muscle flexed beneath her palms as he jerked her higher onto his hips. A thrill skated over her skin as the evidence of his building arousal nudged her bottom. The slightest shift of his embrace and she was tipped from his chest, arms extending and fingernails whitening as she struggled to retain her hold of the smooth skin spanning his shoulders.

One of his eyebrows rose as he leaned in, heated breath mingling with hers, his focus riveted to her lips. "Not that I'm complaining, but are you sure about this?" He angled her head back and buried his face in her neck. The tip of his tongue wet her skin, little circles swirling along the tender skin under her ear. "I mean, you did just wake up. You don't want to eat first? Sorta... build up your stamina?"

She smiled. "Several pangs plague my body at the moment, but not the least of them has anything to do with food." Her lashes fluttered, an exact replica of the warm quivers his moist kisses ignited in her belly. Sparks detonated along the crest of her shoulder, down the inside of her arm to her fingertips as he nuzzled her ear.

"Good. Because I promised your dad I wouldn't take advantage."

Her *father*? Clasping the sides of Rhys' head, she pried him away from her to assess the desire flitting through his darkened gaze. To learn the two men had discussed her condition did not sit well in her chest. Headstrong and stubborn, both relentless in their efforts to tell her what's best... an agreement of terms between them would surely cause her nothing but grief. "At last glance, these were my chambers, and I concluded what activities were contained therein. I suggest you allow my father to remain outside the door where he belongs."

"Check." He jerked his cheeks from her grasp and lowered his lips back to their previous location.

Yet before he made contact, she wrenched him away from her once again. The notion her father could even suggest such a thing frayed the ends of her very last nerve. "And should he be witless enough to ask after our activities, you have permission to tell my father *I* took advantage of *you*."

"There's that sass I love." A corner of his mouth quirked and Rhys shook her hands from his face. His lips parted as he neared and she huffed her annoyance, combing her nails through his hair as he returned his lust-inducing attentions to her neck. "Okay, you about done?"

The man was fortunate he held the secrets to her heart. If not for his persistence, she could have expounded on her irritation for days. "Quite."

"You *do* realize the more pissed off you get, the harder it makes me. You're playing with fire, Faedrah. It's been five long days since I had you." The ends of his beard tickled her skin as he swept an open-mouthed kiss across her chest. "Someone so much as clears their throat outside that door and I'm liable to tear their head off."

A thrill burst in her belly at his whispered confession… that he would want her with such intensity, his needs in perfect harmony to hers. She gasped as his hips bucked beneath her, bit her bottom lip as he jerked her nightgown aside and drew her nipple into the warm cavern of his mouth. His hand curled beneath the edge of her sleeping gown. A flick of his clever tongue and a shiver stole over her skin as he ran his palm behind her knee to the back of her thigh. Every portion of her grew anxious for his touch. Her pulse built to a needy throb, and she rubbed her thighs together to relieve an inner ache.

Fingers clutching her hips, he slid her off his lap to the bed. A twist of his body, and he settled between her legs, urging the cotton of her gown higher upon her waist.

Her breathing grew labored. She perched on the edge of desire and awaited whatever temptations he chose to bestow. He eased both hands under the curves of her ass, massaging and teasing the crease with his fingertips as his lips seared a warm path over and across her stomach. Tingles wound through her limbs at the rasp of his rough cheeks on her sensitive belly. Moisture pooled and a husky moan eased from his throat as the scent of her arousal heightened the anticipation in the room.

Skin against skin, he slithered up the length of her body, dotting kisses along her breasts, his hands sliding higher to shove the remains of her clothing over her head and off her arms. Kneeling between her legs, he skimmed the tip of one finger around her nipple, groaned and thumbed the tight nub until her pulsating need grew and she bucked and writhed under his touch.

She needed more. Cupped his manhood through his leather pants and squeezed to emphasize her yearning. He hissed and his head rolled back on his shoulders. The planes of his stomach tensed as his hips took up a rhythmic rocking against her hand. She fondled the hard length of him, delighting in the little veins that popped and rode the smooth skin leading down inside the band of his breeches.

Jamming his thumbs into the laces on either side of his hips, he jerked and the leather ties gave. A shove of his hands and he yanked the black leather down to his thighs. His cock jutted into the air, flushed and erect. She circled the bulbous head with her thumb and forefinger and stroked a tight band down to the base. A shudder dislodged the set of his shoulders and he fell forward, the solid weight of him pressing her into the mattress as he kicked his pants to the floor.

He placed one of his hands along the side of her head, elbow braced on the pillow cradling her shoulders, and tended her lips with a coaxing kiss. The other snuck down between their bodies, and light shimmered along her spine as he used the tip of his member to prod and caress her inner folds.

Reason fled as she arched against him, increasing the pressure. The soles of her feet sparked and heated. She wriggled and writhed as the embers burst and slid smooth and sleek up her inner thighs.

"Look at me." Rhys circled her entrance, eased the head inside and then withdrew. A whimper scuffed the back of her throat as he denied her fulfillment. The entirety of her form trembled and ached. She fisted the blankets, her core fluttering and a roar mounting in her ears as he thrummed her clit with the rim of his cock. "Look at me, dammit. I wanna watch your eyes when I slide inside you. I wanna see what it does to you."

She grasped his scruffy cheeks and peered hard into the depths of his gaze. Any wish he asked, she would readily grant to have him stretching her, filling her. Quenching her desperate need.

311

A thrust of his hips, and she gasped as he sheathed the entire length of his erection inside her. Love glinted in his gaze as his husky chuckle warmed her cheek. The base of his cock bore down on her cunny, a titillating pressure heightening her arousal. She shuddered and her fingertips numbed as he scooped the back of her head in his hand and crushed his lips to hers.

Flashes cascaded at the edges of her vision. His arm slid around her waist and her back bowed as he cinched her hard to his chest. His hand swept her bottom, fingers dancing along the crease. A firm shove and the angle increased, allowing him to penetrate a fraction deeper. The tip of his manhood bumped a delicate place high inside and her internal walls quivered. Ripples radiated outward to both heat and chill her skin.

"That's it, baby." He ground into her, forcing her thighs wider. Seizing her hip with one hand, he dug his finger into her flesh and held firm, urging her ever nearer the abyss. "Come for me."

A slight rotation, a sweep of that glorious spot and her body ruptured. She was cast into bliss, body and soul. Rhys groaned into her ear as she trembled around him. She clutched his backside with one hand, fingers tangled in his hair as he pumped and withdrew, riding a wave which propelled her higher and extended the force of her orgasm. A sharp inhalation, the tendons in his chest corded and he shuddered, joining them over and again as the essence of his soul warmed and melded with her core.

A moment later, his body went limp atop hers and she chuckled, gently scraping her fingernails up and down his scalp. "I fear you have done yourself in."

"Oh ye of little faith." A minor shift of his hips and she laughed again as the evidence of his unappeasable appetite for her twitched and flexed inside.

The beauty of his artwork shone down upon her face, and she squinted at Rhys' apt depiction of the heavenly bodies. Oh, that they could truly be lost among the clouds. To forget the dangers lying in wait just outside her chamber door. "How long do you imagine we could remain abed without discovery, exploring all the ways in which to bring each other pleasure?"

Pressing up from where he'd planted his face in the pillows, he wagged his brows. "I'll go stack some furniture in front of the door and let's find out."

She placed her hand on his cheek, sweeping the tip of her thumb along his full lower lip. Perchance a day? Perchance several? She would gladly consent to any length to stay entranced beneath the tide of his love-making. "Let us ask a meal be delivered first. Any and every item we crave, and then I shall order we not be disturbed until Helios heralds the dawn on the morrow."

Desire flickered in his gaze, and he turned his head to warm the center of her palm with a lingering kiss. "Lady, you got yourself a deal." Rolling onto his back, he scrubbed a hand over his chin, scratching his face. "And maybe I should shave."

"Do not do so on my account." Sitting up, she tugged her dressing gown from the end of the bed and stood, shrugging the silky material onto her shoulders. "I find the singular delights presented by that soft scruff extremely titillating."

"Oh really?" Pressing up onto his side, he braced his head in his hand, the intensity of his jade gaze warming her skin as she knotted the belt at her waist. "Good to know."

A glance at her tangled hair in the mirror above the dressing table and she smoothed down her unruly waves. "Although a bath before the hearth might be in order."

"I would definitely be into that."

Passing before the wide span of her northern windows, she tugged one of the curtains aside. Too long had passed since Helios' golden rays had kissed her cheeks and, if the weather was mild, a gentle breeze would be welcomed to air out her chambers.

The startling view caught her unawares and her footsteps faltered. She stumbled to the side, clutching the curtain to better steady her balance. "Goddesses wept…" Pressing a hand to her chest, she scanned the desolate terrain. Blackened trees stretched their barren limbs skyward, roots searching for purchase upon the cracked, windswept ground. The heavy shroud of a drab gray haze darkened the sky, the village below sagging beneath the oppressive weight of its invasion.

"What's wrong?" The blankets rustled behind her, and she glanced over her shoulder as Rhys tore a coverlet from her sleeping pallet and rushed to cross the room. Yet the agony over her kingdom's deterioration since last she gazed upon its fertile fields and verdant wood, stilled the words upon her tongue. How could she describe what used to be, against the horror of what had become? "Faedrah, what is it?"

Or how easily her joy could falter and fade as if mislaid by the flip of a coin? Movement caught the corner of her eye and she withdrew a step at the long line of villagers trundling toward the castle, large bundles filled with food and belongings burdened upon their backs.

"Oh, shit." Rhys grabbed the curtain above her hand, wound an arm around her waist and tugged her back to his chest. "I didn't know. I swear to God, I didn't…"

A moment stretched, and he dropped his hand to his side. "The motherfucker just called my bluff."

She turned to Rhys with a frown. Quite certainly, the decline of her kingdom was Gaelleod's doing, yet her beloved spoke as if he and the dark lord were engaged in a game of wits. "What bluff?"

"Don't you see?" Opening his arms to the sides, he turned a slow circle to encompass his artistic endeavors about her room. "He can't get in. Just like when you took off the key, the connection's been severed and it's making him crazy."

Her eyes widened in alarm. "Goddesses' tits." Her brilliant lover spoke true. His efforts to keep her safe had garnered the iniquitous vice of Gaelleod's attentions and, in return, the vile demon had unleashed his ravenous anger upon the entire scale of her homeland.

Her jaw firmed as she stepped nearer the window to better

witness the evil waiting at their gates. Hands fisted, eyes watering as the sharp ends of her nails bit into her palms, she absorbed the full scale of Gaelleod's menace.

If he called her to a war, the monster best stand prepared. A growl of hatred built in her throat. She would not go softly into the night. She would not shrink and cower as the people she loved were cast from their homes under his vicious blight. Not while she held the key, and remained the one person able to stop the evil bastard in his tracks.

"Alert the king and queen I've arisen." She spun from the window and strode straight for the metal stand displaying her short swords, needing the weight of honed steel and the confidence of the hilt in her hand. "Tell them as soon as we're able, we ride for the realm of Seviere."

To be continued...

A Time of Reckoning

Chapter 1

"From there, we shall scour the cliff side, until the entrance to Gaelleod's tomb is revealed." Fandorn smiled, the wrinkled skin near his eyes cracking more than the dry dirt inside the castle courtyard.

Oh, no. Rhys slumped. Aw, *hell* no. Leaning side to side, he searched the bustling bodies for Faedrah, and found her standing a few feet before the portcullis, her head lowered in private conversation with Vaighn.

One guess was all Rhys needed to figure out who'd come up with this bright plan.

As if his stare had somehow psychically tapped her on the shoulder, she glanced toward him and her head snapped up. Her eyes widened then she frowned.

That's right, lady. There was no fucking way.

"Excuse me, my boy." Fandorn nodded toward the gatehouse and the loud discussion growing louder by the second between Denmar and Faedrah's dad. "If I am interpreting the tones of that conversation correctly, my assistance is required by our king."

Rhys jerked his chin at Fandorn as the old geezer wandered off. Seemed this excursion they were about to take had tensions running a little hot all around. But, god dammit. Just about the time he believed he'd finally gotten a handle on this place, *someone* up and changed the rules.

The earth rocked under his boots, and he gritted his teeth against the bone-jarring impact as another Dregg rammed to the ground like a high-speed locomotive. The moldy air gusting off its wings nearly shoved him forward a step. A few blonde strands pulled free from Faedrah's braid, whispering across her lips and dancing around her head like a golden halo, and Rhys clenched his fingers against the urge to cross the distance and tuck those silky tendrils behind her ear.

Sure, she was sexy as hell—one lick of her mouth and his blood was on fire, one wriggle of her tight little body under his hands and his cock grew a mind of its own—but if the woman expected him to willingly volunteer for human pay load duty, she'd lost her damn mind.

The Dregg lumbered past Rhys' shoulder, apparently bent on joining the rest of the fan club crowded around Faedrah's mom, then paused and lifted its face to sniff the air. A skinny forked tongue snaked out and slathered a layer of slime over the quivering slits that doubled as its nostrils. Eyes as dead and empty as a great white shark's locked onto Rhys as the hulking creature swiveled its head.

He braced for the incoming assault, every muscle in his body tense, but still winced as the Dregg released a series of chittering shrieks that pierced his skull like fingernails scraping down a chalkboard.

Jesus Christ. Enough already. Squeezing his eyes tight, Rhys scrubbed his lids with his thumb and index finger before pinching the bridge of his nose. As if this exact same reaction from every other Dregg he'd had the pleasure of meeting hadn't already delivered the message loud and clear. Evidently, the god damn legacy his father had left him manifested in a particular scent. One whiff and the Dreggs picked up on his connection to Gaelleod, hackles raised and fangs bared like a police dog sniffing out some border-crossing contraband.

Fine. That made two of them. Dropping his hand, Rhys leaned forward and curled his top lip to return the creature's twisted sneer. "Yeah? Well, I'm not real fond of you, either."

"Grommel!" Faedrah stormed across the courtyard in their direction, hands fisted at her sides. "Cease this instant!"

Grommel? This thing's name was...*Grommel*? Rhys huffed. How the hell could she tell? To him, they all looked—and stank—the same.

The hairy behemoth broke off its caterwauling, backtracked a step or two and ruffled its leathery wings before lurching toward the rest of the crew. The musty stench of bog water it left in its wake soured the lunch in Rhys' stomach, and he smacked his lips in disgust.

Vaighn swung around to follow behind his sister, ambling toward Rhys at a leisurely stroll, shaking his head and lips compressed as if holding back a smile.

Oh, really? Rhys crossed his arms. Far as he could see, not one god-damn thing about this situation was funny.

The prince stopped beside Faedrah, hand resting on the pommel of his sword, posture slouched as if the dude didn't have a care in the world. "I take it my sister's plan to infiltrate Seviere's Kingdom undetected has left you quite unsettled."

Oh no, not at all. Being dangled over the cliffs by a sentient parachute who just so happened to hate his guts sounded like the best idea ever. Rhys darted a sharp glance at the one woman who could ever get him to agree to something so stupid. "That's putting it mildly."

"I would be happy to entertain any other suggestions you may have to expedite our speedy conveyance to the entrance of Gaelleod's tomb." Flipping an open palm toward the beasts clustered around her mother, Faedrah raised her brows as if they were a bunch of cuddly teddy bears instead of a super-sized mutation between a bat and those fucking flying monkeys from *The Wizard of Oz*. "Nonetheless, the Dreggs have already agreed to our plan.

With their aid, an arrival from the seaward side of the cliffs seems the most prudent course."

Sure, sure. Or they could just save everyone the trouble and go careening to their deaths like a bunch of lemmings right now. Rhys shifted a glower between Faedrah and her brother. "I don't like it. What's our guarantee they won't accidently drop one of us?" Like him, for starters.

"You are welcome to follow on horseback, if you prefer." Vaighn shrugged. "Though such a delay will most certainly ensure you fail to partake in all the fun." Shoulders jerking to attention, he slapped a hand to his leather chest plate like he'd just had the mother of all ball-busting revelations. "Unless, perchance, our four-legged creatures alarm you as much as a Dregg?"

Faedrah smacked her brother's arm, but that didn't stop the two of them from sharing a chuckle at Rhys' expense.

He squinted, bobbling his head. Yeah, yeah, fucking hilarious. "If you ever get to my world, remind me to take you for a ride on my motorcycle, your highness." They'd see then who had the last laugh.

"You worry unnecessarily, my heart. I've ridden with the Dreggs countless times." Running a warm hand down each of his biceps, Faedrah tugged his elbows apart and stepped close, settling her arms around his waist. "Their leader, Reddeck, has sworn his clan's allegiance to the White Queen. For any Dregg to disavow her wishes would be tantamount to sacrilege." Rising on her toes, she pecked his lips. "You must trust me in this. Our entourage *will* reach its destination unharmed."

"If you say so." He curled his fingers around the thick braid trailing down her back and tugged. Still, a little added insurance never hurt, and while she'd been off scheduling this chance to go skydiving with a clan of boogey men, Rhys had been using the time to sort through a pile of discarded weapons in the armory, hoping to finalize his own strategy in sticking an ace or two up everyone's sleeve.

322

"Here." He released her and backed away a step, flipping open the black leather pouch he'd threaded onto his belt. Metal clinked and silver chains snaked between his fingers as he scooped the contents into his palm. "A little something for everyone in the group." Four of the necklaces he handed to Faedrah—one each for her mom and dad, Denmar and Fandorn—though the wizard's was more a souvenir than anything else. Fandorn didn't need a lucky rabbit's foot any more than Rhys did.

Unless, of course, Gaelleod woke up barrel's blazing before they'd successfully murdered him in his sleep. Then it was pretty much guaranteed they were all up shit creek without a paddle.

The fifth, he tossed in the general direction of Vaighn.

The prince snagged the chain in mid-air and held the medallion in front of his eyes, dim light from the gray cloud cover winking off the surface as it spun back and forth.

"Jewelry?" He grimaced, refocused on Rhys and blinked once. "Really, you shouldn't have."

Oh, for Christ's sake. The dude acted like Rhys had just dropped to one knee and proposed.

"Vaighn," Faedrah scolded. "I most vehemently suggest you reconsider."

"It's my signature, dumbass." Rhys nodded toward the swaying pendant. "A protective symbol that might just save your ass, considering there's a good chance we're about to interrupt Gaelloed's beauty sleep." Shrugging, he tipped his head. "Odds are, this little surprise party Faedrah's got planned is really gonna piss him off, but if you don't want it then, hey, no skin off my nose." He reached for the necklace, the corner of his mouth twitching as Vaighn jerked it out of range.

"On further contemplation, perchance my sister offers an alternate perspective." The sigil bounced against Vaighn's chest plate as he dropped the chain around his neck. "'Tis the height of rudeness to refuse a gift so graciously given, despite the repulsiveness of its creator or the hideous nature of its design." He bowed slightly at the waist. "I believe the stakes between us have been leveled, Wizard."

Rhys grunted, his gaze following as Vaighn sauntered off to supposedly check in with Fandorn, Denmar and the king. But his bogus indifference fell flat. Especially once the king pointed at the medallion and Vaighn smiled, nodding in Rhys' direction.

"Wait." He frowned. "Did that asshole just call me repulsive?"

Faedrah chuckled. "Flattering praise, indeed, from the highest ranking member of the royal guard."

Ah. So that's how this game was played. "Yeah, well, your brother's one ugly son of a bitch, himself."

Her musical laughter was drowned out by an ear-piercing shriek and Rhys winced, instinctively scooping her back into his arms. God dammit, being surrounded by this many Dreggs was like standing inside an ambulance bay, all the sirens blaring at the same time.

Grommel broke from the group and the Earth vibrated under Rhys' boots as the Dregg hailed a series of punches along the ground like a rampaging gorilla.

Fucking great. *This* was their ride? Or maybe… Rhys' shoulders dropped a solid inch. "Let me guess. They drew straws, and Grommel just found out he got stuck with me."

The Dregg leader lurched forward and rammed a hand against Grommel's chest. The two scuffled, raising a haze of dirt that blended with the same dull gray as the sky.

"'Twould seem so." Faedrah sighed, sliding her hands along his chest to behind his neck, and Rhys linked his hands in the small of her back as her nails scraped and tingled his scalp. "I'm sorry, my heart." The sadness in her eyes turned them the richest, most beautiful shade of chocolate brown. "Had I known the Dreggs' would find your presence displeasing, I swear—"

He dropped his lips to hers, swept a kiss along the sweet slope of her mouth and dove in for more. No. None of this was her fault. And he'd be good god-damned before he stood here like a dick and let her carry the guilt over something that had always been outside her control.

He'd catch whatever she tossed his way. That's what he'd told her. And if jumping through mirrors or, hell, becoming a Dregg's personal special-order delivery is what she wanted, then it was time he strap on a pair and live up to his promise.

The tip of her tongue met his in a seductive flick. Her breathy chuckle washed over him like a warm invitation and his blood pumped straight into his groin. Her arms tightened around his shoulders. He slid one hand down to cup her leather-slicked ass as the full curves of her breasts met his chest.

Jesus Christ, the woman drove him insane. They fit together like a hand in a glove.

He thrust his fingers under the tight weave of her braid; angled her head to deepen their kiss. Her back bowed. She moaned against his lips as their hips bumped, her soft belly cradling the ridge of his cock.

Fuck, as soon as they got back...*if* they came back...he was locking them inside her bedroom and insisting they follow up on those two days of uninterrupted sex.

Someone cleared their throat—Vaighn, judging by the lower register. Yeah, yeah, no public displays of affection and all that shit. Faedrah pulled back, but Rhys shoved her forward, forcing his thigh between her legs.

No one from the court was around and, besides, he didn't give two shits what everyone thought of the two of them locking lips. God only knew what might happen once they entered Gaelleod's tomb. This could be their last moment together, and if Faedrah's brother didn't like it, he could take a fucking hike.

She swayed against him, a sexy whimper catching in her throat, and he dug his fingers deeper into her sweet, round ass. *That's it, baby. I got ya.*

A second, louder, clearing of the throat, and Faedrah pushed against Rhys' shoulders, breaking free of his arms.

God! What the fuck? They couldn't have a few measly minutes?

He ground his teeth and turned, ready to rip a Faedrah's brother a new asshole.

His shoulders wrenched, and Rhys crossed his arms over the way Faedrah's entire family stood nearby, surveying the scene with varying degrees of awkwardness. But his anger didn't dissipate. Not as her dad leveled a fierce glare at them, and most definitely not when Vaighn rolled his eyes and the queen pressed three fingers to her lips, trying and failing to hide a smile.

The king fisted his hands, his jaw so tight it was a wonder he didn't crack a molar. "If you are *quite* finished molesting my daughter."

Rhys cocked a brow. Yeah, the two of them needed to get something straight. Like, right now. It was high time the king either shit or got off the pot.

"I'm never gonna be finished with your daughter. Not ever. If you're waiting for that day, I hate to tell ya, it ain't gonna happen." He clomped forward a step, spreading his arms to the sides. "So whatever punishment you wanna dole out or hole you wanna lock me in, have at it. Just keep in mind your decision isn't gonna change a damn thing." He glanced at Faedrah's wide-eyed stare, shaking his head; aimed a finger at the ground and punctuated each sentence. "I'm here. I'm staying. I love her. You got that? Even when she gets a ridiculous idea in her head that drives me bat-shit crazy, I love her."

Faedrah's jaw dropped. Not a split second later, she squinted, running that delicious tongue of hers along the edge of her teeth.

"So there you have it." Rhys dropped his hands in surrender. "I'm guilty of loving your daughter. Go ahead and convict. But I suggest you rethink the metal bars and chains, because there's no way in hell I'm letting her face-off against Gaelleod alone."

Her dad jerked upright. A tense moment hung in the air before he darted a glance at his wife.

"Well." The queen's eyebrow twitched. "That sounds oddly familiar."

Satisfaction settled in the center of Rhys' gut. He just bet it did. According to the stories Faedrah had told him, once upon a time, the queen had charged straight into Seviere's castle to steal back the key...and the king had gone with her, regardless of his opinions or the bullshit that errand entailed.

Fandorn cleared this throat. "Of a surety, I defer to your ruling, Sire. Yet, be advised, 'twould be wise to have the boy with us. His knowledge and powers will provide an added benefit whilst navigating the labyrinth to Gaelleod's tomb."

"Agreed." Denmar stroked the tip of his pointed goatee, the luster of his black leather eye patch an exact match to the dull sheen of his bald head. "The lad longs to prove his fealty to the crown? What better way than to deliver the killing blow, himself?"

Ha! If that challenge was supposed to bring on a nervous sweat, the dude was in for a rude awakening. Rhys couldn't wait to follow through on their plan.

A low growl rumbled in the king's chest, but he jerked his head to the line of waiting Dreggs. "On with it, then." He spun away, then pulled up short, pointing a thick finger at Rhys. "Hands off the princess."

Yeah, right. Like that was gonna happen. Rhys dipped his chin. "Highness."

He faced Faedrah, but her attention stayed fixed over his right shoulder as she started toward her Dregg. Yep. He'd reserved himself a night in the doghouse, all right.

Snagging her wrist, he stopped her mid-stomp and yanked her shoulder to his chest. "I'm going to pay for that 'ridiculous idea' comment at some later date, aren't I?"

She boosted her chin. "At the moment it's least expected."

And there it was. The flash of anger in her eyes that made him rock hard and aching to be buried inside her. "God, I can't wait."

He chuckled at her exasperated huff, wagging his brows at the sway of her perky ass as she marched off. His gaze landed on Grommel, and he eyeballed the Dregg from the tufts of its pointed ears to the deadly talons on its feet. This entire task force should have their heads examined. Too bad the crazy train had left the station sometime last week.

Closing the distance, he stared the creature straight in its bottomless blank eyes. "Don't get any wise ideas."

The Dregg snorted, wings rustling and snapping like sheets hung out to dry. Rhys turned his back to the creature and squinted as dust and dead leaves whipped into small tornadoes from the down stroke of six sets of veined wings.

A set of hairy hands grabbed his waist, and Rhys seized Grommel's wrists. A bounce on his toes and the ground shrank beneath his feet.

Waves of nausea wadded in a tight ball as they shot into the sky, lodged under Rhys' breastbone and stayed there. The tinny flavor of adrenaline flooded his mouth, and he jerked his knees to his chest as Grommel pin-wheeled right, skimming a notched parapet in the castle wall. "God dammit. You cut that a little close, don't you think?"

A chuffing worked the bellows of Grommel's lungs and Rhys scowled over his shoulder. What the hell was that supposed to be? A Dregg laugh?

He faced forward and his stomach screamed for his throat as they pitched at an eighty degree angle, dive-bombing the charred landscape. Rhys shook his head, jaw locked tight. The shithead was doing this on purpose.

Okay, if that's the way he wanted it. Clearing his mind, Rhys pinpointed the nearest rock, envisioned his target and *plunk!* It bounced off the side of Grommel's head.

The Dregg wavered on the wind, a growl showcasing his fangs, but the risk was worth the disorientation gurgling in Rhys' gut. "Test me again, and I promise you'll lose."

Grommel snuffled his irritation, but leveled out, and the bile scorching the back of Rhys' throat gradually sank like mercury inside a thermometer on a cold day.

Good. He filled his lungs and forced his body to relax, legs loose and swaying with each pump of Grommel's wings. Winding tendrils of smoke snaked up from the ground. The bare branches of the lifeless trees clawed at the sky like in the aftermath of a nuclear explosion. Christ, what a mess. Based on the level of devastation, it would take years for the kingdom to get Gaelleod's poison out of its system.

Ahead in the distance, one by one, the dark silhouettes of five jointed wingspans disappeared over the edge of the cliffs…just like they'd planned. Rhys rolled his shoulders, steeling his nerves for the dive, and shot a warning glower at the hairy monster behind him. The asshole better not test his luck by trying to shear off a layer of Rhys' skin against that uneven wall. If they were doing this, they were doing it his way.

"Let's take this nice and easy." A salt-tinged breeze coasted over his cheeks as they closed in on the horizon. "Easy now." The roar of the waves built beneath the rush of the wind in his ears. "Nice and smooth, and we'll get this done so we can all go home."

Grommel soared over the water and veered slightly left, wing tip slicing the air in a cool glide. Circling back to the group in a wide loop, he flapped once and approached their descent at a less vomit-inducing angle.

"Dude. That was awesome." And Rhys meant it. That the Dregg had taken his comfort into consideration proved Grommel was capable of empathy. Good to know, considering that particular emotion had become something of a commodity these past few days.

The scenery from the ocean side of the cliffs left him speechless, and appealed to the aesthetic of Rhys' artistic eye. A foamy rope of indigo water crashed in a violent spray against the jagged coastline. Veins of mica and iron ore glinted from between slabs of sheer white rock.

He had to admit, Faedrah's country was beautiful and, for the first time, something other than hatred for Leo twisted Rhys' need to make sure he did everything in his power to save her kingdom. This place deserved to be preserved. For future generations. Hell, over time, he could even see himself loving it just as much as she did.

"Fall in behind them and watch the wall." He pointed to the line of Dreggs soaring a few feet ahead and below. If the knot of anxiety in his gut was any indicator, the entrance to the tomb was gonna be a bitch to find. "Time to put on our game face."

He kept his eyes peeled, scanning and rescanning the cracks and crevices as they flew north. Tears streamed back into his hairline and his eyelids grew sticky from the constant wind. Hours passed, the sky changing from mottled gray to an alien coral pink as the sun set somewhere beyond the thick layer of Gaelleod's fog. On his right, the black water stretched into oblivion. To the left, the endless coastline unrolled like a frayed white ribbon. The muscles in his lower back ached from the cranked angle of Grommel's grip and, still, nothing. Not one fucking clue to where his father had holed up underground.

Rhys dug his thumb and index finger into his eye sockets to clear the crusty residue from his lashes. Christ, they were completely screwed unless they somehow stumbled across a miracle. No matter how hard they looked, this was like searching for a needle in a haystack.

Dropping his hand, he tipped his head side to side to stretch his neck, letting his eyes stay closed for a few seconds of rest. After staring at the same god damned wall for so long, everything was blurry anyway. Coupled with the fading light, his vision wasn't doing him a whole hell of a lot of good.

He paused. Now there was a thought. Maybe his blurry vision wasn't the problem. Maybe the problem was he'd been using the wrong sense from the start.

Faedrah had called the tomb a crystal crypt. Since quartz was a mineral… He jerked.

Fuckin-ay, he had a sixth sense at his disposal.

Lowering his chin to his chest, he envisioned a wide beam shooting from his mind, a searchlight tuned in on the mineral composition of quartz. The screen behind his eyelids remained an empty slate, but he tried again, widening his focus just like Fandorn had taught him.

Amethyst…citrine…diamond… The nerves along the back of his head lit up like a Christmas tree, and he grunted. Typical. Leo was the only one with balls big enough to encase himself in the hardest, most expensive substance known to man. Not that it mattered. Now that Rhys had found him, the miserable son of a bitch was done.

Jamming his index finger and thumb into his mouth, he blew a piercing whistle. The tomb was half a mile behind them. Maybe less.

The Dreggs wheeled around and he circled his fist in the air before waving everyone back the way they'd come. Squinting into the increasing darkness, he followed the radar blip in his head, then growled and smacked his fist against his thigh as the route dead-ended straight into the cliffs. Not that he'd expected a welcome mat and doorbell, but *come on*!

He blew another quick whistle to snag Fandorn's attention and jabbed a finger toward the area. "Light it up!"

An orb of wizard's fire expanded in the wizard's hands and streaked across the sky. Rhys blinked to clear the iridescent trail imprinted on his vision as the ball exploded and crackled like a fourth of July firework against the white rock.

Movement caught the corner of his eye, and he gripped Grommel's wrist, leaning into the turn as the Dregg veered left. The heavy beat of its wings stirred the air as they closed in, whooshing like the huge bellows inside the smithy. Inching along the cliffs, Rhys cocked a brow as a set of worn, uneven steps appeared carved in the stone, leading smack-dab to a wide flat ledge. The opening to the crypt sparkled and glinted in the fading light, hidden inside an outcropping that jutted toward the water and curled in on itself like a set of gnarled fingers.

That sneaky bastard. Leo had created the perfect optional illusion to camouflage the entrance.

Rhys scanned the terrain for whatever could've caused the movement, but came up empty. Most likely, it had been some sort of animal, startled by Fandorn's fire. And with night approaching, it was best everyone come in for a landing before risking a broken arm or leg in the process. "Set me down."

The gravity under his boots was every bit as welcome as the release of the strain on his back. Grommel peeled off into the night and Rhys stepped aside to make room for the rest of their party, his arms itching for Faedrah's soft curves, to have her pinned against him, safe and sound, in one piece.

The second her feet touched ground, she rushed forward, grabbed his cheeks and kissed him square on the mouth. "How ever did you find it?" She tossed her arms around his neck and hung on tight. "Goddesses' tits, I believed our cause was lost."

He smirked, opened a palm behind her and, exerting a push, caught a large yellow diamond as it snapped off a formation near the entrance and dropped into his palm. "Diamonds." She released him and he offered the gem to his muse. "Once I zeroed in on them, the place lit up like a neon sign in my head." Her brows crumpled in confusion, and he chuckled. "Like the lights with no flame in my world."

"Ah." She handed the diamond back to him and he hesitated before tossing it over his shoulder. Sure, a rock that size would be worth a pretty penny, but he wasn't about to decorate any part of Faedrah's body with something his father had created.

"Well…" He glanced around the group, all tugging on their clothes and checking their weapons were still secure. "Might as well get this party started."

Fandorn rapped the bottom of his staff against the ledge and the knot of wood at the top sizzled and snapped before settling to the bright glow of a halogen light bulb. Slipping the folded map out from under the rope tied around his waist, he shook it open and offered the parchment to Rhys. "After you, my boy."

Wonderful…but not surprising. Rhys waved off the sketch. He didn't need a piece of paper to tell him where to go. The route was still embedded in his brain, and his better option would be to watch every step. One slip, and he'd officially become the expendable crew member in this landing party.

With a nod toward the rest of the group, he faced the entrance and stepped inside.

The dense void of outer space swallowed him whole, until Fandorn entered behind Faedrah and the light from his staff refracted off the gems in the narrow passage like laser beams.

Rhys blinked to adjust to the bright light and then froze, frowning down at the crystalline dust coating the path in a layer of white powder. Fresh boot prints led off into the distance.

Shit, he'd been wrong. He leaned left then right, peering ahead into the dwindling shafts of light for sign any of movement. That hadn't been an animal scampering along the cliffs. Someone was in here with them. "We've got company. Everyone keep on your toes."

A string of silver chimes sang against the walls, pinging down the tunnel and vibrating the diamonds in a whining distortion. He slumped and pivoted toward the group—Vaighn, Faedrah, her mom, dad and Denmar all equipping themselves with some sort of weapon.

Really? Rhys lifted his brows. Why not just get an air horn? Then maybe they could all do the wave like the crowd at a football game.

Vaighn glanced over his shoulder at the king and queen before refocusing on Rhys. "What?"

"Nothing." *Idiot.* Rhys sighed and started them down the path. So much for the element of surprise.

Though the going was dicey in some spots—the precious rubble like casters under their boots made it easy to slip or twist an ankle—navigating the trail wasn't the biggest hurdle, even in the tight crevices where the breathing room got a little thin. The map in his head remained clear as day and, even better, the welcoming committee had laid out each step. There wasn't any guesswork involved as they approached the gaping chasm and Rhys eyed the glittering bridge comprised of one solid, mind-blowing diamond. While the surface was slicker than shit and measured barely half a foot wide, crossing it didn't even work up a sweat. He placed each boot on the print left in the diamond dust and told everyone else to play follow the leader.

The same was true once they'd all made it to the other side and had to shimmy beneath a monolithic overhang that protruded from the cave like a fucking glacier. As long as the group mimicked his motions and stayed hot on his heels, his position as point man suited just fine.

The only pisser was, asking as much was fucking impossible. The diamonds were razor sharp, and—surprise, surprise—the entire place had evidently been constructed using some sort of spell. One wrong move…the snag of a cloak or the smallest misstep and someone invariably tipped sideways, slicing an arm or a leg or the inside of their palm as they braced themselves against the wall.

If that didn't twist his 'nads enough, the powdery dust was littered with needle-like slivers. If anyone so much as skimmed a section of exposed skin against any surface or, worse yet, inhaled too deep, the outcome could be like burying their face in fiberglass.

Rhys did what he could to make the route less hazardous, melting the biggest shards to a rounded nub or shoving them aside altogether, but just about the time the last of their crew inched through a section behind him, all his work disappeared.

It was like trekking through a living, breathing geode. One that enjoyed fucking with them every step of the way. Each gasp made his muscles tighter. Every curse cranked his anger another notch hotter. They needed to move fast and, at the same time, asking Faedrah's family to hurry up was like handing them a death sentence.

By the time he jumped down from the last tunnel into the

central chamber, Rhys was coated in a layer of shimmering sand. It grated between his fingers and the bend inside his elbows, but he resisted brushing off his arms. The itchy grit would most likely turn his skin into hamburger.

The ledge around the perimeter sloped to a spike-infested pit, the diamonds gradually descending from white to yellow, then green, blue, violet and down to indigo—a lethal sunset that darkened to a midnight sky filled with glittering stars. Low in the center, stretched from the roof to the floor, a thick black column braced the cave like a faceted chrysalis. A bizarre white light pulsed inside, each thrum vibrating through his body, drilling into his head and pressing against his chest like a gong.

That black cocoon had to be where Gaelleod slept...the repeating flash his heartbeat...but not for long.

A quick scan of the dark corners for their absentee host, and Rhys turned to help Faedrah off the high ledge. He nearly popped a vessel at the networked slashes peeling back the tight fit of her leather suit, each one showcasing a seeping red scrape running helter skelter along her arms and legs. Denmar toted a nice-sized gash over his leather eye patch and Vaighn's loose sleeves hung shredded down his arms.

Fuck, what a disaster. The only upside was, this far under, the temperature was cold enough to slow the bleeding, and all Rhys needed was five minutes, more or less. There was no need to get close. A few well-placed fissures, a hard shove and that column would tumble like a house of cards.

After that, he could use the biggest shards to skewer Gaelleod in his bed. Seemed appropriate, considering all they'd been through to get here.

"Let's do this and get the hell outta Dodge." Diamond bits rasped under his boots as Rhys pivoted toward the resonating pillar and Fandorn stepped to his side.

Rhys closed his eyes, centering his focus on the mineral components of the black diamond. The walls of the cave shuddered. A

335

loud *crack* split the ceiling and diamonds rained down like jagged hail. Lifting his hands, he splayed his fingers and pressed harder, using the droning vibrations to burrow deeper, his mind's eye following the path of each zig-zagging fracture down to the source.

A creepy chuckle built in volume, bouncing around the ceiling like some corny Halloween soundtrack. The folds of Fandorn's robes whispered as he closed in and seized Rhys' wrist. "Cease."

He yanked back his power, lowering his hands. Rocks tumbled, shimmering stones clacking against each other as they bounced and rolled into the pit. Vaighn inched forward, sword drawn, followed by Denmar and the king.

Rhys turned one ear to the buzz of dead air and glanced around the walls. Evidently, whoever was in here with them had finally decided to make an appearance.

"Continue on this course, Wizard, and you shall die."

Rhys cocked a brow. Like hell. If he didn't continue *then* they would all die. He squinted into the shadowed crevices, waiting, but nothing moved. "The only people who are gonna die here today are Gaelleod and whoever you might be, unless you hightail it outta here PDQ."

Another laugh danced around the cave, filled with a calculating awareness that tingled the hair on Rhys' arms. "You are the son of my master, are you not? Born centuries afield and returned to this realm through the veil?"

Shit, who was this dude? And how the hell did he know anything about Rhys' life?

"And the lovely Faedrah. Daughter to the bastard king and his prophesied white queen. Heir apparent to the Austiere throne and Keeper of the Key. My, how you've grown into a reigning beauty."

All right, that does it. Every muscle in Rhys' body tightened. The dickwad had just crossed the line.

A deep growl built in the king's chest, and he stomped forward, white-knuckling the hilt of his sword like he was itching to take a swipe. "Show yourself, minion. Let us stare our enemy in the eye before the killing blow of our vengeance is delivered."

Genuine humor saturated the next evil laugh. "You speak of retribution for a kingdom so easily granted. A reign as king that should have never been yours." The flutter of a dingy cape caught the corner of Rhys' eye, and he snapped his head to the left. "The Austiere Kingdom is *mine*, brother!"

A hunch-backed figure lurched from behind the black tower of Leo's tomb. The king stumbled back a step. An ear-splitting clang reverberated against the walls as Vaighn dropped his sword. "F-father?"

Son of a bitch. Rhys sized up the misshapen lump of flesh previously known as Braedric Austiere. Faedrah had told him some of the story surrounding Vaighn's dad. The rest had been filled in by whispers he'd overheard at the castle. Christ, this was the last headache they needed. Evidently, Gaelleod wasn't the only zombie featured in this night of the living the dead.

"You insipid fools. You come here bearing grandiose plans to eradicate the evil from this realm, but you cannot do a thing!" The former reigning prince tossed one deformed hand to the side, the ragged ends of his cloak snagging on the floor as he limped forward. The puckered skin near his mouth twisted in a warped sneer. "Destroying Gaelleod will merely bring ruin to your precious kingdom."

What a fucking asshole. Rhys clamped down hard on the anger blistering the inside of his chest. That was nothing but a bald-faced lie. A last-ditch attempt to mess with their heads so Braedric Austiere could reap whatever rewards Gaelleod had promised him in exchange for watching over his tomb. "What the fuck are you talking about?"

Diamond dust fell from his matted hair to his shoulders as Faedrah's uncle shook his head. "So much power and yet, still, you do not see." He stopped before the pulsating tower, craning his neck to peer up at Rhys from his stooped position.

A chill that had nothing to do with the cool air settled over

Rhys' skin.

"You are from the future, son of Gaelleod. Slay your father now, and your life will cease to exist."

Chapter 2

What? A snort grated the back of Rhys' throat. What the hell kind of bass-ackward logic was that? Next, the asshole would be trying to convince them the only way out of this diamond-infested Venus Flytrap was to hand over the key.

Smirking, Rhys crossed his arms. No wonder everyone hated this piece of royal shit. He glanced at Faedrah and rolled his eyes. Big man thought he was so smart, picking up on their worst fears and then twisting the facts around so they'd buy into his...

Jerking his focus back to Faedrah, Rhys sucked air as his stomach dove for his feet. Oh no. He clenched his jaw against the roar gathering like a volcanic eruption in his chest. Oh, *fuck*, no.

The thin crescent of tears hovering along her lower lashes... the subtle shift in her throat as she swallowed... God *dammit*. Unlocking his arms, he tried and failed to come up with some way to reject the undeniable truth in her eyes. There was no fucking way. What that motherfucker said *couldn't* be right. Not after all they'd been through. Not after coming this far.

"He lies!" Vaighn surged forward and the king grabbed his son's arm, stopping the prince from taking a header straight into the glittering pit of death.

"Long have I awaited the day when I could end the reign of your insurrections." Eyes wild, fists shaking, Vaighn scanned the shards as if searching for the safest route down to the lump of flesh that represented his dad. "I shall enjoy watching the life ebb from your eyes." He snatched his sword off the floor, bouncing forward on his boots like he was prepping for one helluva leap. "Come, father. Let the full length of my blade be sanctified by your blood."

Rhys' fingers curled in on themselves; his heart twisted. Jesus *Christ*. Talk about being in touch with that reality. An absentee father…one who'd handed the people Vaighn cared for most in the world nothing but heartache and pain.

Expelling a slow breath, Rhys shook his head. Seemed he and Vaighn had more in common than he'd ever imagined.

"No, Vaighn." The king faced Faedrah's brother, turning his back toward Braedric to grip his adoptive son's shoulders. "This deformity you see is not your father. Braedric Austiere was lost to us long ago."

A muscle ticked in Vaighn's jaw, his lashes clumped together like they were wet. Rhys cleared his throat and dropped his focus to his feet. He'd known from the start Leo had done everything in his power to wreck Faedrah's family, but watching the outcome of that criminal behavior take shape firsthand? Shit, that pain was like a sharp knife to the gut.

"You are correct about one thing, my beloved Uncle." Vaighn placed his free hand on the king's arm, holding on so tight the tips of his fingers dug into the muscle. "Braedric Austiere is not my father. Not since the day you welcomed me as a son and equal in your family."

The king searched Vaighn's face, nodding. A single tear tumbled and tracked through the white dust on his cheek.

A rasping cackle shook Braedric's shoulders, and he swiped a wad of glistening spit off his chin. "Do not deceive yourself, Vaighn. Your loyal king does not consider you his equal. His daughter ascends to the throne, a seat which has always rightfully belonged to you. The king fears you, my son, and the threat of royal blood that flows through your veins. *My* blood, and the same which bequeaths you the authority of every sovereign throughout Austiere history."

"Shut it, ya right bloody bastard." Denmar lunged forward. "Or I shall jump this crevasse and skewer your black heart, myself."

Rhys glared at Braedric Austiere from under his brows. God, it would be so easy for him to kill the fucker right where he stood. Payback for all the hurt, the anger, the gut-fisting frustration of being ignored. But doing so wasn't his responsibility, and he'd be kicked to hell and back before stealing something so epically important from Vaighn.

The prince closed his eyes, a small smile in place as if what his dad had just said was the dumbest thing he'd ever heard. A last-ditch effort to get Vaighn to switch sides. "Yet, I shall have no rest, my soul shall attain no peace until the sins of my birthright have been avenged." Stepping back from the king, he dropped his arm and nodded toward the mutilated man standing by the column. "I beg you, my king. Sanction this one last favor. Allow me to fulfill my duty as a member of the royal guard. Grant me release from the prison I've borne since childhood, and permit me the privilege of slaying our kingdom's most treasonous enemy."

Well, he got that right. Rhys raked both hands through his hair, linking his fingers across the back of his neck. Toting around the responsibility for a father's actions, watching it destroy people's lives day after day... That wasn't living. Not really. Not when Vaighn had the ability to do something about it, and not when Rhys held that same power in his hands.

"I must refuse, my son." The king shook his head. "I could not bear to los—"

"Let him go." Rhys cocked a brow as the entire group pivoted in his direction. Of everyone living out this nightmare, he understood the most. Nothing...not the future or past...not the heartbreak of a broken promise or even the risk of losing his life mattered to Vaighn. Not when pitted against the safety of his family. Not when the chance to right every wrong he'd been forced to carry was only an arm's length away.

The only thing he cared about was this opportunity to settle a very old score and how, in doing so, he'd be saving everyone he loved in the process.

Dropping his arms to his sides, Rhys huffed a sour breath against the bullshit hand they'd been dealt. He and Vaighn most of all. "It's his life, Your Majesty. Vaighn's a grown man and can make his own decisions." A knot of resentment dug into the base of Rhys' throat. Shit. If only the making decisions part was the worst of it. The final outcome is what really sucked ass. "Besides, if you deny him this opportunity, he'll never forgive you."

The king hesitated, the skin near his eyes crinkling as he squinted. His shoulders fell, and he pivoted toward his wife.

"Be careful, Vaighn." Diamonds crunched as she strode forward and wrapped her arms around her son's neck. "Though you follow your destiny, every moment we are parted your welfare will be foremost in our hearts." His arms tightened around her waist as she patted his back. "We shall anxiously await your safe return."

Faedrah hitched a breath and acidic bile percolated in Rhys' stomach. But he didn't dare look at her. One glance at the misery in her bottomless brown eyes and he wouldn't be able to think straight. And he needed every synapse firing at full capacity if he planned to logically think things through.

Suspending his hand over the pit, he concentrated on the minerals in the diamonds and smoothed a clear path straight down to the center. "Go get 'em, Your Highness. Just do me a favor and come back with the asshole's head on a pike."

A full grin lifted Vaighn's cheeks, and he nodded as he released the queen. "On my honor, Wizard." He turned and then paused, meeting Rhys' gaze a second time. "You have my sincerest thanks… brother."

Rhys' brow twitched and he nearly chuckled. *Well, I'll be damned…* The people in this world never ceased to surprise him.

"You shall fail." Braedric's tone was so off the cuff, so blasé, the statement came out as simple fact. "Gaelleod shall rise and restore my place as the rightful Austiere King, or you will kill him now and your young wizard shall cease to exist...and the line of the bastard gypsy king will fade as uselessly as it began." With the twirl of his cape, Braedric scuttled around the column and disappeared.

"But not before the steel of my blade removes your head from your shoulders." Vaighn took off like a bullet down the slick path, rounded the tower hot on his dad's tail and was gone.

Faedrah's family seemed to take a collective breath as if waiting for...hell, Rhys didn't know. The silence stretched, filled with nothing but the continuous drone of Gaelleod's heartbeat. A second later, the weight of five sets of eyes landed on Rhys. He lowered his gaze to the ground and kicked a green diamond over the ledge. It clacked and bounced against the jagged spikes, lodging between two white tines like an olive in a martini.

Christ, what he wouldn't give for a strong shot of alcohol right about now. Not that it would dull the numbing ache filling the spot where his heart used to be. Or make his decision any less painful.

Propping his hands on his hips, he shook his head. The upshot was, he and Faedrah were royally screwed. To leap back through time and confront Leo in the future was a fucking joke. That idea had suicide mission written all over it. In his world, Rhys' powers weren't a tenth of what they were in this place. Besides, the two of them had already boxed two minutes in that ring and been KO'd in the process. No way in hell was he putting Faedrah through that again. Especially when a good chance existed that's exactly the way Leo would expect them to react. If nothing else was certain, sure as shit, he was counting on Rhys being weak, on running scared in the face of a threat just like he had as a kid.

The resentment of past hurts scrubbed at the scabs over his heart and, this time, Rhys didn't stuff the memories down deep. He let them burn through his chest, let them fuel his decision to move forward in the one way he already knew was best.

Getting rid of Leo here was the safer play. The *only* play they had left. In this time, there was nothing Leo could do to stop his death from unfolding. He was a festering wound waiting to be cauterized, and no one but Rhys had the ability to flatten the fucker where he rested. Besides, whatever potential threats Leo might think to levy on Faedrah once he woke up, however he might choose to blackmail her family, his reign of terror needed to stop. And it needed to stop now. Before his evil infected every square inch of her kingdom and there was no hope of ever bringing it back.

Rhys was the only one who could give her that gift, even if it meant he'd be leaving the only woman he'd ever loved.

He tipped his head back on his shoulders, cheeks expanding as he blew on harsh breath toward the ceiling. Still, he would be leaving her alive, with a family who loved her more than anything else in the world. He would be protecting the woman he loved, and would finally gain closure for all the beatings, all those moments his anger had nearly consumed him…the continuous stream of insults that had reduced him to a worthless pile of shit.

Was that tradeoff worth the loss of his life?

Shit, was there even a question?

Lowering his head, he faced his muse and smiled at the beautiful tears hovering along her lower lashes. "I love you," he whispered. "I'm sorry."

She stutter stepped forward. "No." The queen grasped her arm, but Faedrah shrugged her mother's hand off her body. "Rhys, look at me. You cannot do this!"

Turning toward the black crypt that encased his father, he gathered his power and thrust both hands toward the pulsating light. The ground rumbled in warning. The walls shook as fissures cracked like lightning bolts down the inside of the cave.

"Rhys McEleod! Desist in this madness this instant!" The king bellowed off to his left, but Rhys was way ahead of him.

Gathering some loose shards off the floor with his mind, he jammed them into the cracks zipping down the outside of Leo's tomb. They would brace the structure, but probably not for long.

"Get out now!" The tinkling of cascading rubble nearly drowned out his voice. The entire place splintered and sang like the deafening crash of a chandelier. "I'll do my best to hold it until everyone's clear!"

But, instead of shooing everyone for the exit like Rhys expected, Faedrah's dad lurched forward and placed his hand on Rhys' wrist. "Stop, my boy."

What the hell was he doing? The king's voice was calm, his face relaxed…everything about him the complete opposite to the chaos inside the cave. He pressed down until Rhys had no choice but to reel in the energy tingling through his fingers and lower his arms. "Your death this day is not the fate our Goddesses have planned for you."

Rhys frowned, searching the king's face for answers. Had the dude lost it? He should be whooping it up he'd finally gotten his wish. The asshole who'd stolen his daughter's heart had decided to take one for the team.

"I have just lost one son." King Caedmon placed a tight grip on Rhys' shoulder. "I will not stand idly by and allow Gaelleod's evil to deprive me of another."

Wait… Rhys' frown deepened to a scowl. What did he just say? He turned his head, carefully studying the king from the corner of his eye. Maybe Faedrah's dad was pulling his leg. Or, the more obvious choice, he'd accidently inhaled some diamond dust and it had fried his brain.

The king chuckled, and the warmth inside that sound reminded Rhys so much of Grady, the bitterness scoring a hole in the center of his chest slid up and settled into a hard knot at the base of his throat. He grunted, blinking at the moisture in his eyes.

"My daughter loves you and, for the first time since your arrival, I believe her faith in you is soundly placed." The king smiled over his shoulder at Faedrah's watery gaze before facing Rhys a second time. "You were fully prepared to sacrifice your life to safeguard Faedrah and her future kingdom. A king…a *father* could not ask

345

for more from his daughter's betrothed. You have proven yourself worthy, my boy. I endorse your petition to be wed."

Whoa. Rhys stumbled back a step. Talk about turning on a dime.

He glanced at the surprise lifting Faedrah's brows before surveying the rest of her family, all their faces filled with acceptance, kindness, maybe a little fear over what he might do next. "But…what about—"

"Gaelleod has rested in this crypt for twenty passings of the seasons, my boy. To act in haste would seem a fruitless error in judgment." The king turned toward the black tower, his chin lowering as he scanned it from top to bottom. "A few days to strategize our next course would serve us well."

Rhys scratched his head, trying to process what had just happened. One second he was road kill and the next he was getting married. *Married?*

"I do not believe I have ever seen you quite so dumbfounded." King Caedmon pursed his lips like he was trying to curb a smile. "Without hesitation, you charge forth to eradicate the most perilous scourge the Austiere Kingdom has ever known, and yet now your tongue seems remarkably tied." He squinted. "Has the thought of joining your life with that of my daughter's left you offended?"

Shit. That was the thing about this world. Everything was either black or white. There was no gray area in relationships, especially where the king's daughter was concerned.

"No, no." Rhys ran a hand along the scruff on his cheek. Either way, one thing was for sure. Standing here like a dumbass with nothing to say was a mistake of epic stupidity. "Truth is, I'm not sure how Faedrah feels about all this. I've never asked her if she'd consider spending the rest of her life with me."

The king's brows shot toward his hairline, lips turned down in a shrewd frown. "Well then, perchance you should." He cleared his throat and leaned close. "Yet I caution you to choose your words wisely. They may be the last you are granted without interruption."

"Ha!" The queen propped a hand on her hip. "Curb your tongue, my love. Or an interruption of words may be the least of your worries."

Rhys shared a quiet chuckle with the king. His gaze landed on Faedrah, and he searched her eyes, trying to envision a life without her. Yeah, that wasn't happening. Not if he had any say in their future—their past—whatever the hell this was. It didn't matter. Whether they landed in her world or his, he loved her. Hell, he'd loved her since before he even knew she truly existed. Now that her dad had finally accepted their connection at face value, they could move forward together no matter where they were.

So, married. To Faedrah. The thought spread like a warm blanket over his chest. Fuck, yeah, he wanted to marry her. More than anything else he'd ever done.

"What do you say, Princess?" He smirked. "Wanna get hitched?"

Her footsteps crunched as she neared, his arms open and waiting to pull her close, to cinch her sweet curves against him while his tongue dove inside to sample her clean taste again and again.

Her arm swung back, and his chin snapped to the right as pain exploded through his cheek. The loud smack echoed off the walls, followed by the queen's gasp.

Rhys slowly turned back to his muse, but Faedrah was already halfway to the exit. She jammed a boot into a crack near the floor and climbed through the opening.

The king sputtered, his head rolled back on his shoulders and his booming laughter drowned out the pulsing of Gaelleod's heart. His shoulders bounced and he shook his head as a few more chuckles worked the muscles of his throat.

Ha, ha, fucking hilarious. Rhys scrubbed a hand along his jaw. Okay, that response had to be a resounding *no*.

"Goddesses' tits, my boy!" The king grinned, slapping a hand on Rhys' shoulder. "I daresay you have met your match." Eyes sparkling with mischief, he tugged Rhys into a rough one-armed hug, lifting his other hand toward his wife. "Indeed, I've made the right choice. This marriage shall serve them both well."

* * *

The man's head was filled with horse dung if he assumed for *one heartbeat* she would bind her life to his in matrimony.

Faedrah marched along the serrated spikes of the diamond encrusted passageway, her footfalls determined though the light from Fandorn's staff faded at her back. Why ever would she do something so incredibly daft? A few more strides and the eerie glow of deep gloaming saturated the tunnel. So Rhys could disregard her the moment of his choosing? So he could cast himself into oblivion and leave her heartbroken and inconsolable, a withering rose seated upon the Austiere throne?

"Faedrah!"

If he truly believed she would willingly consent to such foolishness, he could kiss her barren backside!

The channel narrowed and she cautiously braced her palm on to the wall to steady her balance. Nights beyond numbering she had fought Gaelleod's cruel incursion of her dreams only to end dying upon the sharp edge of his dagger. Yet Rhys all but served himself upon a silver platter to fulfill the dark lord's most coveted schemes.

Were those the actions of a man whose heart's desire was to live out his days at her side? She would think not!

"Faedrah, stop! Just wait a second. You're gonna hurt yourself."

As if he cared one way or the other. She spun to face him, whipping a short sword from the baldric at her back. A flashing arc of silver spliced the air as she leveled the deadly tip at his chest. "You wish to die? You crave an ending to our quest?"

Pulling up short, he lifted both hands in a show of surrender. "All right. I get you're pissed, but let's put the sword down, okay?"

Absurd. As if the silver of her blade was of any more threat to him than the down of a feather. Yet she would drive her point home with whatever tools were at her disposal. "Do not order me about as if one thought to my wellbeing is foremost in your mind." Stepping forward, she jabbed the tip of her blade into his chest. A soft chime vibrated against the crystalline walls, traveling the length of the silver into her hand. "You've proven well enough my happiness is not the least of your concerns."

He frowned, withdrawing a step as she prodded and poked. "What the hell are you talking about? Your happiness *is* important to me."

Ha! Twice since their arrival in her realm he had presented himself for execution. Perchance his third attempt would be just the charm. "Then you think me blind? An addle-brained fool?"

"Of *course* not!" Anger glinted in his eyes, sparking with the same verdant starlight as the green diamonds cluttered around their feet. "I just asked you to marry me, for Christ's sake. Not sure about this world, but in mine that question pretty much defines love and respect."

"And yet, at every turn you seek to present Gaelleod the achievement of his goals." She backed him against the wall, and irritation plucked at her nerves as the diamonds behind him melded to a slick sheet of glass. Threatening a wizard of his means was an exercise in futility. Particularly in lieu of his persistent need to do himself in. "Above all, your father stands to gain the exact fulfillment of his desires should your life cease to exist."

"Oh, now hold up just a second. You got that backwards." Encircling her blade in his bare hand, he forced the weapon down between them. "If I die, Leo gets nothing. He needs my body, Faedrah. If I take it away, his plans aren't worth shit."

A rueful smile tugged one side of her lips, and she huffed, releasing the hilt of her sword. Let him have her blade. 'Twas of no use to her if he did not see her point. "As are mine, my love. As are mine."

Backing away from him, she searched his gaze. Did he presume for one moment she did not know? That she had not lived and

349

breathed his same wretched bitterness through Vaighn? "And watching you destroy yourself? Bearing witness to the anguish such deeds would cause in those who hold you most dear? Would that not present Gaelleod the ultimate pinnacle of his desires?"

Rhys hesitated, his fingers whitening around the circumference of her blade.

"Ten years I stood silent while Vaighn struggled to live down the transgressions of his father. Ten years borne of insurrections which were not rightfully his." Her voice caught and she gritted her teeth against the misery bearing down upon her chest. "Vaighn's father did not *leave*. His evil deeds did not disappear into the ether. Braedric Austiere has been with his son every day since the moment of Vaighn's birth…controlling his actions, determining his fate, altering Vaighn's life into something 'twas never meant to be."

Jabbing her finger at the ground, she locked her knees against the impulse to reclaim the distance between them. She refused to allow her beloved to suffer Vaighn's fate. There had been enough misplaced guilt. Enough misery over past hurts. Shouldering such hopeless duties would serve neither of them any good. "I will not have it from the man who binds his life to mine. I will *not*."

But, perchance, her petition came too late. She eased back another step, shaking her head. "Gaelleod controls you even now, my love. You hold within your beautiful, loyal heart the ability to steal from him everything he craves, yet you freely offer him your life as if everything it entails is his just reward."

The tension eased from Rhys' jaw. His shoulders lowered, and the anger in his gaze transformed into awareness a scant moment before his eyes slipped closed.

"If you truly despise him as you say you do, there would be no sweeter revenge than to persevere. Become the antithesis of all that Gaelleod embodies. Best him on *our* terms, and accept the blessings you've been granted by living on in happiness and peace."

Rhys lowered his head and, in the silence which ensued, three heavy heartbeats pulsed in Faedrah's ears. He must accept she had spoken true or every moment they shared moving forward would be tainted with bitterness and loss.

She would not permit their life together to start in such a way. Braedric…Gaelleod…the evil plaguing her kingdom had already overshadowed the joy bestowed upon her brother. She would not stand idly by and let its filthy taint go unchecked.

"God dammit." Rhys' chest rose with a deep intake of breath. He glanced down at his hand and turned the sword as if, for the first, realizing he held it in his fingers. His focus lingered along the blade before he lifted his gaze to hers. "I never saw it that way."

"Indeed." She crossed her arms, arching a shrewd brow. Yet the mystery remained how he planned to proceed moving forward. "And now that you do?"

A grunt bounced his shoulders and he flipped the sword, offering the hilt in her direction. "Whatever we decide, I'm gonna do my best to give Leo hell. I choose to fight…and live."

Thank the nine. She slumped as the weight of her declaration eased from her shoulders. Her heart would have certainly been lost had he not consented, though chances were high they would have hounded each other until some or another settlement had been reached.

She grasped the hilt of her sword, casting a gentle smile toward the man she loved. Yet instead of releasing the weapon, he jerked her close, slipped one arm about her waist and hauled her to his chest.

"So, now that we got that worked out, you gonna answer my question?" The fingers of his other hand dove into her hair, and he angled her head as if he longed for the taste of her lips.

The whisper of his breath spread a seductive warmth through her body. A firm wall of muscle met her stomach as she relaxed inside the tight band of his arm. He widened his stance to cradle her hips and her pulse spiked, his palm easing down to cup her bottom and apply a generous squeeze.

An edgy impatience mounted between them, their bodies

swaying as they perched on the edge of a kiss. She slid her arm about his shoulders to pull him down to her lips, but he would not relent. Not until the words he hungered for had been formed by her tongue.

His brow twitched, and she bit down hard on her bottom lip. Only one response would grant her release from this desperate need and, to keep him with her, she would gladly submit. No danger in either world compared to agony she faced of forging ahead without him, and she closed her eyes to await the moment they would finally be joined in a kiss.

"I accept."

Chapter 3

Faedrah's eyes slipped closed as the strength of her mother's embrace tightened about her shoulders. The unbound sheets of the queen's white tresses slid glossy and sleek beneath her palm, and Faedrah curled her fingers in their silky texture, hugging her mother back just as fierce. The slightest tip of her head and the scent of night blooming jasmine filled her senses, mixed with subtle warmth and the familiar perfume of her mother's skin.

"Oh, that the Goddesses had granted us another way."

The strike of her father's boot heels continued their nervous pace under her mother's bare whisper, and Faedrah squeezed her eyelids to thwart the budding threat of her tears. Chances were high, once her sorrow arrived, it would not cease, and she would not allow herself to assume the worst, regardless of the grim circumstances she and Rhys were about to face.

"The future has not yet been set. Let us not despair an outcome Rhys and I will strive our utmost to avoid."

However much they had struggled to reject the truth...no matter the wrath of her father's anger or Fandorn's pursuits to aid in their quest, none could deny the path before them had been set.

She and Rhys had been offered no other choice but to return to his world and battle Gaelleod in the future.

Yet, with this decision, a bleak despondency had settled about them like an unshakable shroud. 'Twas no guarantee the strength of Rhys' powers would follow him through to his world and, in taking such a leap, the likelihood Faedrah and Rhys would never return had continued to grow thick and foreboding in the air.

Her father's footsteps ceased, and despite the hopelessness Faedrah warred to keep from invading her heart, a gentle smile graced her lips as she envisioned the way he habitually raked his hair back from his brow. "Can we not delay this leave-taking but a day or two longer? Perchance, given more time, we can ferret out a more optimistic course."

With the parting of a reassuring squeeze, Faedrah released her mother and withdrew a pace to find the king standing across the throne room, facing the vibrant magenta sky glorifying Helios' descent through an open stained-glass window.

Several days had passed since their sojourn to Gaelleod's crypt, and though they'd discussed the topic at length, tarrying long into the night, nary an alternative had made itself known.

She neared the window and slipped her hand around the king's upper arm, leaning the side of her head against his shoulder. "To what end, father? We have delayed long enough and at our kingdom's expense."

Beneath the splendor of the radiant sky, the Austiere fields lay blackened beyond recognition. Leafless trees reached skyward amid tendrils of acrid smoke, their putrid odor wafting from fissures rent upon the barren ground. The once thriving forest beyond had altered to a hard black slash, vacant of all life save whatever vile spawn sought sanctuary in Gaelleod's malicious fog.

"We cannot allow the dark lord's plague to run rampant throughout the entirety of our lands." Faedrah brought her other hand to her chest and fisted the golden key in her fingers. Lifting her head, she turned to better study the profile of her father's face. Had it truly been less than a fortnight ago she had longed for escape? To cast aside his concerns in lieu of seeking her fate?

What a fool she had been.

Regret built as a heated weight at the base of her throat, and she quickly snapped her focus back to the inhospitable view. What a silly, spoiled little girl. How could she have ever regarded this white castle perched high atop the sprawling mountains as a prison? What manner of discourteous entitlement had she harbored to imagine her privileged life as a curse? If now given the choice, she would have happily agreed to remain sheltered within the safe haven of her parents' home.

Unfurling her fingers, she stared down at the mysterious treasure cradled in the center of her palm. She'd once craved the forbidden fruits of the key's enigmatic secrets and, in doing so, had opened a doorway leading to her fated half. Though her life would be lost without him, at what cost had she made such an impetuous decision? Only to become the figurehead guiding those she loved to heartache and ruin? To watch her kingdom fall to its knees before an enemy of invincible doom?

She had longed to be the savior of her people and, instead, she had led them straight into Gaelleod's inescapable trap.

"Majesties. I've found something."

Faedrah turned from the window, as did her father, to find Fandorn entering the throne room through a side door. His foot-falls were hurried, his gray robes training behind him, his hair a wild mass of tangles about his head. He carried a large leather-bound tome in both hands and brought it to a decorative table along the wall, dropping it with a resounding bang. "Look here."

The binding crackled with age as he flipped to the center, and Faedrah hastened to close the distance as he aimed a rigid finger at an illustration bound on the right-hand side. "Have you seen this dagger, my child?"

The queen strode up behind her, along with her father and Rhys as Faedrah stared, unblinking, at the page. Goat-headed forms writhed in ecstasy down either side of the diagram and, in the middle, a large silver blade dripped crimson with blood, an inverted pentagram cast in gold upon the hilt.

'Twas the same curved blade she'd seen in her nightly visions...
and the same Gaelleod had cruelly plunged into her beloved's chest.

Faedrah closed her eyes against the horrifying reminder and
spun away. "Indeed. Yet, I've not the occasion to view it firsthand."
Blinking, she turned back to the table and locked on to Rhys, and
her heart rebelled as an anguished understanding filled his gaze.
"'Twas shown to me in a dream. You bring us the dagger Gaelleod
employs to complete his rite of transformation."

The king muttered a curse as the queen's shoulders fell. She
peeked askance at Rhys before addressing the aged wizard. "What
does this mean, Fandorn? Have you found its location?"

"I have not, my queen." One of the wizard's bushy eyebrows
rose, though he kept his attention pinned to Faedrah, and she shivered as a dire warning tempered his words. "I fear this instrument
of the dark lord's vile incantations has been secreted far outside
our reach." He reached down with one hand, and dust wafted into
the air as he slammed the cover, shuttering the image from view.
"Gaelleod's knife contains a dark magic which spans far beyond
the limits of our kingdom, and is the only blade promised to
withhold the power and capacity to kill him."

Faedrah snapped her focus to Rhys. He'd withdrawn to pace
before the open armoire, the veil aglow with shimmering light,
the dark-blue curtain crumpled aside in preparation for their leap.
As if sensing her perusal, he stopped and met her gaze, and her
heart skittered forward at the unyielding determination etched
upon his face. "Well, then, we'd damn well better go find it. Based
on Faedrah's dreams, I'm guessing the bastard's got it with him
in the future."

She would gladly offer her life in payment to safeguard those
she loved, a sacrifice to secure the wellbeing of her kingdom and,
deep within his eyes, she knew. Rhys, as well, was prepared to take
what necessary steps to protect her people.

Yet, to pilfer the treasure Gaelleod valued above all other? To
steal inside his lair and slaughter him with the very object meant

to secure his rule? A harsh breath left her lips over the outcome of such appalling odds.

Perchance, if she and Rhys stayed true…if they stood united, their hearts forged by the purest of intentions, all would not be lost.

She had to believe as much. No other reassurances remained.

His chin lowered the slightest degree as he searched her face. Torchlight from the sconces set about the room winked off the silver vambraces encasing his forearms. Magic ignited to spark and sizzle along his hands. "Our time together isn't over, Faedrah. Not by a long shot."

A small smile came unbidden to her lips, and she nodded. "I know, my heart." Still, the question remained. How many passings of Helios' bright face were left them? How many tender moments before their time of reckoning drew nigh? "And there is much yet to be done."

She stepped toward the armoire, but was waylaid as the king's large hand grasped her shoulder. He spun her to face him and a breath left her throat as her father whisked her into his arms. "You *shall* return to us, daughter." Cupping her head to the hard wall of his chest, he centered her cheek over the steady beat of his heart. "Swear it to me now. Swear to me you will return unharmed or I fear I shall order you remain in this realm."

Wrapping one arm about his waist, she fisted the soft folds of his shirt. "I shall do my utmost to try, P'pa."

His muscles tensed beneath her palm. Holding her tight, he placed a firm kiss upon the top of her brow and then thrust her away, his footfalls brisk as he crossed the room for his gilded throne.

Stamping down the urge to follow and request one last embrace, Faedrah pivoted back to her mother. The queen offered her hand, and Faedrah clutched it in hers as they joined Rhys before the armoire.

"No mother has ever been more proud, than I." The queen grasped Rhys' fingers, pausing a moment before relinquishing her hold on Faedrah and linking her hand with that of her betrothed.

"The king and I owe you an unpayable debt. We love you both."

Placing a tender kiss upon Faedrah's cheek, the queen drew the curtain, shuttering Faedrah and Rhys within the magic of the veil. The strike of the queen's footfalls faded against the high ceiling as she crossed the room.

Silence droned in Faedrah's ears, at odds with the turmoil cascading through her heart. A breath stayed lodged within her chest as she lifted her gaze to the mirror.

Dim light cast the majority of the opposite room into shadow. Yet still, the corner end of a low, well-appointed sleeping pallet rested silently within a shaft of moonlight. A large, woven reed mat, much like those commissioned for use in the sparring room, lay centered upon a glossy hardwood floor. Two thick dressing gowns had been spread atop the blankets, awaiting their need, and Faedrah took heart her uncles had followed through on their promise to keep the veil well within the safety of their reach.

Rhys brought the back of her hand to his lips, the scruff of his beard prickling her skin. "You sure about this, Princess? It's still not too late to change your mind."

So that Gaelleod could reign victorious? So he could torment her kingdom throughout a horde of unending years?

Straightening her shoulders, she darted a firm glance at her betrothed. "Quite."

A curt nod, and he firmed his grip on her hand. "Whenever you're ready, then. I'll follow your lead."

With a parting peek toward the heavy curtain at her back, Faedrah filled her lungs to their capacity and they leapt.

"Are you kidding me?" Wizard Oliver smacked his palm to his forehead, crinkling the diminutive piece of parchment pinned to the lapel of his silk sleeping shirt. "Rhys killing Gaelleod equals suicide?" He sighed and rubbed at a spot between his brows. "This time travel business is such a pain in the ass. I swear to God, there isn't enough wine in the world."

358

"Psst." Sir Jon drew Faedrah's attention with soft hiss, nodding in Rhys' direction. "What's he doing?"

She glanced to where her beloved perched beside her upon the padded edge of a wicker settee and her nails instinctively dug into the stiff, woven reeds of the armrest. A single silver spoon lay before him on the low table, unchanged in form or function, Rhys' eyes darting along the length as if the utensil withheld the secrets to the cosmos and all it contained.

Shaking her head at Sir Jon, she forestalled the urge to run her palm down the hunched tension of Rhys' back and placed a silencing finger to her lips. Since the moment their unceremonious tumble through the veil had announced their arrival, her beloved had been like a man possessed. First waylaying all greetings in favor of demanding the use of a black writing instrument so he could scrawl the sigil of his signature upon every wall of her uncles' island abode. Insisting no words pass between them until he'd scribbled that same protective badge upon slips of paper and commanded each person to affix them to their attire.

Ordering Sir Jon to bring him the nearest piece of silver so Rhys could disappear inside his mind and try to ascertain what, if any, residual powers had accompanied him into this realm.

Even as the witch, Violet, and Sir Todd had stumbled sleepy-eyed into the large, airy common area of her uncles' home, Rhys' had remained distant, his gaze devoid of the dangerous passion Faedrah had come to know and love. Though he'd cast an unruly glare toward the interruption and, as if seeing them for the first time, scowled toward the spotless glass panes doubling as the outer walls of the structure, once Sir Todd and Violet had found their seats, Rhys had mentally vacated the room.

The last item on Faedrah's agenda was to interrupt her beloved's meditations.

A dubious lift of his brows, and her dark-haired uncle levered up from his cross-legged position at Wizard Oliver's feet. "Wine it is, then. As much as we can drink." He padded to the far wall, the bottom edge of his loose cotton trousers flopping atop his bare feet, swung open a low wooden cabinet and selected a bottle from the latticed shelf. "And in case anyone cares, I'm cracking open the good stuff."

Rhys muttered a curse; his gaze narrowed. A frustrated breath heaved his shoulders, and Faedrah clamped her jaw tight as he raked a hand through his hair.

The pop of a cork, and crystal chimed as Sir Jon slipped the stems of two wineglasses from an overhanging rack. After conveying his burdens to the table, he took a circuitous path back round to the cupboard and used both hands to bring forth four additional glass goblets.

Faedrah studied the cursive F etched into the sides of the delicate stemware as Sir Jon set about doling out the libation. Mayhap her uncle was right and a draught of strong wine would do them all good…particularly given the horns of her current dilemma.

Whilst she welcomed her beloved's foresight in ensuring Gaelleod be kept unawares of their arrival…and the added benefit inherent in Rhys' signature guaranteed his father would be powerless to hone in on the proximity of the key…unease had grown to the weight of a millstone around her neck. One that continuously increased in circumference and thickness the longer she occupied her seat.

Precious time had passed as her beloved stared, unspeaking, at the silver spoon resting upon her uncles' table, and frustration all but simmered in the air about him as the utensil transformed not one bit. Moreover, with his distraction, the telling of their excursion to Gaelleod's crystal crypt had been left to her, and she worried her explanations over the cause behind their subsequent failure had been somewhat marred in translation.

"So, from what I'm hearing, the bastard's got you by the shorthairs."

"Indeed." She nodded at Sir Todd, the tension in her shoulders slackening a degree. Thank the nine, 'twould seem her account of their time in her world had carried the clarity she intended. "Our hair is decidedly short. Razor-shorn, in fact, and we are in sore need of any succor you may see fit to offer us. We must do our utmost to mask our incursion of Gaelleod's domain if we withstand one chance at delivering the strike of our killing blow."

"Hold on a second." Wizard Oliver sprang forward in his seat, a sharp finger aimed at the plush rug tickling the soles of her feet. "What are you saying? Since you can't do away with Leo in your world, the two of you are planning head to over to his place to kill him in this one?"

"That's it precisely." Faedrah paused, studying the array of stunned faces staring back at her as Sir Jon offered her a glass of claret.

The witch Violet paled, tucking her feet beneath the glowing screen propped open atop her thighs, the elongated width of her seat shrinking her stature to that of a dormouse. Sir Todd lifted his brows and expelled a short puff of air.

Rhys grumbled and shook his head, though his attention never wavered from his labors.

Faedrah frowned. "I fail to see the reasoning behind your hesitation. Does not your world wish to be rid of the nefarious nature of Gaelleod's evil deeds?"

"Well, of course we do, sweetie." Violet reached across the wide arm of her chair to apply a supportive squeeze to Faedrah's wrist. "But in our world, this little discussion we're having is known as pre-meditated murder. We have laws against it, especially since we can't prove Leo McEleod has done anything wrong."

Wizard Oliver fell back in his chair, eying the level in his glass as Sir Jon dispensed him a measure of wine. "There's no way in hell any of us are walking into Leo McEleod's house." Reaching out with one finger, he pressed the bottleneck down until the red liquid had glugged to the rim. "Not to mention what could happen if you and Rhys are actually successful. Heaven forbid, you're caught and the motive gets out. If the case went to court, any sane jury would lock you in the loony bin and throw away the key." He snatched the glass from his lover and downed half the contents in one breath-stealing swallow.

"The operative word here being *if*." Sir Todd squinted, one arm lying crosswise atop the thin cotton shirt encompassing the girth of his protruding belly, the other hand stroking two long, slender braids plaited into the wiry beard on either side of his lower lip.

"Todd." Violet shot a warning glower at her mountainous other half. "Get serious. If Faedrah and Rhys went anywhere near Leo, there would be witnesses. The evidence against them would be stacked from here to Mars. We all know the guy has put the screws to half the Chicago police force. Not to mention the way he's beefed up security ever since—"

With an abrupt jerk of her shoulders, she reigned in her tongue, and dread slid like an oily serpent through Faedrah's stomach as the witch cast an uneasy glance toward the top of Rhys' head.

"Ever since *what* has happened?" Edging forward on the settee, Faedrah set her wineglass upon the table. Full disclosure to any events that had passed whilst she and Rhys were absent from this realm was paramount. Hedging for the sake of civility was a luxury none of them could afford to take.

Sighing, Violet shook her head and tapped a series of lettered squares on the mystical portal balanced upon her lap. She spun the device and lifted it to the left arm of her chair, offering Faedrah full view of the screen. "Read it and weep."

Faedrah's brows shot up the same distance her heart plummeted in her chest. The glowing display depicted a picture of Rhys' beloved Grady, smiling with as much warmth and acceptance as the first time Faedrah had looked upon the butler's face. Yet the element which sent alarm tingling through the hair at her nape, was the accompanying image of a hale and hearty Leo McEleod, shown slightly lower inside the screen and to the right.

She peeked askance at Rhys before her snarl of outrage had the chance to escape. 'Twould seem her love had been correct in his assumptions regarding the black plague invading her kingdom, the same as he'd rightly deduced Gaelleod's connection to the key. Whilst the beauty of her lands all but withered and faded, Leo McEleod had reaped the rewards. He'd grown stronger in this world, revived. The strength of her kingdom had been stolen in exchange to reverse the deterioration of his bodily form.

She gathered the apparatus from the arm of Violet's chair to better read the small lettering surrounding Grady's likeness, her grip growing tighter about the frame with each passing of the vile lies unfurling before her eyes.

Though the recanting did its fair part in relating the truth of Grady's death, the details behind his murder had been skewed to a story of infuriating madness. The broken glass found scattered around his body, followed by her and Rhys' fateful disappearance, put the onus of culpability squarely on Rhys' shoulders.

Lifting her eyes from the screen, Faedrah firmed her jaw. Gaelleod had named Rhys as Grady's executioner, stating the horror over Rhys' violent outburst at the McEleod estate had been too much for Grady's age-worn heart to bear. In the days since, Leo McEleod had employed a regiment of mercenaries on par with that of the royal guard to safeguard his immoral dealings, and requested any news of Faedrah and Rhys' whereabouts be sought by the authorities with persistence.

She closed her eyes. How like Gaelleod to twist the events to better suit his needs. How cunning to play the victim, subverting his wickedness in trade for placing the blame at his son's feet. Yet this distortion of the facts did not hinder her desire to rid both worlds of the dark lord's degraded mongering. If anything, it only heightened the bitter tang of hatred which thickened and soured upon her tongue.

"Heed my words well." She blinked and settled her gaze upon each member of their entourage, in turn. "Rhys and I go forth with the blessings of Austiere's devoted king and queen. Regardless of the dangers inherent in our task, neither he nor I shall renounce this last chance we've been given to be rid of Gaelleod's infestation. By the blessed tears of the nine, we shall endeavor until we are no longer able, and concede what end the goddesses have preordained as our fate."

She offered the all-seeing portal back to the witch. "Help us or not, our goal here remains the same." Yet, with this exchange of hands, as Violet met Faedrah's gaze, a quiet understanding passed between them, and Faedrah swallowed hard at the telltale breaking of her heart.

What that she could save her friends the weariness of such a troubling decision. What that she could turn the tide and spare them all this perilous harbinger they faced.

Not one soul in either realm should be made to bear the burden of her responsibilities. Least of all, the loyal companions she'd called upon in this room. "But, be it known, we shall respect whatever verdict you choose to offer, and accept with grace and thanks the aid you've granted us thus far."

"Well, hell." With a roll of his eyes, Wizard Oliver tossed his head. "When you put it that way, how are we supposed to say no?" He muttered a curse before lifting his wineglass in her direction. "Of course, we'll do whatever we can to help you. For God's sake, doll, you should know that by now."

She smiled softly and nodded, adoration for her uncle growing stronger with each beat of her heart.

"Yay!" Jon grinned, softly clapping his hands. "I'll call ahead and make sure the plane is fueled and ready to go." He popped to his feet. "Oh, and we'll need something to wear." He frowned, tapping a finger against his lips. "What *does* one wear to stop the apocalypse?"

"I'll handle communications." Violet's fingers flew across the black board on her lap and she tapped once, twice, thrice as her focus darted across the screen. "Ollie, I'm gonna need your credit card. We need to set up a base of operations. Someplace deep underground."

Faedrah eased back in her seat, shaking her head. Now that they'd consented to join the campaign, 'twould seem her friends' enthusiasm had formed a mind of its own.

"Leave that to me." Sir Todd's gravel-laden voice cut through her musings as he slapped his hands against the armrests and stood, and Faedrah squinted at the colorful runes encasing his forearms as the first inklings of an idea sprang to mind. "Several of the boys have been grumbling for a while now it's been too quiet. I'll place a few calls, put out the word whoever's interested in raisin' a little hell should meet us at the bar."

Faedrah smiled, nodding her thanks. 'Twould seem she'd been correct in her assumptions regarding Sir Todd's allegiance to a steel-horsed *gens d'armes*. Their support in facing Gaelleod would provide an added benefit, indeed.

"Make sure they know how to keep their mouths shut."

Everyone froze; Sir Jon's eyes enlarged to the size of saucers.

A slow swivel of her head, and Faedrah's jaw came unhinged as Rhys held up the silver spoon, twisted and bent beyond recognition. She placed a hand atop her chest in stunned amazement, yet her joy over her beloved's accomplishment wilted as quickly as it had bloomed.

Something untoward glinted in Rhys' eyes. A troubling storm which bespoke his anxious discomfort.

Faedrah held a breath, biting her bottom lip.

A twitch of Rhys' brow, and the light chime of silver echoed against the rafters as he tossed the warped utensil to the table. He collapsed against the settee and his chest rose with a heavy sigh. Raking both hands through his hair, he linked his fingers across the back of his neck. "Shit, Faedrah. That took everything I got in me. Looks like we're in for one helluva fight."

Chapter 4

Faedrah lifted her chin as the door hasp slipped into the lock with a soft *click*, yet she did not turn her gaze from the serene view spread out before her like a regal tapestry. A fair breeze fluttered the filmy drapes framing the open glass doors of the bedchamber, and centered just above the faint, dark line of the inky horizon, Selene dipped her toes into the sea. The moon goddess' pearlescent face shown down upon the black water. The cascade of her milky white tresses rode the undulating waves, frothing and hissing as they neared. And as Faedrah stood listening, silently waiting, she could've sworn the barest hint of Selene's playful laughter frolicked through the thin, long-necked trees.

The soft cadence of Rhys' footsteps neared as the wash of the tide met the sandy shoreline in its eternal kiss. The melodious ring of fine crystal caressed the quiet as he set their wineglasses upon the rolled-top writing desk on her left.

Dawn would break soon and, with it, Helios would herald the day. Perchance, this rising would signal the last occasion his nine starlit daughters allowed Faedrah and her beloved to bask in the glorious rays emanating from the sun god's face.

A pair of warm hands landed atop the dressing gown blanketing her shoulders, and her eyes fell closed as the sweep of two supple lips brushed her hair back from her brow. "Thanks for giving me a minute. That article was a bitch to digest."

'Twas only fair she petition Violet to permit Rhys to read the truth of his father's deceit firsthand, though this did not staunch the regret Faedrah had suffered whilst agonizing hatred had filled her lover's gaze. Each passing of his eyes over the glowing screen had stretched unbridled fury increasingly more taut across his handsome face, and the words she had tried to offer in consolation had been botched by her inept tongue.

Unable to bear witness to the torment he endured, shuttering that same cold rage inside her breast, Faedrah had left the frenzied activity of the common room in search of a moment's peace.

The comforting heat of Rhys' palms slid down her arms. The edge of his jaw met her shoulder, and he wound his arms about her waist to tug her back against the hardened muscle of his chest. "Hey. You know what we need?"

She recognized exactly what desire lingered in her heart, though given Rhys' predilection for love-making, her doubts were high he spoke of the same thing. "A grand miracle?"

'Twas anyone's guess the escalating potency Gaelloed's power had achieved in their absence, how sharpened the edge of his magic had grown at her kingdom's expense. A shiver stole through her body, and Rhys cinched her tighter in his embrace. If the rehabilitation of the dark lord's appearance echoed the enhancement of his skill, she and Rhys were bound for a battle to test every wit and reason they contained.

"Well, yeah, that too. But I was talking about a long hot bath." His lips traced a searing path down the side of her throat. He pushed the collar of her dressing gown aside with the edge of his jaw and little sparks tingled her skin as he nibbled the crest of her shoulder. "Some time alone, just the two of us, on the off-chance we can forget about everything for a while except why the hell we're doing this."

She smiled. A relaxing soak would surely lead them in one direction, and despite the unfortunate timing, Rhys brought forth a valid point. Untangling his arms from about her waist, she threaded her fingers through his, palm to palm, and lifted the backs of his hands to her lips.

In reigning victorious, how many young lovers would be gifted tender moments such as this? For what more reason could they implore the goddesses' divine blessing than the endowment of everlasting love?

Clutching his hands to her chest, she curled her fingers more securely between his knuckles. A soft laugh shook her shoulders as he firmed his grip and held on to her just as fierce. So much control lay hidden within his hands. She lowered them back into view. So much potential this world held just beyond his reach.

A flip of her wrists, and she loosened her hold, stroking her fingertips down the calloused landscape of his palms. Given the time and effort he'd expended warping that damnable silver spoon, his magic remained, flowing through his body, and yet he'd experienced difficulty tapping the source.

But, why? She frowned and traced her thumbs along the deep creases bisecting his skin. If her suspicions regarding Gaelleod's abilities held true, the inhabitants of this world had been fed a jagged lie and magic was, indeed, a part of this realm. So what obstruction stood in Rhys' way? And, even more vital, what steps, if any, could they take to remove it?

She brought one hand up and held his coarse palm to her cheek. "Tell me."

The heave of his sigh along her back...the way he dropped his arms and withdrew a pace conveyed he understood exactly what information she requested. But she must know the truth. If only to clutch at any last strands of hope or salvage what small certainties were left them.

He plucked one of the wineglasses from the table and tipped the rim to his lips; his throat shifted as he swallowed. "I can see it." The burgundy line within his glass angled dangerously near the lip as he studied the wine in a beam of moonlight. "Christ, I can almost feel the vibration of each mineral in this room." Shaking his head, he pivoted toward the armoire and ambled toward the veil.

The thick sleeves of his robe had been shoved to his elbows, the belt secured in a snug slipknot about his waist. Yet the seams were strained due the width of his chest and shoulders, and the folded collar formed a deep vee atop his smooth, rippling flesh. "When I was in your world, it was like each molecule was a grain of sand. They were loose and easy to manipulate. All I had to do was reach out and scoop them up." A sweep of his hand through the air and he fisted his fingers before his face.

The slightest tip of his chin, and he squinted at the mirror's shimmering surface. A low rumble of discontent issued from between his clenched teeth. The muscles in his forearm flexed as he dragged his fingers over his eyelids to pinch the bridge of his nose. "Here it's like all the sand is stuck together. Like, in order to move one grain, I gotta lift the whole god-damned beach."

Faedrah's eyebrow twitched. 'Twas a true testament to his resilience and the strength of his formidable powers. Despite the odds, the magic he'd labored to summon had been successfully invoked a short span ago. "And the silver spoon?"

"Don't get too excited." He dropped his hand to his side. "I found a snag."

Whatever did he mean? She studied him from the corner of her eye, frowning, and he searched her face before his shoulders slumped in defeat. "An imperfection in the silver. Sorta like…a loose thread in a piece of fabric. Once I noticed it, I was able to pick at the edge until it lifted enough for me to give it a good, hard yank." He rolled his eyes, sighing. "Only problem is, it took me forever to find it, and no guarantee says Leo's knife is gonna have that same flaw."

Indeed. Faedrah crossed her arms, chewing the inside of her cheek. Given the nature of Rhys' powers, the blade Gaelleod used during his vile ceremony was their most logical target. Once revealed, Rhys must do his utmost to gain control of it, though it was doubtless a treasure Gaelleod coddled and protected above all else. Certainly, one kept free of blemishes and stains.

Nonetheless, they could not afford to dismiss any idea presented them, however trifling it may be. "Perchance such an imperfection could be inflicted upon the silver, allowing you to gain sway over its abilities."

"Maybe." Rhys shrugged, returned to his spot near the table and lifted her glass, offering the wine in her direction. "Either way, once we're at Leo's, we'd better have our shit locked and loaded. Considering the time it'll take me, coupled with the shock and awe Leo's prepping to launch at our asses, I'll be lucky to get in one clean shot."

She nodded, lips pursed in contemplation as she accepted the glass. 'Twas a small flicker of hope in an otherwise bleak situation. Yet if her years under Denmar's tutelage had taught her anything, a successful war campaign relied heavily upon the element of deception. Mayhap Gaelleod's preparedness could be exploited to their advantage. They could draw upon his arrogance…do the opposite of what was expected.

Emerge from the shadows when not anticipated. Appear weak where we are strong.

She hummed, running the tip of her tongue along the sharp edge of her teeth. Many factors would be at play during the rite of the dark lord's incantations. If close enough, perchance one *shot* would be all she and Rhys required to sabotage the outcome of Gaelleod's schemes.

Her jaw firmed in determination. If nothing else, they could use what chance remained to wedge a vexing thorn in Gaelleod's side.

"Then we shall do our utmost to make one shot count." She tapped the side of her glass against Rhys' with a light *clink*.

He huffed, his gaze riveted to hers as he joined her in a hearty swallow, and Faedrah delighted in the mischief caught by the light of Selene's moonbeams, glinting within the depths of his piercing jade eyes.

"Christ, it turns me on when you get pissed. Come on." He clasped her hand in his and tugged her toward the far corner of the room, pressed his back to a wooden door and wagged his brows as they entered the privy.

Applying the tip of his elbow to a small switch upon the wall, he flooded the room with bright light.

Faedrah stumbled to a stop. A heartbeat passed before Rhys glanced over his shoulder, and his low whistle echoed about the gray-veined marble denoting the room. Two pedestal steps lead to a large, sunken wash basin, so vast and deep four or more of them could have easily lounged about inside. "Shit, the things I'm gonna do to you in that tub."

Arousal spiked in her belly. Her imagination ran rampant with all the ways Rhys relished applying his able mouth to her skin.

He leaned over to twist two silver knobs protruding from the wall and water thundered from the spigot. Steam rose into the air like the mists which oft hovered among the high mountain peaks near her home. A quick yank to the knot at his waist, and her brows shot heavenward as his robe coasted down the length of his arms to crumple in a heap near his feet. "Remind me at some point to send Oliver and Jon a big ol' basket of fruit."

Faedrah lowered her chin against a smile, pausing to absorb the measure of her lover's naked form from the side. The smooth rounded cap of his shoulder tapered to an arm honed by might and years of hard effort pounding steel. A long, fixed ridge flanked his torso, at complete odds with the ladder of eight well-defined grooves which stepped down the tiers of his ribcage. The line of his back dipped inward with a slight curve, dotted by a tempting dimple perched atop the tight flex of his backside. A rope of corded muscle arced down the front of his hip and, beyond, dark hair formed a mouth-watering trail starting just below his navel, and ending in a nest of dense curls which framed his well-hung manhood.

"Enjoying the view?" Rhys cocked a brow and pivoted to fully face her, and his unabashed sexuality ravaged every feminine wile she contained.

A whimper eked from her dry throat. Her palms grew anxious to explore every hard-edged curve; her tongue starved to taste the heady flavor of his skin. Yet whilst she longed to shed the dressing gown preventing her such pleasures, the same warning she'd fought to deny since his enticing invitation, pealed like the strike of the Apex bell in her head.

Numerous passings of Helios' bright face had elapsed since the time of her womanly course. For her and Rhys to so recklessly lose themselves in throes of abandon could initiate a result neither of them were prepared to undertake.

He seized the belt at her waist, and her hands met his chest as he jerked her against the unyielding tower of his body. "I'm gonna lick every delicious inch of you." His lips danced near. Her knees all but gave as he dipped his head to skim the tip of his tongue up her throat. "I'm gonna make it so that no matter what bullshit Leo throws at us, you never forget this night."

A throb pulsed hard and fast between her legs. Her nipples peaked against the soft cotton folds of her robe. The tight cinch of her belt went slack, and her breath caught as the heated caress of his fingers stroked a downward path along her belly. Sweet Goddesses wept, the man kindled the yearnings of her body with more skill than the bard plucked the strings of his lute.

He buried his scruffy cheeks in her hair and her head fell back. Warm tingles sparked and sizzled along her skin. She pulled her bottom lip between her teeth and bit down, relishing the slight sting as he nuzzled the shell of her ear. "Rhys, we cannot."

"What the hell are you talking about?" His words were clipped, a grating rasp thickened by desire. "Shit, I'd like to see anyone bust in here and try to stop us."

Her back bowed. The sides of her dressing gown brushed past her thighs to be replaced with the hot press of rigid muscle. "The timing is not right, my heart." One of his arms threaded about her waist and he yanked her to his hips, his arousal thick and stiff between them. "For us to continue may result in the conception of our heir."

He froze, yet he did not withdraw from her, and as his deep exhalation warmed her hair, she wrapped her arms about his neck to keep him near.

Water splashed and swirled over the trip of her pulse in her ears. The steady thump of Rhys' heartbeat instilled a bittersweet ache in her chest. Of all the nights they must abstain this, by far, would be the cruelest...on the eve of impending doom, when all light and love could be forever banished from their worlds.

"I'm not going to lie to you, Faedrah. The thought of being a dad scares the shit out of me." Rhys pulled back from her, releasing her waist to cup her cheeks in his hands. "And there are a lot of things in this world people can use to prevent pregnancy. Hell, I'm sure Oliver and Jon would move heaven and earth to get us anything we wanted." He lowered his forehead to hers and Faedrah's heart leapt as magic glittered and sparked in his gaze. "But when it comes to you, I'm a greedy son of a bitch. You should know that by now. The last thing I want is a layer of latex between us. Not tonight. Not after knowing how fucking good you feel without it."

He closed his eyes, the fringe of his lashes two dark fans atop his shadowed cheeks. His teeth clenched with such force a muscle spasmed in his jaw, and Faedrah curled her fingers in his hair against the urge to crush her lips to his and let their passions soar toward whatever bliss awaited them...the consequences be damned.

"But I'm not convinced any of that counts for squat." Rhys blinked and lifted his head. His gaze dropped to her mouth, and he swept the ball of his thumb across her lower lip. "Remember that day in the cave? When you told me the best way I could beat Leo was to live life to the fullest?"

An ember flared and burned bright in her heart, and she nodded inside the safety of her lover's hands.

"Well, I made you a promise that day. What kind of asshole would I be if I let Leo force feed me those words?" He cocked a brow. "So, here it is. You were right, Faedrah. But you were right about more than just me or any guilt Vaighn might be carrying around because of his dad. Truth is, I'm over letting Leo suck the joy out of every fucking second. He doesn't deserve it. And, god dammit, I'm sick and tired of him always being one step ahead. The buck stops here. Right here and now. With you and me and whatever kids we might make."

Tears burned, and Faedrah dug her nails into the muscles of his shoulders as the truth of his words arrowed home. She and Rhys had been granted a rare blessing through their bond. One refused the prior descendants of his bloodline.

If the worst were to happen, Gaelleod would one day endeavor to fill her womb with his successor. What better way to circumvent his father's ploy, to begin afresh and protect them all than for Rhys' to gift her his true child? Their child, conceived in love, born pure and free of Gaelleod's ill-begotten curse.

Rhys tucked his hands inside the collar of her dressing gown and urged the sides from her shoulders, and Faedrah released him to let the sleeves tumble past her fingers to the floor. Enveloping her in his strong embrace, he swept a tender kiss across her lips. "As much as being a dad might scare me, I'm not stupid. I get how this might be our last chance, our *best* chance to hit Leo exactly where it'll count the most." He thrust his fingers into her hair, his thumb propped under her chin to ensure she remain devoted to his gaze. "I'm not about to let that rat bastard win. Do you understand me? Not now. Not in the past. And, most definitely, not in the future."

And neither would she.

His eyes flew wide as she leapt into his arms. Circling her legs about his waist, she held on to her beloved with all her might. A warm tear snuck from between her lashes and traced down her cheek. "I love you, Rhys." His courage and commitment could

374

ultimately save her kingdom. "More than Helios' bright diamonds number in the sky."

He chuckled and palmed the length of her hair, rocking her side to side. "The feeling's mutual, Princess." A smack of her bare backside, and she jerked back from him in surprise. "Now no more doomsday prepping. Together, we're gonna go kick Leo's ass and then we're heading back to the castle to get married."

A smile bloomed, and she shook his shoulders. "Agreed."

He smirked, yet the devilish curl of his lips did not mask the sharp bite of hunger in his gaze. She released the tension in her thighs and he grunted, jostling her onto his hips.

His pupils dilated. The tip of his tongue skimmed his bottom lip.

With a teasing arch of her brow, she laced her fingers behind his neck and shimmied farther down his torso.

Their centers met, the head of his manhood a delightful pressure prodding her folds, and her internal walls quivered as he dove forward to capture her lips in a searing kiss.

His hips shifted as he strode forward. The solid muscle of his thighs bumped the curves of her bottom as he climbed the steps and lowered them into the bath.

Water eddied through the ends of her hair, tingling her scalp. The heated line rose to tickle the crease of her bottom as Rhys shuffled beneath her, his hands curled behind her knees to keep her straddled atop his hips.

The ridge of his cock slid sleek and smooth along her hidden pearl and she gasped, slapping both hands to his chest. His soft laugh was decidedly evil. The glint of desire in his gaze, wicked beyond compare. He ran his splayed fingers up the sides of her waist; cradled her breasts in the wide dip between his fingers and thumbs.

A sweep of those calloused digits over her nipples, and they peaked and hardened. Sparks glimmered near the edges of her vision. The water licked and fluttered against her skin. His second taunting caress of her breasts, and a shudder dislodged the set of her shoulders. She slipped her hands behind his neck and wrenched him to her chest.

The angle between them deepened and she writhed, fighting the buoyancy of the water to remain seated against him. Rhys drew her breast into the hot cavern of his mouth. His hands met her shoulders and his hips jerked. Heat expanded low in her belly, trickling into her legs, and she tossed her head, arcing into him.

His low moan shivered the hair on her arms. The enthralling swirl of his tongue sent fireflies dancing down her spine as he nipped and suckled.

Rhys seized her hips; his thighs widened. He forced her knees farther apart, and her muscles trembled as he floated his hand up her inner thigh. His middle finger circled her entrance. His thumb tapped and rubbed her aching bud. She grabbed his wrist to force him deeper, but he resisted.

His other hand rose to the base of her ass. His fingertips teased and stroked her higher, his cheeks hollowing as he pulled her breast deeper into his mouth.

A whimper caught in her throat, and she swayed, setting a mounting rhythm. Her core spasmed as he dipped the tip of his finger inside. "Shit, you're sexy. I love how I can make you come with just my hands."

She glanced down to find his heavy-lidded gaze glinting with arousal, his jaw tight and teeth clenched. A furious rap of his thumb and she tensed. The quick thrust and curl of his finger inside her, and a loud rushing built in her ears.

Shimmers ignited and zipped across her skin. She hissed, her arms shaking, her body perched upon the edge as Rhys wrenched his thighs closed and sheathed her onto his rigid member.

She sharply inhaled and he groaned as she convulsed around him. The light dimmed and she cried out as the entirety of her being was pitched toward the heavens. He rolled his hips, filling her fully. Her internal walls spasmed and she fisted his hair as he plunged all the way to the base. His lips found hers and water splashed as he lifted and slammed her to his hips again and again.

A second wave of euphoria grew as Rhys ground against her. Tremors gripped her form, and she shuddered as a vast pulse surged. Ecstasy detonated throughout her body. Quivers heated and cooled her skin. She reached behind her with one hand and he roared, his hips rising from the water as she stroked the underside of his erection.

His warm essence burst through her core. She braced her hands upon the hard planes of his stomach and rocked, hoping to extend the pleasure of his orgasm. Starlight glittered in her fingertips, the soles of her feet. His hips rose higher and he gritted his teeth. A deep throb ricocheted and he roared a second time as his cock twitched inside her.

Shuddering, slowly lowering himself into the water, he blinked and his cheeks expanded as he blew a harsh breath. "Dammit, woman. God *dammit*, how is it even possible that sex with you keeps getting better and better?"

She laughed, rolling off his hips to stretch her languid limbs along the length of his body. He lifted an arm about her shoulders, dragging the tip of his thumb down her cheek as she nestled her head on his chest.

Trailing the backs of her nails down the little bumps of his ribcage, she snuggled closer, following the path of one raised vein as it angled down the inside of his hip. "How long, do you surmise, 'twill be before we reach the pinnacle of our love-making?"

He peeked askance at her from beneath the thick fringe of his lashes. "Not a clue." Lifting his foot from the water, he curled his toes around one of the silver knobs and twisted the first...and then the second...to the right.

She circled her thumb and index finger around his manhood, and answering sparks of pleasure flared to life within her as his flesh firmed and stretched inside her grip.

"But I got my heart set on one thing, Princess." A suggestive bounce of his brows, and she grinned as he flipped from the water to blanket her with his heated body. "I'm damn sure gonna try and find out."

Chapter 5

"Nod if you can hear me."

Rhys kept his focus pinned on the dark hallway at the back of the grungy biker bar, rubbing the heel of his hand over the gauze pad and itchy medical tape stuck to his left pec. What the hell could be taking so long? Faedrah had swapped spots with him in Buzzer's tattoo chair over an hour ago.

"Rhys, are you there? Hello?" Rustling echoed through the tiny mic Violet had told him to plug into his ear. *"Damn,"* she whispered.

Rhys shot a quick glance around the room. Christ, he should've had his head examined for agreeing to Todd's suggestion this motley crew ride as back-up over to Leo's. While the brawn was there, the brains end of this operation seemed a little iffy. Shit, if Rhys had to guess, he'd place bets nine out of ten of these dudes had a rap sheet a mile long. All around, the biggest priority seemed to be catching a buzz-on, and having them around Faedrah wasn't sitting all that well in his gut. Not that he'd been given had a lot of choice. With Nate MIA, his short list of friends added up to a big fat zero, and Faedrah had insisted Todd's Harley riding *gens d'armes* would be the ideal stand-ins for a battalion of palace guards.

Rhys raked a hand through his hair then grimaced as the high-pitched screech of speaker feedback drowned out the thump of AC/DC's *Highway to Hell* blaring from the dented jukebox in the corner.

"God dammit." He tore the wireless earbud from his ear and glared at Violet through the cloud of cigarette smoke ballooning up from the mosh pit of mismatched tables crammed in the middle of the club.

She waved a hand then pointed at her headset. A jiggle of the attached microphone curled in front of her lips, and Rhys sighed as he plugged the com device back into his ear.

"Well? Are you getting the feed or not? You didn't answer me."

"Yeah, yeah, I got it." He adjusted his back against the bar, shaking his head as she spun around to face the long narrow table Todd's cronies had set up on the other end of the bar, opposite the hallway leading to Buzzer's tattoo parlor. Her fingers clicked something into one of the keyboards before she wheeled her chair farther down her bank of networked monitors.

Rhys shifted his attention back to empty hall. One patch of skin was just like the other, his ass. He huffed. Buzzer may have fooled everyone else with that statement, but Rhys hadn't bought into his bullshit for a second.

Crossing his arms, he leaned to the side as three leatherbacks crossed his line of sight. Okay, fine. No one could argue Faedrah's idea to get matching tattoos had been a stroke of genius…least of all him. One he should've seen coming the second Forbes' private jet was wheels up for Chicago and she started asking after the *veneficus* tats inked along the undersides of his arms. But the buttery smooth softness covering every inch of his muse didn't come anywhere close to a normal woman. Especially when it came to the mouth-watering slopes of her breasts. And the image of her baring that flawless flesh for another guy? The idea of Buzzer eyeballing that perfect mound of skin?

Shit. Rhys squinted at the hallway, willing Faedrah to walk through the door. God dammit, he should've never left her alone in that room…wouldn't have if Violet hadn't insisted he step outside and get suited up. He knew better than anyone how addictive Faedrah was. How one taste of her was never enough. The night they'd spent locked behind closed doors on Forbes' island had forever pounded that reality into his brain.

Those two luscious globes had filled his hands like they'd been molded by Faedrah's sex goddess specifically for him. His cock twitched, and he inched his boot to the right. She'd been wet when he slid inside her, hips gyrating at the perfect speed. Whimpers had caught in her throat right before she convulsed, and she'd clamped down so hard around him he'd practically died and gone to Heaven.

Gritting his teeth, he ripped the bandage off his chest and balled up the gauze before tossing it aside. Fuck, she'd returned every single one of his needs with an urgency that only made him crave her more. In exchange, he'd taken his damn sweet time memorizing every inch of her, hoping by doing so he could somehow imprint her taste and fresh clean scent on his brain so he would never forget.

He slipped the black t-shirt Jon had handed him off the bar and crammed his arms into the sleeves, worked the collar past his head and tugged the hem down to the waistband of his leather pants. But the best, by far, had been the way she'd snuggled against him in bed. Her hair had covered his chest like a soft blanket threaded with silver, their legs and arms tangled while they whispered and giggled about stupid stuff.

That night their bodies had been so in tune, they'd gotten punch-drunk on sex. Or maybe it was the desperation that had heightened their libidos. Deep down, they were both trying to cling to a moment they might never see again.

He lifted the leather jacket off the stool on his right and shrugged it onto his shoulders, adjusting the Nero collar as he took another sweep of the room. The three men who'd crossed in front of him stopped at the back corner booth near Violet's surveillance set up, and nodded at Todd and Oliver who were knocking back a beer. The one sporting a long brown ponytail spoke a few words and Todd flicked a hand toward the table.

381

Rhys grunted. Evidently, Violet's husband ran this organization like some mafia godfather. No one made a move without the boss' say-so, and good thing too, since that loyalty was pretty much the only thing stopping Rhys from marching across the bar and down that fucking hallway so he could kick open the door to Buzzer's inner sanctum.

Five more minutes…counting down from four minutes ago.

He'd seen the hungry glint in Buzzer's eyes when Faedrah had approached him about getting tatted. Not that his reaction was any big shocker. Unlike most of the club's members, the tattoo artist was second generation. Young enough to be sniffing around where he wasn't wanted. Besides, any man would have to be half-dead not to notice how she lit up a room.

The second their entourage had stepped inside the dingy interior of the bar, conversations had stopped mid-stream. Heads had swiveled; jaws dropped, and the black leather cat suit Jon had strapped Faedrah in had popped the gears of every red-blooded male of legal age.

Rhys resettled his back against the bar, arms crossed, and counted down the seconds in his head. Whether or not she'd picked up on Buzzer's interest, Faedrah was too polite to say anything… had too much style to offend the guy by asking a favor and then backpedaling. Even if he was in there flirting with her, eyes all bugged out of his head and drooling like a horn dog, she would treat him with respect. Her supposed "duty" to Todd demanded it.

Unless, of course, the skeeze ball got grabby. Rhys smirked. If that happened, well then. An evil chuckle shook his shoulders. She'd make it so that no woman was in danger of getting poked by Buzzer's needle for a good long while.

Movement caught the corner of his eye, and he slid his focus to the left as two of the dudes slumped into Todd's booth. The third swung a chair around and straddled the seat. The five men settled into a conversation, the one at the end hunched over the back of his chair, tatted forearms balanced on the table. The matching leather patch stitched across the back of his vest had been stamped in red gothic script with the word *Crucibles*. Beneath, another black patch displayed the gang's emblem—a grinning skull sitting on a metal cup surrounded by flames, the phrase *Can you take the heat?* stamped below in that same blood red script.

The three newcomers turned their heads in unison and locked on to Rhys. The music cut out, and clinking glasses mixed with raspy laughter filled the bar until the chest vibrating thump of *Dirty Deeds Done Dirt Cheap* crackled from the speakers.

Yep, that's right. Rhys clenched his jaw, meeting each stare, one after the next. He was the prick who'd dumped this pile of shit in their laps, the first born and only living son of the asshole they were going after. He was also the douche bag who was about to lead their gang straight into hell, Faedrah bound and gagged on the back of his bike like a sacrificial lamb led to slaughter.

A harsh breath blurted past his lips. But what the hell did they expect? He'd been the first one to argue this scheme she'd cooked up was crazier than a bag of cats, but the woman refused to listen. If they thought he hadn't already boxed four rounds in that ring, they could kiss his hairy white ass. She was proof positive showing up at Leo's uninvited would knock the fucker off guard. And, hell, maybe she was right. After all, it wasn't like anyone else had any bright ideas about how to get them inside.

Disgust flooded his mouth and Rhys sneered, smacking his lips. Manhandling her in front of dear old dad is where things were bound to get tricky. The thought alone was enough to burst an artery in his head. But it wasn't like someone else could do it… not that he would've trusted anyone who volunteered. He was the only one who could guarantee she wouldn't get hurt while being rough enough they could convince Leo the act was real and Rhys wanted to switch sides.

Whether or not Leo bought into the act? Well, that was still up for grabs. But one thing was for damn sure. Leo would never count on Rhys showing up with Faedrah in tow as a peace offering.

Faedrah entered the room and Rhys pushed up from the bar. Thank God. It was about fucking time. She turned with a smile and nodded her thanks as Buzzer followed behind her, one of her hands pressed to her chest like she was about to break into *The Pledge of Allegiance.*

She pivoted back around and met Rhys' gaze through the dim clatter. Her eyes glittered with awareness, but she didn't smile, and his shoulders dropped as she held up a finger for him to wait a second. Shit, now what?

Fisting his hands, he kept his focus on her as she glanced around the room, located Oliver, Todd and the members of his gang in the corner booth and started in that direction. Okay, good. Rhys eased the air from his lungs. Whatever she was after, at least she was headed for people they trusted.

She placed a hand on Todd's shoulder and he sat back from the conversation, glancing up at her face. Lowering to eye level, she moved her hand to his forearm and her lips started moving.

Anxiety jabbed Rhys' gut as Todd frowned, leaning away from her. He narrowed his eyes as the other dudes shifted uncomfortably in their seats and traded raised eyebrows around the table. Oliver crossed his arms with an emphatic bounce and mouthed, "No."

Aw, fuck. This did not look good.

Faedrah paused, staring at Oliver. She shifted her attention back to Todd and kept talking, her heels lifting from the floor as she leaned in. He shook his head and slashed a hand between them, but whatever he said back to her was hidden by his beard.

God dammit, what the hell was she doing? Rhys shuffled his boots, shoulders high and tight, every synapse in his brain screaming for him to get over there and find out.

The guy with the ponytail sat forward in the booth and spoke. Rhys stepped from the bar. Faedrah jerked her head around, hesitated and then nodded.

Uh-uh. No chance in hell. Rhys strode forward and skirted the nearest table. Whatever she'd just agreed to wasn't happening. Not unless he was included in the decision and *especially* not since her suggestion seemed to royally piss off Todd.

The big guy pointed a thick finger across the booth, mumbled something and ponytail shrank back in his seat. Faedrah stood, slamming her fist on the table. Heads turned; conversations halted. Rhys shouldered past a group of riders and wound through the crowd, pushing for the other side of the bar.

Todd gripped the edge of the table and shoved his bulk from the booth. Faedrah stumbled back, lifting her chin in defiance. Oliver scrambled to follow, but the guy seated at the end snagged his upper arm and held him in check.

God dammit! Rhys tossed a vacant chair aside, jerked his shoulder from someone's grip and kept moving. What the hell was going on?

A nod from Todd, and the other two men slid from the booth, arms crossed, creating a human blockade in case anyone got it in their head to interfere.

A violent rage built, clawing at Rhys' gut. His legs filled with lead and the world inched to a stop as Todd gritted his teeth, swung back and Faedrah's head snapped to the right as he rocketed his fist into her face.

"What the fuck are you *doing*?" Rhys leapt forward, flipping a table out of his path. Blinding rage seared the edges of his vision. Glass shattered; feedback shrieked and Violet squawked in his ear.

On instinct, he zeroed in on the large silver belt buckles of the two riders and *shoved*. A gap appeared between them, and he slid through. Shouting and chaos erupted as he leapt onto a table and skimmed his hip along the top.

His feet hit the floor, two lunging strides, and he rammed his shoulder into Todd's stomach, tackling the fucker to the floor.

"Wait!" Faedrah screamed on his right. He clamped his hands around Todd's throat and squeezed. God dammit, the asshole would never touch her again. "Rhys, cease this instant! Sir Todd did as I asked!"

Rhys lifted and slammed the asshole down to the ground. Hands grappled for his wrists. Fists pounded his back and shoulders. The lights flared and pops ricocheted around the room. Sparks rained down, stinging his face as an arm wrapped around his neck and wrenched him off of Todd's waist.

"Rhys, stop!" Violet shouted. "Get your shit under control or you're gonna tear down the entire building!"

Two sets of knees pinned his arms to the floor. Boot heels dug into his legs as bearded faces swung back and forth over his head. Faedrah shoved between the bodies and clasped his face in her hands. "Be still, my heart. Please, do not fight them."

A red welt covered her left cheek. Blood poured down her face from the gash under her eye. God *dammit*. Rhys squeezed his eyes tight, grinding his teeth. He was gonna kill Todd. Christ, they never should've come here. The second his arms were free, he was gonna make it so that asshole would never hit anyone again.

"I asked Sir Todd to strike me." Faedrah leaned down and dotted kisses over his face, his eyelids and lips. She braced her forehead against his. "We must make every effort to forestall Gaelleod's suspicions. A minor injury now could ensure our later victory."

Her words slammed into his brain and his body went limp. A *minor injury*? Had she lost her damn mind? He blinked and searched her face. "Faedrah, what in the hell are you talking about?"

She smiled, though it came off lop-sided, and moisture trickled from the corner of her left eye. "I knew you would never strike me. Nor would you agree to Sir Todd inflicting me harm. Yet we must do our utmost to ensure the dark lord believes the sincerity of our ruse. What better way than for me to appear before him bearing the insult of your anger? 'Tis a small price to pay in exchange for the deliverance of our worlds."

Mother…*fucker*. He closed his eyes, shaking his head. God dammit, the woman made his heart crack open right in his chest. Too bad, one of these days, her antics were also likely to throw him into cardiac arrest.

But she was right. Deep down inside, he knew she was right. He growled, pounding his fists on the floor. None of this would work unless Leo saw it with his own two eyes. The best thing... the *strongest* thing they had going for them was their love. So that was their play. To appear weak where they were strong from start to finish. And shit, after what she'd just gone through to prove it, he wasn't about to let her down.

"Son of a bitch," Violet muttered. "Rhys, I'm gonna kick your ass. Dammit, you fried my hard drive. "

Faedrah gasped and sprang back from him, her lips parted as she spun toward Violet's computers.

Wait...what? "Hold on. Get off me." Rhys jerked his arms and legs and, the second the pressure disappeared, he sat up to follow Faedrah's line of sight.

Smoke wafted from the three monitors Violet had networked on the table, mixing with the bank of cigarette smoke hovering near the ceiling. The hi-def sound system she'd plugged into the wall sizzled near the outlet. The speakers buzzed, the sound warbling like she'd tapped into some bizarre alien transmission. Beer dripped off the nearby tables, the mugs shattered. The light fixtures on either side her equipment flickered and popped.

A belt buckle snapped, and the guy standing next to her lost his jeans to around his ankles. He mumbled a curse, slapping his hands over the crotch of his tightie-whities.

"What the hell did you do to my club?" Todd groaned and pushed to sitting, rubbing a hand around his neck. He shot a scowl back and forth before aiming a finger at Rhys. "You're paying for the damages."

What the...? Rhys swiveled toward the bar and followed the line of destruction. A charred black channel ran diagonally across the room, starting where he'd been standing and leading all the way to where Todd had punched Faedrah, up the wall and past Violet's station to the ceiling. "Well, I'll be damned. Looks like I'm back in action."

That was…at least as far as his muse was concerned, since everything a foot or so outside the path appeared intact. Then again, that seemed right on the money. His powers had always been connected to Faedrah, and when it came to her and keeping her safe, apparently the roadblock between fantasy and reality remained more of a two-way street.

"Well, bucky for you." Violet lifted a keyboard off the table, sighed and tossed it aside with a rattling *clack*. Leaning down, she righted a chair with a grunt and stepped onto the seat. "It's forty minutes to zero hour and I'm down, people." She crossed her arms, tapping the toe of her army boot as she squinted at Rhys. "Time to empty the saddlebags, fellas. I need every cell phone, iPad and laptop we got."

Chapter 6

The piston-popping rumble of fifty-plus hogs practically dislodged the stars, bouncing off the palatial homes and drowning out everything except the tight heat of Faedrah's thighs clamped around his hips.

She'd been right, though. Rhys gunned the engine and smirked as the *blat-blat* of his Indian peeled back the summer night like a hot knife slicing through butter. Showing up at Leo's with Todd's crew heavy at their backs was a good thing. In fact, it fucking rocked.

In the past, going anywhere near his childhood home had always been a bitch, and doing so with his muse trussed up like a Thanksgiving turkey on the back of his bike was the epitome of every bullshit disappointment he'd faced inside those four walls. Seemed only fair he snub his nose at Leo's bogus respectability by announcing their arrival in the most obnoxious way possible.

And if the neighbors called the cops, who gave a shit? An ear-splitting growl inched up on his left, and Rhys glanced over as Todd's chopper closed in, the big guy's eyes hidden behind a set of aviator shades, gray beard trailing over his right shoulder. If they got lucky, whoever phoned in the disturbance would hopefully complain enough, a squad would be dispatched to Leo's to investigate.

Rhys bounced his brows and pulled in the clutch, revving the engine until it red-lined and a chest vibrating *bang* shot from his tailpipe. Because he and his muse weren't sneaking in tonight. Hell, no. This time, they were coming at Leo balls to the wall with a wild side of heavy, fine-tuned carburetor.

The edge of Todd's moustache twitched and he leapt forward, peeling around Rhys in a wide right-hand turn, one hand near the ground and waving half the crew to follow.

Rhys shifted into a lower gear and wrapped his fingers around the back of Faedrah's knee as they coasted to a stop at the corner.

It'd only been two blocks since they'd pulled over, and already he missed the soft cushion of her breasts against his back, the warm band of her arms around his chest, but she'd insisted on being tied up before they got too close.

Snapping those handcuffs around her wrists had been so fucked up, he'd bungled it the first time. Even though he knew full well the key was hidden inside her sleeve just in case things went sour, he'd still left them too loose. Same with sticking that wadded rag in her mouth and securing it with a bandana.

Bracing his foot on the ground, he checked the quiet street for oncoming traffic. Not that there was any. It was nearly midnight and, this late, everyone in Leo's affluent north shore neighborhood was most likely tucked in bed for the night.

Faedrah wriggled close, turning her cheek to his shoulder. Her legs squeezed him on either side, and an unexpected chuckle worked the muscles of his stomach.

God, she'd been pissed. The second that bandana had slipped past her chin and dropped to her neck, she'd arched a brow at him meant to shrivel his balls. Too bad her irritation accomplished nothing but making him hard. He'd just crossed his arms and cocked a brow right back at her, only breaking their stare-down after she'd threatened to call Todd over to handle the job.

Yeah, Rhys wasn't about to let that happen. If anyone was tying her up, that person would be him and only him.

Todd's right-hand man rolled to a stop beside them, dipped his chin and revved his bike. A few leaves fluttered down from the trees lining either side of the boulevard. A Schnauzer barked inside the lighted interior of a glass patio, front legs braced on the back of a padded chair, but he might as well have been singing Pavarotti. Rhys couldn't hear a damn thing.

Half a block ahead, the McEleod estate sat back from the street on the right, two high globed streetlights illuminating the front hedge and either side of the drive. The plan was to wait until Todd had circled back around, parking his men along the street until the entire block was covered. This was as much a tactic at intimidation as an added guarantee the back stayed clear. If this high noon standoff went down the way they'd planned, Rhys and Faedrah would need a clean exit.

If not, well then, none of it would matter...except for Faedrah. Rhys ran his hand back and forth along her thigh. She'd still be alive and under Leo's thumb, which was where the rest of the Crucibles came in.

Todd had given his word the second Rhys and Faedrah made it inside...*if* they made it inside...his crew would take out Leo's security. Afterward, if the whole works had blown up in Rhys' face, Todd had also promised to do whatever was necessary to get Faedrah back to the mirror and home, where she'd be safe, even if that meant losing some of his men in the process.

A single headlight rounded the corner a block down. The tinny flavor of adrenaline flooded his mouth, and Rhys' stomach took a swan dive for his boots. He inhaled, cheeks expanding as he pushed all the air from his lungs.

God, this was gonna suck. He should've listened to his gut and just told Faedrah to stay behind. A visual of *that* conversation set up shop in his head, and he rolled his eyes. And do what to stop her? Be exactly like Leo and lock her up so she couldn't escape? Besides, if he stood one chance in hell at knocking Leo's lights out, Rhys needed her there. And if they were doing this, if they were seriously facing the end of forever, there was no one he wanted with him more than his muse.

A pop of the clutch, and a breeze ruffled his hair as he started them down the street. It was the fucked up circumstances that had his balls twisted in a knot. Shit, just the thought of Leo being anywhere near her pissed him off…not that this did him a damn bit of good.

Rhys ground his molars, his nostrils flared. He'd hoped that would be enough. That the idea of Leo touching her would set off some sort of chain reaction. But in those forty minutes before tip-off, while he sat staring at a belt buckle on the bar, no matter how hard he kept that visual in his head, his efforts amounted to zilch.

Christ, it was most frustrating hand he'd ever been dealt, even though he understood the problem the second the dust had settled inside the club. Faedrah wasn't in any real danger. Shit, at that precise moment, she'd been trading hugs with Oliver and Jon. Rhys' heart knew it, his head knew it and, apparently, so did his magic, because the short gap to using his powers had stretched back to the San Francisco Bay Bridge.

He met Todd in the center of the block and they slid to the curb, parking their bikes wheel to wheel. Most of the gang followed suit while a few drove on ahead to fill in the rest of the block. Which meant, to come out on top, Rhys had no choice but to place her in harm's way. He had to put Faedrah directly in the Leo's path, and gamble with everything that had ever meant anything in his life.

He closed his eyes and sighed. Loving her the way he did, Christ only knew if he could do it.

A door on the side of the house swung open, spilling a block of yellow light onto the sidewalk leading toward the garage. Two suits exited, dressed identically in black, wearing the same set of dark sunglasses. They stopped about halfway down the lawn and folded their hands.

Jesus *Christ*. Amusement tightened Rhys' stomach as he killed the engine. Evidently, they'd just entered the Matrix.

"*I'm up as of ten minutes ago.*" Violet spoke in his ear and he jerked his focus to Todd. "*Everyone's in position. I'll stay with you as long as I can.*" She paused. "*Good luck, Rhys.*"

Todd nodded and shut down his bike. Sending up a Hail Mary, Rhys swung off his seat to the ground.

"I love you," he whispered, squeezing Faedrah's thigh.

She winked, and the urge to jerk that damn bandana off her lips and dive in for a taste, to kiss her and beg for forgiveness before they even got started, nearly made him call the whole shit mess quits right there.

He gritted his teeth and pivoted toward the house. The last engine cut out down the street, and the immediate silence was almost as loud as the deafening roar that had escorted them in.

Leo's front man cocked a brow. "May I help you?"

Rhys huffed. "Cut the crap. Leo knows why I'm here." He reached behind him and grabbed Faedrah's arm, yanking her off the seat. She whimpered, and something inside his chest cracked as she tripped over her feet and stumbled forward, falling to her knees on the grass.

Son of a bitch, she was one hell of an actress. For a split second, even *he* believed he'd shoved her. "Now be a good little watchdog and tell Leo I brought him a gift."

The front door creaked open, and Rhys swiveled his head left. Leo stepped onto the stoop, a maroon velvet smoking jacket resting on his shoulders, the soft light from the streetlamps catching on the satin lapels. Black slacks hung in starched creases down to his shiny black shoes. Ruddy color tinted his cheeks, his eyes were clear and exacting, and fresh crop of brown peach fuzz sprouted from his head.

Well, looky here. *Perfect.* Seemed as if Leo hadn't just been using the life he sucked out of Faedrah's kingdom for a little boost. More like he'd siphoned off enough gas to level the tank back to around the age of fifty.

No wonder the area surrounding the castle looked like shit. That much energy had to be addictive. Rhys was counting on it.

He smiled. "Hi, dad. You look…better."

Leo's focus flicked to Todd, back over to Rhys and down to Faedrah. One side of his lips curled in a calculating smirk. "Rhys, I'm offended. There's no need for all this." He waved a hand toward the street. "You didn't think I'd welcome you and the lovely Faedrah back into my home with open arms?"

Ha! Nice. "Consider my friends as insurance." Rhys tipped his head toward the bikers, paused and jerked his chin toward Leo's goons. "You know how it is."

"Ah, yes. A necessary evil for a man of my means." Leo's attention returned to Faedrah and one of his eyebrows rose. "I'm afraid you have me at a disadvantage. Did I hear you say you'd brought me a gift?"

Fuck, yeah. Check number one off the list. Confused is exactly the way they wanted Leo. Now, if Rhys could just stay in the driver's seat for number two. He shrugged. "A gift in trade is probably more accurate. I'm interested in making a deal."

Leo hesitated. The night stretched, and furry little creatures everywhere scurried for cover as his head fell back and he let loose a hair-raising cackle. "Oh, Rhys, you slay me. Truly, you do." His Adam's apple slid up and down with his chuckle, the muscles working on either side of his scrawny throat. "I believe you've come here under false pretenses, as if you withhold something I cannot just reach out and take. Though, I must say, I've thoroughly enjoyed watching your struggles, enough they've caused me quite the delay." He peeked at Rhys from the corner of his eye and a dangerous pressure built low in Rhys' gut. "I take it your sojourn to Faedrah's homeland didn't merit the outcome you'd anticipated?"

Asshole. They'd just see about that, wouldn't they? "You sure there's nothing I got that you need?" He strode forward and wrapped Faedrah's braid around his fingers. Taking his cue, she screeched, tipping back, leaning into his palm as he tugged on her hair.

"And this?" He fisted the gold chain and yanked until the tension was tight around her neck. "It's cool with you if I just snap this beauty off right here?"

The lead Matrix wannabe stepped forward, reaching for his breast pocket, and Leo whipped up his hand. "Don't."

That's right, fucker. Rhys smirked. Life was pretty shitty when someone had ya by the balls. "I got everything you need right here, *dad*."

He pulled the chain harder and Faedrah gasped, the muscles in her throat straining, body stretched on her knees. All he had to do was pop his thumb and Leo's connection to her world would go up in smoke. After relying on the added pep for so long, it was anyone's guess where that would leave him. Not Leo's happy place, based on his knee jerk reaction. "But I'd be willing to give it up for the right offer."

Faedrah shook her head, weeping. A moan rolled up her throat and she fought to speak around the gag. "Nuh. Nuu-uh!"

Oh shit, was she really gonna make him go there? "Shut up!" He shouted inches from her face, and then clenched his jaw against a smile as Leo squinted. Hands down, the woman was a damn genius.

"You would forsake your beloved Faedrah?" Leo withdrew a step, a cunning gleam in his eye. "In exchange for what?"

"Life." Rhys lowered his chin, staring straight at Leo from under his brows. "Power." He let the word hang in the air. "I was a god in Faedrah's world. I had everything and I liked it. You don't need me. As long as you have Faedrah and the key, you could live another hundred years in this reality." He flexed his arm and she pushed to her feet, shaking, her chest heaving like she was out of breath. "She refuses to take me back through, so you deal with her. She's your problem now. Let her have the next son. Give me what I need, and I'll stay the hell out of your way."

Leo pursed his lips, the first hint of suspicion narrowing his gaze, and Rhys snatched his chance to dangle the bait a little deeper.

"That surprises you?" He laughed, cinching Faedrah tighter. She squeaked and danced around on her toes. "You never got to know any of them, did you? Never took time out of your busy schedule to spend two minutes with your sons." He gritted his teeth. "Well maybe you should have. After all, we *are* related. I'm not sure why it's so fucking hard to believe we would want the same things."

One of Leo's eyebrows rose, and the delight shining in his eyes shot sour bile up the back of Rhys' throat. "Perhaps I've underestimated you. A negotiation, then." He refocused on Faedrah and grinned.

Magic prickled in the tips of Rhys' fingers, and he stomped on it like an ant. Christ, if Leo caught wind of his powers before they were ready, they were screwed.

"Yes, I like that." He glanced around the yard. "But not here." Turning for the house, he opened a flat hand toward the doorway. "Please, do come in."

Bingo! Whether or not Leo had bought into the lie didn't matter. He wasn't ready to play *Let's Make A Deal* any more than Rhys, and was an idiot to think Rhys would believe one fucking word out of his mouth. But he'd invited them in, with enough brains intact to play out their next move. That's all they'd been after.

Rhys kept a tight hold on the chain and pressed his arm into Faedrah's back, but she planted her feet, fighting him like hell.

He shoved and she edged forward, wriggling and squirming until they'd reached the stoop. Hauling her inside, he met Leo's fake smile. "Let's stash her someplace safe. If memory serves, you've made some improvements to the basement."

Leo pushed the handle closed and shrugged as if whatever Rhys wanted was all the same to him. "Very well."

He walked them past the staircase to the door opposite his study, waved a palm over the lock and twisted the knob, standing aside as Rhys wrestled Faedrah down the stairs.

Electricity lifted the hair at Rhys' nape as Leo stepped off the bottom riser and slithered past them, leading the way down a dank hallway that ended at another locked door.

Water dripped off to the left in a steady splash. Glee twinkled in Leo's eyes as he glanced over his shoulder. "I think you'll find the accommodations to your liking."

His gaze dropped to Faedrah, and he winked, swinging the door wide.

Rhys thrust her into the room. One step over the threshold, and she stomped on his foot. He cursed a blue streak, hopping sideways. A quick spin, and she rammed her shoulder into his ribcage.

He roared, pin-wheeling his arms, and stumbled back. A maniacal laugh built, echoing off the concrete walls. Rhys fisted his hand and swung, hoping the misdirection had worked and he'd connect with Leo in time.

His arm froze mid-punch. Faedrah's shoulders wrenched upright and she sucked air through her nose, her body stiff as a board. A current tingled over Rhys' skin. The ground disappeared beneath his feet, and he clenched his jaw as the air thickened, a dense pressure lifting his arms to the sides like he was about to be crucified.

"I cannot recall the last time I've had such fun." Leo rubbed his hands together, striding forward. A flick of his finger, and Rhys flew back. A grunt punched from his lungs as his spine slammed the concrete wall. "In fact, I daresay this has been so enjoyable, I'm nearly sad to see it end."

"What the fuck are you doing?" Chains rattled overhead, and Rhys twisted his shoulders, yanking at his arms as a set of shackles snaked down from the ceiling. "God dammit, I thought we had a deal."

Leo tipped his head back and laughter burst from his throat, so freakish and abnormal it doused the room in a layer of slime. "Oh, come now, Rhys. I believe the time for our little game has passed. Do you think me a fool? You are no more willing to give up the princess than I."

The iron cuffs snapped in place and Rhys hissed as the air

decompressed, his arms jerking in their sockets as his full weight dropped a solid foot. His toes danced around a drain in the floor, and his stomach knotted at the dark red stain ringing the outside.

"But do not worry yourself." Leo crossed to his altar and flipped open a thick book. "I promise to keep your beloved close until she's outlived her usefulness."

Heat flooded Rhys' veins. Pinpricks numbed his fingers and, this time, he welcomed his magic like Faedrah's kiss. *Just a little more, fucker. Bring it on and we'll get this done.*

Leo lifted his hands to the sides and the candles on the altar flared. His lips whispered some bizarre incantation, and a pulse point throbbed in Rhys' skull.

A black cloud formed in the empty space over Leo's book. Shadows crept into the corners of the room, swirling and thickening. Rhys glanced at Faedrah and she blinked. A tear rolled down her cheek, but she didn't move.

The acidic flavor of ashes dried his tongue. A drone buzzed in his ears, and he gritted his teeth. Shit, they were so close, but he needed more, to have his powers barrel in like a freight train if they hoped to make it out of this clusterfuck alive.

Reaching inside the empty void, Leo licked his lips. The candles flickered and the flames altered to the violet glow of a black light. He stepped back, lifting out a curved, silver knife.

Yes! Rhys expelled a harsh breath, puffed a few times and filled his lungs, searching for any imperfection in the silver, any flaw he could find. His magic fizzed and sputtered at the edges. He narrowed his focus and *shoved*, but the god dammed knife refused to move.

Turning from the table, Leo resumed chanting, his voice pitched both high and low, two octaves at once. Whispers of otherworldly voices joined in, and Rhys' stomach lurched; Faedrah shuddered. He thrashed at his restraints, growling.

Leo lifted his eyes to Rhys, empty and filled with black. The tempo of his incantation grew faster, the voices frantic. He balanced the knife on his fingertips and closed in. The blade glowed, and Rhys tried to fling it across the room.

Stopping before Rhys, Leo grabbed the handle and his chanting cut out. "In many ways, you were the pinnacle of my creations. I certainly hope you don't take offense. Your death is nothing personal."

Pushing the zipper of Rhys' jacket aside, he lifted the knife overhead and plunged it toward Rhys' chest.

Rhys squeezed his eyes closed and braced. A small percussion rebounded against his eardrums, and he flinched. A second passed…then a couple more. He peeked at Leo through one eye and the tension in his arms went slack. Holy shit, it had worked.

The tip of the knife poked Rhys t-shirt, piercing the fabric, but the blade had stopped dead in the air.

"What have you done?" Leo swung the knife back and jabbed it toward Rhys a second time. And then a third. "*What have you done!*"

He scrambled for the collar of Rhys' t-shirt and ripped off a wide strip in one swipe. His eyes bulged at the raised ink of Rhys' signature, tattooed over Rhys' heart. Nostrils flared, Leo seized Rhys by the throat. "Do you think this will stop me? Do you truly think I shall not find another way?"

Yeah, good luck with that plan, asshole. Rhys grimaced and faked a cough. "God, Leo, your breath reeks. What up, major halitosis?"

Faedrah grunted, her eyes wide. She shook her head and then rocked back on her heels as a full-throated laugh burst through her gag. Gasping for air, she bent forward at the waist, stomping her foot as another round of laughter shook her shoulders.

"Right?" Rhys chuckled along with her. "I swear to God, the dude stinks worse than Fandorn."

She nodded, laughter tears streaming down her cheeks, Rhys' stomach cinching tighter over her amusement the more Leo stammered and fumed like some bratty kid.

He bounced the knife handle in his hand, strode toward Faedrah and wrenched her head back. "We shall see how you fare without your lovely muse."

Everything in Rhys' world slammed into focus. His back arched, wrists straining against the shackles as lightning bolts exploded down his spine. Light crackled from his hands. The shadows shrieked and scampered for the corners as his body buzzed like he'd been shot with a thousand volts.

A smile twisted his lips as he lowered his chin. Every piece of metal in the room, every mineral down to a molecular level was his, dammit. They all belonged to him.

An evil chuckle rumbled in Rhys's chest, and Leo shook his head. "This cannot—"

"Now, Faedrah!" Rhys aimed a sharp beam of energy straight at her handcuffs. Her hands jerked free at the same moment Rhys shoved at his restraints.

The shackles split with a metal *clang*. She drove her elbow into Leo's stomach, tangled the gold chain around her fingers and yanked. Leo bellowed. Rhys' feet hit the floor, he ran two steps and jumped as she flung the key into the air.

An earthquake rocked the ground. Cracks zig-zagged through the foundation. The walls shook and the candles toppled. Melted wax sprayed and sparks smoldered on the black tablecloth covering the altar. "No!" Leo shrieked.

Rhys snagged the key, spun and punched both hands forward, throwing everything he had into the knife. It flew from Leo's hand, but he thrust both arms up, stopping the blade in mid-twirl.

Gritting his teeth, Rhys dragged the knife to eye-level, pushing harder, aiming the tip toward Leo's chest. Heat built at his back. Flames sputtered and licked at the air. Leo's face grayed. His skin sagged. He panted and curled his fingers as the nails lengthened and yellowed.

A moan wound up from Faedrah's chest and her legs wobbled. God dammit, her memories. Her parents had said she might lose them. She staggered back, tearing the gag from her mouth, and dropped her head into her hands.

"Stay with me, Faedrah!" Rhys grappled at the knife with his mind. Leo growled and the sharp end spun back toward Rhys. "God dammit, don't you leave me!"

She shook her head, blinked and glanced around the room. Her eyes landed on Leo, and her jaw firmed as she peered past his shoulder and locked on to Rhys. "Never. I shall never leave you, my heart."

Hands fisted, she went up on her toes and sprinted straight for Leo, jumped and rammed both feet into his back. Rhys roared, pouring the last of his power into the knife. It twirled as Leo careened forward. Rhys grabbed the handle and jammed it all the way into Leo's chest, down to the hilt before giving it a hard twist.

Leo stumbled back, fell and scrambled away, crab-walking and flopping around like some possessed, disjointed body. He smacked into the burning alter and his hands fluttered and slapped at the knife. Hot wax streamed onto his head. The black bled from his eyes, streaking down his face.

Flames snaked over his clothes. The stench of rotting flesh filled the air and Leo screamed, thrashing. "I may die in this realm, but I live on in mine!"

Beams of blue light shot from his fingers, from his eyes and gaping mouth. His back bowed off the floor as fire enveloped his body. Rhys dove for Faedrah and knocked her to the floor, covering her head with his arms. The shadows screeched. The air was sucked from the room a second before a bone-jarring detonation lifted and slammed them back to the ground.

Debris pounded Rhys' back and legs. Dust and smoke filled his lungs, and he buried his face in the soft slope of Faedrah's neck. Coughing, holding her close, he waited as the tremors subsided.

He lifted his head and ran his hands over her cheeks, her shoulders, down her sides and back up again. Ashes floated past his shoulder and caught in her closed lashes. Black smudges covered her forehead and cheeks. "Are you all right? Sweet Jesus, Faedrah, can you hear me?"

She wheezed and waved a hand in front of her face. "I am fine, my heart. None the worse for wear."

He slumped back on top of her and crammed his arms under her shoulders, squeezing her tight. "Thank God. For a second there, I thought I'd lost you."

"I am afraid you are still burdened with my presence."

He chuckled and leaned away, cupping the top of her head so he could wipe the grime off her forehead with his thumb. "Holy shit, we did it. We won, Princess."

She smiled. "I did not harbor any doubts that we would."

"Rhys? Oh my God, are you there? Just…say something. Todd's coming. He should be there any second."

"I got ya, Violet." He dropped his lips to Faedrah's, and damned if he didn't give two shits about anything else other than the fact she returned his kiss.

Footsteps thundered down the hall and the blown-out frame of the door slammed open against the wall. "Rhys!" Another round of bricks fell from the rafters.

"Over here!" The weight holding Rhys in place eased up as Todd and a few members of his crew dug him and Faedrah out from under. He sat up and scanned the basement, but there wasn't much left…unless he could count the pile of cremated ashes that had once been Leo.

Rhys pushed to his feet and offered Faedrah a hand up, kicked a smoldering beam out of the way and high-stepped over a pile of cinderblock. He nudged the black mound with the toe of his boot and his brow twitched. No way.

Leaning down, he picked up the silver knife and swiped it back and forth over the side of his hip to clean off the oily residue. Faedrah wound her hand around his bicep and leaned in, and he glanced at her, flipping the blade over and back. "What the hell are we supposed to do with this, now?"

She frowned, and the confusion in her eyes made him hesitate. "For all my efforts, I cannot recall its significance."

Shit, he forgot. The key. Unless he got that chain back around her neck, they'd be stuck here…her kingdom, her mom and dad and everyone who loved her in that world would be gone from her memories.

Sirens wailed somewhere off in the distance, and Todd glanced up at gaping hole in the floor of Leo's study. "Later. It's time we hit the road."

"Yep." Rhys shoved the knife into the back waistband of his pants and faced his muse. "Just one last thing." He clenched the chain he still had wound through his fingers and closed his eyes, searching for any defect in the gold. The broken ends helped, giving him the perfect place to start, and the middle of his hand got hot as he concentrated on melting the links together.

He opened his fingers and, all things considered, the necklace looked pretty damn good. A nod down at his work, and he dropped the chain around Faedrah's neck.

Todd muttered a curse, bracing his legs as another earthquake shook the ground. A few more chunks of concrete tipped from the walls and shattered. White dust hissed from between the cracks and a row of books slid off the overhead crater, flapping and bouncing as they landed.

But Rhys kept his eyes on Faedrah, watching…waiting…hoping he hadn't fucked up the key's magic and everything they'd been through would fall back into place.

She grabbed his arm and pressed two fingers to her forehead, squeezed her eyes tight and shook her head. The rumbling eased up and she lifted her gaze to his—aware, sharp, the perfect chocolate brown. "I remember…" She searched his face. "The two of us floating amongst the stars."

The mural he'd painted in her bedroom. Damn straight. He smirked. "Floating, huh? That all you remember?"

One of her eyebrows rose, and he crossed his arms as she ran her focus up and down his body. "If memory serves, you and I have agreed to be wed."

Yep, his furious little muse was back, and apparently reliving everything they'd done in her bedroom since she seemed to be mentally tearing his clothes off. He strode one step forward, snuck an arm around her waist and jerked her to his hips. "That's right, Princess. And don't you ever forget."

Epilogue

Denmar released the catch and the sand bags creaked, swinging to and fro over the narrow wooden beam at the gate of the Gantlet.

Faedrah sighed, searching the far tree line to either side of the large audience gathered beneath the white canopies staked upon the lawn. Royal blue pennants woven with the silver crest of the Austiere Kingdom caught and fluttered in the warm autumn wind. Green and floral garlands hung draped in a colorful display around the chairs and heavily-laden refreshment tables. Liveried servants batted at flies as they bowed and coursed through the crowd. Every able noble within her father's rule had arrived to celebrate this joyous occasion and, yet, she could not displace the lingering disquiet burdening her heart.

Two full cycles of Selene's passings had lapsed since Faedrah and her beloved Rhys had returned to the realm of Austiere. Two cycles of the moon, whilst every soul had rejoiced, the woods and surrounding lands had begun to heal and preparations for this long-awaited day had consumed the entirety of the kingdom.

Following her and her beloved's victorious purge of Gaelleod's foothold in the future, Sir Todd and his loyal band of steel-horsed riders had hastened their troupe to the home of her two faithful uncles. There, amid tears of farewell and heartfelt promises to one day return, Rhys had passed to Wizard Oliver and Sir Jon the silver blade Gaelleod had employed during the rite of his immoral transformations. Whilst both she and Rhys were hard-pressed to let such powerful magic vacate their watchful eye, the goddesses would not allow such an object safe passage through the veil. Rhys and Faedrah been left no choice but to take heart her uncles had vowed to secret the blade inside the armoire.

The moment they had returned to the castle, she'd removed the golden key from around neck, locking away both sides of the veil and the dangerous power contained therein.

Yet, in this realm, Gaelleod and his lost blade remained.

Faedrah closed her eyes, smiling softly over the impatience of the confident warrior threatening to take hold inside her. She stepped past the first bag and paused. Many hours Rhys had endeavored to locate Gaelloed's most treasured instrument of evil, toiling long into the night beside Fandorn whilst they combed through the castle's library. He'd lead several excursions into Gaelleod's crystal crypt, the days long spent exploring the tunnels, enough Faedrah had become accustomed to her beloved entering their bedchamber coated in diamond dust, his dark hair shimmering like a sea of stars. Still, for all his efforts, the dagger's location remained shrouded in mystery, and though Rhys used a portion of his powers to ward the tomb of Gaelleod's undead sleep, he would not allow for the entrance to be sealed.

Though his appeal contained a treacherous risk, neither the king nor queen nor anyone in all the realm dared to argue his request the doorway remain open. How could they when Vaighn had yet to reemerge from within that warren of diamond littered halls?

Another step, and Faedrah slipped past the second bag. Each morning as Helios had announced the beginning of a new day, she had hoped for the best and, each night, as the sun god set, her brother's rightful place within the kingdom remained vacant. For a time, Faedrah had insisted they postpone her contest in the Gantlet. Of all her brothers at arms, Vaighn was Austiere's true champion, stalwart of heart and fealty, unbested with his able sword, and she could not rightfully accept the Austiere crest until the two of them had contested.

Her heart slowed as she envisioned her brother's smile, the devilish mischief glinting in his eyes. What that she would give to have him taunt her? To have him enter the sparring room, his hair a tousled mess and his clothes unkempt after a long night tossing the bedclothes with a courtier?

Out of love and the deepest respect for her brother, she had continuously deferred...until the goddesses made known to her they had other plans in mind.

The swing of the final bag formed a steady rhythm in her mind, and she widened her stance, unsheathing a short sword from her back. A fortnight had passed since the expectation of her womanly course, and before Rhys confined her to lazing about the castle...before the grand announcement of their upcoming arrival had spread to every ear in the realm, she would follow through on this day. She would do the one thing she could to honor her brother, and take his place as the King's right arm until the joyous moment of Vaighn's return.

The crowd quieted. A soft breeze tugged a loose strand from her braid and she smiled as it tickled across her lips. Her first opponent lingered near, hidden behind the foremost wall on her right. The scent of his sweat and leather chest plate gave his location away.

The knock of an arrow, the creak of a bow, and her second opponent made himself known. Straight ahead, he kneeled behind the low defense of a free-standing partition. Silver hummed as the third withdrew his sword, and she lowered her chin, targeting his position high atop the rope bridge. Once engaged in combat, she could locate the fourth and fifth from that vantage point with ease.

Filling her lungs, she awaited the swing of the bag, then dropped to one knee and rolled beneath it, using the unexpected maneuver to mask her advance. The first arrow loosed with the recoil of a bowstring, and she dodged left, knocking its aim off-kilter with her sword. The crowd *ooohed*. A smattering of applause accompanied their praise. She sprinted dead on for the archer, batting his arrows from the air, veered right at the last moment and charged for her first contender. His brows shot toward his hairline at her misdirection, and she used the beat of his surprise to leap and rebound off the wall.

Her boot heels rammed his shoulder. He staggered sideways and an arrow *thunked* into his leather shield. She landed behind him, flipped to her shoulders and pinioned her legs toward the backs of his knees. His full weight slammed to the ground from the force of her kick. A second well-aimed thrust at his shoulders, and she sprang to her boots as he careened face-first to the ground.

A sickening crunch accompanied his fall, and he turned his head aside, one hand holding the bridge of his nose and blood gushing down his lips. "Submit, milady. I submit."

The tip of an arrow glanced off her shoulder, and Faedrah hissed, spinning for the edge of the Gantlet and the high wooden arm that extended toward the crowd. A length of rope dangled from the top, swaying in the breeze, and she leapt with all her might, body extended, and snagged the cable in mid-air.

The audience cheered, ducking low as she swung toward the tents. A careening swoop through the center of the Gantlet and she flipped, soaring aloft to gain hold of the bottom support rope of the bridge.

Her momentum spun her under and around, and she brought her knees to her chest as her side slammed her opponent's hardened chest plate. Pain ricocheted through her body. His back rebounded off the side hand rope, and he flailed his arms, tipping forward as the hit swung her under and back up behind him. A hard shove with her boot as she crested the hand rope, and he flipped like a piece of lumber, tumbling head over heels to smack the ground.

The rope bounced beneath her boots as she landed, and she peered down at the guard's prone form.

A wheeze leaked from between his parted lips, and he put a hand on his chest. "Submit."

She twiddled her fingers at him and raced for the end platform. Arrows whizzed past her head. A glance at the maze below, and she located the last two guards, each waiting behind the innermost ends of two opposite, identical walls. A narrow gap stood between them, forming the entrance to the Table of Doom.

A spring off her toes and she flew through the air, arms spread high, one leg bent as the floor rushed up to greet her. The crowd gasped as she landed and tucked onto one shoulder, rolling forward to disperse the impact to her legs. Dodging left then right, deflecting a hailstorm of arrows, she ran full force toward the archer, sprang hands over heels and *smack*, slapped the side of his head with her blade as she landed.

He flinched at the blow and she leveled the edge of her sword across his neck, bent in a crouch behind him. "Load your bow. Two arrows, please."

He hesitated and she pressed her blade deeper. He sharply inhaled as a bead of blood rolled along the sharp edge toward the hilt.

Muttering a curse, the archer reached for his quiver, knocked back a set of arrows and she squinted, leveraging her threat on his neck to set her sights on her two remaining targets. Yet she must be crafty, aim high enough to clear the walls.

Faedrah pressed her knee into the archer' back and tipped the bow back until the angle was pitched toward the sky, warranting her satisfaction. "Release."

The arrows flew from the bow, two black streaks against the lofty clouds, arched gracefully toward the ground and, a moment later, two identical howls of agony echoed from behind the walls.

A smile graced her lips, and she dug her blade deeper. "Are we moving forward the easy way or the hard way?"

"Easy, Your Highness." The archer glanced at her from the corner of his eye, disgust curling his lips. "I submit."

"Right, then." She stood and tousled his hair before jogging toward the Table of Doom. A hearty round of applause showered from the crowd amid cheers and piercing whistles. A glance left then right as she passed through the gap and a chuckle shook her shoulders as both guards bowed low, muttering their surrender. The first one's foot had been pinned to the floor by her arrow and the second grasped his sword arm, the thick black staff protruding from between his bloodied fingers.

Sheathing her sword at her back, she dipped her chin at Fandorn, standing in the center of the table, and strode forward to stand before him. Full dress regalia adorned the king's tall form, awaiting her arrival on the wizard's right and, beside him, the queen had donned her gray leather warrior's ensemble in homage to Faedrah's ascent through the guard.

Rhys stood to the left of Fandorn, his black leather waistcoat and breeches stretched across his muscular frame, sunlight winking off the silver vambraces he'd crossed before his chest. A dark scowl pleated his brow, and he shook his head. "Okay, that sucked."

Faedrah laughed. Her beloved had given his solemn vow he would not employ his powers to interfere in her final test, yet to remain no more than a bystander had surely stretched his nerves to the limit of their extent.

Tipping her head toward the slight injury peeling back the leather atop her shoulder, she arched a brow at her beloved. "A slight nudge to that arrow would've earned you much in the way of my favor."

Rhys unlocked his arms, clenching his grizzled jaw. "Don't start with me, Princess. It was hard enough to just stand here and watch. Though with the way you move, I gotta hand it to the guy. It's a wonder he got anywhere close."

Her mother smiled, linking her arm with that of the king. "Your father and I are so very proud of you, Faedrah."

The king cleared his throat, nodding. "Indeed, my daughter. No father in all the realm could ask for more from his kingdom's future queen."

"Yeah, yeah we're all thrilled Faedrah just tried to get herself killed." With a roll of his eyes, Rhys stepped forward and turned about to face Fandorn, taking his place on Faedrah's right.

Darting a sidelong glance his way, she pursed her lips against a smile. "Speaking of things starting anew…" She lifted her hand and placed it upon her belly. "I have joyous news of which you should be made aware."

Rhys froze; slowly swiveled his head. A magnetic current vibrated the silver at her back as his face flooded a deep red. "Are you kidding?" He pivoted to fully face her and grabbed her upper arms, his hands trembling, glanced back at the Gantlet and expelled a harsh breath. "Tits of the nine, Faedrah! Are you crazy? Going through the Gantlet pregnant?"

She rolled her lips to curtail a laugh. Her beloved's use of their effrontery never ceased to tickle her heart.

The queen gasped and slapped a hand to her chest. Her rosy smile bloomed, and she softly clapped. "A babe! How wonderful!"

The king sputtered, swiping a hand down the front of his face. "Helios wept, my boy." He chuckled and shook his head. "Did you just now conclude the woman you're about to marry is as headstrong as her mother? Of course, she would contest in the Gantlet before making you aware of her condition." He tossed that same hand in the air as if he'd long since relinquished any chance at winning an argument with an Austiere queen. "That decision makes perfect sense."

"Oh, my God." Rhys whisked Faedrah close, gathering her in his strong arms. He dotted kisses over her cheeks, her lips and forehead, then thrust her away and applied a gentle shake before another round of his ardent kisses heated her skin. "Sweet Jesus, I hope it's a boy."

Faedrah closed her eyes, her heart taking flight as her beloved cupped the back of her head in his warm hand. "Sure as shit is slick, taking on another Austiere woman will kill me."

The king and queen shared a chuckle, and Rhys leaned back to search Faedrah's gaze. "My crazy, beautiful, stubborn as hell muse."

He brought his lips to hers and she gladly met his kiss. "Just wait until we're alone, Princess. You're in deep shit."

Faedrah's pulse skipped over all the delightful ways her beloved might exact revenge for such an offense, and she quietly laughed as he applied a firm squeeze to her back side.

Fandorn cleared his throat. "At your majesties' pleasure, shall we begin?" With a nod from her parents, he called the courtiers to order, and Faedrah smiled into Rhys' eyes as the wizard opened his hands to his sides. "We are gathered on this auspicious day to witness the joining of two hearts bonded in love."

Acknowledgements

No author sees a book through to publication without an army of fierce allies at her back. To my agent, Dawn Dowdle of Blue Ridge Literary, you are part agent, part mentor, part therapist and part fairy godmother. I can't thank you enough for your support.

My heartfelt thanks to talented editor, Charlotte Ledger, who waved her magic wand and granted one of the greatest thrills of my career by contracting this series. Epic love and thanks to Alexandra Allden and Lizzie Gardiner for their outstanding artistic eye and unending patience while designing the covers for this series.

A big thanks goes out to several friends, without whom this story would not have reached its full potential: Arial Burnz, Vonnie Davis, Mackenzie Crowne and Rachel Brimble for their keen attention detail and helping me center my characters.

To the three folks who inhabit the halls of my lunacy and provide a limitless fountain of love and support—my husband Scott, my son Jack, and my daughter Lily Belle. Without you three, I would simply cease to exist. Lastly, to my readers. Thank you for choosing this story. I hope it finds you happy and healthy, and that all your fairy tale dreams come true.